COURT

OF

WANDERERS

COURT

OF

WANDERERS

RIN CHUPECO

SAGA PRESS

LONDON SYDNEY **NEW YORK** TORONTO NEW DELHI

SAGA PRESS
AN IMPRINT OF SIMON & SCHUSTER, INC.

1230 AVENUE OF THE AMERICAS, NEW YORK, NEW YORK 10020

First Saga Press hardcover edition April 2024

SAGA PRESS and colophon are trademarks of Simon & Schuster, Inc.

Simon & Schuster: Celebrating 100 Years of Publishing in 2024

For information about special discounts for bulk purchases, please contact Simon & Schuster Special Sales at 1-866-506-1949 or business@simonandschuster.com.

The Simon & Schuster Speakers Bureau can bring authors to your live event. For more information or to book an event, contact the Simon & Schuster Speakers Bureau at 1-866-248-3049 or visit our website at www.simonspeakers.com.

Manufactured in the United States of America

1   3   5   7   9   10   8   6   4   2

Library of Congress Cataloging-in-Publication Data has been applied for.

Library of Congress Control Number: 2023951942

ISBN 978-1-9821-9574-8
ISBN 978-1-9821-9576-2 (ebook)

For Lil—
you're still a mad lad.

REGRET

Remy complained, of course. Of the bad roads and of the storms that came upon them without warning, the winds stronger than they were accustomed to, even within rain-drenched Aluria. Of the way the carriage jerked them about at intervals, the way the vampire horses yanked their coach along at a dizzying pace, eschewing comfort for speed. Variations of *Malekh, slow the fuck down, you're jolting Xiaodan out of her bloody seat* frequently left his mouth, his language growing more colorful and more desperate as the days went by.

Malekh said nothing, and the more he said shit-all, the more Remy whined to make up for the silence. The vampire lord never rose to his bait. On the rare occasions he remained inside the carriage with them, he merely folded his arms across his chest, leaned back with his eyes closed, and pretended Remy wasn't there. For the better part of the journey, he stayed on the driver's perch outside where his helhests, undeterred by the rain and the fog, raced on down the path.

It had been four days since they'd first set out from Elouve, and Remy still didn't know where the hell they were; Peanut and

Cookie could run from one end of Aluria to the other in a week if their masters wanted them to. On at least three occasions now, Malekh had halted the carriage inside some forest, uttered a terse *stay here* to him, and was off to Light-knows-where for a couple of hours. No badgering could convince him to tell Remy where he'd been, once he returned.

Malekh hadn't stopped at any villages or towns to rest, choosing to keep vigil outside the carriage at night while Remy managed a few hours' sleep within. And despite all his whining about seeing to her comfort, Xiaodan slept through it all anyway, never once waking to join in Remy's grievances.

Her head was currently in his lap. The rest of her was stretched out on his right, short enough that the soles of her feet were settled comfortably against the side of the carriage door. Her eyelids fluttered every now and then, and he hoped that she was dreaming of something better than where they were. Her heartbeats sounded loud to his ears, irregular as always.

She'd fallen asleep almost as soon as they'd left Elouve, and nothing could rouse her. Malekh checked on her frequently, his nonchalance over her condition Remy's only assurance.

There was only so much he could moan about when the scenery was beginning to blur together and his nitpicks about the roads' conditions were the same day in and day out, so eventually Remy stopped griping and started talking about anything else that tickled his fancy. Like whether or not plants had feelings. Or if bugs waged little insect wars with one another like humans did. Or how many undead chickens it would take, theoretically speaking, to defeat a vampire. In his nearly a thousand years of existence, surely Malekh had the answers to these and other philosophical questions.

Remy was just goading Malekh, really. He thought about shutting up. Silence had a far better chance of improving matters between them.

He did not shut up.

Sometimes, when he ran out of hypotheticals with which to annoy the vampire lord, Remy talked about how his father, the Duke of Valenbonne, was overseeing Aluria's defense in fresh new horrifying ways since assuming the position of lord high steward. How Queen Ophelia had permitted him to continue Dr. Yost's experiments on the mutations despite her obvious reluctance. Edgar Pendergast had played his hand well. Sending his creatures against the First Court vampires and whatever other mutations that still haunted the lands was better than sending in her Reapers. The queen did not want to incur more losses from the latter when the former was designed to be expendable.

Malekh likely already knew this, given his and Xiaodan's close friendship with Her Majesty, but Remy nattered on anyway. He was to serve as Valenbonne's spy for when the eight courts eventually convened—classified information he was supposed to withhold, but Remy no longer gave a fuck. So he'd told Malekh about how his father had manipulated his way back into power and how he intended to create an army of creatures devoted to him alone, using Yost's bloodrot to command their loyalty. How Lord Valenbonne's manservant, Grimesworthy, had been his prototype, a colossus mutation masquerading as a human servant.

Malekh said nothing. He crossed his arms and closed his eyes and checked on Xiaodan and his undead horses and did everything else but respond to Remy, widening the distance between them that had begun when Remy killed Malekh's brother Naji.

Remy was almost relieved when the ambush broke the tension. He spotted the approaching mob in between thunderclaps on the fifth night, when the rains were worse. A dozen at least, many wearing the red robes that declared them minions of the First Court. The rest wore plain, threadbare clothes stained in some mixture of mud and dried blood—victims from previous villages that had fallen to the horde, convinced to take up their former predators' cause after turning. Lightning streaked the sky around them, keeping Remy from using his Breaker at will.

It didn't matter. His daggers could cut through vampire flesh just as well as his scythes did, even if they weren't as sharp as he'd liked—he'd had no time to whet them back in Elouve, and he'd bitched about that, too. He plunged one into the eye of an undead attempting to pull itself in through the window, and then another through its chest. The vampire gurgled once, then let go.

It didn't matter to Malekh either, who tore through the other kindred with a ferocity that contradicted his usually precise, analytical style of fighting. He cut through the throng quickly; Remy could see nothing of his attacks in between the brief flashes of light, the explosions of blood erupting from their bodies in the aftermath the only indication that there had ever been a strike.

Remy had barely gotten his arse out of the carriage when he saw there were no vampires left. Malekh was thorough.

A faint creak told him that the vampire lord had returned to his position on the carriage, taking up the reins once more.

"Malekh," Remy said.

The winds howled, but he knew Malekh could hear him.

"I can understand why you're choosing to give me the shitty silent treatment, but I don't believe this is a natural storm. It feels like the one at Chànggē Shuǐ when Vasilik attacked."

Still nothing.

Remy was losing his patience. "We should wait till it passes. There could be more out there worse than this lot, and Xiaodan isn't in any shape to deal with further surprises."

He heard the puzzled whinny of the helhests when their master made no move to urge them onward.

And then Malekh's voice, quiet and gravelly and well missed, penetrated through the barrier between them. "Rocksplen is up ahead."

HE'D TOLD the innkeeper that they would be needing two rooms for the night, only for Malekh to interrupt, saying that they required only one, the biggest the inn had if you please, and that he would be compensated handsomely for the trouble. The innkeeper's eyebrows climbed as he took them all in; Malekh as noble and as regal as ever, cradling the sleeping Xiaodan in his arms, and Remy, who still had enough self-regard to turn beet red. As if they needed more attention, what with the helhests loitering in the nearby woods just out of sight and the new rumors swirling of fresh vampire attacks within King Hallifax's kingdom.

Once Xiaodan was snug and warm inside the surprisingly large bed they'd been provided, Malekh had left without another word. Logic told Remy that the man intended to scour the area, find any other vampires from the group that had tried to waylay them, and see whether the storm was as unnatural as suspected.

It rankled that Malekh hadn't bothered to tell him any of that.

But Remy sucked it up.

For a *generous* fee he was sure Malekh wouldn't mind paying, he ordered a very expensive dinner—prime roast beef and *fresh* vegetables, even—sent up to their room so he wouldn't have to leave Xiaodan, who continued to dream. Once he'd had his fill, he'd asked for a bucket of water and a clean cloth and retreated behind a small screen to wash off the stink he'd accumulated over the last few days.

He no longer wore Reaper black, only traveling clothes chosen from his own wardrobe. Officially, it was because he was on a covert mission for Her Majesty. Personally, it was because he didn't realize how much he hated that damnable color until he'd had the opportunity to stop wearing it. And after days spent inside the cramped carriage, he should have relished in the idea of finally spending the night in a soft bed with goose feather pillows, but he was too keyed up to rest.

He stretched out beside Xiaodan and listened to her heartbeat for a while; an arrhythmic cadence contrasting with the steady hum of the downpour outside. He touched her cheek, relieved to see her expression relaxed in slumber, that her sleep was at least free of nightmares. The fringe on her forehead was starting to look uneven. The last thing he'd expected a vampire to need was a hair trim.

"He's angry at me," Remy told her. "Not that I blame him." His gaze drifted back toward the small window, watching the darkness beyond it. Minutes passed before he realized he'd left his last thought unfinished.

"I don't know if I can forgive myself, either," he said.

HE MUST have fallen asleep shortly afterward, because Remy woke up to a body sprawled on top of him. His first instinct was to shove, anticipating an attack, but strong hands pinned his wrists down, and no amount of struggle could wrest him free.

"Remy." It was a soft whisper, the voice familiar and loved.

"Xiaodan?"

The vampire straddled him, holding his wrists against the covers. She was wide awake now and staring at him with a ravenous look he knew all too well.

"Please," Xiaodan whispered. Her hold on him slackened, no longer keeping him immobile, though she remained on top of him. She looked eager and needy and beautiful.

Remy's hands found her waist. "Take all you need."

He groaned when he felt her fangs bite down against his neck as she slaked her thirst. Her hands burrowed underneath his shirt, fingers fumbling with his braies, pushing them down.

She drew back momentarily. "Remy," she breathed, "are you sure?"

It felt oddly touching that, even when she was not herself, even when she was fighting for self-control, she still thought to ask.

He reached up and cradled her face in his hands, watching those gorgeous brown eyes soften for him. "Never wanted anything more, my love," he said, and gently guided her mouth down to his.

SHE FELL asleep soon after, still sprawled on top of him after finding her completion. Remy could only manage a tired laugh, his hand stroking at her hair. There was more color to her cheeks now, her pallor less sickly than before, and he hoped it was enough until they reached the Third Court.

He left her under the blankets while he staggered off to find something to clean her and himself with. That done, he disposed of the soiled linen and stopped by the wash basin to scrub at his face, feeling the stubble he'd accumulated over the last few days and wondering if he could pester the innkeeper for something to shave with.

He turned, and his heart nearly stopped at the sight of Malekh at Xiaodan's side, pulling the rest of the covers over her. "The fuck did you come from?" he choked out.

Malekh nodded at the now-shut window. "Keep it locked next time."

"You didn't join us."

The lord's gaze drifted toward his fiancée's sleeping face. "She needed someone gentler tonight."

"And you don't?"

The vampire's golden gaze was back on him. "I have an urge for something rougher."

"So I'm good enough to talk to now?" Remy asked, stung and still a little horny. "Now that you want to wet your cock you're going to—"

Malekh's teeth sank into his shoulder, and Remy shuddered. "It would have been irresponsible to vent all my pent-up frustrations on the road with Xiaodan incapacitated. I have been very patient, listening to all your aggravating talk about . . . insect wars. Chickens." He actually sounded pained, and the heat inside Remy only escalated. "I amused myself with the many different ways I might otherwise keep your mouth occupied on the journey here."

"So you wanted to rush all the way here because you were *raunchy* and Xiaodan couldn't—"

Malekh kissed him again, and this time Remy finally shut up.

NOT ON the bed, Malekh had said. They might wake Xiaodan, despite the latter having slept through terrible roads, a thunderstorm, and an ambush.

They wound up breaking the dresser, the only other furniture of note in the room. It was staved in now, having been slammed into the wall behind it so hard that the wood had broken from the impact. Remy was certain there were still a few splinters lodged in his hip. Worth it, though; he was sore in all the right, satisfying ways, and some of the hardness had left Malekh's expression, however slightly.

"Did I hurt you?" Malekh's voice was rough, husky.

"No," Remy said, slightly dazed. He'd been deposited back onto the bed, where he'd immediately planted himself face-first onto the pillow. His right arm throbbed; he'd bitten down hard on it, worried that he'd shout the place down.

Normally Malekh would take up watch beside the window as was his habit, always on guard. Instead, Remy heard him moving around the room; a minute later, he felt a piece of cloth against his backside, warm and soothing. The lord then found himself a spot beside Remy, hand combing slowly through his hair. It felt like he was waiting for Remy to speak. And for the first time since leaving Elouve, it almost felt like he was willing to listen.

"Some days I wonder if I really should have left Elouve," Remy mumbled. "Don't know why I'd think that. Only Elke and Riones ever liked me, and I'm not even sure Giselle ever did. I was just a rare specimen she could parade on her arm and flaunt to the rest of the ton. Someone she could taunt Astonbury with."

He paused. Malekh still said nothing.

"You said the courts look down on familiars," Remy continued.

"The more militant of them, yes. Doesn't stop them from taking humans of their own."

"You've barely spoken a word to me. You have every reason to despise me for what happened to—to . . ." Remy couldn't even bring himself to say Naji's name. "But you agreed to bring me along. I could have stayed in Elouve if you didn't want me here—"

"That isn't the case." Remy felt the man's hand tighten against his hair. "And you would not have been happy in Elouve, for all your hesitation about leaving."

"Why?" The words hung thick in his throat. "I would have hated myself in your place. I shouldn't have let her use me to—I'm a liability. I can't—"

Malekh yanked his head up—unexpected enough for Remy to start in surprise, but not enough that it hurt. Not enough to protest when Malekh's mouth came crashing down on his.

The kiss was forceful, starved. And when Malekh lifted his head back up and the words came, they were harsh and angry, as they had to be. "Don't you think I know how difficult it is to wrench your mind free, having spent the greater part of a century as a thrall to the Night King, unable to disobey him even as he sent me to kill in his name? I don't blame you for Naji, Pendergast.

The blame is on me. I should have ordered him to stay with Lady Whittaker at the farmstead. I failed Naji, and I failed you."

Remy stared at him. Not once during the journey had he thought Malekh's silence as guilt. "There was no way for you to know that the Night Empress was my mother. I won't sit here and watch you punish yourself for that. The only sin you've committed is ignoring me and letting me think you didn't want me along."

There was no mistaking Malekh's reaction this time, eyes back to a bright gold as if they hadn't broken the damned furniture already. "Xiaodan and I will always want you along." He bent his head, and for a moment, despite his soreness and bruised back, Remy thought he was ready to go again, and his exhaustion fell away in anticipation.

Instead, he felt the lightest of touches on the side of his neck where Malekh had bitten him. The lord shifted to give him a more comfortable position on the bed. "Rest tonight," the vampire said quietly. "It will take us a few more days to reach my court, but I intend to stop by Libéliard along the way." The hand lingered; a thumb grazed at the spot where his neck met collarbone, and Remy shivered without meaning to. "Close the shutter behind me."

He was out the window before Remy could yell at him to use the door like everyone else. Grumbling, he went and locked it, then slouched back down next to Xiaodan, who slept blissfully on. His hand wandered to the spot where the lord's hand had been, then jerked back when he realized it.

"Bastard," he muttered, not without affection and a good amount of relief.

2

TRANSFORMATIONS

Malekh settled accounts with the innkeeper the following morning, and the sorry state of the dresser was resolved with generous portions of gold and copper. The latter accepted payment with little fuss, he and Remy surreptitiously avoiding eye contact.

It was a strange night. Remy had dreamed of his nanny, Miss Grissell. She was singing the Tithian lullaby she'd taught him as a child. The song once put him at ease, before his mother had used it to invade his fucking mind. He'd bolted up from bed, panicked and still groggy, only to be pulled toward a hard chest and a gruff voice by his ear, telling him to go back to sleep, and to the warmth of Xiaodan cuddled at his other side. She was still sleeping when dawn arrived, but Malekh was gone again, leaving Remy shivering slightly from the cool morning air.

The bulk of the villagers' fears, as far as Remy could determine, was focused on the rash of attacks sweeping the border between Aluria and Kerenai, the latter being King Hallifax's kingdom—a good five hundred miles away, though the distance did nothing to ease their worries. "No attacks around these parts," said one of the inn's other patrons as Remy took time to enjoy one last drink before departing. "Not yet at least, thank the Light." Remy thought about the ambush only the night before and silently disagreed.

The helhests were where they had left them the previous night, damp from the rain but pleased to see them. Malekh laid Xiaodan gently down inside the carriage. Remy paused by the side door.

"You said that we were heading to Libéliard?" It was a larger town than most, tucked into the northwestern part of the kingdom some hundreds or so miles from Rocksplen, and they were likely to reach it sometime that afternoon if Malekh allowed his horses freer reign. But it was an odd decision, considering how adamant Malekh had been about avoiding human civilization since starting out.

"Eugenie has set up shop there. She'll know more about what's been happening at Hallifax's borders." Malekh frowned. "I'm not sure I like the news coming out of his territories, but I want to separate what's true from the exaggerated."

"How'd you even know that she was at Libé—was that why you were skulking about the village last night?"

Malekh looked at him like he had never skulked a day in his unnatural life and was insulted at such a suggestion. "Eugenie has contacts in every village along the trading routes between here and Kerenai. It was only a question of ferreting out her contact in Rocksplen and gleaning the information from them."

"Suppose it would be nice to have a roof over our heads for a second day running." Remy liked Eugenie. The resourceful information broker was likely to know what was going on before anyone in Elouve ever caught wind of it.

Still, he lingered before climbing inside the coach. Malekh paused, watching him with a raised eyebrow.

"I had second thoughts about leaving Elouve," Remy admitted. "But I'm glad I'm here. Wouldn't have missed it."

"And we are glad for your company, Pendergast," Malekh said, moving to pat Peanut on the head.

The rains had since abated. Malekh had found no other vampires lying in wait, leaving them without answers as to the storm's true nature. The fog was still shit, with Remy's visibility down to no more than several yards beyond the carriage window. But Malekh seemed to know where to go despite the soupy haze, and both Peanut and Cookie soldiered on without hesitation at breakneck speed.

No other vampire hordes accosted them, leaving Remy with little else but Xiaodan and his own thoughts for company. He stared out the window and reflected on the First Court, on his mother.

He didn't want to think about having to kill Ligaya Pendergast. He didn't want to think about her song in his head, about being so powerless that he'd killed Naji.

Xiaodan shifted in her sleep, pressed the side of her face against his hand, and murmured something into it.

"You worry too much," Remy told her, resisting the urge to kiss her cheek. "I'll deal with it when I deal with it."

It took a little more than three hours to reach the town of Libéliard. Remy had never been here before; it was not in an area vampires were known to frequent, with a dash more sun than most places in Aluria. Already the rains were letting up, the fog lifting, and the clouds looking marginally less gray than before.

Libéliard itself was a bustling place, a nexus of trade. Just like in Ankersaud, merchants and peddlers were a constant presence, most traveling from the northern and eastern kingdoms to sell wares not often found in Elouve. Eugenie seemed to thrive when keeping herself at the center of human activity, an unusual lifestyle for a vampire. They threaded their way toward Eugenie's domicile, which turned out to be one of the larger residences in town: an impressive two-story brownstone made from a combination of whitewashed bricks and adobe.

As always, Eugenie was somehow dressed for both camouflage and attention. A protrusion of peacock plumes formed a nest atop her head, and her dress was sewn with hundreds of trimmed feathers in every color known to man. She soon had Xiaodan stretched out on a comfortable-looking bed, fussing over her form.

Paolo, her companion, was as crotchety as ever. He held a tray bearing several hot beverages, wordlessly proffering a mug to Remy with a welcoming grunt.

Eugenie affectionately brushed a strand of hair out of Xiaodan's face. "The poor girl. She's young by our standards, but already she's been through so much."

"It's very good to see you again, Eugenie," Remy said quietly. "I wished it was under better circumstances."

"There is much to do," the woman said, "and I am sure that Lord Malekh here is already quite pressed for time. Saracosa is gone, milord, as are many other villages."

Malekh stared at her. Remy was reminded of their first meeting, when she'd told them that Brushfen had been razed to the ground and its villagers killed. "Overwhelmed by kindred?"

"Yes. The majority of Hallifax's soldiers have retreated to his stronghold at Wycaff, prepared to defend it and their liege to the death if necessary. But every village and town between there and Derila to the north has been reported lost to the waves of vampires who had emerged out of nowhere and had laid waste to their lands."

"Since when?"

"We only received confirmation of this an hour before I sent a pigeon to my Rocksplen informant." Eugenie shook her head. "By all accounts, it was a massacre. Far, far worse than what had transpired at Brushfen. My source at Saracosa was fortunate enough to get out before the worst could befall him, and only because he was already near the borders at Parhi when the attacks began. You can speak to him if you'd like. He's reliable, and has a cool head in desperate situations, and is currently fortifying himself with our ale reserves in the kitchen. He's quite shaken—he had good friends killed before his own eyes in a coordinated attack."

"But so quickly?" Remy asked hoarsely. If only Wycaff, Kerenai's capital, remained standing in between, then that meant over a hundred miles had been taken by vampires in the space of one night.

"First Court," Malekh said tersely, an answer more than a question.

Eugenie nodded. "There was no mistaking their scarlet robes, milord. Perhaps it would be better if you spoke to him directly, if you can forgive his state of inebriation. It is not something that I would wish on any human to endure, sober or not."

Leaving Paolo to keep vigil over Xiaodan, they made for the kitchen. The informant in question was by the pantry, a nearly empty tankard of ale in his hands. His clothes were muddy and bloodstained, and he stank as if he'd been rolling around in a pigsty. But even in his distress, he was mindful of where he stood to keep the mud off Eugenie's clean floor.

He took a swig from the tankard and nodded abruptly at them as they approached. His demeanor was calmer than Remy had expected, but there was no mistaking the haunted look in his eyes. His hands shook slightly as he tipped his head back to finish the dregs.

"Mason," Eugenie said, in a gentle voice. "There are some patrons of mine who would like more information about what happened in the north."

"What can I tell them that they cannot already imagine, Eugenie?" the man asked wearily. "Would you like me to recount how people were torn limb from limb by those vile crimson fiends? How they lapped up the children's blood, toyed with the villagers who attempted to crawl away, taking their lives at the very last moment in horrible, painful ways? Demons spawned from the darkest pits of hell, one and all. I wish them all dead with every fiber of my being. Could you spare another tankard, milady? I still cannot wash the taste of copper from my mouth."

Eugenie wordlessly passed him a second bottle. The poor man downed it all in one go.

"We can do little now to save those villagers," Malekh said, "but trust that we will do our utmost to prevent more deaths. What of the kindred that attacked? How large was the horde? How did you learn that the same had occurred in the other towns?"

Mason squinted up at him. "You're one of them, aren't you?" he asked accusingly, but with none of the anger. "One of those fanged bastard nobles who want peace with the rest of us. Well, that peace is dead, milord, after everything I've seen. I wasn't the only one of Eugenie's people sequestered up north, just the one that got away. It was Rylen who came riding in with his horse all tuckered out, panicked and sounding the alarm. He'd just come from Ferilwen, he said, and the only reason they held out long enough for him to get away was because of all the soldiers coming in from nearby Lufthan on their way back to King Hallifax, a pox on his name for all eternity. Rylen had gotten a couple of those men drunk hours before, learned that Hallifax was pulling them back into the capital because of 'certain incidents farther north,' to quote him precisely. They knew little themselves, only that the king was adamant they return to the capital immediately."

He barked out a laugh. "Turns out the vampires were only three quarters of an hour behind the regiment. Vampires and one hideous mutation that spewed poison. They were all silent, moved like strung-up marionettes, he said. Didn't matter; they killed quick enough. Rylen barely escaped with his horse. Rode nonstop until he arrived at Saracosa, and even then, he beat the ghouls by only two hours. Enough time to relay to me everything he'd been told, before we were attacked in turn."

He shuddered. "Rylen thought he'd gotten away, but he didn't, milord. They must have gotten to him—some bite or mark that festered. Minutes before the vampires showed up, he turned. Didn't realize what was happening himself. Thought he'd go into a frenzy, but it was far worse than that. He—" The man gulped. "He started growing. Massive-like, with awful scales popping up all over his body. His skin melted off before he even had time to scream. He looked like . . . them. Like some creature of the deep, eyes like hell. They turned him, I know they did."

"No. They couldn't have." Remy leaned forward, knuckles white against the table. There was *no way* the First Court could've gotten their hands on Dr. Yost's formula to create mutations of their own . . .

. . . Or could they? Vasilik, Malekh's former lover, had acquired a colossus of his own, using his own blood to make it his perfectly obedient thrall. Before his death, he had hinted at an alliance with the Night Empress herself. Any secrets he might have gleaned from Remy's father, he could have passed on to the court he served.

Malekh had already come to the same conclusion, several steps ahead of Remy besides. He grabbed Mason by his shirt collar.

"What are you doing?" Eugenie exclaimed.

But Malekh was already forcing the man's head back, ripping part of his shirt in the process to reveal a deep, ugly-looking gash that started from the man's collarbone and retreated farther down his chest. It was putrefied and decomposing rapidly before their eyes, flesh sloughing to reveal bubbling sores underneath.

"Mason," Eugenie gasped. "The good Light, Mason, what did they do to you?"

The man stared helplessly back at them. "Impossible," he

rasped. "Rylen took a swipe, but there was no mark on me when I arrived. It can't be—Rylen got it different. Lost his mind before he started mutating. They overwhelmed Hallifax's towns. I'm—no. Got to warn everyone. Got to—got to—"

His face shifted—literally, as if something had burrowed beneath his skin and was scurrying up the side of his cheek under the flesh. The veins on his neck began to stand out, bulging forward as if they were a separate organism of their own.

"I'm so sorry, Mason," Eugenie whispered and lifted her hand. Remy hadn't noticed it before, but her nails were long and sharp.

The man's head dropped to the floor, shorn of neck. But even then, his body continued to tremble and shift, the muscles in his arms bunching up and swelling to double, then triple their sizes.

"Stay back, Eugenie," Malekh ordered, though the point was moot.

"We have to evacuate the whole town," Remy said, Breaker already in his grip. He slid the knifechain out, the spike attached to the other end swinging. "We need to at least get it out of this place before—"

He felt the sudden rush of heat from behind him as a great burst of light illuminated the room, and his instinct was to duck and cover his face with one hand while the other raised Breaker in anticipation of some new blow.

Lightning sizzled past them in the space between him and Malekh. It struck the still-transforming Mason, obliterating his body in an instant. It was a familiar brightness—one Remy had seen indirectly many times before.

He turned.

Xiaodan stood in the doorway, hands on her hips and glaring at them like they were all somehow at fault. Her eyes were a blazing gray. Beside her was Paolo, looking discombobulated.

There was a faint noise from the floor where Mason's head lay, still moving and groaning, still transforming. Xiaodan leveled a finger at it. Another burst of light exploded at the tip, effectively blowing it into nothingness. Her arm wavered.

Malekh caught her just as she slumped to the floor, unconscious once again.

"I don't understand," Eugenie quavered into the silence. "You said that she was no longer able to summon the sun."

"That's what we thought. This changes matters. You must ask the captain in charge to inspect everyone in town and monitor those with suspicious injuries. It's clear to me now that some of the mutations attacking the villages were born in this same manner." Malekh paused, his gaze straying back to the floor where Mason had been. "I'm sorry about your informant."

Eugenie sighed heavily. "He was dedicated until the very end. If you hadn't been here when he had . . ." She shuddered. "I'm friends with the commander stationed here, and I shall send word to him immediately. I would not wish the same fate for this town as Brushfen and Saracosa. What do you intend to do next?"

"Any hope of treating Xiaodan lies within my laboratory at the Fata Morgana. And if the borders between Hallifax's kingdom and Aluria are about to be overrun, then we must act quickly to prevent both First Court vampires and mutations from finding their way here." Malekh carefully deposited the unconscious Xiaodan back into Paolo's arms.

"My heartfelt apologies, milord," Eugenie's lover said. "She jumped up and tore out of the room before I could stop her."

"None are necessary. Any precaution you'd taken would have done little to slow her down."

"All the same, I shall guard her better this time."

"I've intercepted more than just a few messages from the Alurian queen, milord," Eugenie said after Paolo had carried Xiaodan away. "Hallifax may have abandoned most of his kingdom, but Queen Ophelia has committed several regiments of Reapers to the safety of the villages he's left behind. Any still standing, at least."

"I do not think Reapers alone will be enough to combat this threat, Eugenie."

The woman smiled faintly. "It's rather ironic then, that Lord Valenbonne brings his own mutations to shore up Alurian defenses." She carefully slid a slippered foot across the wood, probing for ashes. "Xiaodan is quite thorough," she observed sadly. "Mason had no family to speak of, but I would like a memorial commissioned for him, even with nothing to bury."

"I didn't know my father had made more mutations," Remy said, stunned.

Malekh's gaze was hard. "It's a mistake to bring those creatures to the borders."

"Aluria currently lacks the forces to defend their territories, and Queen Ophelia has bowed to the pressure. To spare both Reapers and soldiers the risks of war by sending these monsters in their stead, I suppose." Eugenie shuddered again. "Unfortunately, this isn't the only bad news I bring. Cao Fanglei reached out to me two days ago."

The vampire lord visibly tensed.

"She wished to tell me that the eastern borders leading to Situ will be well defended under her clan, and that she has already sent overtures to Queen Ophelia. She has invoked your alliance with Aluria as one of the reasons she has decided to aid the humans."

"We are not currently under any official alliance with Aluria."

"She says it does not matter." Eugenie cleared her throat. "I took the liberty of, uh, perusing the contents of her letter, just in case. She was rather put out that you chose to visit the other court leaders these last few days while she was resigned to only a message from you. She has been in contact with the other remaining courts regarding your request to convene, and they have unanimously decided to gather at the Allpriory."

"No," Malekh said immediately.

Eugenie reached into her dress and rummaged inside a pocket, finally pulling out a sheaf of folded parchment.

Malekh said nothing, his expression stony. When he made no move to take the proffered letter, Remy took it in his stead, unrolling the paper and scanning it quickly, lest the Summer Lord wrest it away.

As much as you detest the place, there are decided benefits to holding our session where it would be well defended against what the Night Empress may throw our way, Cao Fanglei had written. *The meeting is to take place two weeks hence. I hope that you will deign to make an appearance before then, but our decision is final. Was it not you who called for a parley in the first place? Was it not you who argued for cooperation, to give up our individual pride to work together against this new incarnation of the First Court? Or do you still fear the Godsflame?*

We expect you there, Lord Zidan. You can even bring your lover with you, if you wish. It would be most amusing to see Raghnall throw a conniption once he discovers the man is a Reaper.

3

COOPERATION

"What's this Allpriory that Eugenie mentioned?" Remy asked as Malekh prepared the helhests to leave. They'd spent the night at Eugenie's residence, which, in contrast to the woman's own wardrobe, was all muted hues and tasteful decor. Fortunately, Eugenie lived near the outskirts of town, with a small path leading into the forest that proved valuable for ferrying both informants and undead horses in and out without detection. Remy, Xiaodan, and Malekh had shared sleeping quarters, though the latter never showed up for bed.

Xiaodan still hadn't woken. Remy had struggled not to lie awake all night with worry.

When he'd finally slept, he'd dreamed of Miss Grissell again, only this time she was leaving because his father was a right bastard prat and had sent her away when he'd heard Remy singing his mother's lullaby. The man's only saving grace was that he'd paid her enough that she'd never need to work again. This had made Remy feel guilty as a child, though Miss Grissell had insisted it wasn't his fault, that she'd miss him so terribly and oh how proud she was of him. Her expression in the dream was as loving and affectionate as he'd remembered, brown eyes filled with tears. He'd come awake after that to find Xiaodan wrapped around his torso, and it had taken several minutes to gently disentangle himself from her embrace.

"And this Godsflame," Remy went on. "Why are you determined not to meet them?"

Malekh shot him a sour look. "The Godsflame is a *what*, not a who. The Allpriory was once the headquarters for the First Court and the Night King."

Remy faltered. "Ah. And is there no way to hold this meeting elsewhere? Why are they so adamant about it?"

"The Godsflame is one of many unusual features within the Allpriory. It's a pillar of fire tended to by a noble vampire clan whose responsibility is to keep it burning. The first vampire was said to have been forged within its conflagration. Kindred who have lived long enough can walk into its fires to augment their abilities."

"Like compulsion? Or controlling the weather, like the one who brought the rains down at Chànggē Shuǐ?"

Malekh nodded. "It does not come without risks. More vampires would perish in the flames than emerge from it with newfound skills. Longevity has little to do with that success, though it is believed that living for centuries increases one's chances of survival."

Remy could only imagine. To throw themselves into a pillar of flames would have required a bravery very few possessed. "Ever tried it yourself?"

Malekh fixed him with a disapproving look. "I have found little inclination. It is not worth the endeavor, given the other consequences."

"*Other* consequences?"

"Even if a vampire emerges alive from those flames, their mind may never be quite the same. The fires can renew their bloodthirst, and they may be more prone to violence as a result. Something within the Godsflame takes a piece of them away in exchange for strength." He turned away. "Fanglei thinks that Xiaodan could benefit from the Godsflame. But I do not wish to imperil either her health, her life, or her sanity on so slim a possibility."

"Which is why we're heading to your laboratory at the Third Court?" Remy squinted at the horizon, as if he could perceive from that alone how such a court's castle might look. Perhaps tall, dark, and disgruntled, like its master.

"We can reach it by day's end if we hurry." Malekh gave Peanut one last affectionate stroke. "If you wish to gather more supplies, now would be the time to procure them."

It was a good idea, even if it had come from Malekh, so Remy ventured into the town's marketplace in hopes for better sustenance than the simple bread and dry beef jerky he'd been subsiding on along the road. He'd seen a bulk of sweet ham in one of the stalls when he'd passed earlier and was feeling the need to indulge, with a few bottles of wine for company.

There had been a noticeable increase in soldiers nearly overnight. Libéliard already had its own barracks, but the men that patrolled the streets had not been there when Remy and his companions had arrived the day before, which meant the captain had taken Eugenie's warning seriously. An outpost leading into the town had been erected, and travelers who'd only just arrived were being questioned by the sentries. Remy figured they would need to leave before the soldiers turned their attentions to their little group.

There was no mistaking the lapels the men wore, nor the royal insignia of Aluria so clearly embroidered on their shoulders. They'd been sent by Queen Ophelia—or perhaps by his own father, acting in Her Majesty's stead.

His suspicions were confirmed when he idled by a market stall, inspecting some onions while two privates conducted a hushed conversation nearby. The plaza was noisy enough that eavesdropping would prove difficult to anyone else, but Remy's bloodsharing with Xiaodan and Malekh had given him certain advantages that even bloodwakers couldn't replicate.

"There's nothing here to defend," one of the men was grumbling. "They sent most of the Reapers up into Kerenai territory, so you know that's where the real action is. What good are we doing staying here, listening to these villagers chattering about their day without realizing the danger close by? All we do here is check them for signs of bites. Clerks could bloody well do that."

"Lord Valenbonne's insistent about it. Captain Gareth announced some stricter measures yesterday, but that's to be expected. Surely you can't be serious about wanting to fight those undead buggers up north. Lord Valenbonne says they're from the First Court, and ten times as deadly."

"Valenbonne's been obsessed with First Court vampires for decades, Sloan. He'll say any vampire is a First Court vampire just so he can grind them down to dust. I've already applied to join the Reapers, but I can't make a name for myself while I'm stuck in this backwater town."

"You'd best be careful what you wish for, Jaren. Once Commander Gareth's positive we can prevent those bloodsuckers from trickling in, he says that Lord Valenbonne intends to bring the rest of us on reserve here down to Meridian Keep."

Meridian Keep, Remy thought. Former nest of the Second, so-called Court of Beauty. A five-hour ride from Libéliard on regular steeds.

"Our contingent will be moving out soon, and if you don't get yourself killed or worse, you can bet you'll be getting your silver scythes soon enough." The man glanced over to where he'd been standing, but Remy was already walking away, heart pounding in his chest.

"The logic is sound," Malekh conceded when Remy told him what he had overheard. "Your father may have his faults, but he knows strategy. It's feasible to suspect that there are already vampires who've made it past the barriers they're enforcing between Ophelia and Hallifax's kingdoms, and Meridian Keep is the most likely place for them to be. At least Valenbonne was wise enough to instruct his men to check the villagers for any signs of mutation in the other towns."

The idea of more hidden infected like Mason sent a spike of alarm through Remy. He tugged his collar closer to his neck, uncomfortably aware of the faint love bite Xiaodan had made on one side, and of Malekh's in the other. "I've no doubt that my father would return to the Keep even without proof of a new infestation within. It's the site of his old victories against the Second Court, and he would leap at the chance to repeat his successes. A glaring accomplishment so early in his career as the new lord high steward. He'll even oversee the regiments himself."

"Do you wish to join him?"

The question took Remy by surprise.

Malekh's gaze was still on Cookie's flank. He didn't even look in Remy's direction. "You were trained as a Reaper. Your father's rise to power has likely reflected well on you, and any accolades you achieve on the battlefield will only increase your esteem and reputation with your colleagues, no matter how dismal you believe their regard for you is. It would be a good opportunity for you, for your continued future in Elouve. What are you doing?"

Remy was chortling, slinging his arm over Cookie's mane to keep himself upright, sharing his mirth with the undead stallion. It felt good to laugh for a change. "That's horseshit and you know it. They don't care about how well I fight. They'll think of something else to find fault over, make up some new affront. I'm done with their politics and with their prejudices. If you're worrying on my behalf, don't. I am already among the peers who matter."

Remy let go of the helhest and folded his arms. "I'm already among my peers," he repeated, because the fool was likely to misinterpret him again. "I'm where I'm supposed to be."

Something shifted in Malekh's face. It was not quite a smile—not quite anything, really—but his gaze lost some of its edge, softening his profile. "We'd best leave in the next several minutes. If they know your father, then some may recognize you by face."

Eugenie bustled out with Paolo, the man carrying a wooden basket under one arm. "More sustenance for your journey, Remy," she said cheerfully. "Malekh has not been feeding you enough. Paolo bakes the tastiest pastries—he's made a fresh batch right out of the oven. Please take them with all our gratitude."

"We should at least pay you." The smell of fresh bread that wafted out made Remy's stomach rumble.

"You have done so much for us already. And we are friends, are we not?" She bustled off to consult with Malekh one last time. Paolo handed Remy the basket.

"How do you do it?" Remy was unable to help himself. "You—you're not kindred, and—"

"I'll croak one day and leave her alone?" Paolo was blunt, as always, though something in his harsh voice sparked an emotion in Remy that he couldn't understand. "And you're thinking about how that might look like with you, with them?"

"It—it's crossed my mind."

"I love her enough not to meddle with the parts of me that make me myself. And she loves me enough not to demand that I do. Might be I'll change my mind, might be I won't. Might be I'll change enough on my own that wanting to turn and be with her is what makes me me. But that's between her and me and no one else, ain't it? Here. Have this meat pastry before you go. It's best when it's still hot."

Remy obeyed; it was fantastic. "You should start your own bakery."

There was a glint of amusement in Paolo's normally apathetic gaze. "Too busy carving out cane frogs for Eugenie to make a regular go of it."

"It was *you* who made all those horri—those souvenirs for her stall?" Remy asked, appalled.

"Better money than bread could ever make us." He turned to nod at Eugenie, who drifted closer.

"I believe I know the whereabouts of the young Fifth Court vampire with an affinity for metalwork," she said.

"Elke?" Remy clasped his hands to hers. "Do you know where she is?"

"I have an inkling of where she went after leaving Elouve, but nothing to confirm just yet. I will send word to Malekh at Fata Morgana once I know more." Eugenie squeezed his palm. "And as a symbol of our friendship, I won't even charge you for it."

THEY SPOTTED larger groups of soldiers after heading northwest. Malekh kept to the side roads out of view, and the helhests were quick enough that Remy supposed they were nothing more than a blur from the soldiers' perspectives. Peanut and Cookie were excellent at sidestepping obstacles and avoiding the areas where the legions gathered, covering swifter ground along the smaller paths instead.

Remy's departure from Loxley House had been civil, but rather cold. Whatever the old man's motivations had been, even if he had created these mutations out of some perverse desire to protect Aluria, Remy could never forgive him. No one, save Malekh and Xiaodan, would ever believe that he hadn't been privy to his father's and Dr. Yost's experiments, and Edgar Pendergast had taken advantage of that to keep Remy silent.

Midway through the afternoon, Remy felt the carriage slow

down, the undead horses trotting to a stop. Curious, he poked his head out the window. "Anything the matter?"

"There are more kindred afoot." Malekh's voice was low, angry.

"That's never stopped us before."

"It is with your father's soldiers, not us, that they are currently fighting with."

"What?" Remy scanned the clearing before them and saw nothing.

"A few miles ahead," Malekh said. "They're spread out across the plains, and it will prove difficult for my helhests to pass through without finding us involved."

"Are you saying we don't have a choice?" Remy glanced worriedly down at Xiaodan.

"We are far enough from the border that there should not be any sizable covens in the area. Certainly not enough to commit any full regiments. But Meridian Keep lies within this territory."

"So he was right? There *are* First Court kindred hiding there?"

"If so, it is crucial to stamp them out. We will stay close to the battle and determine our next course of action from there. But I would appreciate it if you stayed in the carriage and remain by Xiaodan's side in the interim."

Remy sighed heavily. "Don't take too long."

Malekh, he was dismayed to learn, was right, as the noise of armed steel clashing became more apparent over the next few minutes. There were Reapers at the fray, fighting alongside the royal soldiers; Remy could see the familiar black coats, the fire lances they shot unerringly into the vampires they met head-on. There were perhaps a hundred and fifty, two hundred of the undead, but most wore nondescript brown robes that gave none of their affiliation away, hoods pulled over their heads to hide features. None of them wore the scarlet robes he detested.

But the vampires were not the worst things on the battlefield, and Remy now understood why Malekh had wanted to linger.

There were mutations aiding the human army; four that he could count. They were all likely sprung from the same test tubes that Yost tinkered with, fifteen feet tall and made of painful-looking sores and tumors, covering their bodies like trypophobic nightmares in lieu of skin. They were hairless and devoid of clothing, though they had no observable extremities. Their only variations lay in their number of limbs, ranging from three to seven and stuck at random points on them like afterthoughts.

Remy had fought colossi before. It was jarring to see the hulks fighting *for* them this time.

One of the behemoths lumbered forward, seizing an unlucky vampire by the throat and dashing his head back on the ground. The other colossi were adept at similar acts of violence. The hunters were taught to fight with swift precision, to kill as cleanly as possible. The behemoths, on the other hand, tore their prey apart with silent gusto. It was horrific to watch.

Even worse than the foul hulks was Grimesworthy. Unlike the other Rot-infected, the large man still maintained his human facade, still dressed in his valet's uniform, but nothing about the way he was slamming his fists into the vampires, literally punching them into pieces, indicated any humanity inside him.

The Alurians appeared to be in control of the situation, so Remy did the smart thing and remained inside the carriage, watching as the enemies diminished in number. It didn't take long after their arrival for the surviving vampires to realize they were outmatched, many turning tail and fleeing before more of the mutations could get their hands on them.

One vampire was far too slow. He blinked out of view and then reappeared again with Malekh clutching at his throat, but he continued to fight like a caged lion, snarling.

Something whistled through the air toward them, and before Remy could shout a warning, Malekh had already jerked out of the way. Not so the vampire captive, who made a harsh gurgling sound as a crossbow bolt plunged through his throat. He fell and was abruptly yanked out of Malekh's grip by Grimesworthy.

Without so much as a change in expression Grimesworthy lifted up one meaty fist and began pounding the vampire into the ground, the rhythmic and steady blows a horrific contrast to the mess he was inflicting, not stopping until his victim was no more than a bloody smear.

Even Malekh was stunned by the colossus's calm ferocity. Now he sprung; a hard shove sent the hulk skidding a few feet forward. The manservant released his grip on the corpse and turned to confront the new danger.

"Hold!" A voice thundered through the open plain. "Grimesworthy, heel!"

The man striding toward Malekh was nearly unrecognizable to Remy. As an invalid, Edgar Pendergast had been sour and angry at the world, riddled with illness and spite; if lemons had arses, they could have passed for his portrait. But no longer bent and confined to a wheelchair, Lord Valenbonne was now in the peak of health for a man in his sixties—the good-looking, stately features he'd once been known for returned, with the step and surety of one thirty years younger. He carried a battle-axe loosely in his grip; the other held the crossbow he had shot the enemy vampire with. His smile was broad. He had a full head of hair now, dark like Remy's but more impeccably arranged.

Much to Remy's dismay, Dr. Quintin Yost was with them. The stocky doctor strode after his patron, looking eagerly around him like the carnage was some exciting carnival to behold.

"Lord Malekh," Edgar Pendergast greeted, stopping several feet away. "My apologies. My manservant, you see, has been trained to recognize all vampires as the enemy, but to his credit, I had little idea that you would be gracing us with your presence today. Grimesworthy, return."

The hulk lowered his arms, coming to full rigidity for a few moments as if rigor mortis was trying to reassert itself over his undead body. Failing, he trotted back toward his master like a beloved pet. Valenbonne raised his axe, and the other mutations, too, came lumbering. Remy took note of the repugnance plain on the other Reapers' faces, their lack of surprise. How many times had his father flexed these displays of power that the others had long become immured to the sight of, even disgusted as they were?

"The vampire you slew was acting like he was under a thrall," Malekh said icily. "I was trying to verify his condition."

"If it is details about this particular horde that you seek, then I am more than happy to provide you with everything you wish to know. I have already ferreted out their lair, my good sir. This was not our first battle with this wretched group. I have interrogated far too many of them for my peace of mind this week alone, and all my suspicions have since been confirmed twentyfold. Villages in Kerenai have fallen due to foul mutations, and we have contained the threats so far with Yost's improved antidotes. You'd best believe that I will not allow the same to occur on Alurian soil."

Lord Valenbonne jerked his thumb toward the east at some distant landmark only he could perceive. "These fiends have been roosting at Meridian Keep. Perhaps these kindred believe themselves the next generation of that doomed clan, though most of these vampires are far from comely. At least Declan Aughessy and his minions looked like they could be the pretty concubines of the Night King—pretty before I'd lopped off their heads, at least. I presume that my erstwhile son remains with you?"

Valenbonne had been infirmed for much of Remy's life, but even then, he'd been crafty and cunning, not one to let things pass unobserved. The old man's gaze strayed toward the carriage Remy sat in, though it was half-hidden by the trees and nearly invisible had one not known where to look. "Are you there, my boy?"

There was no hiding now; already the man was walking toward them, gleeful at having deduced correctly. Remy alighted quickly from the carriage before Valenbonne could draw up beside it, turning to his father with grim regard. "Sir."

On the other hand, Anthony Castellblanc, the Marquess of Riones, was a much more welcome sight. The man let out a happy yell when he spotted Remy and came bounding over. His head was freshly shaved, but he otherwise looked the same as the last time Remy had seen him. "Aphelion, what a fortuitous surprise!" he called out. "I would shake your hand, but I'm not quite presentable at the moment." He gazed down ruefully at his bloodied lance. "I thought you were making for the Third Court's domains. Didn't you have a greater head start, what with those stallions of Lord Malekh's?"

"We had to make a quick detour farther north."

"Ah, that whole bother with King Hallifax?" Yost shook his head sadly. "A shame. We could have evacuated the villagers nearer to Alurian territory, had His Majesty thought to send us word. Those poor people. 'Tis why I offered to come along. My assistants at Elouve are well equipped to continue with the necessary inoculations and safeguards, but you can never be sure of what you can learn on the battlefield." He patted Grimesworthy's hand fondly.

"You look well enough, at least, Remington," Lord Valenbonne said, casting a critical eye on him, and Remy resisted the urge to draw his coat tighter around himself to hide the small marks on his neck. "Given the reports from the northern border, I would not be surprised to find this region awash in all manner of bloodsuckers soon. Begging your pardon, of course, Lord Malekh."

"No offense taken," Malekh said acidly. "Did any of these vampires tell you why they were taking up residence at Meridian Keep, or did your manservant take liberties with them before they could?"

Valenbonne chuckled. "They were all as enthralled as the vampire you caught, and despite Grimesworthy's tender care, they gave nothing away. The only mindless drivel they spouted over and over was that *she* was sleeping within the castle, and that *she* would wake and bring everyone else into her fold."

"They looked to be villagers." Malekh nudged aside the robe of the vampire that Grimesworthy had so gruesomely killed, revealing the blood-soaked simple clothes of a traveler, spartan garbs rather than the expensive regalia that so often marked one from the Court of Beauty. He blinked out of view, and Remy turned to find him on one knee, studying another corpse. "When Zelenka was attacked, many of those vampires were newly made from Brushfen, pitted against us by one of Vasilik's lackeys. It would not be surprising to see the strategy duplicated again."

"But why would they be here? The towns in the area are well defended, but they did not seem inclined to attack any of them."

Valenbonne paused, considering. "So you think they are here for some other purpose." He nodded his head thoughtfully. "Of course. Hallifax, that miserable bastard. These were *his* villagers, not ours. These must have made it past the border long before we were made aware of what had transpired at Kerenai. But if they aren't here to attack, then what use does the Night Empress have for them?" Valenbonne smiled, a bloodthirsty sight. "But it does sound like my former wife lies within Meridian Keep, as I thought. Perhaps this is the regiment compelled to protect her."

Remy felt his chest constrict. "You cannot be certain she is there," he rasped.

"She was dead before you knew enough to remember her, Remington, but surely you can feel her. I can. I feel her malice from miles away, and it points me toward that damned castle. She is hiding inside those walls, I am sure of it." Edgar Pendergast turned to Malekh. "We aim to reach Meridian Keep before nightfall. Perhaps you might care to accompany us. Speaking of the Second Court's lair—a fine job you made of Giornovo. Politics prevented me from avenging the Lady Annalisa, but if the reports that reached me were true, you were far more brutal than Grimesworthy, for all your displeasure at how my manservant disposes of his opponents."

"We have pressing business elsewhere," Malekh said tersely.

"And what about you, Remington?" Valenbonne grinned at Remy. "Would you think to leave your poor old father in danger? Turn down the chance to see your mother again?"

"We accept your invitation, milord," came the soft, faint voice from behind him. Xiaodan stood, frail-looking but otherwise unrepentant.

"Xiaodan," Malekh said. "You need rest. There is nothing in Meridian Keep that is worth our—"

But Xiaodan shook her head. Her hand was pressed against her chest, fist clenched so tightly that Remy was afraid she would carve a fresh hollow between her breasts. "Lord Valenbonne is correct," she said. "The Night Empress lies within the castle. I can feel her heartbeats as if they were my own. And I must find her there and see to finishing what we both started."

4

MERIDIAN KEEP

Nothing could convince Xiaodan to change her mind. "No amount of sleep and rest will help me now, Zidan." Her heartbeats had slowed, and she was perfectly composed, like she hadn't been in a coma for four days running. "Whatever she did at Elouve, she took something from me. Possibly my sunbringing abilities, maybe more. And I won't be whole again until I take it back."

"Xiaodan—" Malekh began.

"There's a reason she's hiding out in the castle instead of invading Hallifax's domain herself. There's a reason she hasn't shown herself in the last several days when she could have used my convalescence to strengthen her hold, make herself a much more visible presence to intimidate the kingdoms. She did not leave that fight unscathed either."

"And how do you know all this?"

"I can't explain it. I just do."

Malekh made an exasperated sound. "And on the chances that you are incorrect?"

"If my assessment is incorrect, then I give you leave to spirit us out of the castle whenever and however you deem necessary—but not until we can confirm my words aren't true." Xiaodan smiled sweetly, and it was a beautiful sight to behold for Remy after the last few days of watching her pale, listless face. "I am sure that my strong, wise fiancé would be more than up to the task."

Malekh only grunted. "If your fiancé was as strong or as wise as you like to believe, he would have taken you back to the Fata Morgana regardless of your theories."

Even fresh out of a prolonged unconsciousness, Xiaodan was still clever about getting her way, and soon all three of them sat inside the carriage as it raced east with the rest of Lord Valenbonne's army. The helhests were clearly impatient at having to match their pace with the slower and very alive horses that the soldiers preferred, but Malekh thought it prudent to remain with the humans.

The rest of the regiment kept themselves well away from the undead stallions. Remy didn't blame them, because Peanut and Cookie looked like the exact archetype of cadaverous steeds that lich lords would ride into battle, coal black and red-eyed and massively skeletal. But the men kept an even farther distance from the mutations following after them, the beasts easily able to keep up despite their bulk. Save for Riones's enthusiastic welcome, they were silent regarding Remy's unexpected appearance, though that was better than their usual derision.

Malekh said they would reach the castle in another two hours at the rate they were traveling, and for the first time since being told what a helhest was, Remy wished the steeds could go a little faster.

"You could have gone with them," Malekh added. He was staring out the window with his arms folded across his chest, not looking at Remy one bit again.

"What?"

"You could have gone with them. Your father clearly wanted you close by."

"Is this your roundabout way of saying that you don't like my company?"

"Don't be absurd. I would not have been offended, had you chosen to ride with him."

Remy looked down at his lap, unable to hide his grin. "I prefer it when you're sweet like this."

"Pendergast."

"I'd be much obliged if you'd stop acting like I've had to turn down something better, because you're both the *something better* I would have rejected, had I gone with my father. Did you know that Riones accepted the job I refused in Elouve? I wish him all the best, with no regrets."

"If that is your wish" was all Malekh said in response. He continued to look out the window.

"I should fall asleep more often," Xiaodan marveled lightly.

"Are you okay?" Remy asked her quietly. "Malekh is right. You're in no condition to be confronting anyone, least of all my moth—the Night Empress."

"I'm weaker than I want to be, but strong enough for anything else." Xiaodan stretched, faint cracking sounds coming from numerous body joints as she did. "I would be lying if I said I was at my best. But something tells me I'll never be at my prime strength again if I don't confront her while she's just as weak."

"We are risking a lot on assumptions, Xiaodan," Malekh said gruffly.

"You would have put your foot down right from the start if you didn't think I had the remotest chance of being right." Xiaodan reached to take his hand, and then took Remy's with the other. "Thank you," she said softly, "I know it wasn't easy looking after me these last several days—incidentally, how long was I asleep?"

"Six days," Remy supplied.

"What? I've been useless for almost a week?"

"Give or take a few hours, including when you woke up long enough to blast one of Eugenie's mutated informants into nothingness."

"We were at Eugenie's?"

"You don't remember? You sunbringed him into nothing and then collapsed afterward. Or is it 'sunbrought'? 'Sunbrang'? I—" Remy stopped. Xiaodan had frozen, stock-still despite the moving carriage. "Xiaodan?"

She turned to him, her eyes filled with tears. "I still have it?" she whispered. "I didn't lose it? I still have my . . ." She bowed her head, pressed her hands against her face, and, to Remy's shock, began to cry.

XIAODAN HAD composed herself by the time Meridian Keep came into view, the castle rising up above an enclosure of trees like a big black vertical stain against the clouds hovering behind it. "I apologize," she said. Remy and Malekh had taken turns holding her until the worst of her weeping had passed. "I don't know what came over me."

"S'all right," Remy said.

"Have you ever had to live with something you thought was a detriment your whole life, only for it to become such an integral part of you that it felt like you were missing a piece of yourself after it was gone?"

"I've never had to contain the fucking sun up my short arse," Remy said, "but I understand."

Xiaodan laughed at that and gave him a light peck on the cheek. Then she looked down at her hands and focused.

"I'm trying, but I don't feel anything," she said, though she didn't sound too upset. "Is it because I haven't regained my full strength yet, or . . . ? I should be able to. Eventually. I just need to figure out how."

"We could learn quicker if we returned to Fata Morgana," Malekh said, ever stubborn.

"You're still not going to get me to change my mind, love. I need to be at Meridian Keep."

The castle in question had seen better days. It must have been a beautifully imposing fortress once, befitting whatever fancy shit the Court of Beauty had been known for. It had graceful arches and high lofty towers even more majestic than the palace Queen Ophelia resided in at Elouve.

But the white ivory exterior had turned gray and bleak over the years, and thick rows of ivy had overrun the walls. It was an overgrown briar patch run amuck, and nothing about it suggested habitability. There were the remains of a moat surrounding the castle, the trenches long since drained of water. Thick roots grew from the ground, nearly as large as tree trunks, and Remy wasn't sure he wanted to step into that tangle of branches and vines. They were more effective than the moat would have been had the latter retained water, blocking the approaching army from the castle's entrance.

The severity of the infestation became clearer within yards of the main doors. The overgrowth did not come from the forests surrounding the structure, but from somewhere within the Keep itself.

"Seems to me that something else has occupied the castle after the Second Court's demise," Malekh said quietly.

"How did this escape our notice?" Remy's father sounded disgusted. He turned to Riones. "Did Astonbury not send scouts here on occasion, should any more vampires return to reclaim the territory?"

The marquess winced. "I don't think so, milord. The castle itself is in an isolated region of Aluria, with no nearby towns or villages to be threatened. He must have thought it best to leave it be."

Valenbonne snorted. "Please. He thought to ignore Meridian Keep because it was the site of one of my major accomplishments, and he did not wish to be reminded of that fact. No use dwelling on his incompetence now. It would have taken years for the briars to overcome the castle like this. And yet we've been oblivious all this time."

Xiaodan was looking up at the turrets, a determined look on her face. Already she was clasping her cloak around herself, as if bracing for the inevitable.

"What is it inside this place that you're worried about?" Remy whispered quietly to Malekh. "I don't think it's just the Night Empress."

"There was a reason the Second Court was known as the Court of Beauty. It was not a coincidence that most of its members were fair of face. The Night King initially created the Second as his personal harem. But in the years before it fell, there were rumors of Aughessy, the former Second Court king, and some of his clanmates using other methods to enhance their looks."

"Some blood ritual?"

"No." Malekh gave the grounds around them a pointed look. "The Godsflame was not the only feature that the Allpriory possessed. A sacred tree called the Fount once grew within the temple, purportedly blessed with healing properties. It was consumed by the Godsflame eons ago, and we believe it was what gave the fires its special abilities. Their similarities are . . . striking."

"There's a damned vampiric tree inside the castle?" But it made sense. There was nothing nearby that would justify the thickness of the roots and vines snaking out of Meridian Keep. "If it was in the Allpriory, then what the hell is it doing here?"

"Another mystery that needs solving."

Lord Valenbonne only rubbed his hands together after being

informed of the possibility, looking anticipatory. "And here I thought you kindred could no longer surprise me. I should have suspected that there were more secrets within their vile lair." He ran the blade of his axe against one particularly massive root, looking thoughtful. And then, before anyone could stop him, he swung.

The axe cleaved into the thick bark. Crimson liquid spurted out from the fresh wound, staining the nearby ground.

"What are you doing, milord?" Riones gasped.

"Seeing if there is something to the story before we risk our lives any further. We may be allies now, Lord Malekh, but I make it a habit to confirm such matters with my own eyes." Valenbonne examined the edge of his weapon and then smiled in satisfaction at the sight of the wine-red sap trickling down the blade. "'Tis true, then. I have heard of similar tales from the southern islands, where—" His mouth twisted briefly. "No matter. We cannot allow this to infiltrate Alurian lands. I should have burned that castle down to its foundations years ago."

"You underestimate the extent of these unnatural woodlands, milord," Xiaodan said wearily. "I have never seen one myself, but Malekh told me they are called bloodwood, capable of ensnaring humans and draining them of blood as a vampire can."

"And how many of these exist that you know of?" Valenbonne demanded.

"Two. One at an old vampire stronghold, and one within the Whispering Isles." Malekh gazed at Valenbonne. "You don't look surprised by this."

"You are right. Such rumors were why King Beluske turned his attentions to Tithe. He did not relish the idea of a vampiric outpost south of his territories."

"He did not live long enough to see such a conquest realized," Dr. Yost murmured. "His daughter was a much more benevolent ruler and spared the survivors, but the damage was already done."

"I thought Tithe was overwhelmed by spates of vampire attacks and that Aluria had rushed to their aid," Remy said slowly.

His father chuckled, but the sound was strangely bitter. "I am not one to trust those who put things down in books and claim them as history, lad. They've always been the finest liars I've ever known."

"Do you mean to say that this . . . thing is self-aware, Lord Malekh?" Riones asked, looking back up at the castle with a faintly worried expression.

"If you ask whether it possesses a mind of its own, then no. But it does not need sentience. It hungers in the same way these mutations do—bereft of thought, acting only upon instinct." Malekh pointed at something that lay half-hidden within the high tufts of grass, and Remy saw, to his revulsion, the carcasses of both a horse and its rider. The corpses must have been recent, for it had not yet been relegated to bone, but what remained was shrunken, the bodies drained of blood.

The marquess shuddered. "What benefit could vampires achieve by harboring such a monstrosity? Some means of defense, perhaps?"

"Most kindred avoid this creature entirely. Only the most desperate allow it succor on their lands. These vampiric trees feed on blood but can be redirected and harvested with some care."

"Which means that these bastard Second Court vampires could have used it as a repository of sorts?" Lord Valenbonne made a sound of repulsion. "A means to keep them fit and fattened when their human supplies run low, *and* for their vanity. Perhaps you would oblige us with the best means to kill it without unnecessarily endangering the lives of my men, Lord Malekh?"

"Fire," Malekh said shortly. "As large as you can make it, although that may not be enough. Chopping these roots will take too long, given their immensity. The ones that you see lying tangled outside the castle are part of its safeguard. The thickness

serves as armor. If you wish to kill it quicker, we will have to venture deeper within its lair, where the bark is thinner and much
more vulnerable. But . . ."

"But?" Valenbonne prompted, when Malekh did not speak for
some seconds.

"But if the Night Empress is within the castle as we believe and
she commands it, then it will likely defend her to the death."

"What reason would a vampiric tree have to bond with my
wayward former wife?"

"The bloodwood is given to compulsion just as much as any. A
sentient being may bend it to their whim—what it takes from its
victims to sustain itself can easily be transferred to a host of their
choice."

"And if she was severely injured during our last battle," Xiaodan
added grimly, "this would be an easy way to rejuvenate herself."

"Then let us act quickly." Lord Valenbonne hefted his axe.
"I have been inside Meridian Keep before and know the lay of
the castle. The bulk of my soldiers will remain outside to keep
watch, building bonfires, should we need to fumigate what hides
within—or burn the castle forthwith, should it come to that. Some
Reapers and I will enter; a dozen to man the lower floors, the rest
to venture into the heart of where the Night Empress presumably
lies in wait—and there, we shall kill two birds with one stone."
He paused. "None of the mutations for now, save Grimesworthy.
They remain clumsy when fighting in close quarters, though Yost
is working to refine that. Would you like to take command of
our manservant, Remington? Your blood runs freely through his
veins, as mine does."

"Nothing would disgust me more," Remy said sourly, and his
father chuckled.

Malekh nodded. "Take heed when it comes to your Reapers,"
he cautioned. "There is no telling if she is capable of compelling
them against her will, even in her weakened state."

"I shall take that into consideration." Lord Valenbonne went off to issue more commands. Xiaodan and Malekh remained where they were, staring up at the castle. "We can still leave," Malekh murmured. "It seems to me that Valenbonne is fit to handle this matter on his own."

But Xiaodan shook her head. "She's in there, Zidan. I can feel her." Her eyes hardened. "Whatever it is she took from me—my strength, my sun—I want it back."

Malekh looked at Remy. "And I suppose you feel the same way?"

"Not necessarily. Any situation in which I have to fight alongside my father makes me uncomfortable. The last time was not a pleasant one."

"Pendergast—"

"I am fine," Remy said, waving his concerns away with what he hoped was cheerful ease. "If Xiaodan says she needs to be here, then I'll be here with her—and you."

Valenbonne returned with the Reapers that were to accompany them inside, Riones among them. Grimesworthy lumbered behind them, much to Remy's dislike. From the look on the other hunters' faces, they shared the feeling.

Malekh drew out his saber and turned toward the entrance of the castle, where thick roots and vines barred their path. "Cut down only the ones that impede our way," he instructed. "And brace yourself for any attacks."

It took an hour for them to cut through the bark, the latter falling away to reveal darkness and even more unearthly tangles of bark and foliage. Occasionally a root or trunk would react poorly to their attacks, lashing out with sharp vines to stop their progress, and more than a few Reapers sustained some minor injuries before they were able to create a small clearing and step inside.

"It seems that Meridian Keep has no wish to entertain visitors," Valenbonne murmured.

Any furniture left standing after Valenbonne's attack on the castle years before did not survive the wrath of its latest occupant. Bits of broken wood lay on the floor, along with the remnants of whatever decor had once graced the place. Writhing vines and ivy covered every inch of the walls. It was like walking into the hollow of a monstrous oak rather than a castle. Even the stairway had been overcome, the roots assuming roughly the shape of the steps but leaving none of the original intact.

"Stay alert," Valenbonne barked at his men. "No telling what surprises she has in store for us."

They received no further resistance from the tree while they were on the landing. Now they traveled up onto the second floor and down a long hallway bereft of anything but more twisted roots. Malekh clearly viewed this as a bad sign, eyeing every piece of rubble they passed as if it would rise up and grab them.

Valenbonne paused to survey a broken picture frame, one of many that had once hung from the Keep's walls. The portrait had long been ripped to shreds, and all that remained to be seen was part of a face, a scrap of cloth from which blue eyes looked back at them. "Kurdashev," he said dismissively. "I would recognize that pompous gaze anywhere."

They encountered more resistance here, but the roots were slimmer and easier to slice through. There was only one accessible chamber on the floor whose entrance had not been tapered over.

Remy heard the heartbeats long before they entered, a much more regular rhythm than Xiaodan's. The walls seemed to shake from the volume of it, the closer they approached.

Within the inner sanctum, an immense cocoon hung from the ceiling, covered in more bark and twisted branches. It was ten feet tall and half as wide, and the heartbeats grew louder as they drew nearer. Something thrashed and twisted beneath its surface, as if it lay trapped within and was fighting to escape.

Valenbonne swore. "She's inside that damn thing. Reapers, draw your weapons."

The hunters obeyed, a faint humming noise overlaid against the heartbeats as their fire lances charged up.

"What now?" Remy's father asked. "Do we wait for it to burst from its recesses like some demented butterfly, or are we free to stab into it without retribution?"

"The tree knows that we are here. It allowed us to breach its sanctuary, to make it this far. I will not be surprised if it was a deliberate trap."

"What do you think, Remington?"

Remy blinked. "I—I don't—"

"Come now," Valenbonne encouraged. "In your years of fighting vampires, and then the last few weeks against the Rot, surely you have some ideas."

Remy glowered, not wanting to be put in such a position in front of the other Reapers. "It would be much more practical to retreat immediately from here and burn down everything else as we do."

"But then we wouldn't know if it truly is the Night Empress hiding within her little chamber, now, would we? Don't you want to be sure, boy?"

Quietly, from somewhere else, someone began to sing.

It was a familiar lullaby; one that Remy had been taught as a young child, a melody his mother sang often while he'd been in her womb. He had sung it himself when he paid his respects to the dead, or on the occasions he'd been alone and drunk and depressed enough. But the song had taken on a far less fond association the moment the Night Empress had used it to lull his mind, take over his body, and attack Malekh and Xiaodan. And Naji.

An odd lethargy was coming over him, his thoughts sluggish.

"Remy?" Xiaodan asked, sounding alarmed.

"I can hear her," Remy rasped, staggering back. "I can hear her singing."

Valenbonne reacted quickly. He turned, lifted his axe, and swung it hard against the cocoon, cleaving an inch or so deep into it. Again and again he attacked, the heartbeats stuttering with every blow until, finally, the husk broke in half.

There was a corpse lying inside it, a fresh kill drained of blood. The threadbare clothing it wore told them that this was another turned villager, though shrunken and drained of blood like the corpses outside. Even in death, the face was pulled back in a snarl of surprise as if its killer had come upon it unawares, its fangs protruding from a slack mouth.

It was not the Night Empress.

A snarl of frustration from Valenbonne; a curse from Malekh. "Where is she?" Remy's father demanded, just as the vampire lord said, "She used her own people for sustenance."

The song continued. Remy dropped his Breaker and clasped his hands to his ears, fighting back despite knowing the inevitable. Already it was burrowing inside his mind, that *everything is going to be all right, let me take care of you, my sweet child—*

"Above us," Xiaodan said suddenly. "She's above us. We must—"

There was a crackling of brittle branches from the ceiling.

Xiaodan disappeared, reappearing in front of Valenbonne just in time to block the hand about to claw at his face. She shoved back, the attacker crashing into the wall across the room, but easily righting itself as if it had taken no damage.

The Night Empress did not look as she had during the battle at Elouve. She wore her dark hair long and loose, though the locks were tangled up about her, matted and flat against her head. Her dark skin, the same shade as Remy's, was stained with the same wine-red liquid from the tree. Her eyes were unnaturally golden, and her crimson robes muddied. She was still heartbreakingly beautiful, but she looked thinner, her cheeks hollower. There was a strange languor about her that reminded Remy of Xiaodan's illness, like something was wasting her away.

Vines covered the lower half of her body, puncturing her flesh. They throbbed as if they were alive, moving with her, extending long enough to offer little restriction. Crimson liquid flowed within the near-transparent stems, funneling into her.

She ignored the other Reapers and vampires, turning to Remy. *My love,* she greeted in her voice but not through her mouth, the affection in her voice at odds with her horrific appearance. *How well you've grown.*

"No," Remy rasped. "Don't do this. Please don't do this."

"Your fight is with me, not him," Xiaodan snarled, planting herself between Remy and the Night Empress.

The woman's gaze moved back to Xiaodan, hate twisting her features.

She moved, and Xiaodan followed. Both reappeared at the center of the room in blurs and stuttered glimpses. Faint bursts of light sparked whenever they made contact, as if currents of electricity ran through them both.

"Start burning the vines," Valenbonne barked. "Let no branch or root go unscathed!"

Malekh's saber flashed, cutting down the branches and vines encircling the lower part of her body, every attack cutting more foliage from her.

The Night Empress lunged for him as well. Xiaodan blocked her path.

A sudden luminescence sprung from where their fists met, the room awash in a painful brightness that made Remy instinctively cover his eyes.

He heard a screech, and then more crackling as the vines around the Night Empress unraveled—

—and large bat-like wings sprouted from her back, filling the length of the room. The Night Empress rose, winds whipping through the chamber from the force, sending them skidding backward.

"Now!" Valenbonne shouted.

The Reapers aimed their fire lances at the Night Empress, shooting rapidly. The woman avoided their blows, but the walls behind her were set aflame by their efforts. She snarled and blinked out of view, only to reappear on top of one of the hapless Reapers. The man screamed as her fangs bit hard down on his neck, blood bursting in a fountain up from the wound.

Valenbonne was already running, axe swinging. The Night Empress released her grip on her victim and evaded her former husband's attack. She was on him next, but Valenbonne managed to drive his weapon in between them just in time to ward off her bite.

And then Grimesworthy was by his master's side, swinging his fists. They missed the Night Empress completely; she reappeared several feet away, fangs still bared, coiled to spring.

Snatching Breaker from the ground, Remy whipped the knifechain free and spun it in the woman's direction. She turned and easily caught the spike but did not attack. Something in her monstrous expression softened when she found Remy's gaze.

Child, the voice crooned in his head.

"Mother," Remy whispered. "Please."

My Remington, the Night Empress said, *he broke my heart.*

With a roar, Valenbonne attempted to strike her from behind, but the Night Empress glided out of range and released her hold on the knifechain. With a final wail, she shot out through the ceiling, destroying the barrier to swoop up into the sky. Bricks and stone rained down, and there was nothing they could do but watch helplessly as her form vanished among the clouds.

In her absence, the tree around them came alive, writhing and lashing out. One impaled a Reaper's shoulder, and he screamed in agony. Vines wrapped around Remy's foot. Their tips opened up to reveal jagged teeth on their ends as they tried to clamp down on whatever part of his skin they could reach. He drove one of Breaker's scythes down on it and cut himself free, and he fancied he heard a shrill scream from somewhere within the castle in response. More of the vines began to envelop the other fighters, and there were cries from among the Reapers who were not as fortunate at avoiding their bites, the tree's many incisors digging into their flesh.

The room was filled with smoke, making it difficult to see as the flames from the hunters' fire lances began to spread. "Retreat!" Malekh commanded. He was a blur, reappearing behind some of the still-trapped Reapers and expertly divesting them of their vined opponents, pieces falling to the floor after several strikes with his saber.

"You heard him!" Valenbonne snapped. "Fall back!"

The fire had spread to the lower floors, and the soot burned at Remy's eyes as they stumbled back down. Behind them, the ivy-encrusted stairs crumbled, and Riones had to take a flying leap to safety as the ground underneath him fell away, Malekh catching him easily at the landing. Remy looked up, spotted parts of the ceiling that had not already been demolished by the Night Empress beginning to give way. Years of overgrowth had weakened the structure; without the vampire tree's strength holding it upright, the castle itself was crumbling.

They made it out without a moment to spare, the Reapers stationed outside dragging some of their injured comrades away just as a horrible, wrenching sound filled the air, an agonized roar of a beast that had just been slain.

They continued to run as the castle collapsed. Floor by floor it came crashing down, the sound like a terrible hurricane.

It was over in a matter of minutes; nothing remained of Meridian Keep beyond one wall left standing against all the odds, seated in rubble and detritus. But of the strange vampire tree, nothing remained; its roots and branches shriveled as the flames took hold, disappearing into the still-burning fires.

5

THE FATA MORGANA

They burned the dead Reaper a short distance from where Meridian Keep still smoldered. It was a new Alurian policy, Riones had told Remy. No one who had fallen to a vampire's bite was allowed burial within Elouve's graveyards, fearing a repeat of the chaos when the Night Empress had attacked the city. "Don't want anyone else rising from their graves," the marquess said sadly, watching as the body of his comrade was consigned to kindling. "Seems like all we've been doing lately is attending funerals."

"How have you been faring?"

"Work has kept me busy, and there's been much of it. Curse Feiron, by the way. The man was so busy playing lackey to Astonbury over the years that he let all the paperwork pile up for me to worry over. Did you know that there were thousands of missing children from both Aluria *and* Kerenai, and Feiron neglected to act upon it? I have you to thank for this, too, by the way."

"Pardon?"

Riones grinned. "I know you were offered the position—I was

expecting that, given what you had to go through for it. Imagine my surprise when they presented the job to me instead. Your father said little, but I'd suspected you turned it down." He sighed. "That said, even with all this piddling paperwork, I must admit I am enjoying hammering the Reapers into better shape using policy rather than field training."

Remy smiled. "I am unsuited to the role. Yours is a well-deserved promotion." He glanced back at the castle, or what was left of it.

"The good Light, Pendergast—what *was* that creature? Was it truly the Night Empress? I have never seen a vampire that could manifest such wings!"

Remy hadn't either. The looks of shock on both Xiaodan's and Malekh's faces when they had beheld her new form told him that their encounters with such kindred were few and far between.

"Are you certain?" Lord Valenbonne demanded of Malekh, clearly agitated. "There is no other foul evolution that your kindred ever undergoes to produce . . . that?"

"None that I am aware of," Malekh muttered, almost to himself. "The First of the Vampires was said to have borne wings, but they resembled an eagle's rather than a bat's."

"It wasn't the damn tree's doing." Valenbonne spat on the floor. "No one from the Second Court ever sprouted bloody wings!" He turned. "I want a dozen more scouts surveying the area. If either the Night Empress or her coven are sighted, they are to report to me immediately. I want this region secured. Little use in protecting that if we do not root out the rest still hiding in Aluria."

"We will take our leave as well," Malekh said. "I need to return to my court and make my own preparations."

Xiaodan was still awake and alert. Unlike the others, who persisted in distancing themselves from the smoking rubble, she perched atop the sole remaining wall, looking about with a contemplative gaze.

"I don't know," she said when Remy approached her, before he could even voice his questions out loud. "I could be wrong, but it *felt* like she took a bit of the sunbringer into herself. She had none of my tolerance for it, and it weakened her." She glanced ruefully down at her hands. "The light that sparked between us—that was not my doing. I'm beginning to believe that, had I brought the full force of the sun on her at Elouve, we would both be dead. It must be what Lilith did to kill the Night King." She shivered at the thought. The shadows under her eyes were darker, and there was a faint tremor in her limbs as she shifted. "But I hesitated, and that might have saved my life. And now, I am sorry to have put you all in danger. Again."

"I chose to be here." Remy looked down as Xiaodan had reached out to take his hand. "She tried to use me to kill you. She used me to . . ." He choked before he could say Naji's name. "Let's go back to Malekh's court, wherever it is. We'll need his beautiful mind for this."

She managed a faint laugh. "If you thought Chàngge Shuǐ was impressive, wait until you see the Fata Morgana. It's rather well suited for Malekh."

"That's what I was afraid of."

Lord Valenbonne approached Remy only just as the army was ready to depart for the northern border. "Seems like recent events have not dulled your association with these court vampires." He said it conversationally, as if he were discussing something as trite as the weather. "I trust that you've told them little else of Alurian politics."

"Of course not," Remy lied.

Valenbonne smiled like he didn't believe him. "As the Third Court king intends to make haste for his court, I'll be sending word to you there. You remember our usual signals?"

"Yes, sir."

"Good. I presume Lord Malekh and Lady Song are still adamant about meeting the other surviving courts to discuss their next steps against the First. The Sixth Court leader has proven tractable, at least. They have offered to defend the eastern borders. Keep a close eye on these clans. Learn who among them will be steadfast, and who must be cut down with the Night Empress."

Valenbonne chuckled. "It's not too late for you to join us as we move to finish securing Hallifax's territory, my boy. It should be easy enough to stamp out the rest of the vampire rebellions while their mistress still licks at her wounds, and Yost's vials have been effective with the mutations there. Hallifax will forfeit those lands soon enough, and we can add them to Aluria once we have ended the unrest. Queen Ophelia is impressed with you, my boy. There would be title and prestige awaiting you, but none of that, should you continue to travel with these vampires, even if they are court leaders. You could be the lord of more territories, far more than as the next Lord Valenbonne—"

"Armiger," Remy said, unable to stop himself. "Not lord."

"What absurd nonsense are you spouting again? You are a *lord*, and that is far more—"

"And this, Father, is why I know that everything you say is engineered to benefit yourself first and foremost. If you cannot even allow me the dignity to be called a title of my own choosing that impacts you little, then you will not care to do more. I will remain with the court nobles."

"Are you still frustrated that I sought to use your blood without permission?" Valenbonne gestured at Grimesworthy, at the other horrifying creatures waiting patiently for their master's next orders. "This was always your problem, Remington: your inability to see what is good for the kingdom. Aluria has benefited from our work, and she shall continue to do so in years to come. You should be pleased."

"Pleased?" Remy was shouting, and he no longer cared about the way heads turned in their direction, hearing his every word. "Did you think I would be pleased when you forced me to wield Breaker at seven years old, mocked for my every mistake? When you abandoned me in those caves to take the queen's ear before Astonbury could? To whore me out to every willing woman in the ton to find the secrets he was unwilling to provide you with? For all your talk of sacrifice and of seeing to the safety of Aluria, you neglect to mention that it was *I* you were constantly sacrificing!"

"You dare speak to me this way?" Valenbonne snapped. "I protected you from those who conspired against us! I taught you everything you needed to ensure your survival, and *this* is how you repay my goodwill?"

"The same goodwill that you showed Mother?" *He broke my heart*, the Night Empress had whispered to him. Remy didn't trust her, but he believed the pain in her voice.

Valenbonne's face was red with rage. He took a step toward him, but just as quickly, Malekh stood next to Remy. "We are ready to depart," he said calmly, as if he had heard nothing untoward between them. "Lord Valenbonne, we shall be taking our leave."

"We are indebted to you for your help, Lord Malekh." The Marquess of Riones did not move quite as quickly as the vampire lord, but it was not for wont of trying, and he was slightly breathless by the time he reached the older man's side. "A Reaper's work is never done, as they say. Should you require any assistance from us in turn, I am sure that Queen Ophelia would be most pleased to hear from you."

"I would be glad to establish more frequent communications with Her Majesty as soon as we are settled back at my court." Lord

Malekh bowed to him and then to Valenbonne. He gave what he likely thought was a light tug at Remy's arm, nearly yanking him off his feet. "Let us go, Pendergast."

Remy gave Riones a quick nod and turned. He ignored his father completely but felt the man's eyes on him the rest of the way back to their carriage, where Xiaodan and the helhests waited.

XIAODAN HAD tried her best to stay awake but succumbed to exhaustion only minutes after they had left the Alurian army behind. Malekh sat inside the coach with them, allowing the helhests to select their route. Xiaodan's head was on his lap this time, and the unassuming way the man was saying nothing was making Remy itch.

"I should not have lost my temper," he finally blurted out, too impatient to let Malekh broach the topic first. "He's the commander of the army now, and all he can think about is how we haven't rebounded from the years when Astonbury was in charge—"

"He's refused to call you *Armiger* all this time?"

Remy hesitated. "Yes. He said that it was a frivolous fancy, and that I would grow out of it soon enough. When I did not, he'd taken to calling me *Lord* deliberately, as if daring me to contest him. Today was the first time I pushed back."

"Seems to me that everyone else needed to hear it, then."

Remy glanced at him, startled.

"But perhaps I am biased. I am no stranger to turning against my own sire. I know the strength that requires, to challenge someone to whom you feel beholden but who has hurt you nonetheless. And it took me far longer to stand up for myself than it took you."

"I must be hearing things," Remy said hoarsely. "Is it the hunger talking? I have not seen you eat since we started—um, other than what you took from me."

"Eugenie was kind enough to supply me with blood to refresh myself with. But it would be best to prepare yourself once we arrive at my holdings, though. There are a few in my court who were excellent chefs when they were human, and you shall be needing sustenance soon enough."

Remy stared at him, but Malekh kept his gaze on Xiaodan's sleeping face. "The furniture I keep at the Morgana," the lord added languidly after a significant pause, "is far sturdier than that at the Rocksplen inn," and this time it was Remy who jerked his eyes away, flushing.

"I shouldn't have yelled," he muttered. "I don't know what came over me, doing that in front of the other Reapers—"

"You are dealing with the possibility that there is more to your mother than even we know, if her wings are any indication. Your father is weathering the same shock, hence his attempts to take forceful control of the situation, and of you."

"What do you mean by that? Is my mother more than just kindred?"

"There is little to say there that is not speculation on my part," Malekh said slowly. "Once more information is at hand, you will be the first to know."

"Somehow, it feels all the more worrying when you say it that way."

"In any case, I have taken samples of the bloodwood sap. We may learn more of its origins once we return to the Morgana and my laboratory."

It was a relief to finally spot the Third Court castle when it loomed into view—and then Remy did a double take, goggling at the sight. Where Chànggē Shuǐ had been a beautiful albeit abandoned cluster of Qing-ye architecture surrounded by obsidian towers, Malekh's domain was an overly detailed monstrosity that would not have been out of place in some of the self-indulgent, overwritten gothic fiction that Remy still enjoyed. It looked exactly like the type of dark citadel villains cowered within; imposing black towers devoid of light stood starkly against gray skies, and Remy thought the stench of decay and blood could thrive here from ambiance alone. It looked far too large, like a city of near-Elouvian proportions.

As their carriage approached, the sides of the fortress folded out, revealing more secreted within. The outer walls lowered unexpectedly, each one like its own drawbridge, as if the castle was unfurling in all directions. The result was not unlike layers of onion slowly peeling away, though Remy did not think that Malekh would welcome the comparison.

No. Not quite an onion. The fortress wore its multilayered walls like armor. It would be highly effective against anyone attempting a siege against the Third Court castle.

Remy hadn't even noticed until the fog lifted high enough that the Fata Morgana was situated in the middle of a lake, and they would need to traverse a narrow bridge to reach the castle—another mechanical device fashioned by complicated cogs and wheels that rose up from *beneath* the water's surface to permit them passage, and would no doubt slide back into its depths once they had crossed. Remy was no expert, but he thought it was a tempered combination of silver and steel, possibly the same combination Aluria used to manufacture fire lances: some strong alloy that could withstand immersion underwater without fear of rust, much like his Breaker.

"Her Majesty would kill to make off with your bridge," he said, impressed. "Silver is a rare enough resource, and I'm surprised no one's tried to poach it from you."

"Some have tried," Malekh said darkly as they made it past the crossing. It promptly folded up behind them and sludged back into the waters.

The *real* castle past the lowered walls was still just as black and as brooding as its exterior—because of course Malekh would strive for a symmetry of design. What annoyed Remy, however slightly, was the absence of any grinding mechanical noises expected of something of this size and scale. The whole place functioned like a well-oiled machine, dutifully tended to forestall any breaks in the mechanism, and while he was used to Malekh being hyper-efficient, it was staggering to think of the energy and labor required for their maintenance.

The inhabitants of the castle were not what Remy had envisioned, either. Waiting for them by the entrance was a motherly-looking woman, stout and pleasant, with a farmer's wife's air about her. With her were several youths still too young for Remy to determine if they had the ageless appearance that outed a vampire heritage.

"We've been waiting for you since this morning, milord," she chided Malekh. "Carmen was in such a state, fearing that you'd run into some fresh trouble."

"Was that why you chose to raise the outer wards?"

"I had no way of asking your leave to do so, but you've always said that we must make snap decisions in times of uncertainty. And Graf and Solis have been reporting unusual sightings of vampires in the area. We thought it best to err on the side of caution. Something did happen, didn't it?"

"A bloodwood at Meridian Keep, and the Night Empress in repose within."

The woman winced. "The Second Court's old lair isn't all that far. I shudder to think that she would be so close. Did you kill her?"

"Not yet."

"More's the shame." The woman peered at Remy and smiled. "And is this the young Reaper you wrote would be visiting us? Hello, dear one. My name is Agatha. Quite a pleasure to meet you,"

"The same, ma'am," Remy said carefully, "though I can't say most vampires would be delighted at the chance."

"Nonsense. All are welcomed here at the Morgana. It would be hypocritical of us to turn anyone away."

"He doesn't really look like much, after hearing all that about him," one of the youths said, examining Remy critically. "Reckon I can take him out in a fight."

Another beside him snorted. "You ain't good enough to beat me yet, so don't be shouting your mouth off elsewhere, Renzo. *I* can take him on better than you can."

"Renzo! Barnabas!" Agatha said sharply. "Begging your pardon, Armiger Pendergast. These boys are a trial even on good days, and they've been chomping at the bit to catch sight of their first Reaper. You're a rarity here, as you say, but I will ensure they and the other children don't bother you much."

"It's no trouble, milady," Remy said, smiling. "I know what it's like to be a wayward youth myself."

"I have rooms ready for you. A beautiful view of Lake Reidwele below us, and a bit of the Galeos Sea out on the horizon. Sanlea is quite pleased to hear that another human has arrived. She used to be the head chef for King Arsentil, you know. The best in all of Lusenig, she'd always boasted, though I imagine those places have long been forgotten now, as was the king."

Malekh left them briefly to take Xiaodan from the carriage, while the other boys trotted off obediently to see to the helhests' needs. Agatha sighed heavily upon spotting the sleeping Fourth Court heiress.

"The poor mistress," she said sadly. "Can you cure what ails her, milord?"

"I will," Malekh said with quiet confidence. "In time. Has anything of note transpired while we were away, the intrusion of other kindred in our lands besides?"

Here the woman fidgeted. "Well, Lady Fanglei of the Sixth has been sending us letters as of late, and has been quite persistent in demanding an answer."

"Have you responded?"

"No, milord. I thought it more prudent to await your arrival."

"Good. Continue to give her no reply. Pendergast, come with us."

Remy gave the woman an awkward bow, then followed Malekh. As he had thought, the Fata Morgana's interior was built to be as forbidding as it had looked from the outside. The windows were small, the walls made of rougher but sturdy material, and he was unsure if they were painted black or if the color was natural.

But all of that was offset by the furniture. Like the pieces at Chàngge Shuǐ, they were comfortable and well used. There had been attempts to introduce white, silky curtains in some of the rooms they passed. Some even had tasteful floral patterns, and Remy was certain that Malekh's input had not been asked for there.

There were vases in every room containing different varieties of flowers that added color to the walls. Where portraits of austere-looking ancestors would have hung within the long hallways like they had at Loxley House, there were bright landscape paintings depicting happier scenes: children playing, horses cantering merrily across fields, farmers tending to their crops. The chairs, slightly worn but not in any terrible state of disrepair, came in practically every size and shape.

Where Chàngge Shuǐ had been sparsely inhabited, the people living here were enough to make up a good-sized town. There were soldiers sparring in the courtyard who stood to attention and smartly saluted Malekh when he and Remy passed. There were workers and craftsmen in abundance, carting wood, hard metals, and other resources to and fro, and Remy spotted a forge near one of the gatehouses, large enough to have satisfied even Elke.

There were vampires that could have passed for ordinary townsfolk. Remy would not have known they were kindred if not for the sudden hint of fang whenever one laughed, which they often did. They wore clothes better made than in other villages he'd been to and were busy mending outfits, selling wares from stalls, or standing about, engaged in animated conversation.

There were children; so, so many children. Remy did not think that they were vampires, but they ran freely among the kindred without fear, laughing as they played games on the cobblestones.

"You're liable to catch flies or worse with your mouth open like that," Malekh noted calmly. They were climbing up a third set of stairs, leading to the upper floor where Remy suspected Malekh and Xiaodan's chambers lay, but he kept glancing out the windows at the people below.

"Your castle's facade is exactly how I imagined it would be. But the rest . . ." Remy waved a hand around vaguely, "I never thought your home would be so . . . cheerful. Or brimming with people who look rather ordinary. I mean, I shouldn't have been so surprised."

"How so?"

"Xiaodan said your castle resembled you, and she was right. You pass yourself off as cold, but in truth, you're kind. Generous enough to allow all these people in."

Malekh stopped walking, and Remy yelped when he bumped into him. The vampire lord stared down at him, expression unreadable.

"That wasn't meant to offend," Remy added quickly, but couldn't help an, "I know how prickly you can get when anyone so much as implies you have emotions just like the rest of us."

The man gazed at him for a minute longer, then turned abruptly to resume his walk without responding. Remy followed him into a room he immediately recognized as a laboratory—one larger and much more fully equipped than what the Third Court king had overseen at Chàngge Shuǐ.

Men and women in pristine white coats immediately dropped what they had been working on, and lined up to greet Malekh.

"My lord!" One man stepped forward, a ginger-haired youth with bright green eyes and a nervous, excitable air who did not look all that older than Remy and was unquestionably *not* kindred. "You're back! Given all the reports we'd heard, we were worried that—" he faltered, eyes moving down to the figure Malekh carried. "Has Lady Xiaodan overspent herself again, milord?"

"As is her penchant, yes."

The others were already moving, practiced and sure. By the time Malekh had laid Xiaodan gently down on one of the feather beds at the far side of the room, they were already strapping odd devices on her arms and hands. One had placed a small, gelatinous-looking bag on a small table beside the sleeping girl and was sliding a needle connected to it through a long tube into her skin. All worked with a familiar measure that told Remy they were used to treating Xiaodan.

"You would do well to rest yourself, milord," the redheaded man told Malekh. "I can tell that you've traveled long without much sustenance of your own."

"I can spare a few more hours."

"Be that as it may, you must take the time while milady is asleep to see to your own needs. Farfair and Daskell should be back soon with fresh blood for everyone."

"I have more than enough on hand."

"I don't see a—" The doctor's eyes flicked to Remy, and a sudden blush turned his face as scarlet as his hair. He swooped down so low that his head practically touched his knees. "Ah, b-begging your pardon. You must be the young Reaper Pendergast. Spencer's the name, but I go by Speck for the most part." He gestured at the others. "Beatrix, Tinsley, Roald, Wits, and Yusuf. We oversee the laboratory in his lordship's absence. I meant no insult—"

"None taken," Remy said quickly. "And thank you for taking care of Xiaodan. She's always been a little headstrong."

Speck swallowed a sudden spurt of laughter. "That she is. She has given us no end to worry whenever she—" He flushed again. "Not that it's not within her right, knowing the responsibilities she takes on, on our behalf."

"Find me again, should her condition change," Malekh said, sparing the young doctor any further embarrassment. "You are right. It would do me good to recuperate so that Xiaodan will have little fault to find in my own condition once she wakes."

Another of the physicians, Wits, nodded happily. "Leave her to us, milord," she said. "She'll be up and about in no time."

They all looked too busy tending to Xiaodan to be further acquainted, so Remy bowed low and followed Malekh out of the room. The Summer Lord said nothing else, stepping back into the hallway, walking some ways along it before stopping at the only other door that Remy could see along the corridor, opening it to reveal a large private chamber waiting within—no doubt the man's personal quarters, one he shared with his fiancée.

"Should I look for Agatha?" Remy asked, not without a trace of self-consciousness. "She mentioned rooms being prepared for me, and I shouldn't be imposing when—"

He was yanked forward without warning into the room with Malekh as the latter closed the door shut behind them. "You still talk too much," the Third Court ruler said, and just as quickly, Remy found himself pressed against the wall, Malekh's mouth on his.

"I thought you were angry about my opinions of your castle," he gasped out once he finally came up for air.

"If you thought that was enough to make me angry at you, then why did you talk incessantly for days?"

"To get your attention."

"You have it. Will you turn me down?"

Remy watched the slight tightening of his mouth, the rigid way he held himself as if bracing for rejection.

I'm not okay, Remy thought. *Xiaodan isn't okay, and no matter how hard he tries to pretend otherwise, neither is Malekh.*

"I won't," he whispered.

6

TRAINING

Remy woke, attempted to crawl out of bed, landed flat on his face instead and cursed Malekh.

Grunting, he staggered to his feet and limped his way to the washing area, where he rinsed his mouth, took care of his morning toilette while bent over the basin like an old man and cursed Malekh. Someone had been considerate enough to bring up all of his belongings, leaving them just outside the door, but Remy cursed Malekh all the same.

"Fucking prickstick," he grouched, though there was no one else in the room to whinge at. He'd wanted to wash up first, but the bastard hadn't been willing to wait, pointing out that they could simply bathe afterward. They hadn't gotten much cleaning done then, either.

Once more, the lord had murmured, voice deep and husky, *just once more.*

"Arsehole," Remy muttered as he attended to his long-delayed bath. His backside twinged as he sank down into a tub easily built to attend three, then groaned at the thought of Xiaodan and Malekh sharing it with him next time. "Fucking titmouse."

Remy Pendergast was many things, and useless after orgasms was one of them.

It hadn't helped that he'd woken up alone, either. He'd dreamed about Miss Grissell for the third night running, this time watching him when he was thirteen, training with Breaker while his father yelled things like, *Hold it higher, do you want to slice your own head off, boy,* and, *Don't let the chain go slack, you fool, any kindred worth his salt would be pulling out your entrails by now.* And that was certainly odd, because she'd left the manor long before he'd ever begun his novitiate. Yet there she was, fury blazing from her dark eyes as she watched him practice, and something felt wrong about the way she was looking at him . . .

Somewhere within the vestiges of his consciousness, he felt Malekh rubbing his back, murmuring something soothing before sleep dragged him back into oblivion. Remy suffered no further dreams after that, but with the morning came Malekh's absence again.

He wasn't as sweaty or as mucky as he'd expected. Malekh must have cleaned him up when he'd passed out. His hand reached up to his neck and felt small stabs of pain when his fingers grazed over the bite marks the lord had left there.

"Fucking shitfuck," he said aloud, grinning.

The soak felt good on his aching body. He hadn't noticed it earlier, but there were pipes running through the room pumping in heated water through the walls. It was an innovation Elouve had yet to adopt—Remy was used to cold baths in Kinaiya Lodge because he had no valet at his service and it took too long to warm anything up. This was far more efficient than servants running up and down floors carting buckets, at least.

He changed into a fresh set of clothes. He briefly considered leaving Breaker behind, before deciding against it. Nothing looked out of the ordinary in Malekh and Xiaodan's room. There were some potted plants by the window, no doubt Xiaodan's choice. A carefully organized desk near the bed was likely Malekh's. There were two pairs of gold rings on the dresser, and Remy wondered why neither ever thought to wear them, as their engagement was no secret.

The Fata Morgana had far more advancements than just the heating system for their baths. An attempt to visit Xiaodan at the infirmary-cum-laboratory had been firmly blocked by the doctors, with Wits apologetically suggesting that he take the time to familiarize himself with the rest of the castle instead. Remy followed his advice, keeping his steps slow and short. He noted that the kitchen had an ice room not unlike the yakhchāl that Malekh had proposed for the Ministry, though used for better things than storing cadavers—meats and blood, apparently. They kept their wine there as well, and one of the stewards offered him a glass. It was light and refreshing and of an excellent vintage, putting Remy in an even better mood.

He was impressed by the castle fortifications, even more so when the chief engineer explained it to him. "The magic all happens here," Matsuo explained, stabbing at the blueprints of the Fata Morgana's exterior. "The outer fortress isn't just made to defend the main castle, it's built to sacrifice the exterior walls if necessary. And then over here it's chock full of catapults, pitch storage, cannons—everything you can think to throw at an enemy, we've got it and more besides."

There were ramps that could be lowered from the ceiling easily to allow those with infirmities to walk up the floors instead of suffering through stairs. There were glass houses that enabled residents to grow fruits and vegetables not otherwise possible due to the poor weather outside. The castle was even larger than Remy thought; there were small mills within the premises, which a helpful vampire told him were for manufacturing both paper and silk—one of their many means of income and another reason they were self-sufficient, their exports in high demand.

That there were so many friendly vampires was another concept Remy was trying to come to terms with. He saw kindred and humans alike working together, laughing together, living together. Small wonder Xiaodan and Malekh had thought coexistence was possible.

It wasn't fair to *still* be lusting for someone who had tried to fuck him to death only the night before. Not fair that this was all such a goddamn turn-on.

Fortunately, Malekh wasn't around for Remy to indulge. The lord was likely in the laboratory, taking charge of whatever treatment Xiaodan needed, which meant Remy was going to have to keep himself amused until he was summoned. That galled him a little. He knew they would call for him the instant Xiaodan was awake, and certainly he didn't know enough about healing to be of any use there, but it didn't make him want to be there any less.

He felt a quick tug at the small satchel slung over his shoulder, where he kept his money, and reacted on instinct. His hand seized a small bony wrist, attached to a boy no older than ten or eleven. He had a shock of black hair and bright blue eyes, but there was no mistaking the small pouch he'd procured from Remy's bag that his fingers had closed around.

"Bugger that," the boy said, and kicked Remy hard in the shins.

Remy's knees buckled, still weak from the previous night's excesses. He let go, and the boy scrambled away.

"Halt, you little snot!" Remy shouted and gave chase. No one else paid them attention, and he was gaining ground by the time the boy rounded a corner and made for an isolated gatehouse. Remy grabbed the back of the boy's shirt before the latter could make it safely inside, and the waif was light enough that he could lift the boy up so that they were face-to-face.

"Is thieving what your lord's been teaching you to do in this castle?"

The boy's feet dangled a good five inches off the ground, but he scowled like he wasn't in trouble. "I only did it on a dare," he mumbled. "Wasn't anything to it."

"A dare?"

The boy pointed back toward the gatehouse, and Remy saw a group of youths peeking back out at them. He recognized two of them as the duo who'd been with Agatha when he had first arrived.

One of them, Renzo, gave him a cheerful wave like nothing was amiss, but the other one, Barnabas, was frowning. "You got lucky," he grumbled to his companion.

"Luck had nothing to do with it. Hand it over."

Still glowering, the other boy reluctantly forked over a few pieces of copper.

"You were betting on whether I'd catch your thieving friend?" Remy asked.

"I'm not a thief," the boy he was holding protested. "I'm just good at stealing things."

"Do you even know what *thief* means, lad?"

"He means that he doesn't do that for a living," Renzo supplied brightly, pocketing his earnings. "It's more of a pastime."

"Not sure that makes things better." Remy set the boy down and reclaimed his pouch.

"They said you've been traveling with Lord Malekh and Lady Song for a while," another from the group spoke up eagerly. "And you're a Reaper!"

"They never let anyone jaunt about with them," another added, almost in a hush. "Not with anyone who ain't of our court."

"Why not?" Remy asked.

The youths looked at each other, and a few shrugged. "Lady Song said that they want humans and kindred to live together," one of the girls said, "but it doesn't mean that those outside can be trusted yet. She said it'd take work, what with people out there not wanting 'em to succeed."

This time, the looks they shot his way were riddled with cautious suspicion. He regretted bringing Breaker with him.

"It would have been easier to just ask rather than steal my money," Remy said.

Renzo inched forward, his eyes still on Breaker. Remy expected a question about the weapon, but what came out of the boy's mouth instead was, "Is it true that you and Lord Malekh and Lady Song are lovers?"

Remy remained standing out of sheer will. His first impulse was to tell them that was none of their business.

"Yes," he said, and it felt oddly freeing to say out loud, even if it was to a group of children who should have known better. It was like he'd announced himself to be long-lost royalty; their faces looked awed. "I'm not complaining, mind. Did Lord Malekh tell you?"

Barnabas shook his head. "Didn't need to. You've got more hickeys on your neck than bites during mosquito season. When you live in a castle with kindred, you know who's courting who. And I overheard Agatha saying she had a room ready for you near ours, 'cept she brought your stuff into Lord Malekh and Lady Song's private chambers because His Lordship asked her to."

"Lord Malekh didn't break his fast this morning," the same girl from before added. "But he stepped out for a bit before heading to the labs, and he looked properly fit and well. He was wan and sallow last night." She, too, gazed pointedly at Remy's neck.

Remy cleared his throat several times. These little shitheads were nosier than he thought. "You all seem familiar with your lord's comings and goings."

"He and Lady Song are away most days now," Renzo said sadly. "But they don't tell us much about what they see out there. All the battles they've been in."

"We take interest in what they do," another boy said importantly. "How else can we help defend the Morgana if we don't know what's going on hereabouts, yeah?"

Remy considered this. "I've been in a few of those fights. How about I tell you some stories?"

Their faces lit up like candles at a convent. "Really?" Barnabas asked gleefully. "Like the time Lord Malekh fought the Second Court? Or the time Lady Song punched that fellow from the Seventh?"

"I wasn't around for those, but I can tell you about the ones I've been present for."

"And maybe show us how to fight, too?" another youth asked eagerly, staring brazenly at Breaker. "Like with that stick on your back, Armiger?"

"Who told you to call me *Armiger*?"

"Lord Malekh did when he came out this morning. He sent a letter to Agatha before you lot arrived, but he reminded us to make sure."

Bastard, Remy thought, warmth pooling in his stomach. "I can't show you how to use my Breaker. It's not a weapon you just stumble upon. But if you've got some staffs or sticks handy, I can show you how to defend yourself."

This wasn't how he'd been expecting to spend his morning. Perhaps this was how it was to have younger siblings, though he thanked the Light his father never had other children.

They told him their names (Barnabas, Renzo, Claus, Felicity, the hobbyist thief Caidnson "but only his mum calls him that cause he's Caid to the rest of us," Emma, Breislin, Samhein), and they were all human save for Renzo, the only child within the Fata Morgana who was a cambion, like Xiaodan. They'd received training from some of the soldiers, but not much.

They found an assortment of staffs to arm themselves with, and Remy showed them the proper way to wield them. "People don't expect speed from me when they see me holding a weapon like this." He spun the Breaker quickly in his hand, and the children oohed when the scythes flicked out. "Whatever weapon you choose, practice with it constantly until it becomes an extension of your own body. You need to know where it strikes, what it will hit before you even attack."

They'd attracted an audience. A crowd had gathered, and Remy had tensed, though the onlookers were curious rather than hostile. No one thought it odd to have a stranger teaching their younglings the finer points of weaponry, though Remy supposed it was not completely out of the ordinary, considering their vigilance over the castle fortifications.

"You're very good with them," one of the observers complimented him after he'd called for a short break.

"I haven't had enough experience with children to know," Remy admitted.

The man who'd spoken was darker than he was, with a short crop of black hair and easygoing brown eyes, though taller by a couple of inches. The stranger stuck out his hand. "The name's Salvador," he said. "Always good to find a fellow kababayan in these parts, though I was rather taken aback to learn you were a Reaper."

"A fellow what?"

The man chuckled. "And a kababayan unfamiliar with the mother tongue. It means *countryman* in Wikaan, though they call it Tithian nowadays."

"You're Tithian?"

Salvador grinned, revealing hints of fang. "Was I wrong to presume the same?"

"On my mother's side I am, yes. I . . . I've never met another Tithian before. Certainly not kindred. You're a long way from home."

"As are you, though Agatha told me that you grew up in Elouve. You must have if you're a Reaper, given those painful-looking scythes." He looked around with a smile. "This is my home now.

One of the strays Lord Malekh took in, more fortunate than some others. If you've got time away from your affairs here at the Morgana, come and have a drink with us. There's five of us here at Lord Malekh's court. Agatha knows where to find me. I can tell you a thing or two about the Isles over several bottles of lambanog."

"Armiger!" The youths had returned, Caid tugging at his shirt. "We're ready for more training, but you promised to tell us about all the adventuring you've done with Lord Malekh and Lady Song, too."

"Please?" Samhein added eagerly. "How many bad vampires have you slain? Have you killed any bad humans, too?"

Remy didn't tell them about the battle at Elouve; it still felt too raw to him. He regaled them instead with the fighting at Chàngge Shuǐ, an easy crowd-pleaser—less than a score of Fourth Court vampires facing nearly a thousand attackers, some of them colossi, led by a feared Fifth Court vampire. He might have exaggerated Malekh's and Xiaodan's exploits in the retelling, but the youths and many of the adults were spellbound. Remy gave them a good show, shaking Breaker at times for emphasis.

"So there we stood atop the waterfall, facing one of the biggest fu—biggest *creatures* I'd ever seen. My friend Elke is a master blacksmith and had reforged her lance to shoot lightning instead of fire. She aimed it at the colossus, timing it just right so it hit the water as we jumped. The fall would've killed me, but Lord Malekh grabbed me before I could so much as move and leaped off the cliff, dragging my arse along with him."

"He wanted to see you safe," Emma said in a hushed tone.

"That he did," Remy agreed. "We thought we were out of danger. But the Fifth Court vampire attacked while we were airborne. He lashed out with his sword"—Remy jutted the scythes into the air, mimicking the attempted blow—"straight for my heart."

His listeners gasped. "Did you survive?" Claus quavered, immediately followed by an irritated "Are you daft? Of course he did" from Breislin.

"And then what happened?" one of the older men demanded.

"Lord Malekh saw it coming and did the only thing he could—shoved me out of the way and took the strike in my stead." More exclamations of dismay. "We fell toward the castle, and I used Breaker to land safely and out of danger." He whirled his knifechain toward a nearby tree, the links swinging easily around a thick branch to demonstrate his escape. "Malekh was injured, but that didn't stop him from engaging the Fifth Court bast—*kindred* in battle. Your liege is a brilliant tactician, the best I'd ever seen in a fight—"

The air felt just a little bit colder, and a hush fell over the crowd.

"—although perhaps that is being far too generous," he allowed. "Truthfully, he's not all that formidable. He cheats a lot, and tends to insult people for an unfair advantage. He's not as fast as you might expect considering he's getting on a thousand years—"

"That may be so," came the amused voice behind him. "I do prefer being slow and thorough if it will make them squirm."

The marks on Remy's neck felt hot, like warning beacons. "How is Xiaodan?" he mumbled, lowering Breaker.

"As well as can be expected. She is not in any danger, if you are worried about that."

"She must not be, if you've condescended to venture out of your lab."

Malekh let out a low chuckle. When Remy finally spun to face him, the vampire lord reached out and laid a hand on his cheek, heedless of everyone looking on. "I hadn't seen your face in a few hours," he said calmly, "and I thought to check on you. I expected to find you asleep in our chambers, not entertaining the youths with your tales of bravery."

"W-was it necessary to say all that with an audience, do you think?"

Malekh ignored him. "Our cook is put out with you. She laid

you a sumptuous breakfast, and you have yet to show yourself at her table."

"I'll go and offer my apologies." Remy turned to his new charges, who were clearly disappointed that their session was over, but also absolutely fascinated with the way their liege was treating their instructor. "We'll continue this another time," he said gruffly.

"We will?" Renzo asked, perking up. "Tomorrow? I want to learn how to whirl a huge chain too!" and the others chimed in with a chorus of agreement.

Remy departed after making his promises, not surprised when Malekh fell into step with him, everyone watching them leave. "Of all the places within my keep to find you," the lord said. "You were training the younger wards?"

"They tried to steal my money. Only fair to make them suffer for it." Remy scowled. "Despite my being bloody fucking sore."

"I will need to return to Xiaodan's side briefly, but I can attend to your aches now."

"Somehow, you always end up making them worse rather than easing them."

"Should I leave you be today? Agatha still has your rooms waiting."

Remy's gaze met his. "No," he muttered. "If I can't visit Xiaodan and there's little change in her condition, I wouldn't mind wasting an hour or two learning more about your court. But if you think you're going to be anywhere near me so soon, I'm going to hit you with your own vaunted, *sturdily built* dresser."

"Do you wish to take control next time?" Malekh asked, slow and deliberate.

It took awhile for the words to make sense, Remy's jaw dropping when what Malekh was offering finally dawned on him. "I—I assumed that you—when was the last time . . . ?"

"Not since my time at the First Court, excepting Xiaodan."

"What? But she doesn't have a—" Remy nearly swallowed his tongue as his imagination supplied him with the answer. "So you're saying . . ."

"I am not averse to it, with the right persons."

With the right persons. Fucking Light, why was Remy the blushing sod here?

"I did not mean to make you uncomfortable," the Summer Lord finally said, after a silence that lasted for some time.

"I'm not!" Remy nearly shouted, worried he would take back the offer, because it felt significant somehow. "I *would*, but . . . maybe after Xiaodan, or we can discuss it again another—"

"Whenever you are ready," Malekh agreed, unflappable.

Sanlea, whose skills Agatha had raved about, had prepared a table groaning with grilled sausages, freshly baked loaves, cheese omelets, berries, and avocado slices, and a sweet cream mixed with honey that she called yogurt. Remy protested it was all too much, even as he tried his damnedest to eat his way through everything, and Sanlea was suffused with pleasure at his praise.

"Not every day that I can receive a compliment from a Reaper, milord," she said with a lovely laugh. "Back in my younger days, we used to share horror stories of how they feasted on vampire hearts to take our strength and speed for themselves."

"Only during the Light's Evenmas," Remy said solemnly, and joined in their laughter.

He ate, and Malekh sat across from him and watched him eat with an inscrutable expression that made Remy's stomach flutter. "You don't need to accompany me. I look like a glutton, stuffing my face while you have nothing."

"I took more than my fill last night."

Remy shoved a whole omelet into his mouth, but his slovenliness did nothing to lessen the faint gleam in the man's eyes. "Why can't I visit Xiaodan yet? I thought you said she was out of danger."

"Yes, but there are no guarantees that her health can be

restored to what it was." Malekh's eyes wandered to an empty spot at the table. "We try to keep the laboratory here as sterile as possible, and that includes limiting visitors. I am more concerned about when she finally awakens. Now that Xiaodan realizes that she can still bring out the sun, she will keep pushing her limits to prove her capabilities."

"And she's going to ignore any warnings we give her." A stray lock of hair had fallen over Malekh's face, and it had been irritating the shit out of Remy since they'd both sat down. He reached out and brushed it away, sliding it back behind the lord's left ear. Sanlea saw and smiled beatifically at them. Her acceptance of him—hell, the easy acceptance of so many of the inhabitants of the Fata Morgana—was something Remy was trying to acclimate to. It felt nice.

"I could ask her to take certain inhibitors," Malekh said. "They would prevent her from exerting herself, whether she likes it or not—"

"Regardless of whether they actually work, you *do* know she would murder us both for even suggesting it, right?"

They smiled at each other. Or rather, Remy smiled, and Malekh's face grew a hair less creased. "You're not wrong," he said. "But at this point, I will gladly take that risk if it prevents her from harming herself again. I would not like to see a repeat of what happened at Elouve. It reminded me far too much of what Lilith had to do to stop Ishkibal."

Remy's grin disappeared. "Malekh, I—"

"And I will tell you again and again that it was not your fault until you finally believe it. If you wish to honor Naji's memory, then do so with a clear conscience."

"He wouldn't have wanted you shouldering the guilt, either." Remy's finger traced a slow, short path across the lord's cheekbone. "Where did you bring him?"

"I thought it best to lay him beside his human sweetheart,

Anastacia. Naji spent more time in Chànggē Shuǐ than he ever
did here, and I thought he would prefer it better. He would not
have wanted you blaming yourself, either, to toss and turn in your
sleep at night."

"I wasn't sleeping badly because of that." Remy hesitated. "I've
been having dreams about my old nanny." He scowled at Malekh's
arched eyebrow. "Not like that, you bloody degenerate. She's the
closest thing to a mother I've ever known."

"They did not seem like fond memories, judging from your
restlessness."

"They are. It just feels unsettling to dream about her now, out
of the blue. I could have told you if you didn't keep on disappearing come morning. Could've thanked you, too, for looking out for
me," he added grudgingly.

"I rise early, and you need the rest. There are many things that
need attending here."

"I like it. This castle of yours. I wouldn't mind spending more
time here."

"I would have expected Chànggē Shuǐ to be more to your taste."

"I enjoy them both. The crowds here don't affect me as much,
because the people are different. Far more welcoming than any
other place in Aluria I've been to. And I appreciate the effect this
place has on you."

"And what might that be?"

Remy took his time chewing on his avocado slice, hoping
he would let the comment pass, but Malekh continued to wait.
"You're gentler here. Not that you aren't elsewhere, but it's
clear. It's like you feel freer to indulge in happiness in the Morgana."

"I thought you said you didn't want me anywhere near you.
This is not helping."

"Well, if you're going to fall back on your old habits of fasting
and taking poor care of yourself whenever you attend to Xiaodan,

then," Remy said, glowering at a nearby strawberry, "I ought to be on hand to make sure you have something."

Malekh's thumb pressed down the back of Remy's hand. "I intended to give you some rest tonight. I thought to ask if I could draw more blood from you, run more tests to determine exactly how our bloodsharing affects you. Beneficial as it has been to your health, I would like to know of any unforeseen side effects it might bring. The laboratory at the Morgana boasts better equipment than the one in Chànggē Shuǐ. The results would be far more accurate after a good night's sleep and regular sustenance."

"And now?" Remy croaked, looking up.

Malekh held his gaze. "I suppose sleep and sustenance can wait until tomorrow."

"Milord?" Speck, the ginger-haired scientist, scuttled into the kitchen, looking mildly panicked. "There's been a problem."

Malekh half rose from his seat, letting Remy go as he did. "I told you to call me only when Xiaodan's taken a turn for the worse, Spencer—"

"Oh, no! No milord, it's not like that. It's just . . . Lady Xiaodan's missing. Vanished from her bed when we weren't looking. Thought you ought to know."

7

WINGS

Malekh didn't seem too concerned about Xiaodan's disappearance, but his irritability told Remy that she'd pulled this stunt before. A hunt was currently underway, though Malekh had returned to the laboratory for a moment to go over her most recent test results. He'd told Remy that she would make herself known to them whenever she felt ready to, that it was usually best to leave her be in the meantime.

Remy was not of the same disposition as Malekh. He remembered all the times he'd gone off to sulk—which in his case often meant getting shit-faced drunk—only for Xiaodan to find him anyway, cajole him out of feeling sorry for himself, and get something sobering into him. Though the last time, it was him sobering up inside her, which worked well enough. He ought to look, in any case.

Easier said than done, as Fata Morgana was two-thirds the size of Elouve, intimidating by that measure alone. He had little inkling of Xiaodan's favorite spots here, or any special hiding places known only to the locals. But, glancing up at the spire above him, the tallest structure within the fortress, he thought he could hazard a good guess at where she was.

The guard on duty was only too glad to show him the way to the top. Unlike elsewhere in Fata Morgana, the tower held no ramps—too narrow, too high, and too remote for the residents to access, as he was informed it was not in use.

The winds were stronger up at these ramparts, and the cold made Remy's teeth chatter. The steeple was tall enough to graze the dark clouds overhead, but the fog below swamping the plains prevented anyone on watch here from seeing into the horizon for approaching hostiles. It was probably why no one kept watch here. Malekh undoubtedly used other means to alert his people of any enemy sightings.

He was alone. There was no one else around, and Remy thought that he'd gotten it wrong, until he could hear the faint sounds of a heartbeat. It took a few minutes for him to puzzle out where the source was coming from, finally looking up with a quick flash of insight.

Xiaodan sat on the roof above him, carefully perched on the angled stone tiles and so quiet that he wouldn't have noticed if not for her heart. She was as still as a weathervane in a storm's eye, gazing out into the vastness below them while the winds whipped her long hair forcefully about her.

She'd been crying. Remy couldn't even begin to describe the sheer melancholy on her face, at the wistfulness there.

"Malekh's worried about you," he said.

"Zidan knows where I am. He's giving me space." The quick look she shot his way indicated that Remy should have followed suit. "How did you know I was here?"

"I seem to recall someone at our first meeting saying they would climb the highest tower they could and shout into the wind when they were feeling out of sorts," Remy responded, refusing to budge. "I was worried about you."

"I'm all right. You didn't need to come looking for me."

"You always sought me out when I was in a foul mood or was trying to drink myself into oblivion, insisting that I would do better with the company. I'm just repaying the favor."

She flickered out of view and reappeared beside him, her gaze still on the mist surrounding the castle below. Her hand was cold, but Remy quickly warmed it, slipping his fingers in between hers. For a long moment they both said nothing, gazing out into the plains.

"Zidan's not going to be happy with me," Xiaodan finally said.

"I know."

"Especially once he learns I've been up here for close to an hour, trying to channel the sun again."

"I know."

"I couldn't. You said I was able to do it back at Eugenie's, but I don't remember that. I can't even manifest so much as a spark. But I won't stop trying. And Zidan won't like that."

"I know."

"I thought you'd be angry too."

"I'm not sure Malekh's as mad about this as you think. He knows you better than I do, and *I* know you're likely to be stubborn regardless." Remy ignored the glare she shot his way. "He understands, but you could at least let him set the pace for you."

"You're actually agreeing with Zidan? Am I dreaming?"

It was Remy's turn to grump. "We don't fight *all* the time."

"It's foreplay for you two. I find it both heartwarming and alluring." Xiaodan ignored his glower. "I took being the Sunbringer for granted. I thought its absence would improve my health, but I'm not so sure anymore. My heart doesn't feel any stronger for its lack. I don't even know if I can stand strong against the First Court."

"And I don't give a fuck about the Night Empress or her court if it means putting you at risk. We can't keep relying on you to defeat her. Malekh and I will just have to work harder to take the burden off your back." Remy lifted her hand, pressed it against the side of his mouth. "But you have to give yourself time, too."

Xiaodan's fingers shifted, and Remy let go so she could move them down his neck, the tips cool against the bite marks there. "These look rougher than they should be."

"He's been taking out his worry for you on me, yes."

She tilted her head up toward his, and Remy kissed her. He had missed this. He'd missed her, and he would have been content staying up on that windy rampart, kissing her for hours despite the bracing cold.

"I suppose I can return now and listen to his lecture," she said after a while.

"When you need time alone, I would appreciate it if you could find a more accessible spot than this," Remy grumbled.

A glint of mischief appeared in Xiaodan's dark eyes. "We could always jump down."

"Absolutely the hell not," Remy said, breaking out into a sweat despite the chill. "Unless you start sprouting bat wings yourself, and even then, I'd rather use a hundred flights of stairs."

Xiaodan froze, looking at him like he'd just told her he could sprout feathers out his rear. "You're right," she whispered. "She *did* do that, didn't she? Hold tight, Remy."

Remy had no time to stop her, because he was already clinging on for dear life, Xiaodan having only enough consideration to check if he was safely secured to her person before quite inconsiderately jumping off the spire.

Remy's screams were swallowed up by the winds as they plummeted down, his throat raw by the time Xiaodan landed with the gracefulness of a cat. His head was still spinning when she anchored her hand even more securely around his waist and took off running back into the direction of the castle courtyard, the world blurring around him.

By the time everything had stopped swiveling around, he was flat on his bottom, the ground finally stable underneath him. They were at one of the mills. Workers stared curiously at him as he staggered to his feet, still tottering. "Xiaodan," he managed to say, "we weren't so pressed for time that you had to throw us off the fucking—"

"Why take the longer route when I could simply jump some hundred feet down and arrive here in seconds?"

"That is not the point!"

Xiaodan wasn't listening. She was waving frantically at one of the workers: Salvador, the Tithian vampire he'd talked to earlier.

Salvador glanced questioningly at the dazed Remy. "I'm glad to see you up and about, milady, though I believe Lord Malekh has been worried about you."

"Zidan can wait," Xiaodan said dismissively. "I apologize for the abruptness, Salvador, but I was hoping that you might tell us all you know of Wikaan vampires."

Salvador looked surprised. "Err, you mean like me, milady?"

"You were bitten by an Altruscan vampire during the turn of the century, so that's not quite what I was asking. I meant the kind of kindred prominent within the Whispering Isles before the Alurians renamed it Tithe. You're a historian, so I thought you might know more."

Salvador nodded, a bright smile breaking out on his face. "It's been awhile since I've talked to anyone about any of my scholarly pursuits. Yes, I was a student of Tithian lore, but if it's kindred you wish to learn more about, I'm afraid there's little to know of Wikaan kindred even before Aluria invaded."

"And why is that?"

"The vampires of the Whispering Isles learned to survive by

pretending to be human themselves, milady. It was said that the First of the Vampires had established another ruling clan within the islands. It was their lineage that Ishkibal warred with, believing them to be one of the many threats to his rule. Lord Malekh would know more. As one of Ishkibal's generals, he would have fought the Wikaan vampires—ah, Tithian kindred, I mean—all those centuries ago. But it's harder to do battle when your opponent has no desire to face you on the field—they used guerilla tactics to keep themselves hidden from his ire. The eastern and northern kindred clans fell to Ishkibal's forces, but the Wikaan survived against all odds."

"Did the Wikaan vampires possess bat-like wings?" Xiaodan asked.

"Xiaodan." Remy was stunned.

"So they say," Salvador confirmed. "Wings of varying textures and shapes, I believe. I know disappointingly little, for all the information I've tried to procure in the years since." Salvador grinned, a hint of fang protruding. "In ages past, being a Tithian vampire was a symbol of royalty—few were permitted to be turned. Unlike the vampires of the Eight Courts, who believe in multiplying their species at will."

"A symbol of royalty?" Remy echoed.

"They were called mandurugo. They can choose to pass down their abilities to their kin—their leaders were called babaylan, I believe, but Tithians use it nowadays as a title rather than any proof of kindredship. One of the few monikers that survived to the present day, though many are unaware of its true origins. It's not even a question of birth, milady. You can be born of one and still not be worthy until the babaylan decide to make you their heir. Unfortunately, even if the war with King Ishkibal didn't whittle down their numbers, then the Alurian invasion would have, if not obliterated them entirely. I'm impressed that you know of even that small detail, milady—no babaylan has ever emerged from Aluria's—" Salvador broke off. "Are you all right, Armiger? You're looking pale."

"We need to find Malekh." Remy was finding it harder to breathe. *"Now."*

"YOUR BLOOD tests are in order," Malekh said, leaning back against his chair with a frown. "If your main concern is that you are going to sprout wings and fangs and fly away like the Night Empress did, you are safe."

"She bit me at Elouve." Remy paced the floor, his mind running a mile a minute. "She must have, if she could control me."

"She doesn't need to bite you to compel you," Xiaodan pointed out gently from her spot on the bed. Much to Remy's relief, Malekh had asked the other scientists to leave the laboratory to give them some much needed privacy. "She compelled Malekh without it."

"She might have." Remy's fists clenched. "How can I know for certain that she hasn't tried to give me some of her blood? If she wants to pass this onto me without my consent?" His voice rose, angry and fearful. "She was never turned by a vampire. She already was one herself. Those damned wings were proof she was descended from the Whispering Isles kindred. What if I become like her? What if I turn into kindred? What if I turn on the both of you—"

"You won't." Xiaodan left the bed, her arms now wrapped around his waist. "Zidan is certain. He would know the best out of all of us. As Salvador said, had she truly passed anything down to you, she would've lost her own abilities. Inheritance is not something they take lightly."

Remy gulped in a lungful of air. "But what if eventually passing them to me has been her intention all along? What if she succeeds? I think I'd rather kill myself before—"

"We will not allow it to happen," Malekh said sharply. His hand was on Remy's face, his hold firm. "Do you hear me? We will never allow that to happen to you."

Remy dragged Xiaodan closer. His other hand tightened on the front of Malekh's coat.

All his life he'd been desperate to cling to any part of his mother, to imprint memories of her on himself so he wouldn't forget as he grew older. And now, the very thought of sharing the same blood as her, with the same consequences, terrified him more than anything else.

REMY TRIED to put it behind him in the days that followed. Malekh had pointed out that there was little to be done and worrying about it now would change nothing until they could uncover more information.

So he took to training the sprouts more seriously. The youths didn't have enough experience yet to be comfortable with sharper-edged weapons, so Remy put them to work with staffs, wooden sticks, blunted practice swords. He hadn't thought he'd make a good teacher; he only had his own experience training with his father and then the Reapers to fall back on, but while Valenbonne had been a hard taskmaster and an unrelenting disciplinarian, Remy tried to temper his instructions with a kinder touch, giving his charges the space to make mistakes to analyze afterward.

Some of the other adults had also asked to be trained by the third day, and Remy obliged. He'd never been placed in charge of his own squadron before, unofficial as this was. It was oddly satisfying.

"You make it look easy," Xiaodan said on the fourth morning.

She had grudgingly stayed at the infirmary until the doctors determined her fit to leave, and today marked her first day of freedom.

"Can you beat Lady Song, too, Armiger?" Renzo called. "She and Lord Malekh'd be the only ones that can give you a good raking through, yeah?"

"If this is them liking me, I don't want to know what it's like for them to hate me," Remy muttered, earning a laugh from Xiaodan.

"Do you want to?"

Remy looked back at her inquisitive face. He'd fought Malekh many times before, but he'd never had to face Xiaodan in a sparring match. "All right, but I'm not looking forward to getting my arse handed back to me with my pupils looking on."

"You're underestimating yourself again." Xiaodan grinned. "Don't worry, I'll be gentle."

She was brutal. The Fourth Court vampire's idea of a spar was to jab him lightly on his sides, forcing him to block the blows whenever he could, then grab his face when he grew tired and plant a wet, sloppy kiss on him when his guard was fully down. It became their means of keeping score, which made it harder for Remy not to concede defeat at every bout. The hoots and friendly ribbing grew louder after he barely managed to keep Xiaodan from kissing him a *fifth* time.

"It's not much of a fight if the armiger *wants* to lose, milady!" one of the women called out, and the laughter was contagious. Remy felt giddy, light on his feet, and not because he was making a good impression.

"Why so quiet now?" Xiaodan teased. Their fighting exhibition over, she'd wrapped his arm around her shoulder, looking healthy and happy and beautiful and still checking him worriedly for any bruises.

Remy couldn't stop grinning. Times like this, he could almost— almost—forget about his mother. About his own cursed lineage.

"They're right. Feels like I won, anyway," he said, and kissed her this time.

He was still getting his share of ribbing when Salvador invited him to the Tithians' domicile that night. The men lived in several cabins they'd built at the outer courtyard, spacious and comfortable enough for their needs. They were sprawled in chairs outside their respective homes, which Remy learned was a nightly habit of theirs. They'd initially been offered rooms in the castle when they first came to the Morgana, Salvador had explained, but they'd turned them down. "Too luxurious for our tastes. We'd asked for something with a nice view of the night sky instead, and Lord Malekh obliged."

"Did you all live in Tithe when it was an independent kingdom?" Remy asked curiously, already tipsy. The Tithians drank as hard as they worked. They'd offered him a liquor they'd brewed themselves, an eye-watering concoction called lambanog that had Remy choking and pawing at his throat at the very first sip, while the others knocked the foul liquid back like it was water.

"Tithe," another named Allan snorted. "*Alurians* call it Tithe. Wikaan was its original name. Even that they eradicated until there was nothing left. So few remember nowadays."

"I heard Geoffrey telling the others about the Night Empress." Salvador's face was a picture in sympathy. "Said that she was Wikaan, too? That's why you and Lady Song were asking me about Tithian lore?"

Salvador held up his glass. "Here's a bit of information, then. Apparently babaylan had a ritual where they transferred their authority to another by sharing lambanog." He took a swig and laughed. "Always thought they made up the occasion to drink themselves insensible."

"Still not sure about this alliance with Aluria that Lord Malekh wants," Josefin said with a scowl. "But if he really believes it's the key to peace . . . Queen Ophelia has been working with the Tithians to reconstruct their kingdom, I hear, though it'll still be a mere shadow of what it once was."

"I can tell you what little I know," Salvador said. "The bat wings, for instance. It's not quite that."

"What do you mean?" Remy asked.

"There'll be more than one pair on her, at her strongest. Mandurugo supposedly possess multilayered wings, and I suppose she was severely weakened if you've only seen one. You asked about how they pass down their abilities. That's commonly through their children—Wikaan are devoted to their families—but from what I've gathered, the heir must be willing to be turned and the sire willing to do the turning."

Remy took another sip, trying to hide his nervousness, his relief. "So they can't pass it on to someone who refuses?"

"That's what the legends say, though without any firsthand accounts I can't really confirm that. Sounds like it's been something you've been thinking hard about, though. I thought Lady Song would be willing. Or is it Lord Malekh who's resistant?"

"Resistant to what?"

Salvador looked embarrassed. "Ah, pasensya. Thought you were thinking about, uh, you and the Third and Fourth Court leaders. Because you're human and they're . . . I assumed that you were going to let them, at some point."

"I—no. Or rather . . ." Remy paused. "I haven't talked to them about it."

"Didn't mean to bring it up," Salvador said apologetically.

"No apologies necessary," Remy said, then took a huge gulp of the lambanog. This time, he didn't even feel the burn.

"Night's still young," Tonio said cheerfully, tipping a new bottle Remy's way. "Up for another round, Armiger?"

They were right. It was far too early to be thinking. Remy shoved his tankard toward him. "Just one more," he agreed.

"I AM not drunk," Remy said, keeping himself very still and steady.

"You are impossibly drunk," Xiaodan said with a slight, crooked smile. She was cross-legged on the bed, watching Remy cross the room in what he hoped was a straight, sober line. "I could smell you before you even stepped foot inside the castle. The Tithians must really like you, if they're breaking out their most expensive liquor on your behalf. I could hear all the merriment through the window."

"We weren't that loud." Light, but the Tithians loved to sing. Mother's tits, that was right, he'd sung along with them. "You've drunk their lump—their lamba—limsa—"

"Their lambanog? It's not quite to my taste, but Selim and the other carpenters sometimes buy it off them. Said it strips bark clean off, better than any tool they've got."

"Ah." Remy reached the side of the bed and paused. "Do you want to turn me?" he blurted out.

Xiaodan looked startled. "Remy, why—"

"Because I might let you," Remy said in a rush, because maybe he *was* drunk. "I might want to. I don't want to—I don't want to be eighty and hunchbacked and liver-spotted while you and Malekh . . . I'd be a blip in your lives, and you'd forget me soon enough. I'm selfish, but I want to be more than just a mayfly in your—"

"Remy." A split second was all it took for Xiaodan to send him onto the pillows, her finding a spot on his side. Her arm encircled his waist. "Go to sleep. We can talk about this in the morning."

"I would," Remy mumbled. "If you asked me to, I would."

Xiaodan looked at him for a few seconds with both fondness

and sadness. "I know," she sighed and stroked his hair. "But I'm not asking, Remy. Go to sleep."

HE WAS at Miss Grissell's funeral, seventeen and alone, the whispers loud to his ears as he paused by her coffin, head bowed. He was sober here, at least.

Only his nanny's brother was brave enough to approach him, already old enough to be his grandfather. "She was proud of you," he said softly, voice full of tears. "Used to cut out news clippings of your exploits. More than once she'd march to the *Wayward Post* offices and demand they recant something they'd said about you. Was successful a couple of times, after she invoked your father's name. Always enjoyed it whenever you stopped by to see her, even after her mind started going."

"I didn't visit her enough," Remy said.

"You did more than you ought to," Miss Grissell said. "More than he would have wanted. I'm glad there was someone in your life you could rely on, however brief."

Remy turned.

Miss Grissell was standing by the doorway, smiling at him like she wasn't dead inside the casket before him.

"Blue eyes," he said.

"What's that, love?" asked whoever was pretending to be his nanny.

"Lanacia Grissell had blue eyes," Remy said. "And in these bloody dreams, yours are brown."

Miss Grissell opened her mouth to speak.

Then he was standing outside the caves at the Dà Lán, the dead children Vasilik had turned, piled at his feet. Light danced across the ground before him, the clouds above parting briefly to allow the sun passage every few minutes.

I am sorry, Miss Grissell said, an odd accompaniment of echoes now augmenting her words. Before he could say another word, black wings spurted from her back, the wispy white hair transforming into tangles of the same shade; he saw eyes that were brown for only a moment more before they turned to him, now red and burning and bright.

8

WITHIN DREAMS

Malekh's solution had been to dose Remy with some foul-tasting tincture that threw him into so deep a slumber that no dreams could intervene. It left a faint aftertaste of something bitter and burnt in Remy's mouth, not unlike when he'd overimbibed with cheap mead. He complained as frequently and as loudly as he could but took the damned medication in the end, because it was better than picking up that dream where he'd escaped it. He didn't protest when Malekh took more blood from him, despite result after result coming up negative in his favor.

Xiaodan's solution was to keep Remy busy during the day so he would have little time to dream at night. She was at home in the Fata Morgana just as much as she had been in Chànggē Shuǐ, and the people here treated her like their other leader, like she was already Malekh's wife. Remy still took to training the children in the morning, but afternoons were spent visiting the mills and the foundries, watching men and women dance on grapes to produce the sweetest liquor or gathering a certain shellfish species native to the region to produce the beautiful purple dye for cloths that they sold at markets like the one in Libéliard, which explained Malekh's familiarity with the place, Eugenie notwithstanding.

He spent most of his free hours trying to be useful, pumping water out of the natural wells from underground rivers and lakes beneath the castle, harvesting fruit from the vineyards and greenhouses, even learning to milk the cows. Sanlea delighted in having him in her kitchens. His own cooking was too simple and spartan, a drawback of the bachelor's life he'd led in Elouve, but he did know his way around a knife.

Remy's solution was to pretend nothing was wrong and get fucked instead.

Neither Xiaodan nor Malekh complained. They were methodical, practiced. They stripped him easily of his clothes, wasted little time in removing their own. A slight push sent Remy onto their bed, and he fell willingly. Their bedchambers had been the first place he'd learned to trust them fully with himself.

He felt their hands lift him up, felt the warmth of Malekh behind him even as Xiaodan settled herself over his body. He felt their mouths all over him, their touch welcoming and needed.

The more logical thing to do would've been to sit him down and talk about it. Reassure him, because that's what Xiaodan would have done. Run other tests to prove that Remy didn't have any goddamn mandurugo's blood running through him no matter who his mother was, because that's what Malekh would have done.

Instead, Malekh kissed his way down his neck, adding more love bites to the others he'd already left there, and then it was Xiaodan's turn to mark Remy with new ones of her own. They knew how to work him. Remy still wondered what they saw in him, that they could be so kind.

They might still opt for the more reasonable routes tomorrow: Xiaodan earnestly trying to convince him things would be fine, Malekh hooking him up to Light-knows whatever contraptions within his laboratory to learn every secret his blood could divulge.

But for now, this was what he needed.

He wasn't used to the cuddling, though.

He was accustomed to it with Xiaodan, who liked to worm her way through every available breathing space that lay between her and him, like he was her only source of warmth. He was *not* used to it with Malekh.

"What are you doing?" Remy asked when the mattress dipped until Malekh's weight was settled comfortably against his body and Xiaodan's. Malekh did sex, but he never did the bed.

Malekh grunted. It was his fiancée who responded. "It's not like he wasn't staying with you before we even knew about those dreams you were having."

"He always flees in the morning like some blushing chambermaid, so I wouldn't know."

"How do you know how blushing chambermaids flee, Remy?" Xiaodan asked, curious.

Remy reddened. "I don't! The last thing I needed was more gossip about m—"

"Would you like me to leave, Pendergast?" Malekh interrupted.

"Of course not—"

"Because I am more inclined to stay when it is silent."

Remy glared and grumbled, but quieted. Xiaodan only grinned broadly, flinging her arms around them both and somehow managing it despite her slight form.

This is all I need, Remy told himself.

Malekh was still there the next morning. Xiaodan was asleep, her weight a comfort on his chest. Unexpectedly pleasant, Remy thought, and gazed at Malekh until the latter, eyes still closed, shoved a pillow into his face and told him to stop staring.

All of it helped, in a way. Malekh's sleeping tincture probably was the most effective of the lot, though Remy wasn't keen on telling the lord, lest he up the dosage.

He didn't want to think about it. Didn't want to think about his mother, and why she'd been haunting his dreams. He dreaded going back to sleep, comforted only by the knowledge that he never went to bed alone. Staying busy helped stave off the brief periods of melancholy whenever Remy had enough time to himself to think.

Like when he was showing the youths the best way to position a bow in close quarters with an enemy and he'd thought of Giselle. Before he could shunt those thoughts away, he'd remembered how she'd always preferred him with a bow rather than with Breaker or a sword; he had a fine-fitting form whenever he drew the nock back, she'd said, that emphasized his biceps and the spread of his shoulders. She'd bought arrows for him, goose feather–tipped and expensive, and when he'd protested that hitting a target was not dependent on the decorativeness of the projectile but on the surety of the mark, she'd only laughed and said she liked spoiling him either way.

He'd told his charges to practice on their own for the next half hour with the bullseyes he'd set up along the courtyard, having had the foresight to close off the perimeter to discourage other residents from walking into any rogue arrows. Then he'd walked a short distance away to lean against a wall and gather himself.

He didn't miss Giselle, and it was a cruel thing to say. He was sorry that she'd died and he would always blame himself for it, but he tried to find something in the years they'd been together that he wished to have back, only to find those memories wanting. There was nothing of her he could remember that wasn't about his own guilt.

He thought about the Lady Daneira, about the people who'd hung from the gallows in the capital because they'd been accused of consorting with him, though he hadn't even recognized any of them by face.

The pain in his chest was like a hammer striking bone. Remy clutched at it, waited with slow breaths until it went away.

It was easy to forget when he was away from Elouve. And just like in Chànggē Shuǐ, Remy felt the familiar tug here at the Third Court, the desire to stay.

It would be easier if they turned him.

They told Remy Xiaodan was at the spire again, so he took the winding stairs up. At the top he saw Xiaodan, silent with her hands clasped before her in the familiar gesture of one of her fighting forms.

She was beautiful to look at, always had been. And when she finally moved, going from one stance to the next with a fervency to her paces, Remy felt a familiar lump settling in his throat, remembering everything that had brought him here with her, everything that had happened to make them love each other.

She paused and brought her arms back to herself, curving them as if she was holding something invisible inches away from her, and closed her eyes. Many weeks ago, it would have brought out the blinding light she could harness, the one she'd always referred to as the sun. But the space between her hands remained empty. He waited for her as she stood there, unmoving, as long minutes ticked into a quarter of an hour. He could tell from the rigidity along her shoulders that she was straining, as if steeling herself for some powerful blow.

And then she relaxed, let out a soft noise that sounded like a sob.

Remy waited for her to acknowledge him. And when she did, her smile was bitter, brown eyes glassy with tears.

"I'm not going to stop trying," she said.

"I know."

"Speck said I needed to rest for another week before attempting this again."

"I know."

"I didn't want you and Zidan worrying."

"You know we'd worry more that you're hiding this from us. And if Malekh hasn't been actively trying to find you all this time, then he probably already knows where you are and what you're doing."

"How did you get so good at reading us?" Xiaodan hiccupped.

"How did you get so good at reading me?" Remy held his arms out, and Xiaodan flew to them. She didn't cry again, but Remy held her all the same, waiting for her heartbeat to slow as much as it was capable of. She sniffed, looked past his shoulder. "I don't know what else I should be doing," she said. "It's not like I can spend the whole day inside your laboratory unless I can annoy you while I'm there."

Remy scowled, not bothering to turn around. "Can't you ever announce yourself first?"

"I didn't want to intrude until I had to," Malekh said calmly.

"Speck and the others say to heal, but that's what I've been doing for years. Decades." Xiaodan dashed angrily at her eyes with the back of her hand. "I've been doing nothing but trying to heal, and it's never going to end. Not as long as I've got Lilith's heart." She pressed her hands over her chest. "I want to do more than just wait to get better."

They were handling it all wrong, Remy realized. The tinctures, the distractions, the sex.

"I need to talk to her," he said.

Xiaodan paused. "Remy—"

"You know it's what I should have done when we realized she'd found a way to infiltrate my dreams. She could have controlled me, used me to attack either one of you, but she didn't. This feels different. Like that wasn't her intention. Maybe there's a way to get back your sunbringing abilities if this is hurting her as much as it's hurting you. I can find out."

"And what if she's only biding her time, trying to lower your guard so she can compel you completely this time?" Malekh demanded.

Remy looked down at Xiaodan's concerned face, at the strain in Malekh's expression. He regretted having thought he was nothing more than a passing fancy to them, someone to forget with the passing of time.

"She's my mother," he said, which was not an answer and yet the only answer he could give.

MALEKH TOOK precautions, as Remy had expected him to. His methods left little to be desired, though.

"Is all this necessary?" he asked gingerly, tugging at the straps the doctors had attached to his body, slightly self-conscious at being half-naked in a room full of acquaintances.

"It is if we intend to learn when your dreaming cycle begins," Tinsley told him cheerfully. "There's nothing invasive about the procedure, if you're worried."

"Sounds pretty bloody intrusive if you all intend to eavesdrop on my sleep."

"Oh, we won't actually see what you're dreaming about. We'll only know when it starts through the increase in your heartbeats and subconscious eye movements." He gestured at the odd machine the straps were connected to. "If the Night Empress does anything, we can easily bring you back awake."

"Malekh doesn't even fucking sleep." Remy glared at the lord, who was making some last-minute tests on his contraption, loosening the wraps and tightening wires. "How would *you* know anything about dreams?"

"Sleep is a necessity for humans, but kindred are capable of it," the man responded calmly. "*Sleep* is not quite what we experience; it is more a state of senseless inactivity. And since I lead a court of both humans and vampires, I thought it important to study the mortal waking and sleeping cycles to better understand and accommodate their well-being."

"You've been sleeping beside Xiaodan and I the last several nights," Remy said.

Malekh shot him a blank stare. "Was that not what you wanted? Or would you rather have me flee again like . . . a blushing chambermaid, was it?"

"Forget it," Remy muttered; already a bright red, trying to ignore the curious looks from the doctors—and the particularly gleeful ones from both Xiaodan and Wits.

"Human sleep moves between two distinct states of passivity and activity," the lord continued. "We've detected with some level of certainty when one slips into the other, and we'll be monitoring for any unusual changes in your patterns. While these vary from person to person, there's little time for us to gauge your habits, so we'll be using the median we've learned from previous studies."

"You've done this before?"

"Some humans here have been gracious enough to volunteer. But for the most part, our research was conducted mainly on felines."

"Cats? You've been fucking testing this on ca—"

"They were not subjected to undue stress during the testing. The opposite, in fact, was our prerequisite for successful results. And if your current aggravation stems from the fact that we have used cats to improve the process—"

"You're more nervous about this than I am," Remy said with some surprise.

Malekh's expression did not change. "The machine is perfectly safe, if that concerns you."

Remy lay down and tried to find a much more comfortable position on the cot. "So I just fall asleep, and that's it?"

"That's it," Speck confirmed.

"Bloody hard to do that when you're all watching me." He was going to get failing marks in *dreaming* of all things, something that was surely normal to fear and possible to achieve.

Malekh glanced at the other doctors. Speck was quick to take the hint. "We'll come back when you're asleep," he said, giving them a merry wave as he began ushering the others out.

Xiaodan settled herself by the side of the cot, but Remy was having none of that. "If this blasted contraption isn't going to do much, then it should be fine for her to lie down beside me, right?"

Xiaodan was already moving before Malekh could give his permission, plunking herself happily by his side. "Don't worry," she said, taking his hand. "I'll be here the whole time."

"As will I." Malekh had positioned himself beside the machine, as close to them as he could manage. Remy just grinned at him.

"You think we three can fool around for a bit while we wait?" he asked, in a bid to ease the tension. "You two put me instantly to sleep that way."

"Pendergast," Malekh warned.

"Just a suggestion. Your fancy machine's got a nice thrum to it. Might feel nice to have me or Xiaodan against—"

"I have a syringe full of a sleeping medication that can have you under in twenty seconds. Do not tempt me into using it."

"Does that mean you're at least considering it?"

"*Pendergast.*"

HE WAS standing inside Kinaiya Lodge, staring up at the portrait he had there of his mother. It didn't matter that he'd already had the residence up for sale, his possessions stored with his solicitors' firm for safekeeping. It didn't matter that the lodge itself was still undergoing repairs, half-burnt from when an Elouvian mob had tried to destroy the place and drag him off to the gallows. Everything was exactly the same as when he'd lived in it, from the succulents on his shelves to the watercolors on his walls to the empty bottles of wine littering the common room from when he'd sunk into an alcohol-soaked depression, adrift and alone in his misery.

He realized that he was already dreaming when someone said behind him, very quietly, **It should not have had to be this way.**

She was so much like her portrait on the wall that it hurt Remy's heart to see her. She looked almost human now, dressed in Elouvian clothes instead of the crimson robes he'd always seen her wear. Her bat wings were gone, tucked away somewhere and invisible from where he stood.

She, too, was looking up at her own picture, just as beautiful as she'd been painted, and whatever it was she saw in the face looking back at her, there was a faint quaver in her voice that took him by surprise.

"Why were you using my old nanny to talk to me?" Remy asked.

Was I? The Night Empress sounded surprisingly startled. **I did not realize it. All I wanted was to watch you. She was kind. She was who I should have been to you.**

She stepped beside him, her eyes never leaving the painting. This close, it came as a shock to Remy that she was shorter than he was by several inches. Out in the battlefield, inside Meridian Keep, she'd somehow seemed taller, larger than life. Her arms were bare, and he wondered about the absence of the First Court mark that should have been etched onto her skin.

Gone when I returned from death, the woman said, as if reading his mind. I'd allowed them to mark me. **For protection, they said, when in reality it only made me a target. But perhaps I was not in a condition to give my consent, for they had already compelled me in some small way then.**

"And afterward?" Remy asked.

Afterward, I learned of Aluria's treachery. That they had not come as saviors, but with intentions to utterly annihilate Wikaan. That my own husband had known and said nothing to me. And my choice became clear.

Both fell silent for a while, Remy quietly reflecting on her words.

These plants need watering, the Night Empress said unexpectedly.

"I was away frequently," Remy said. "Elke often let herself in to do so for me and feed the cats."

Far less than either of you should. My Alurian ivy can live forever with the proper care. Between you and your friend, it will not last another ten years.

"That—that was *your* ivy?"

The plants at the manor were all under my care. Did you not take some saplings from there before you moved?

He could only nod, speechless. The Night Empress stood over the succulents, inspecting them carefully. She made no move to touch him, this time keeping her gaze carefully averted. Oddly, the rejection made him feel resentful.

"And now you can't stand looking at me."

Never! The word shot out of her like a cannon, as if that was all it took to bring her bottled emotions out into the open. Her hands unclenched, arms rising to the air in frustration. Remy had done that in the past, recognized her gestures as ones he'd done himself.

"My father—"

Do not speak of him. The words were cold and hard. But when the Night Empress finally turned to him, her eyes were lined and weary, as if even agelessness could not keep back the years that had passed between them. **You are with them. The Summer Lord and the young heiress.**

He heard the question she wanted to ask. "They seek an alliance with the humans. They have no desire to start another war when there can be peace. A war that you've been trying to hurry along."

They seek an alliance with the humans, she echoed his words, her lips twitching as if she were smiling to herself. **Even you speak like kindred now.**

"Why are you here?" Remy burst out, tired of them dancing around each other. "Why won't you leave us alone? You could end this. You could parlay with the Alurians—"

No. There was no forgiveness there, none of the curiosity that was there moments ago. **They destroyed my home. They will pay.**

"Well, now you're destroying my home. Everything I love, everything I've known—you'll take that all from me just as they've taken from you. It will never end, Mother. You compelled me, like the First Court once did you. You made me kill someone I cared about."

I'm sorry. I didn't know. For the first time, he saw doubt in her dark eyes. Her chin dropped. **I don't want to do this**, she said. **I don't—**

He heard the sharp crack her body made when it stiffened without warning, as if unseen hands had seized her. She cried out in alarm, and Remy grabbed her shoulders without thinking. He heard a murmur of voices blending into a harsher, guttural sound without words.

Even as he held her, he saw the wings rising from her back, and then another pair underneath the first, sleek and beautiful and horrifying. She looked up again, and her eyes were no longer the brown that had alerted him to her true identity, but a bright bloodred.

And then hate hit him like a thunderclap. It was *her* hatred pouring into him, her fury and pain directed at all the wretched mortals, those murdering, traitorous *monsters*. No, she would never forgive, not until she saw every one of them dead.

I will protect you, the Night Empress said, and her wings unfurled even farther.

And then Remy was awake again, Malekh's hands around his shoulders, shaking him firmly. Xiaodan watched them, eyes wide.

"You started shaking uncontrollably," the lord was saying. "I had to resort to a stimulant to bring you back."

"No," Remy gasped out. Remnants of the dream still clung to him, as did his mother's hatred that felt like it could be his own. "She'll protect me, but she'll kill them all," he whispered, and then burst into hysterical laughter.

9

A MATTER OF PIGEONS

T he letter came bright and early a few days later, carried in by the world's most hideous pigeon.

Remy was not particularly invested in the concept of pigeons as a whole. He knew they could be trained to fly thousands of miles to deliver correspondence of utmost importance and were often gray or white with feathers and a beak, as were most birds.

This one was scarlet, with an angry black streak through its backside. Its eyes were an uncomfortable shade of crimson, and it somehow managed to have the aforementioned beak *and* fangs at the same time, small canines apparent only when it squawked. The combination would have been more comical had the pigeon not turned out to be a miniature horror show, nearly biting a finger off the castle's bird keeper when it thought he came too close.

"This isn't your doing, is it?" Remy asked, gaping at the little hellspawn.

Malekh's brows drew low over his eyes; you could bury treasure in the wrinkle on his forehead. "We're not keeping it overnight, Vernon," he said. "It's not a creature you'll want resting in our rafters. Send it on its way."

"But we haven't even taken off the message, milord." Vernon pointed at the vampiric pigeon's clawed feet, where a rolled-up sheet was still attached.

"There's no need. Send it back as soon as you can, unless you'd like to see it feasting on the rest of the coop."

"Are you sure?" Remy asked, watching the undead bird fly away. There were worse things, certainly, but the idea of violent vampire pigeons somehow felt repulsive. "It could be important."

"It belongs to the leader of the Sixth Court, and I'm not interested in what she has to say," Malekh said brusquely.

"There are *more* pigeons like that?"

"If we are fortunate, we will have little need to meet the rest." Malekh looked at Vernon. "Do not allow any more of her messengers within the keep. Fanglei was never good at training them not to attack when they were hungry, and I doubt that has changed."

The Sixth Court ruler's pigeon did not bring another letter the next day. It did summon more companions to keep it company, and all took roost in the upper beams of the castle hall. They were silent, watching the people below with their bloodred gaze.

"I thought you said the castle was well fortified?" Remy asked, mouth full of cheese-and-onion omelet.

"None of the openings are wide enough for kindred to go through, however successful their birds are."

"They could drop in poison. Or mutated rats. This Sixth Court leader might've found a chink in your castle armor."

On Malekh's instructions, a few of his men sent the pigeons scattering with several well-aimed sandbags.

"The Sixth Court ruler seems . . . persistent," Remy said, watching it all unfold.

"There is nothing she has to say that I wish to listen to." Malekh had been making it a habit to accompany Remy while he broke his fast, though he and Xiaodan often partook of their meal in bed the night before. Xiaodan tended to sleep for another couple of hours, though she no longer slipped into a coma-like slumber.

Remy helped himself to a buttered slice of bread. "You're going to have to talk to her eventually if you intend to convene the other kindred to discuss the First Court. You seem pretty settled here, though. Not once have you told either Xiaodan or I to make our preparations to leave for wherever this meeting is." When Malekh didn't say anything, Remy looked at him in surprise. "Are they to gather here at the Morgana?"

"No. We do not make it a habit to invite outsiders to our respective strongholds."

"So why aren't we heading off to wherever we ought to go?"

"The neutral territory I had proposed was not to the others' taste."

"So they're opting for somewhere else?" Remy paused. "That temple Eugenie mentioned? The Allpriory? But why? They despised the Night King just as well, even if they had the temerity to blame you for freeing them from his influence."

Malekh looked faintly amused. "You look ready to fight them all. I would not have thought you so eager to leave, especially since you will need to present yourself to them as our familiar."

Remy scowled at him. "Every day we squander is to the Night Empress's advantage."

"Do you still dream of her?"

Malekh knew he hadn't. Remy had resumed taking the lord's tinctures. Any offers on his part to try again had been soundly rejected by both vampires, who had been far more shaken by his reaction after waking from his last dream than he had. "No, but I think we should make another attempt before we leave."

"It's too dangerous."

"She didn't harm me. She said she wouldn't. I just got a little overwhelmed, is all. She was . . . kind, like she gave a shit about me as her son. At least, until the end." Remy scowled. Something about the encounter nagged at him, though he couldn't remember what. *They destroyed my home,* the Night Empress had said, and it didn't sound like she'd been talking about him or his father.

"There may be a way to allow Xiaodan and I access to your dreams," Malekh said softly. "If you are determined to see this through, then at least let us allow us a chance to confront her with you."

"Last I remember, she has a tendency to be a lot more homicidal when either of you are around."

"Just because she remembers you does not mean she will always be kind."

Remy stared down at his half-eaten bread. "She can't do this," he said. "Waltz into my head and tell me she misses me, just for her to leave, like everyone else."

"Not everyone, Pendergast. Some of us have no intentions of leaving."

Remy looked at Malekh. The vampire lord had no breakfast to eat, and was instead watching the people around him, though his gaze remained averted from Remy's.

"I know," Remy said, then proceeded to stuff the rest of the bread slice into his mouth.

Several loud thuds resounded across the dining hall. A few people were scrambling backward, staring in dismay at the sudden volume of bird droppings that had spattered onto the tables, rendering their meals inedible.

Malekh muttered something under his breath and pushed his chair back to stand.

"I can help," Remy offered, swallowing quickly.

"It shouldn't take long. Don't you have charges to teach this morning?"

"This Sixth Court ruler is bothering you more than you let on. You're not usually this pissed unless it's about me or Xiaodan."

"And that is *my* problem to deal with." Malekh surprised him with a quick, hard kiss. "I will find you again once I've settled matters with her messengers."

Remy trained the youths for the next hour. Barnabas and Renzo were arguing again, and it occurred to him that only one of them would grow old one day. He remembered Salvador admitting that he'd thought Remy had plans on being turned.

The idea terrified him. He hadn't stayed with Malekh and Xiaodan to be made kindred, but, as his father had pointed out in the past, he never thought that far ahead. He would grow old and die in the natural course of things the way other humans did, and that was that.

But Wikaan vampires could pass down blood to an heir of their choosing.

The heaviness gathering in the pit of his stomach refused to go away.

"Do you always sulk like this after giving them lessons? I thought you enjoyed teaching them." Xiaodan had appeared. Her hands were warm when they touched his face, despite the misty day. "Is something the matter?"

"Just thinking." Remy's gaze wandered toward the other people in the courtyard. Now he saw a couple holding hands, one human and the other clearly kindred. He saw mill workers chatting, some fanged and others without. He saw deceptively youthful-looking vampires unafraid of the daylight, sparse as it currently was, chatting with humans who looked older than they were. When you lived with kindred, questions like Barnabas's were natural to ask.

"Why me?" he asked her, not for the first time.

Xiaodan studied him carefully. "Why not?" she countered.

"Surely you and Malekh had talked about possibly turning me at some point, but neither of you ever broached the subject to me."

"Are you willing?"

"I was so sure that I wouldn't. But . . ." He hated it. That he'd been so cocksure in the past, finding the idea repugnant. And

now he was considering throwing away all his long-held principles because he was a randy fuck who wanted to stay in their bed
for at least another century, wanted to be with them longer than
the life he'd been given.

"You were so adamant about not wanting to," Xiaodan pointed
out gently. "You were prepared to die rather than explore the possibility."

"Well, when I thought I was dying at the cave in the Dà Lán,
I took the cowardly way out. I told you and Malekh to save me,
whatever the consequences."

"It's not cowardly to not want to die, Remy. Many chose to
be kindred exactly because of that. We would never ask you to
do something you hated, even for us. Eugenie and Paolo make
their relationship work. If anything, I suspect knowing that their
time together is limited allows their love to flourish even greater. I
hope to have the same with you, and I know Malekh does, too. A
love *of your own choosing*."

But Remy remembered that Paolo hadn't set anything in stone,
either. *Might be I'll change my mind, might be I won't,* he'd said.
"So neither of you wish to turn me?"

She looked up at him and smiled. "I would be dishonest if I
said that I wouldn't jump at any opportunity for you to be with us
longer. But you know that not even I can guarantee that, given my
own health. I could die before you."

His grip on her tightened. "The fuck that's going to happen."

"I know you're afraid that we're wasting time with you, and
that is the furthest thing from the truth. We treasure every moment spent with you like each one is an eternity." Heedless of who
was around to see, Xiaodan tugged his head down to hers.

"How do you always know the perfect thing to say?" Remy
mumbled when they finally broke apart.

"Probably because I haven't yet been completely sated from
last night and want to rectify that." Xiaodan smiled and kissed

his ear. "Malekh's far too busy to be of any use to us today, and I've already forgone my undergarments," she whispered, pressing against him.

Remy could feel it. "Fucking Light, Xiaodan."

"It's not the Light that I want you to be fucking right now, Remington."

A shrill scream broke the mood. A flock of pigeons raced overhead, their shrieks unlike any sounds Remy had ever heard a fowl make. People were staring above, pointing and gesturing, but most were trotting back into the castle, trained to seek cover at the first signs of trouble. Frowning, Xiaodan watched the birds disappear into the clouds. "She's here," she said abruptly.

"Who's here?"

"Fanglei." Xiaodan was already striding toward the gatehouse.

Remy hurried to keep up. "Where are you going?"

"I want to speak with her before Zidan can get his hands on her. There are some things I would like to discuss first." She glanced back at him. "Fanglei is a persistent old biddy, but she's the closest thing we have to an ally among the other courts. While her clan isn't a threat to us at the moment, it's unlikely that Zidan would allow her inside the Morgana. You'll be meeting her soon enough, so we may as well make our introductions now."

THE LEADER of the so-called Court of Cultivation did not look anything like Remy expected. For one thing, she was old—genuinely old, with a wrinkled face and silver hair wrapped in a tight bun behind her head. She was dressed in a homespun robe that appeared ordinary and inexpensive to his eye, and carried with her a cane without any decorations to mark her status. She looked like a grandmother from one of the smaller villages in Situ rather than a vampire powerful enough to lead her own clan.

With her was another anomaly, an old man with a bent back and a squint who also looked about her age. He wore large spectacles and a pair of breeches that hung down to his knees, revealing skinny legs and a pair of walking sandals stained from travel. His shirt was no better. It hung loose on his lanky frame and was spotted with faint bits of mud and dirt.

Even more puzzling were the other two by their side. One was a youth no older than Remy, with a shock of dark hair, green eyes, and an agelessness that proved him kindred. But the older woman beside him was not, though their coloring was similar enough that they were surely related. She was . . .

And then Remy did a double take, staring.

"Remy?" Xiaodan murmured.

"That's the Lady Rotteburg. One of the matrons of the ton. What in the hell is she doing here?"

All four were having tea. There was a small cooking fire atop a large rock suitable enough to serve as a table between them. The old woman was pouring thick herbal liquid from a metal teapot into two wooden cups before them, the steam rising rapidly. Lady Rotteburg looked up when they approached and paled when she spotted Remy.

"About time one of you showed up," the old lady said good-naturedly. Even her voice sounded grandmotherly, low and husky and just this side of nasal. "We've been here nearly an hour—quite rude of his lordship to keep visitors waiting for so long. Would you like some tea?"

"Fanglei makes the best chrysanthemum blends," the old man said heartily.

Xiaodan said, "Perhaps next time, milady. But surely any matter you wish to discuss is of no small importance, for you and your companions to have traveled all the way here from Situ?"

"Well, my letters didn't work. Your fiancé is still as stubborn as a mule." The woman beamed at Remy. "And you're the famous

Reaper. Remington Pendergast, was it? Your exploits are known to us, yours and your father's."

Quick as a wink, she disappeared from her perch and returned to view only inches away from him. Xiaodan seized her wrist before the elderly lady could reach out and touch Breaker. "Fanglei," she warned.

The old woman clucked her tongue. "While it is a relief to see you just as quick as ever, I am rather put out that you think I would harm so much as a hair on this young lord's head. I have had many, many run-ins with the Pendergasts and this weapon. I merely wanted to see if it was still as sharp as I remember."

"It is, and you may refer to him as *Armiger*, not *Lord*."

"Very well." The woman bowed low. "My name is Cao Fang-lei, and the doddering old fool behind me is my husband, Si Daoming." The old man waved cheerfully at them. "It is not every day that we see a Reaper in the company of a court ruler. What might a Pendergast be doing within Morgana's walls, Lady Song?"

Remy saw Xiaodan hesitate; they had yet to discuss the specifics of his role. "I'm their familiar," he volunteered.

Xiaodan looked mortified. Fanglei's mouth dropped, and her companion lowered his teacup to blink at him. The youth looked at him curiously, but Lady Rotteburg held herself still, looking at him with something akin to sympathy rather than the derision he was expecting.

And then the Sixth Court ruler laughed. "If you intended to impress us, my young armiger, then you have succeeded. To call yourself a familiar of theirs so proudly—the other courts will be intrigued." Her eyes danced. "Ah, to be young again. I had not thought either you or Lord Zidan would be the type to indulge, milady, though I've always had high hopes for you."

Remy was starting to wonder if what he'd said was the right call. Even Xiaodan was blushing.

"You can bring him to the Allpriory if you'd like. The others are bringing their own human submissives, though none quite of the prestige of your young Reaper. Alas, I have none of my own, save my foolish husband in tow. I understand your fiancé's reluctance to talk to me, but surely he knows that it is inevitable. It was he who called upon us to convene in the first place. The location should not be as important."

"Meeting at the Allpriory is significant, Fanglei," Malekh said coldly from behind her. "And you realize it."

The Sixth Court couple startled. Lady Rotteburg gasped, and the boy nearly bolted from his seat. Remy as well. The vampire lord was leaning against one of the trees behind them with his arms folded, one foot braced against the trunk behind him.

"Glad am I to see you too, Lord Malekh, but first." Fanglei gestured at the rest of her companions. "Lady Rotteburg tells me that she and the armiger are already acquainted."

"In a fashion, yes," Remy said, carefully neutral.

"He is being far too polite, Lady Cao," the human woman said, rising to her feet. "Like many in Elouve, I, too, was vocal about my displeasure regarding his perceived status as a cambion. Many a time, I discouraged my charges from associating with him in my misguided belief that I could save them from corruption."

"Charges?" Xiaodan asked.

"She chaperoned the first-year debutantes and served as their duenna," Remy supplied quietly. "Though her assessment of me is not entirely without merit. I had a reputation beyond just being a supposed dhampir."

"It colored my assumptions of you all the same when it did not for other rakes that come to mind. I am glad for the chance to apologize now. I do not expect you to accept it, given my own hypocrisy."

"I do not understand."

Lady Rotteburg laid a hand on the youth's shoulder. "This is Lord Lorien Tattersall, my son."

"Beg pardon?" Remy goggled at the boy. Lady Rotteburg had been one of the ton's foremost and most influential spinsters, with nary a scandal to her name. Someone may as well have told him that the moon was made of cauliflower.

"I was away from Elouve these last few years, and he was my reason." Her voice grew heavy in sorrow. "He is the son of Redwald Tattersall. Lady Cao was kind enough to take him under her care."

"Redwald Tattersall," Malekh repeated slowly. "He was Aughessy's right-hand man."

"And a much more sensible kindred than the lord he served, though even he was unable to prevent the Second Court's destruction," Fanglei sighed. "He perished during the Alurian campaign, and I had no idea until a few weeks ago that he had an heir, which puts me in a predicament. As you know, the other leaders have plans on reviving both the Second and Fifth Court in a bid to replenish our numbers, but we agreed not to meddle in their selection of successors until the council was officially in session. As the Alurians left the Court of Beauty with no survivors, Lord Lorien is likely to inherit the clan, but it would look quite suspicious if he was to turn up at my side."

"But not if they turn up at mine, given the responsibility they want to foist on me," Malekh said dourly. "*Was* it a coincidence, Fanglei?"

"I defended the borders between Aluria and Situ longer than I stated to Queen Ophelia. It was then when we happened upon Lady Rotteburg's estate, under attack by some of the Night Empress's coven. The young boy fought fiercely alongside us, and he looked far too much like Redwald for me not to notice."

"Was there any reason for the coven to attack you, milady?" Xiaodan asked.

"Perhaps they learned of my son's identity."

"Surely you would not be opposed to offering them sanctuary? As the incumbent hierarch, you would have the final say in selecting new court leaders. The others would have little reason to protest."

"While you remain behind the scenes, pulling their strings to your benefit?"

"No!" Lorien exclaimed, speaking for the first time. He jumped to his feet. "I am grateful to Lady Cao for everything she's done for my mother and I, but if I intend to lead any court, I will do so with a clear conscience, without using my position for ill or for favors. Mother taught me better than that."

Fanglei chuckled. "Just like his father would have done."

"I am not averse to taking him in as a ward for the moment," Malekh said. "But is it wise for a kindred youth to hold a position of such authority with little experience, despite his father's reputation?"

"It is our law, Lord Malekh. If you are keen on changing them, it would do you best to become our hierarch first and take charge of the Allpriory."

Malekh's jaw tensed.

"The First Court may have been sundered, but the temple will always endure, whether you wish it to or not," Fanglei said smoothly. "And for as long as it stands, there must always be a king to grace its court. You know that the others would jump at the chance. That they agreed to offer you the title is no mean feat. And yet here you are, rejecting such a wonderful prize."

"I am not like the other court leaders."

"Perhaps it is why we chose you. You know the rules, Zidan. You cannot dismiss them so easily. The others would rather you assume the throne if they cannot claim it themselves. You are respected. They know you will be just, despite whatever grudges they've had against you in the past."

"Zidan," Xiaodan said, eyes wide as she spoke aloud what Remy was still trying to understand. "Is she saying that they want you to be the next king?"

"That is exactly what I am saying," Fanglei said impatiently. "We have been trying to hand the throne over to Malekh for centuries now, but this stubborn old goat would rather pretend that the Allpriory does not exist. The title is not a purely ceremonial one. You will be in a position to dictate the laws among the courts. The other clans distrust one another, and you are their compromise. The Allpriory cannot stand dispossessed."

"Let the others fight for the right of it, then," Malekh said harshly. "I am content with the Morgana. Nothing awaits me in the temple but ghosts best left forgotten."

"You would allow someone like Raghnall charge instead, and undo all the progress you have made with the mortals? Even Yingyue shall be coming. As far gone as her mind is, she, too, understands the gravity of the situation."

Malekh was silent. Fanglei sighed. "You are not the only one who holds foul memories of the Allpriory. We were far from grateful when you and Lilith broke the chains that bound us to him, though in truth we have much to thank you for. But if you continue to reject the title, it is only a matter of time before they fight for your place, and that fight will be a vicious one."

"Why are you so invested?"

"Because you are not the only kindred leader who would like to know peace in these lands. Perhaps the other courts would have been content to let the throne remain empty for longer, had not this Night Empress emerged. They do not want another Ishkibal. Perhaps after she has been vanquished from whatever darkness she was spawned from. But for now, we need someone in charge, and I'd rather it be you than Raghnall or Yingyue or Hylasenth. And even without such a threat looming, the others are already trying to seek advantage of the situation. Do you know that Raghnall intends to have three of his kindred enter the Godsflame?"

Malekh's eyes narrowed. "They cannot do so without unanimous agreement."

"If you had thought to read any of the letters I've been sending you over the last several days, you would have known that." Fanglei turned to Xiaodan. "Your ancestor died within the Allpriory's walls, my child. Are you not interested to see what the great Lilith had fought so hard to accomplish? Her heart beat then just as strongly as yours does now. It would be a shame not to visit and see if your malady can't be cured there."

"Thank you for your concern, Lady Fanglei," Xiaodan said politely. "Though I'd rather defer to one of my beloveds on this, seeing as it was he who fought with her against the Night King. He knows all too well the sacrifices she made."

Fanglei shrugged. "We shall be meeting in two days' time. If your fiancé does not arrive by then, we shall call a referendum to discuss another successor. They could vote to give it to the Night Empress herself, for all I know, if her claims to King Ishkibal's throne prove stronger than your betrothed's. Will you at least offer to take in Lord Tattersall and his mother?"

"They will be safe with us."

"Then that is enough—for now. Let us go, Daoming."

The old man was already clearing away their cups, using the leftover tea to douse their fire. Fanglei stood with a soft grunt, leaning heavily on her cane. "Think about it, Zidan," she said. "It would be ridiculous to seek an alliance with the humans if you cannot even forge a unity with the other courts. I trust that you will make the right decision."

And then, before either Xiaodan or Malekh could interject further, both of the vampires disappeared, leaving the faint smoke rising from the remains of their campfire as the only testament of their visit. Remy looked up when he heard sudden sounds of screeching and spotted a flock of red-eyed, fanged pigeons leaving the Fata Morgana, disappearing among the clouds.

10

A NEW ROT

An argument had broken out between Xiaodan and Malekh, who had both taken up completely opposing stances from what Remy had expected.

"You cannot seriously think to have them bully you into the Allpriory," Xiaodan said heatedly. Her irritation did not stop her from kissing Malekh thoroughly while she lay sprawled on top of him, naked. Fighting while fucking was a concept not entirely new to Remy, but the vampires made it look so natural. He himself lay sprawled beside them, too exhausted to do more than listen.

"They are not bullying me," Malekh's voice was rough, harsh with need. "Hylasenth is a stickler for tradition and resistant to change. Raghnall and the others are far too reckless, and your mother is in no shape to be making decisions. We cannot allow them to establish a new Second and Fifth Court without a proper vetting of its interim leaders. Their choices will not be based on merit, but on personal favors and promises to win their votes."

"You all but agreed to go when you consented to take in Lord Lorien and Lady Rotteburg," Xiaodan accused him. She had not stopped moving on top of Malekh, though she was panting a little. Remy realized idly that their ongoing disagreement was making them both even *more* aroused.

Malekh grasped Xiaodan's hips and thrust hard up into her, and both groaned. "We have no choice. I have little say in what the majority of the courts elect to do, as it should be by law. The only way I can override any of their decisions is to take charge of the Allpriory, as Fanglei had proposed."

"Which is out of the question. I cannot allow them to bring you to a place that repulses you, Zidan. I don't care that they don't understand."

"I am no longer as averse to the idea as I once was."

Xiaodan stilled. "What were your findings regarding my bloodwork?"

"Why would you ask about—"

"You spent the better part of the day in your laboratory before Fanglei arrived, which means that if you changed your mind by the time we met her, this was due to something you'd discovered there. Out with it. You promised that you would hide nothing of my condition from me."

Malekh grunted. He pressed up into her again, and Remy watched Xiaodan's eyelids flutter. "It is of little consequence," the vampire lord said. "All theoretical and nothing proven. But I'd returned to studying the tests I'd conducted on Lilith's original heart centuries ago."

"Wasn't your original hypothesis that being a cambion helped me survive the procedure?"

"Yes. I also reread the autopsy results of the two kindred before you who had attempted to use her heart and died in the undertaking." Malekh closed his eyes, allowing Xiaodan to resume control over their movements. "Lilith herself walked into the Godsflame and emerged from it with her sunbringer abilities. It was the reason the Night King marked her a threat."

"Are you suggesting that I walk into the Godsflame myself and see if I can recover Lilith's abilities in the same way?"

"No. The chances of failure are high, and I will not risk that of you. But the clan that guards the temple and tends to the Godsflame is an offshoot of the same clan Lilith ruled. They were the most zealous of her followers, who pledged to remain and protect the place where their mistress had died. It stands that they would be the most knowledgeable of the Godsflame's properties. If there is any clan in the world who would know to heal you, it would be them."

"My condition is not so dire that I would force you to that place."

"I will get over it."

"No," Remy objected from his side of the bed. "We won't let you."

The lord's gaze flitted to his, his expression still hungry. "Come here," he said, in a tone that brooked no argument.

Remy was still tired, but he shifted nearer anyway. He saw Malekh bare his teeth, heard Xiaodan's breath hitch, and knew they were close. "Xiaodan's right," Remy persisted. "Why must it be at this Allpriory?"

"Fanglei believes that the Night Empress will target the temple before long. Seizing it would further cement her position as Ishkibal's successor. The presence of the other court leaders would make such an undertaking far more difficult. They intend to fight her off there. Fanglei implied as much." Malekh's fingers were soft as feathers against Remy's stomach. "The temple clan, too, would know more of the Wikaan that the First allegedly sired at the Whispering Isles."

Remy's chest was heaving. "I'm not going to let you use your logic games to fool us into traveling to that damned temple when you've always been so against—"

"I have refused to dwell on my past for centuries, and that refusal has done me no favors." Though Xiaodan rode him now with much more violence, Malekh's hand on him continued their practiced rhythm, and it was making it harder for Remy to think. "Fanglei is correct. I must return to the temple and face what I left behind, if I am to finally seek closure *and* the information I require."

Xiaodan arched her back and cried out wordlessly. Remy saw Malekh stiffen and grip her hip harder with his other hand; any other lover would have had their skin bruised from the force alone. Xiaodan fell on top of him, kissing him languidly, but the lord's hand never strayed from Remy, still stroking.

"Are you sure about this?" Xiaodan whispered.

"I am." Malekh reached up to cup her face tenderly. "We can leave Pendergast here for the moment and—"

"I'm bloody coming with you, whether you want it or not," Remy said heatedly.

"Do you know where the Allpriory is?"

"Of course I don't. None of the Alurians do, else my father would have been laying siege to the place years ago."

"It lies within a cave, Remington. You can see why I have reservations about bringing you along."

Remy froze. "Not much of a castle if it can all fit inside a damn cave," he finally muttered.

"The cavern is thousands of feet high and many times as long. You could fit half of Elouve inside it."

Remy brightened. "Oh."

"If you ignore all the stone above you," Malekh added dryly.

"I can. If it bothers me, I can always run back out screaming, but if it's not so enclosed a space, I think I can stomach it. And don't give me that look," he added irritably when Malekh continued to study him with a worried frown. "I'd at least like to see it first. I will *not* permit you to leave me behind again. If you are adamant about facing your past for your own peace of mind, then allow me to do the same."

"I suspect Zidan is doing this for us far more than he is doing it for himself," Xiaodan murmured.

"Then it's settled. Should I talk to Agatha and inquire about the proper behavior required to be both your familiar?"

The vampires turned to him. Xiaodan pulled herself off her fiancé, and Remy noted with awed fascination that the man was still hard, and Xiaodan still eager. "What?" he asked defensively.

"Barnabas said that the Reaper had been telling everyone in the Morgana he was our familiar," Malekh said. "And I realized that the Reaper in question knows nothing about what that term actually entails."

"You told me that some of the courts still looked down on humans, but that I would be better off being treated as one rather than just as an emissary from Aluria."

Remy was flat on his back, Xiaodan settling over him just like she had with Malekh only seconds before. He could feel Malekh's breath against his ear. "Do you know what being a court familiar entails, Remy?" Xiaodan asked.

"I . . ." Remy gulped. "You said it was no different from any other human relationship, save for the biting."

A low chuckle from Malekh and a giggle from Xiaodan. "A familiar, yes," the former said. "A *court* familiar is far more complicated. Are you aware of the stories of the First Court? Of the Night King's seraglio?"

Remy's face flamed red. He knew the Second Court had begun as the Night King's personal harem, and while Malekh had never mentioned anything specific about it, the man *had* been one of the king's most favored.

But there was no shame on Malekh's face as he talked. "Vampires are oft to demand public displays of loyalty from their familiars, especially those they are intimately involved with. You would be obliged to prove that on occasion, as will others in similar positions. Old customs die hard, especially within the Allpriory, and certain traditions are still practiced there in deference to the place."

Remy swallowed. "I—are you saying you want me naked in there or something like that?"

"Would you be amenable?" Malekh's voice was far too close to his ear.

"I—I'm not averse to it if it's what's required," Remy said, and saw the slight widening of Xiaodan's eyes, the temporary stilling of Malekh's hand before it drifted down Remy with more urgency than had been there before. "But only with the two of you. I don't want anyone else touching me."

"We will not ask for what you are not comfortable with, but it may be good to show you some of those traditions now, lest it shock your sensibilities later." Xiaodan's voice was breathy. "Being a familiar is not always about exposing yourself. Sometimes, it is about pampering and praising. Like . . . like caring for a sweet puppy." She laughed when he shuddered beneath her.

She lowered her face down to his, her dark hair falling across his shoulder and pooling down. With deliberate slowness, she took his wrists and pinned them above his head. A whisper of fabric later, and Remy could feel his wrists wrapped in his own discarded shirt. "May I?"

"Oh," he said, and swallowed. "*Oh.*"

They trapped him in bed for the rest of the night, and for all their excitement they were soft to him, and slow, and sweet, even as they taught him to be pliant and willing.

They're going to ruin me for humans, Remy thought, and then, *They already have.*

He thought about growing old and leaving them anyway, and pushed those fears away to close his eyes.

—

ANOTHER PIGEON made its way to the Morgana's keep the next day, and fortunately it was not one of Fanglei's carnivorous pets. Malekh carefully broke open the seal and glanced over its contents, a slight twist of his lips his only reaction. "This is for you, Pendergast."

Found a friend of yours moping about a place that holds bitter memories for her, the message read, the looping script he recognized as Eugenie's handwriting. *I do not think she wishes to be disturbed, and I have chosen to honor her request. Perhaps she will feel differently with you.*

"It's Elke," Remy said, relief a river through him. "Eugenie found Elke."

"And judging from the coordinates she's provided, Elke appears to be staying inside Dracheholm Castle, the former stronghold of the Fifth Court."

"But that's in ruins now. Why would she choose to return somewhere she was so badly abused by her own clan?"

"It is not uncommon to look for resolution in the place you need it most. She is braver about it than I have been."

Remy glanced back at him. Malekh's expression remained shuttered. "Do you think she would mind if we paid her a visit?" he found himself asking. "Or do you think it'd be better to leave her be?"

"She is one of your closest friends. You know her desires better than I would." Malekh took back the letter and calmly held it over one of the torches, watching as it caught fire. "But were I in her place, I think I would appreciate the company."

"Will it delay our travel to the Allpriory?"

"What remains of the Fifth Court fortress lies in the same direction as the temple. With the helhests, it will not delay us for more than half a day at best, depending on how long she wishes to remain at Dracheholm."

"Thank you," Remy said gratefully.

The paper burned quickly to ashes. "We'd best make our preparations. There is no telling how many more First Court vampires ply the roads in between."

Remy packed quickly; he'd brought very little to begin with, and he wanted little time for Malekh to change his mind about their going. They were not due to leave for some time yet, so he'd come down to give the sprouts another good drubbing. Later, as a reward for their progress, he told them a story about the first time he'd faced off against a mutation in Aluria with Elke, which was received with no small measure of awe.

It was when the youths had dispersed and the crowd was melting away that Remy caught sight of the Lady Rotteburg, looking set on waiting for him. Sensing the inevitable, he sighed and trudged his way toward her, bowing low. "Ma'am," he said.

"I understand if you have no wish to speak with me, and I will gladly leave if you so desire," Lady Rotteburg said, looking ready to hold her ground regardless.

"I did not intend to give you that impression, milady."

"Then you are even kinder than I expected." Lady Rotteburg shot him a half smile. "I want to tell you all I can about the coven that attacked us. Regrettably, I did not see any of their faces, but some were not under the Night Empress's compulsion."

"I was led to believe that they were all controlled by the Night Empress."

"Not all of them, and I thought you should know. I told Lady Cao, but it occurred to me that she might have not said anything, given our impromptu arrival and her abrupt departure."

"You thought correctly," Remy said dryly.

"They had trapped me inside my own home. One did a peculiar thing, while they waited for the coven fighting outside to gain the upper hand: she traced circles on my skin, showed me the spots where they would drain me of blood. On her skin, there was a sigil, but not of the First Court . . ."

The lady hesitated. Before he could push her further, she swayed slightly on her feet, and Remy put out a hand to aid her without thinking, guiding her to a nearby chair. "Thank you," the woman said. "I have occasional bouts of dizziness that I have little control over."

"Was it because of the attack on your estate, milady? I can ask Agatha for some medicine."

"That cannot help me now. I am dying, Armiger Pendergast."

Remy paused, gaping at her. She laughed.

"I was told I would have less than a year to live, and that it will not be very pleasant. That was why I . . ." She paused, struggling to find the words. "It was I who asked Lady Cao if she could bring us to the Third Court's domain. From what she told me, it is Lord Malekh who likely wields the most influence among the courts, and I hope to intercede on my son's behalf."

"You have nothing to fear. Lord Malekh will not go back on his oath to protect you."

"Redwald told me much about him. He had nothing but the highest respect for your lord, and he liked to believe the feeling was mutual." The hard lines on her face softened.

Lady Rotteburg folded her arms in front of her and took a deep breath. "I truly do want to apologize. We—I—treated you abominably in Elouve. Nothing I can say or do can change that, only that I must do better."

"Because your son turned out to be the very cambion you accused me of being?" Remy asked.

Regret colored her gaze. "I would have incurred suspicion from the others had I shown you any compassion, especially given my reputation as a strict taskmaster. It was cowardly of me. You were already embedded fully within Lady Delacroix's good graces by the time I left, and I thought you would have some protection—I am truly sorry, Armiger."

"That's all in the past. I hold no grudges."

"I was selfish all the same," Lady Rotteburg said. "And for Lorien's sake, I mean to be selfish even now. I trust you and Lady Song and Lord Malekh. Please take care of Lorien for me. I am terrified of the thought of him in his own court, with all its dangers."

"Mother!" came a reproachful voice from behind her. Lorien bowed low to Remy. "You shouldn't be burdening the armiger with our problems," he scolded gently. "You promised me you would rest today."

"I—of course." Lady Rotteburg curtsied to Remy. "Excuse me, Armiger."

"I would like to apologize on her behalf," Lorien said quietly after the woman left. "She had always been extremely protective of me, and it is not easy for her to relinquish the decision-making when she has done it for so long."

"She only wants the best for you," Remy said. "It is the way of mothers."

"She insists on traveling with us to the Allpriory. I told her it would be better for her health if she remained here with the Third Court instead, that it would be dangerous, but Light if that woman can't raise hell until her way is had." Lorien's shoulders slumped, making him look far less certain of the boy he was. "She told you about her illness? I was hopeful that perhaps a cure could be found within the temple as well, if the kindred there have access to special tomes of knowledge. It was the only reason I agreed to let her journey with us. I cannot even begin to describe how grateful I am that you have all taken us under your wing, Armiger. I understand that Lady Cao sprung this surprise on you without warning."

"Think nothing of it."

"Mother said that Father often talked of Lord Malekh. Was rueful that the Second Court lord he served could not be as reserved or as responsible as he. The courts have no love for one another, but he said Lord Malekh saved him from death many times without asking for anything in return." Lorien looked down at his clenched hands. "We don't have much, Armiger. I have no vampire allies to fill my court, should they even agree to grant me the right. But I swear I will make Father proud, and that I will honor the debts he has to your lord by fighting with you in turn."

"You don't have to do that."

"I won't tolerate you seeing us as charity," Lorien said stubbornly, sticking his chin up. "I said as much to Lord Malekh this morning, although he looked at me so strangely, albeit without annoyance, I hope."

"I doubt it," Remy said, smiling. "More likely you reminded Lord Malekh of someone else he cared about."

"Oh? When shall we get to meet them?"

"He passed away not long ago."

"Ah. I am sorry for inadvertently bringing up any sad memories."

"I know very little about the workings of the eight courts, but I would think that one of the rules of being a court leader is to apologize as little as possible. Especially when none of it is your fault, and even more so if it is."

"I apolo—" Lorien stopped himself with a huff of irritation. "This is more difficult than I thought."

"You're doing better than you think." Remy gazed up into the sky. A small beam of light had broken through the clouds, and if he could squint long enough, he almost fancied there was a rainbow across the horizon. When the light finally disappeared, Remy turned away. "Fancy a spar?"

Lorien brightened. "I must warn you that I've been practicing constantly for months. Lady Cao says I'm a natural fighter."

Remy trounced him in the end, and even the way the boy scowled and sulked after that felt like something Naji would have done.

A SECOND letter arrived an hour later, this time from Alegra of the Fourth Court. She and Yingyue had already set out from Chànggē Shuǐ, intending to make haste for the Allpriory. She inquired after Malekh and Xiaodan's well-being, and while the warrior didn't quite ask outright if the lord intended to make the same trip, Remy could read her concern between the lines.

"No need for a response," Malekh decided. "They'll know my answer soon enough."

Another pigeon had briefly joined the rest of the fowl in the castle coop, one without a message attached. But one look at the seemingly random orange and red streaks painted on its back was all Remy needed to know.

He waited until the others were preoccupied with the preparations for their departure before quietly stealing away. None of the guards were suspicious. The drawbridge was lowered for him to canter off on Peanut's back onto the plains, the helhest trotting slower for his benefit.

A hooded figure lurked underneath one of the trees on the opposite end of the lake and grunted when Remy approached with the undead stallion. "I thought you would never come," the stranger snapped, pushing down his hood to reveal a youthful face with flaxen hair and brown eyes. "Took awhile to figure out how to send word, given that bloody near-impenetrable fortress you're in."

"Still serving as my father's lackey, I see."

"He pays very well, all things considered." The paint-splattered pigeon was perched on the boy's shoulder. The zweihänder he had taken from Lord Astonbury's corpse was now strapped to his back. "Your father has news. They've put down most of the wayward vampires beyond the northern borders. That part of Aluria is secured, though it will take some time for them to determine just how many villages in King Hallifax's kingdom had survived the purge. He does believe that a few covens escaped long before his men arrived."

"Any mutations they've had to encounter?"

"Dr. Yost's preventative has done wonders. But your father has reason to think that they were but a third of their true numbers. He warns you to stay on your guard. But I am sure you already knew that."

"The fight at Meridian Keep told us as much, yes."

"You do understand that you are obliged to relay any news on your end to me, so I may bring it to Valenbonne? I know you are not as eager to share in what Lady Song and Lord Malekh have divulged to you, but he is convinced that you will be up to the task regardless."

Remy glared at him. "I don't trust you. Even if I am not currently at odds with my father, neither he nor I have reason to think you are on our side."

"Valenbonne trusts me well enough to serve as the middleman. And until you allied yourself with the Third and Fourth Court leaders, you were all for the destruction of the eight clans as well. What has changed since then, I wonder?" The boy grinned crudely.

"Tell my father that Lord Malekh, Lady Xiaodan, and I will be traveling to the Allpriory, where the council is to meet."

The youth stood straighter. "That old First Court temple? I doubt that your father knows its location. And all the court leaders? Even Yingyue?"

"Even Lady Yingyue, despite her health. But don't look to me to provide you with directions. Malekh hasn't seen fit to supply any, but I'm sure my father is resourceful enough to find a way."

"It is one thing to be consorting with vampire court leaders. It is another to be a lamb walking into the lion's den. I have never been to the Allpriory, but I have heard much of its history. However good you are as a Reaper, I doubt you will like the Night King's domain, even bereft of its former liege."

"You claim to know much for one who has no inkling as to where his lair resides."

"Just a hunch, is all." The vampire messenger glanced back at the Fata Morgana. "Probably no better than that overfortified monstrosity. Is it as vile and as forbidding as it looks from the outside?"

"You have no idea," Remy said, straight-faced. "Why so concerned for my sake?"

"Because if anything happens to you on my watch, I'm certain your father will hunt me down regardless of our mutual interests. And I do try to pride myself on doing a job well. I have my own principles." With a faint smirk, the youth turned. "I'll be off to—"

Remy leaped. A quick shove knocked the startled vampire into the tree beside them. The pigeon broke free, making for the branches above them. "What are you—"

"Be silent!" Remy hissed, drawing Breaker out. The fog around them had grown; he could barely see anything beyond a few feet, but there was no mistaking the abrupt, shuffling sounds on their right that told him something else waited nearby. The youth quieted, having heard the same thing.

Remy was prepared. The creature had barely jumped out from the mist toward them when it was immediately bisected into two, parts landing on the ground before them in heavy thunks.

More approached—mutations smaller in size than the ones

Lord Valenbonne had created, but just as inhuman in appearance. Instead of the repugnant sores and lesions that covered their bodies, these possessed a layer of scales that made their skin gleam despite the absence of light. They resembled reptiles, though they walked upright on two squat legs, and in lieu of faces they were mostly snout and jaws with lidless yellow eyes and jagged teeth. They were quick—far quicker than the other mutations Remy had fought before, and he had to dodge several attacks of another before he could counter with one of his own, neatly decapitating it with a swing of his scythes.

"Come no farther!" Remy burst out, and then sagged against a tree when biting pain lanced through his head. At the same time the mutations obeyed, shuddering to a halt.

"How did you do that?" the messenger asked, amazed.

"If you intend to return to Lord Valenbonne and make your report, then I suggest that you do it now," Remy hissed despite the pain, moving to defend Peanut, who had shied behind him without further prompting.

"And what of you?" The messenger had taken out his zweihänder. Remy's suspicion that the youth had taken the weapon as a prize rather than because he knew what to do with it was confirmed in the way he swung it wildly at the monsters closing in on them.

"I can handle this. The fortress will have been alerted by now." Or so he hoped; the fog obscured the mutation's true numbers. With the mist closing in, it was impractical to use Remy's knifechain; the links could get caught against a tree branch or another mutation. He held Breaker close instead and relied on his scythes to prevent any of the scaled beasts from drawing closer, ignoring the throbbing in his mind.

A sudden flash of silver to his right, and Malekh was cleaving his way through three of the mutations in quick succession. "Took you long enough," Remy gasped out.

"I didn't realize we had guests."

"My cue to leave," the messenger said. "You have my thanks, Lord Malekh." And then he bolted out of view.

The pain dissipated, but the creatures were advancing again. Remy shoved his boot onto a scaled stomach, and then sliced through it. A series of entrails tumbled out, and the creature collapsed. "Was it wise to tell him that we'll be traveling to the All-priory?"

"Valenbonne is the closest thing to an ally we have in Elouve. Should the Night Empress stake her claim on the temple, having his mutations nearby should serve as a good distraction. If we provide him with very little information of value, he will grow suspicious." Malekh cut down another scaled foe. "We'll need to return to the Morgana. We have better defenses in place to take them down all at once."

"How?"

Malekh's smile was bloodthirsty and an answer on its own.

"Armiger!" Lord Lorien appeared beside Remy, shoving a sword through another creature's throat.

"I told you to stay at the fortress, Lorien!" Malekh snapped.

"I won't stay behind while you both risk your lives," the man said stubbornly, taking down another monster. "But I believe it would be prudent to make our way back to the Morgana rather than linger here longer!"

With Remy on the helhest and Malekh and Lorien decapitating anything else that leaped close enough to attack, they thundered back across the drawbridge in minutes, the guards drawing it up after them. Undaunted, the lizard-like mutations swam swiftly across the lake, and Remy knew they would reach the outer fortifications soon.

"Hold steady," Malekh said calmly. Once they had reached the safety of the courtyard, he grabbed a startled Remy and shinnied up one of the castle turrets in lieu of taking the stairs. By the time

Remy's teeth had stopped rattling from the abruptness of their climb, they were atop the parapets. "You could have warned me," he sputtered.

"It would have been easier to show you than explain," Malekh said unapologetically. "Hold it steady!" That was to a group of soldiers stationed in one of the guardhouses. They obeyed and made no move to attack, all waiting for another signal from their liege.

More of the monsters were dragging themselves out of the lake, and the fastest were already a fourth of the way up the wall. Only then did Malekh raise his hand and make a gesture.

The guards turned to small levers at the sides of the turrets and brought them all down at the same time.

Several large spikes secreted within the castle exteriors jutted out without warning, impaling nearly all the creatures in a heartbeat. The sharp, unexpected sounds of the steel traps being released from their confinements were loud to Remy's ears. It was like the fortress itself had taken hold of several swords and had lashed out at its attackers in hundreds of fatal blows.

"Amazing," breathed Lord Lorien.

Very few escaped the initial barrage. Malekh gave his soldiers another signal, and the levers were pulled back. The spikes retreated into the wall, and the corpses, without any impalements to anchor them, fell back down to the ground. What scant survivors there were, persisted, but most were shot down by a row of archers manning the towers above them, and soon nothing else moved in the fog.

"You never told me that your castle was a giant fucking hedgehog in disguise." Remy could not keep the admiration from his voice.

"The spikes are coated in Lord Malekh's anti-rot concoctions." Yolanda, the fortress's garrison captain and one of the soldiers in charge of the levers, called out to him happily. "And we've got more that you haven't seen yet. Fata Morgana has never been conquered by outsiders, and never will be."

"I was able to control the mutations for a spell," Remy said quietly. "Do you think—"

"The blood running through the Night Empress's veins are similar enough to yours, but I don't recommend exploring that option further," Malekh said tersely. "And we have other pressing questions. These were unlike any other mutations we've encountered before; smaller but more sophisticated in design."

"They didn't look like they were created by cobbling together random body parts and then hoping for the best," Xiaodan agreed, landing lightly on her feet beside them from her perch above. "And I doubt that these were something Lord Valenbonne created." She was lugging in one of the corpses. Up close, it looked even more revolting, its skin coated in an unnatural sheen and its lifeless yellow eyes staring back at them. Its mouth was drawn back, revealing black tar dripping from its teeth, which sizzled slightly when it landed on the stone ground.

"I thought Zidan would like to have one brought in to study. We do so for every new creature we've encountered, and this is as freshly evolved as they come." Xiaodan frowned. "Zidan, what does this mean? Do you think that . . ."

"I do," Malekh said quietly. "We must be prepared for the possibility that even the Night Empress is familiar with the experiments your father is trying to perfect, Pendergast. These sound much like the descriptions Mason had of the mutation in Kerenai—the scaled creature that turned his friend, and then him. The Night Empress might have found a better way to use these vile mutations in her favor, but not even she would have learned to develop more complex evolutions of these creatures so quickly. It could very well mean someone in Elouve has betrayed your father and has supplied her with this knowledge—or that she's independently found other similar means to control the Rot."

11

DRACHEHOLM

The creature had been duly taken to Malekh's laboratory and dissected. The lizard-like mutation turned out to have possessed a venom that could kill a mortal agonizingly within minutes. Remy blanched at the idea that he could have been poisoned in his ignorance.

Malekh had instructed his soldiers to clear all the bodies outside the Morgana as soon as the fog lifted, and arranged that the lakes surrounding the castle be dredged and tested to ensure the venom had not compromised the waters. "We have nets in the moat to drag the unwanted out," Yolanda informed Remy. "The meshes are wide enough for fishes to escape their confines, but large enough to properly dispose of corpses and creatures alike. Fortunate that this is not where we take our drinking water from."

Many of the other residents were already hard at work looking through some of the fortifications and checking for repairs.

"I want everyone to stay within Morgana's walls until we return," Malekh said to the other commanding officers. "There is no telling what else abounds."

"Do you think that the Night Empress has found access to her own laboratory to create these?" Remy asked.

"It may be less complicated than that. The vampiric tree we burned at Meridian Keep is not the only one of its kind within these lands, though we have taken steps to eradicate the rest. The more ancient of its species have been found capable of not just rejuvenating fatal wounds, but also reconstituting them to better survive the current conditions where it resides. The creatures' venom share similarities to its sap."

"So what you're saying is that these mutations were also part tree? That she stuffed corpses into it, and they turned into . . . whatever those were?"

"An oversimplification, but yes. The salinity levels in their system match samples I've taken from the region in past travels. The Night Empress appears to have been using the bloodwood for more than just her healing cocoon." Malekh frowned. "All the more reason to go to the Allpriory to take samples of the Fount within."

"The Fount? The vampiric tree at the Allpriory?"

"The temple clan views it as an important relic of sorts. I believe its husk remains carefully preserved."

"I could ask the Night Empress about it the next time I sleep." Malekh just stared at him.

"Or we can wait," Remy conceded.

The youths were sad to see Remy leave. "You'll come back and give us more training, won't you?" Caid asked, his eyes hopeful.

"Gaius and some of the men offered to take over your training while I'm away," Remy reassured him. "I won't have any of you slacking off just because I'm not here to track your progress."

"But you will come back?" Barnabas persisted. "We—" He paused and glanced over at his other companions, who nodded. "We're going to miss you," he said, looking down. "You'll return with Lady Song and Lord Malekh, won't you?"

"Once the business with the other courts is done, we'll be back," Remy said, unable to promise more than that, and was immediately drowned out by loud cheers as Renzo and Barnabas pounced on him, followed by the rest of their friends. For the first time since their training, they managed to unseat him, and Remy found himself sprawled on his arse with the sprouts all over him, wrapping their arms around his midsection, his legs, any place they could reach.

"They love you," Xiaodan said with a laugh once the younglings had finally dislodged themselves from him and ran off. Her smile faded when she saw his expression. "Are you all right?"

Remy's throat felt suspiciously tight. "I've never had anyone— anything like this back in Elouve. Even with the other novitiates, no one's ever . . ."

Xiaodan helped him to his feet and slipped her arm easily through his, the move practiced and welcome. "I'm glad it's happening now."

Despite the initial delays, Xiaodan and Malekh were ready to leave within the hour. Speck, Wits, and three other kindred were to make up the rest of their entourage: a pretty woman named Shiragiku, plus two burly fighters named Aunoir and Diethnir.

"Thousands of years of history and information within those walls," Speck said, rubbing his hands happily. "All to be made available to us."

"The number of vampires waiting for us there doesn't worry you?" Remy said dryly.

"Because I'm not kindred? A little. But I am sure it won't be much of a problem. We're under Lord Malekh and Lady Song's protection, after all."

"Where did you find that?" Remy asked Shiragiku, who was holding a fire lance not unlike the ones Reapers carried.

The vampire grinned at him and swung the weapon cheerfully.

"Picked it off one of the hunters some time back and took a shine to it. I see why you Reapers are fond of them."

"This is your last chance," Xiaodan informed Malekh lightly. "We can still stay here at the Fata Morgana and damn to hell with what the rest of the courts decide on."

"You know it is out of our hands, Xiaodan."

"No, this just means you're too noble to bow out and be selfish like I wish you would."

Nothing could convince Lady Rotteburg to remain behind. Lorien had been reluctant to leave her for all his protests against her going, and Malekh conceded that the Allpriory would likely be well defended and a safe enough sanctuary. They had opted to bring the carriage and the helhests to ensure the lady's well-being.

"Please be safe," Agatha said earnestly, pressing several packages into Remy's hands. "A parting gift from Sanlea. Foodstuffs to tide you all over till the Allpriory, and then some." A small crowd had gathered to see them off, the sprouts included, and they waved cheerfully at the departing travelers as they cantered past the gates.

The stallions were as swift as ever, but Remy was growing much more accustomed to their speed, because it took another hour or so after the Fata Morgana was lost to their view before the familiar nausea started settling in. Lady Rotteburg had taken medication that allowed her to sleep off the worst of their breakneck pace, and the ride remained uneventful.

They stopped for a bite to eat around midday—or rather, they stopped to give Remy and Speck a chance to cram a few more pastries into their gullet, and for Lorien to encourage his mother to have a few pieces of bread. The other three had taken advantage of the well-stocked blood supply Agatha had brought for them, despite the marks along Remy's neck as proof of Xiaodan's and Malekh's overindulging the night before.

"We should have more than enough time to visit the ruins

of Dracheholm," Malekh said, looking up at the sky, which was as dark as ever despite the afternoon. They had encountered no other mutations since their departure, and Remy was grateful for it.

"What do we do when we find Elke?" he asked. "I'm reluctant to leave her alone, especially with all these strange new beasts about."

Xiaodan and Malekh glanced at each other. "We thought to ask you if she would be comfortable accompanying us to the All-priory," Malekh said.

"I thought only court leaders and their retinue were allowed to take part in the meeting."

"There are extenuating circumstances where she is involved. She is the only known survivor of the Fifth Court, and by our own laws that makes her its oldest member—and potentially a candidate to be its leader."

"I doubt that she would accept."

"Even so, she has the seniority on all matters related to the Fifth Court. She can make her wishes known at the temple, and they will listen. If she chooses not to travel with us, then we can at least accompany her to one of the nearest towns to see her safely off."

"What possessed her to go to Dracheholm? I understand what you mean when you say she wants closure, but the place is an abandoned ruin."

"There is no rationality needed for it. We deal with grief in different ways, and the manners by which we do so can only be held accountable on our own terms."

It wasn't long before they arrived at what remained of the Fifth Court castle. Like Meridian Keep, Dracheholm was a crumbling edifice that had by some miracle managed to remain upright despite the years and the fires that had gutted it from the inside, turning the gray walls black from soot—and in some parts of the fortress, leaving barely any walls at all. But unlike the Second Court lair, there were no twisted roots or branches of some vampiric tree trickling from its entryways and windows. Instead, the fortress stood faded and forgotten, just like the kindred that had once occupied its walls.

Lorien had been reluctant to remain in the carriage, but agreed that his mother should not be entering the Fifth Court premises, abandoned or otherwise. Malekh had instructed the rest of the vampires to guard them nearby. "We won't be long," Xiaodan told them. "We're only looking for an old friend."

It was clear that numerous battles had taken place within its halls, judging from the partly smashed walls and broken floors when they entered, making their footing all the more precarious. Remy nearly planted a boot right through a rotting wooden plank when he attempted to ascend the grand staircase, the remaining highlight of the castle interior. Both Xiaodan and Malekh fared better, using their natural agility to leap from one solid-looking foundation to the next despite the distance, at times carrying Remy along despite his half-hearted protests.

They found no one else within the crumbling towers, and the rooms were for the most part bare, either stripped by passing robbers brave enough to search for kindred treasure or destroyed by the Third and Fourth Courts long before. Most of the Fifth Court vampires had been past their first century, and so no bones marked their passing, but Remy could spot bits of femur and skull pieces in between rotting furniture and glass. Black cloth still clung to more than a few of them, the only indication that Reapers had died here, too.

"She wouldn't be up here," Remy finally said, berating himself silently for not having realized it sooner. "She was the Fifth Court's best blacksmith. She would have spent most of her time at the forge."

They proceeded to the lower floors, then toward a set of stairs leading them farther underground. Here were the castle dungeons and prisons, and he saw with revulsion that the traces of death were clearer here than in the upper landings. They walked past broken metal bars and stone rooms with rusting manacles. Little of the light outside passed through the tiny windows overhead. The vampires could see well enough in the darkness, but Remy found a torch still braced up against the cold walls and lit a fire to guide his own path.

"He died here," Xiaodan said with grim satisfaction. She walked into one of the gaols and pressed her boot down on a spot on the floor, heel grinding down on it as if she could still stomp down on the Fifth Court leader's corpse. "I killed Etrienne Sauveterre right at this spot. I think it's one of the best things I've ever done."

"Never do that again," Malekh said gravely. "Not even his death was worth losing you."

Xiaodan smiled. "Always the romantic."

"Romantic as my left ballsack," Remy muttered, shivering in the gloom.

The forge was located in a smaller room past the cells. Remy knew enough of Elke's past to understand that she had been a prisoner of the clan more than a member, and the proximity of the gaols to where she had worked was not lost on him. "How exactly did the Fifth Court leader die?"

"I don't have many memories of the killing myself," Xiaodan said. "I tore him nearly to pieces, but that was mostly a blur. I remember feeling him come apart."

"How long did he suffer?" Remy could not quite keep the bloodthirstiness out of his voice.

Xiaodan gazed back at him. "He boasted about what he would do to my clansmates once he'd gotten his hands on them," she said, "going into sordid detail. I delivered onto him some of what he'd fantasized about so freely. So yes, he suffered greatly."

Remy looked around at the shackles and the heavy stains on

the walls and floor. He was wrong. Time hadn't completely erased everything within Dracheholm, though he wished it had. "Good," he said fiercely.

They found Elke perched on a small stool beside the now-cold hearth. She had laid out several tools, all neglected and corroded, on the floor before her and was studying them intently. Occasionally she would pick one up to examine it closely, as if she meant to see whether it could still be of some use, before setting it back down again.

Xiaodan and Malekh hung back, waiting while Remy drew nearer to his best friend. "Elke," he called out softly.

The redhead didn't look up. "It's odd," she said, her tone conversational. "I thought I would be angrier when I returned. I imagined I'd be frightened, that I'd weep. But try as I might, I feel nothing. I've felt more anguish at seeing my old hammer and tongs reduced to worthlessness than remembering what I'd been made to suffer within these rooms."

Finally, she looked up at him and smiled. "I didn't think you would find me so soon," she said. "You are a lovely sight, Remy."

Wordlessly, Remy knelt beside her, folded her into a tight embrace. She clung back, and a faint sob finally burst from her. By the time he had relinquished his hold, she had taken back control of herself, though her eyes were still unnaturally bright. "Did you receive the little present I left you?"

"I've had to leave it with most of my possessions in storage with Lewis and Leeley's. Once I find a more permanent residence, it will be the crowning glory of my mantelpiece."

"Storage?"

"I sold Kinaiya Lodge."

"Oh, Remy."

"Don't *oh, Remy* me, Elke. The place has fulfilled its purpose, and it's time for a change."

"Then what are you doing here?"

"Looking for you, you little minx," Remy said affectionately. "There are fresh mutations about. The Rot may be evolving faster than we feared. Once I learned you were in Dracheholm, did you really think I would make any other decision?"

"I suppose not." Elke glanced back at the hearth, and then at the vampires behind him. "Thank you both for taking good care of Remington."

"We try," Xiaodan said.

"I am glad to see you well, milady. I've had little news of you and Lord Malekh since I left. But I don't suppose that this is merely a courtesy visit?"

"I am afraid not. The other courts are convening at the Allpriory, and they may have plans to bring back the Fifth Court with a new leader of their choosing."

Elke's face hardened. "I do not think that would be wise."

"Neither do we. We are wondering if you might like to accompany us. Perhaps put forth any objections you have."

"It's happening, then? They've finally decided to do something about the Night Empress?"

"It's still undecided whether they'll attempt to take her down or install her as their new overseer," Malekh supplied dryly.

"We found her cocooned inside some fucking vampiric tree, Elke," Remy said, angry. "She had *wings*. And it looks like she's created more mutations herself and bent them to her will. She's turned Kerenai villagers—"

"What?" Elke was staring at him, paler now. "What's this about a tree?"

"We know little of this particular strain," Malekh said. "Only that it's capable of healing wounds—"

"And that it can extract blood for kindred to consume?"

It was Remy's turn to gape at her. "Elke?"

"The bloodwood was one of Etrienne's pet projects, and one that he was the most pleased with." Elke rose to her feet, tugging

Remy back up along with her. "I should have known," she whispered. "I thought that when Dracheholm fell, it had perished in the fires along with it. But I could be wrong. Some seedling, perhaps, or saplings that someone uncovered and borne away."

"Sauveterre created this tree?" Xiaodan asked, aghast.

"Rather a deadlier variation of it. It had escaped my mind these long years. I'd heard no news nor reports of it festering anywhere else, and when I arrived here and saw no traces of it, I made assumptions. But we must go farther underground."

"Underground?" Remy looked around, baffled. "I thought we already were."

"There is more not in plain sight. It's always been like Etrienne to store his revolting experiments in places only he had access to." Elke paused before one of the walls, fingers exploring the crevices within. "I was the only one he made privy to some of his more grotesque inventions. A sign of his devotion to me, he said." She snorted. "He knew I would have little chance to tell anyone else. There was one hidden latch here that he always used to—ah, there we are."

There was the sound of stones grinding upon each other. A portion of the wall slid backward, revealing another dark passageway with steps leading down into shadows. "In the years since, I've tried not to give any of this much thought," Elke said. "I had no idea any other kindred would have found his secrets."

"It seems to me that no one else discovered his hideaway, and your conscience should be clear. If the Night Empress already knew, then nothing would have stopped her from seizing his inventions for her own." Cautiously, Xiaodan stepped through, Malekh following.

"You look happier," Elke said to Remy. "Much better than I'd even hoped. I trust that things have been going well with you and your loves, even if everything else is imploding about us?"

"I've missed you too, Elke."

The vampire kissed him on the cheek. "I thought to find another place to settle at," she said. "But I couldn't stop my own aimlessness, wandering from town to town and finding fault with each, giving myself reasons not to stay. It's also because you weren't there, Remy. I'm so glad you came to find me."

The bottom of the stairs ended at a narrow corridor, which widened into what appeared to be a laboratory not unlike Malekh's, though long abandoned. Remy could see shards of glass and wood littering the floor, shattered and smashed beyond recognition. Few implements remained on their shelves—beakers, measuring cups, syringes. The area was covered in blackened soot from some explosion that had ripped through the place before it had been taken over by the roots.

And the roots grew everywhere. If any equipment had remained after Etrienne died, it had been crushed beyond repair. The thick foliage squeezed its heavy tendrils around all the laboratory's machinery, twisted and crushed in its grip. Some of the large vines still writhed and curled like large pythons.

"Fuck you, Etrienne," Elke whispered into the room.

"There was no sign of this place from the outside," Xiaodan said. "Sauveterre sealed the place better than the Second Court did."

Malekh had his saber out, having pinpointed the tree's center within a smaller room. The entrance was barred by the rest of the roots that covered the passageway, giving them little space to proceed.

"He said fire was the easiest way to kill it," Elke said. "He kept many volatile liquids here, and I don't know if those compounds are still active. Flames could cause another explosion."

"Taking us all out along with the tree," Remy said darkly. "Light, Elke. What was he thinking when he created this damned thing?"

"He sought a means to heal quickly, should he ever sustain fatal wounds, though he never used himself to test those theories. Many a time I saw some poor lackey dragged here, kicking and screaming."

"Did he ever find a way to use the tree as some healing fount?" Xiaodan asked quietly.

"I'm not sure. He claimed that he was close to succeeding. He claimed to have enlisted volunteers to speed up the process, though I doubt any of his test subjects ever submitted willingly. You besieged the castle before he could finish, though I don't think any of your people ever breached this laboratory."

"An explosion looks to have happened here, but not one of our doing."

"Yes, and I should have done a better job of it. In my defense, I'd been near death myself."

"*You* blew this place up?" Remy asked, horrified.

"It looks like a failed attempt, given that his hideous tree survived." Elke smiled briefly. "I didn't want anyone to find Etrienne's experiments and continue what he started. I crawled upstairs and resealed the passageway before your clansmen arrived. Do you remember?"

"I remember," Xiaodan said softly.

"You were kind. You brought me back upstairs, told me to get out quickly while I still could. And I took your advice."

"I'm sorry I couldn't do more."

"You still had Etrienne to worry about. I stuck around long enough to confirm for myself that you'd really killed him. I didn't care what happened to me after that. I just wanted to watch him die." Elke looked at the thick branches covering the walls, at the roots spreading through what remained of the Fifth Court leader's works. "I want to exterminate the rest of his legacy, and I won't leave until I see this tree as dead as he is."

"We need to cut it down as best we can," Malekh said. "The heart of this tree undoubtedly lies within this passageway. Breaking down the walls may cause the rest of the castle to collapse on us. We'll have to do this the harder way."

"Off to work, then," Remy said with a grunt, his scythes jutting out of Breaker with one flick of his wrist.

It was far more time-consuming than he'd expected. The roots and vines thrashed about as they were cut down as they cleared the way into the inner recesses of Etrienne's laboratory. An hour had passed by the time they'd finally carved out a path, and Remy's arms were feeling the strain. "We should have asked the others to assist us," he grumbled.

"Lady Rotteburg's safety takes priority," Malekh said, slashing through a particularly thick trunk.

"Lady Rotteburg?" Elke echoed. "Is that who I think it is? And she's here with you?"

"Long story." Remy chopped down another vine. "I'm sure she'll be more than happy to tell you once we're out of here."

As with its fellow in the Second Court lair, a large cocoon lay at the center of the room they finally managed to enter, thumping and jerking like a beating heart. The tree itself had twisted to conform to the room's size, gnarled and bent but massive enough to take up nearly every inch of space.

"Do you think there's something inside this one as well?" Remy asked with a shudder.

Xiaodan frowned. "There is, but it isn't her."

Malekh had already swung his saber, cutting through the moving cocoon. Three more slashes and it broke open abruptly, portions of it falling away.

Remy could not describe the . . . the *thing* that lay within. It had been human at some point in the past, but its skin now resembled the same rough texture of the tree it resided in. What should have been a face instead resembled heavy grooves on thick bark, as if someone had carved out a semblance of features upon it with a knife. It had tufts of what could be hair on its head, though bald in places, as if portions had been ripped out. Its body appeared fused to the tree's entrails, the outlines of arms evident, but immobile, like some grotesque wooden sculpture left half-finished.

It was moaning. It turned its misshapen head to and fro, clearly in pain. It angled its horrific excuse of a face toward them, sensing their presence. "... *ghsaaa* ..." it groaned, sounding like wind whistling through a hollow instead of a voice. "... *ehlee* ..."

"Wait," Malekh said, when Remy immediately leveled his scythes at it. "It's in no shape to attack us."

"What the hell is it?"

Wordlessly, Malekh gestured at the creature's legs. Remy looked and saw the scaled skin and tail. "The mutations that attacked the Morgana," he gasped out.

"It appears that at least one of them was made within this cocoon," Xiaodan said grimly. "You were right, Zidan. The Night Empress didn't need a laboratory when this one did just fine."

"It's more than just that," Malekh said. "Elke, did Etrienne ever use his own blood for these experiments?"

"... *ehlee*," the thing whistled, the carved sunken hollows that should have been its eyes shifting toward Elke. "... *ehlee* ..."

"Etrienne," Elke whispered, eyes widening.

"Are you fucking jesting?" Remy gasped. "Elke, how can you even tell that it's—"

"*Elly* is what it's been trying to say. It was what Etrienne called me. As if a pet name would forgive everything else he'd done." Elke moved closer. "It's you, isn't it?" she asked. "Or some copy of you, something with your essence stamped upon it. I was too optimistic, thinking you would never survive the ire of both the Third and Fourth Courts."

The figure moaned.

"I killed Sauveterre," Xiaodan said. "All that was left of him was ash and soot."

"Etrienne was always searching for true immortality, a means to return from the dead even after being ashed. I don't know if this is truly him." Elke reached down her boot and pulled out a dagger. "But he's close enough to the original. And we can't let it live."

Nobody stopped her when she thrust the knife straight into the creature's heart. It shuddered, the hole that might have been its mouth opening and closing.

"*Ehlee*," it whimpered.

"Thank you for living long enough to let me finally stab you myself, Etrienne." There was no pleasure in Elke's voice. If anything, she sounded sad. "Rest in peace, and take all your demons with you."

The whole tree shook. And then the figure within it sighed. Its head lowered, its body disintegrating before their eyes until the cocoon stood empty before them.

The dagger was still embedded inside the hollow of the trunk. Elke left it there, stepping back. "We have to burn this," she said in a voice forged from steel. "Everything must be consigned to the flames until nothing remains."

MALEKH AND Xiaodan had been thorough, as if they were accustomed to committing acts of arson on a daily basis. The laboratory had been liberally drenched in a liquid that Malekh had called an accelerant, and Xiaodan had started a small fire within the tree hollow itself, all making their escape in haste before the flames could spread. The fire was not yet evident from where they were standing a mile out from the castle, though the vampire lord said it would take awhile for its effects to take hold.

Lord Lorien was curious, then horrified, once he'd been told everything. Lady Rotteburg took the news with quiet grace. "Redwald never liked him," was all she said.

Speck had been stunned as well, but more disappointed that he'd been unable to see the bloodwood himself. "I know that it's both unethical and terrifying that someone would willingly go so far in the name of science," he said. "Still . . ."

"I am worried," Elke admitted to Remy. She glanced back at the nearby woods. "He talked about keeping trees all over the lands," she said, "or so he claimed. I thought little of it, but you encountered one at Meridian Keep. If there are more of these things, then he could not have done it alone. What if he was working with others to perfect his experiment?"

Remy had little opportunity to answer. A sudden blast had him crouched low on the ground, the sound ringing in his ears despite the distance. He heard Lady Rotteburg gasp.

When he looked back again, it was to see the castle of Dracheholm burning merrily, lighting up the darkening night sky like the world's largest bonfire.

12

THE ALLPRIORY

Always the scholar and absolutely a thief, Malekh had pilfered what he could of Etrienne's notes, bound together in a thick leather journal. They had since resumed their journey, stopping for half an hour to give Remy and Lady Rotteburg time for an early supper and for Xiaodan and Lorien to help Elke hunt after the latter admitted she hadn't taken blood in three days. Remy sat and watched Malekh as he pored through the papers he'd stolen while the hunter finished his meal of bread, smoked ham and, sadly, water.

The other vampires took turns standing guard. Speck was scanning the rest of the journals Malekh had set aside, looking like his name day had arrived early. Unlike her colleague, Wits was stretched out before the fire, more interested in its warmth than Sauveterre's notes.

"You and Speck aren't going to replicate that bastard's experiments, are you?" Remy asked Malekh, receiving a glower for his temerity.

"Even had I any inclination to, little remained of his research to make any reasonable attempt." Malekh turned a page. "Most of his notes were in code. But this is just as much a diary as it is a record of his findings, with far too many entries focusing on his supposed brilliance at achieving what others could not. It is nauseating to see all this arrogance bleeding through to the paper."

"Don't you ever boast of your own studies? Never written anything down where you might brag about how you saved Aluria from succumbing to the Rot or how impressive you look in spectacles?"

Another flat stare from the vampire lord. "They are not *spectacles*, they were crafted to protect one's eyes from vaporous material. And I pursue learning to protect my clan and Xiaodan's; the knowledge gained is a lesser priority." He glanced down at the journal. "All the same, this troubles me. Elke was correct in fearing that there may be more of these bloodwoods. His works make it clear that he experimented in many regions, testing whether climate and soil variables would affect its curative properties. His notes indicate that he had even burned parts of the wood for study. There's enough here to indicate that the creature at Meridian Keep had been another of his creations—perhaps a gift to the Second Court."

"How could they *want* one of those blasted things in their backyard?"

"The Second Court was always the vainest of the kindred. If Etrienne told them it would increase their beauty or improve their youthful appearances, they would have thought little of the repercussions." He paused. "Or, he could have planted seedlings after the Second Court's demise, thinking to take advantage of a place where he could continue his experiments unnoticed. The latter seems more plausible."

"I'm afraid that may be true, milord," Speck said somberly, lifting his head. "There is not much to glean from these writings unless we can decode this cypher, of which I am doubtful. But it seems apparent to me that these experiments were not just an attempt to find immortality, but to also potentially bring one back from the dead. The creature we found within that cocoon is not quite Etrienne Sauveterre, but likely one version of him."

"A version?"

"I cannot fathom a word to describe the process more accurately. The tree had Sauveterre's blood running through it. The Fifth Court leader boasted that much without the need to hide it in ciphers." Speck tapped at an entry in the journal. "It seems to me that one of his objectives was to produce a facsimile close enough in both mind and body to mimic the real thing. As it was his blood powering the experiment, it stands to reason that the thing within would attempt to be in his image."

"Is such a thing possible?" Remy asked, aghast.

"It is difficult to verify. I do not think he succeeded, given the incomplete state of that thing we saw, but . . ." Speck shrugged helplessly. "All the same, this bloodwood serves the same function: to extract blood from its victims to store within itself. Yet it can also be manipulated from within its hollow to replenish another."

"Redwald would not have tolerated such," Lady Rotteburg proclaimed firmly. "His liege was foolish and irresponsible for the most part, but neither cruel nor malicious." She brushed crumbs off her lap and got to her feet. "I think I shall return to the carriage. Hearing talk of what that villain has done turns my stomach."

"My father would have found some inkling of that tree when he torched the place," Remy said after she'd left. "The Second Court doesn't sound like they would have been good at keeping secrets of this scale. Did Sauveterre provide anything at all in his journal?"

"'Subject 2364. Skin scoured off body after twenty hours' immersion, though vital signs remain at satisfactory levels. Psychosis observed at the tenth hour mark, with subject begging for termination at the seventeenth. Subject 0372. Ripped off own arm in an attempt to escape, required sedation. Regrowth of limb after twenty-seven hours, though not without extreme discomfort. Subject 1356. Expired at the seventh bell after eight hours of treatment. Poor natural constitution to be blamed. Subject—'"

"You've made your point," Remy interrupted tartly, sweeping breadcrumbs off his lap. "And as vile as that bastard was, don't you think—I mean, is there anything in that book of his that could be beneficial to us?"

"You want to know if we could use Etrienne's experiments to help Xiaodan."

"Don't say you haven't considered it yourself."

"If the tree could restore Xiaodan to before she'd had to shoulder the burden of Lilith's heart, then I would ask her to do so without further thought," the lord said. "Whether or not it can accomplish such a task *safely* is a different story. You saw what it did to Etrienne's own remains, if that truly was his corpse."

"But it worked for the Night Empress," Remy said quietly. "The tree at Meridian Keep may not have completely healed her, but she was in far better shape than we thought her to be after Elouve. Why the hell wouldn't it work for Xiaodan?"

"That should be Xiaodan's decision to make," the Fourth Court heiress herself said primly, emerging from the woods with Elke and Lorien in tow. "And she has decided that the last thing she wants to be is shoved into one of those damned cocoons."

"Malekh's a far better scientist than Sauveterre," Remy protested. "If there was a chance he could do it without risking your health, then surely you'd jump at the opportunity to—"

"I've already decided, Remy." It wasn't like Xiaodan to be this angry. "It's my choice to make. You can't sit there and pretend that Etrienne wasn't the worthless scum he was, like something he did actually had purpose. Elke shouldn't have to hear that."

"Well, milady," Elke broke in, sounding far too timid for what

Remy knew her to be, "I agree with you about Etrienne, but if there was something he created out of greed that could help you or Remy or his lordship, then there would be no sweeter revenge for me than to see it be used for a better purpose."

"There," Remy said eagerly. "Elke is right. If Malekh could find a way to—"

"Oh, so we've reached a consensus as to what should be done about *my* body?" Xiaodan snapped. "Well, hěn hǎo!" She spun around and stomped off toward a small stream.

"Let me talk to her first," Malekh murmured and was gone in an instant.

"Um," Lorien said awkwardly. "I shall, ah, see if my mother needs anything." He fled to the carriage.

"I don't understand her," Remy grumbled, chastened. "It doesn't matter if it was Etrienne or the Good Mother herself who'd created those bloodwoods. She wants to be the Sunbringer again. If the easiest path to it is using the bastard's work, then why not?"

"Etrienne nearly murdered her, Remy. You can't tell me you wouldn't have done the same if it was you relying on Astonbury."

"I would have gladly kissed Astonbury's arse if it would save Xiaodan's."

"But not for your own."

Remy glared but could find no reason to rebut her words. "Barely a day since you've been back and you're already spouting sense. I hate it."

Elke chuckled. "Tell Lady Song that you've the right to be worried, too. You two have more in common than you think."

Malekh returned several minutes later, and Remy took it as a good sign that he didn't look chewed up and spat out. Xiaodan was still sitting by the stream when his turn came, having taken off her boots to swirl her feet in the flowing water. "Zidan put me straight," she said sheepishly. "I apologize for taking out my frustrations on you."

"Don't. It's been a trying day for everyone." Remy stretched himself flat on his back on the ground. "I should have been more considerate. I know how much you hated Sauveterre."

"It galls me still to think he's the reason I could call forth the sun to begin with."

"I know. But it's your choice. You let me make my choice to accompany you here, miserable as I would have been had I stayed. I shouldn't have pushed you." Remy paused, staring up at the clouds. "I've been thinking about the way you and Malekh have let me choose to remain human."

A soft exhale from Xiaodan. Slowly, she lay beside Remy, looking up at the sky herself. "I wasn't sure what the right time would be to talk about that again. Would you like to now?"

"I could lose to the frenzy, come out immortal *and* crazed." Remy tried to search for any signs of stars when there was a short break in between the clouds. It was easier than looking at Xiaodan.

"My mother is a mandurugo," he said quietly. "She was likely kindred long before she ever met my father. And she married him, even knowing he was a Reaper. Maybe she really did love him. Mandurugo pass down vampirism to their descendants like it's some damned heirloom. So maybe I never had a choice. Maybe there's a chance that I—that I'm already a—"

Xiaodan flung an arm around his waist. "This is one promise I can make," she said. "If Malekh can find a way to use Sauveterre's experiments to make me better with minimal risk, then I'll at least consider it. You're both right. The man can't harm anyone else, and if something of his work can be salvaged to solve my predicament, then it would be stubborn not to try. Does that sound reasonable?"

"It does."

"Good." She leaned up and kissed his neck. "In exchange, I want you to believe us when we say we don't care if you choose to be kindred or human, and that that choice doesn't affect how we feel about you. Malekh will find a way to exorcise any remotely vampiric blood out of you if it comes down to it, you know he will. Every test he's conducted on you so far proves you're no kindred. You could be worrying over nothing."

"But won't you resent me if I—"

"There is no ultimatum with us. We want you however you *choose* to be with us, whoever you are and will be." She grinned and reached up to ruffle playfully at his hair. "So. Has Zidan figured out how long I have to stay inside one of those awful trees yet?"

HE'D FORGOTTEN about his dreams, the dangers there.

They were to reach the Allpriory in the next hour, and everyone was on edge. Malekh and Speck pored through Sauveterre's notes constantly, though there was little else to glean from them, as the Summer Lord himself admitted. Xiaodan was a bundle of nervous energy, flitting from tree branch to clearing to half a mile out from camp and back again, keeping watch for mutations and vampires too selfish to show themselves and provide her with distraction. Elke inspected Remy's Breaker with the same intensity and zeal that Malekh was applying to the Fifth Court journal. Shiragiku, Aunoir, and Diethnir had started sparring with one another, placing friendly wagers on who would come out on top. Worn out from their time at Dracheholm, Remy resorted to a quick nap to conserve his strength while the others worked off their agitation in their own ways.

Except when he opened his eyes again, it was daylight, and he was at his mother's tombstone, shovel in one hand and the open ground before him. The casket lid had already been tossed aside. Remy stared down into the coffin, heart pounding.

He'd dug up his mother's grave before he'd left Elouve. Had wanted to make sure. The coffin had been empty then.

This time, it was not.

She could have been sleeping. Her arms were crossed on her chest, expression placid and peaceful, eyes closed. There was no dirt to mar her face, none muddying the lace and silks she wore, buried in her best clothes as was Alurian tradition. If she'd been laying inside her tomb these twenty-three years past, she showed no ounce of decay to prove it.

There was nothing Alurian or traditional about the wings folded around her, protruding out of her back; black and leather-like, a second pair tucked just below the first.

The Night Empress's eyes opened. She did not move, only watched him. He could sense no aggression from her, no indication that she would attack.

"Why?" he asked.

The Night Empress sighed; her wings shifted. **My dear**, she said.

And then it was nighttime. The grave was freshly filled, and Remy held no shovel. It was still his mother's tomb; LIGAYA BASCOM PENDERGAST, BELOVED WIFE AND MOTHER a familiar sign etched into the stone, and there were the sounds of digging, of scratching, though Remy was alone and doing shit-all.

The ground before him moved, dirt and soil breaking apart, and Ligaya Pendergast crawled out of her own grave, tears and grime in equal tracks down her cheeks. Her mouth opened and closed, taking in gulps of the cold air while fangs protruded from her lips. Her wings were slick, shiny with some peculiar substance, and they beat erratically against her back, as if they were new to her body and controlling them was a struggle. Because it was clear from the expression on her face, the way she lifted her dress and stared down, horrified, at the hole in her stomach slowly closing up on its own, flesh and muscles there knitting

back together at a rapid rate, that this was all new to her in terrifying ways.

Her hands pressed against her now-healed belly, trying to find
something there that no longer was.

Her baby, Remy thought, stunned.

Ligaya began to weep.

"You didn't know, either." Remy whispered, petrified where he
stood. His mother hadn't known until she'd literally crawled her
way out of her own grave.

The scenery changed. They were beside a lake now, though
Ligaya remained kneeling, her hands still pressed protectively
against her stomach.

I was changing, Ligaya said. **I was pregnant with you, and I
was changing. My family used to tell me stories—a strange, fantastical history of our people, of how they once ruled Wikaan.
I never believed it. When I became babaylan of my village, we
held a ritual. I thought naught of it but a formality then. But
when I lived in Elouve, they came for me. Told me what I truly
was. How I was changing. I was frightened. She placed a hand
at her belly. They said they could help me. Edgar—he drew
away from me. If he knew I was kindred, he would . . . I couldn't
tell him. The Alurians would kill me, kill us. He would kill me.
But they said they could help me, and then . . .**

Ligaya lifted her head, eyes red. **And now they will all die.**

And Remy was being unceremoniously shaken awake, Xiaodan looking panicked above him. "Attack?" he mumbled blearily,
still half-asleep. He reached blindly for Reaper.

"No," Xiaodan breathed. "But I could *feel* her. Did she hurt
you?"

"I . . . no." Things were coming back into focus. The woods
around them, their small encampment. Images of his mother remained in his mind's eye; weeping, crawling out from her grave.

Remy licked his dry lips. "I need to ask Malekh something."

Just as he'd thought, the man refused. "It's dangerous enough to have her infiltrating your mind, even when you expect her to. There's no telling what may happen if you attempt to invade hers."

"That's the point. She's *not doing it* deliberately. She's never been able to in the past unless she was in greater proximity to me, and she's even weaker now. I think she only wants to reach out to me to tell me something." Remy sighed. "She was on a lake. I don't recognize the place. She was standing by the shore, looking out into its center. Maybe we can use this to pinpoint where she is before she can attack."

"Describe this lake to me."

Remy frowned. "I remember seeing mountains from a distance. Four, I think."

"All perfectly round, save for the last?"

"Yes, now that you mentioned it. How did you—"

"You are to always take my tinctures before sleeping. You are *not* to contact her again for any reason. I will continue to monitor you once we are at the Allpriory, and should you suffer from any more of these dreams, you are to tell us in as much detail as you can."

Remy scowled at him.

Malekh gentled his tone. "I understand the need you feel to reestablish a connection with your mother, however changed she is now. But until we are certain of her intentions, it is only prudent to implement standard precautions." The mask slipped briefly from the vampire lord's face before hardening again. "I have no wish to lose you, Pendergast."

"I'm not—" Remy hesitated. "I don't want her to get at you or Xiaodan through me," he admitted gruffly.

"She won't."

"How did you even know about the lake?"

Malekh sighed and rubbed his face. "You'll see when we arrive. Fanglei was right, as much as I detest it. There are more reasons now for the Night Empress to claim the Allpriory, and you are one of them."

REMY HADN'T quite understood until they'd arrived at the temple, was disappointed when Malekh reined in his helhest and announced that they had arrived, though there was no castle to be seen.

They were standing on another lake, this one wider than the ones surrounding the Morgana. It was pretty enough, but Remy didn't think it resembled a vampire lair.

"I was imagining something a little more ostentatious," Elke said.

"It is." Malekh had alighted from Cookie and was staring hard at the water. "Does it look familiar to you, Pendergast?"

Remy glanced around. There were four mountains in the distance, three as round, as he'd seen in his dream.

"Can either of you sense her anywhere nearby?" Speck asked nervously.

"That's not how it works," Remy said. "I only know where she is when I'm bloody asleep."

"I don't know if she can hide from me," Xiaodan said, "but there's nothing of her here that I can detect."

"Even so, stay alert," Malekh said. "Prepare for a short swim."

"A short swim?" Remy echoed.

"The Allpriory lies beneath the lake."

So maybe his previous assessment about vampires and water were wrong. "*Beneath?* But that's impossible." The lake appeared over a thousand feet deep from his vantage point.

"It does make for a clever hiding spot." Xiaodan stopped at the water's edge and crouched down. Remy followed.

The water was clear enough to see the shore dropping off

abruptly, the embankment ending in a deep plunge into waiting darkness. "This could be a problem," he said uneasily. "I can swim, but not that far down."

"You won't need to," Malekh said. "I want the rest of you following my lead and staying close."

"And what of me?"

"How long can you hold your breath?"

"I can guarantee two minutes. Three or more, if I'm not panicking. Shall I have reason to panic?"

Malekh whistled. Obediently, the helhests tore away, disappearing with surprising speed. "They'll return to the Morgana. The Allpriory should be secure enough that they'll be nothing but targets here." He grabbed Remy by his coat. "Do you trust me?"

Remy gulped. "I do, but I wish it didn't involve this."

Malekh cracked a quick smile, leaned in close, and kissed him abruptly. "Deep breath," he whispered against his mouth and, just as Remy took in a lungful of air, turned and threw them both into the lake.

It was good to be given *some* warning, because Remy would have started screaming the instant his head hit the water. The vampire lord was just as fast as he was on land, and all Remy could see, thankfully, were bubbles and blurs as the man swam deeper down, an arm anchored securely around his waist. Remy squeezed his eyes shut and let his body grow slack, the rushing loud to his ears. His lungs felt fit to bursting, and he was starting to feel light-headed . . .

And then they broke through the surface, Remy gulping in noisy pockets of air as Malekh dragged them back to shore, releasing him. Remy fell to his knees, shivering but glad to be on solid ground. "I needed more warning than just *deep breath*, you bastard," he wheezed, and looked around.

But instead of cloudy skies, he saw nothing but stone around them. They were in a cave, and a massive one. The ceiling was easily several hundred feet high, and there were torches affixed at points along a wide passageway before them lighting the stone path. Despite the roughly hewn rock walls, the ground had been paved, a startling detail not in keeping with their surroundings.

"Right, of course it's a cave," Remy muttered. Malekh had warned him, but that didn't make it feel any better. Even if the immense expanse of it helped ease his fears, he kept his gaze averted from the ceiling, not wanting to witness all that rock looking back down at him.

Xiaodan and Elke were wading to shore, both in better shape than Remy. Xiaodan was as wide-eyed as a young girl at a country fair for the first time. "You said only the strongest could become part of his court," she said. "Entering his temple—even that was a test to prove their worth?"

"In the court's heyday, there would be traps set along these paths, altered and repositioned according to the Night King's whims so that no kindred went through the same obstacles in the same week. Returning to his court meant running through a dangerous gauntlet each time. He took pleasure in winnowing the weak from his ranks." Malekh was staring at the cave's entrance. "It's no use for you to hide," he said.

Something moved within the darkness, and several figures emerged—eight in number. They wore white cowls that obscured their faces, and their robes were simple and homespun. They carried no visible weapons, but the sight of them sent Remy scrabbling for Breaker all the same.

"We come in peace, exalted Hierarch," one of the approaching figures called out, pushing their hood off their shoulders. It was a woman with dark eyes and hair, youthful in appearance still, though her voice was a deep and strident timber of one who was far older. "We are the Antecedents, a branch of the Fourth, and I am Isabella, Priestess to the Flame. We are pleased to welcome you to our sanctuary, Hierarch. The others have already arrived and are waiting."

"Why do they keep calling Lord Malekh *Hierarch*?" Elke whispered to Remy.

"Because they want him to take over the Night Court," he answered grimly, watching the way Malekh's shoulders stiffened further each time the strangers called him by that title.

Two more of the hooded figures stepped forward, holding out clean linen. "I see that you have at least one human in your retinue, exalted—"

"I am no one's exalted," Malekh bit out, having had enough.

"Very well, milord," said the woman diplomatically. "Come and dry yourselves. A fresh set of clothes will be waiting for all of you in your respective chambers, as will refreshments and food. Let us make haste. The caves are drafty, and it will be better to bring you somewhere warmer, lest the humans catch their chill."

One of the cowled folk took down a torch from the wall, illuminating the path as the group wearily followed their new hosts. Remy was tense, still convinced that this was a trap, his anxiety amplified by the stone walls.

He hated caves. Fucking hated them. But he'd gone through them before for Malekh's and Xiaodan's sake, and he'd go through even more for them now. The trick was not to think about how the walls closed in on him, about the way they towered over his head like they could collapse at any second, burying him underneath.

He bit down on his lower lip until it started to hurt, and only then did he note Malekh's protective hand on his back, Xiaodan slipping hers into his left, and Elke hovering close by his right. "It's nothing," he muttered, embarrassed.

"We know," Elke said. "But we're here anyway."

The cavern passage gave way to one even more expansive, and Remy nearly tripped over a loose stone when he finally beheld their destination.

He was wrong again. The Night Court *did* have its own castle, carved out of stone and built directly out of the walls. It was taller than either Chàngge Shuï or the Fata Morgana, possessed more towers than Meridian Keep and Dracheholm combined. Parts of the fortress glittered at them, though not because of the torches lighting up the fortress from within.

"Are some sections of this castle constructed out of *jewels*?" Elke sounded delighted. "The gemstones on those turrets alone could fund Aluria for decades."

"Will I have to prevent you from prying out those stones when our hosts are looking elsewhere?" Remy murmured.

"Why Remy, how dare you! I was hoping you would serve as my lookout while I made the attempt. Surely they can spare one or two or five hundred."

There were more hooded figures lining the path leading into the castle. All bowed low as Malekh passed, and the vampire looked distinctly discomfited.

The interior of the Allpriory was just as ostentatious. Jewels of every size and shape shone, embedded in intricate patterns on the stone walls. Some had been used to pave the ground, giving it a sleek, marble-like smoothness. Elke's fingers twitched every time they passed yet another unnecessarily luxurious display of wealth.

The temple boasted of no tapestries, but there were murals, many large enough to cover the wall from ceiling to floor. There were scenes of a court in session, with a tall dark shadow presiding over cowering people, and Remy took it to mean the Night Court in its heyday. Others depicted battles, of people being enslaved and carted away while above them that same shadow, sword extended over the villages and towns it had conquered. Another shadow, this time sporting six sets of black wings, was painted emerging from some great inferno behind it, kindred prostrating at its feet.

"The First Who Walks in the Night," Xiaodan explained quietly.

Malekh had no eyes for the decor, or for the impressiveness of the palace. As they entered the grand hall, his gaze was riveted on the empty throne elevated on a dais, obviously designed to be the room's crowning glory. He stood before it and stared for the longest time, his eyes as hard as the diamonds covering its armrests.

Remy understood, and so did Xiaodan. They stood on either side of him, looking at where the Night King had once reigned, and all the misery he'd inflicted since. Malekh remained impassive, like the man had not once knelt before that same throne as a slave and an executioner for the deceased vampire king.

"Let's go," he finally said, nothing in his voice giving any of what he felt away.

13

AN ARGUMENT
AT BREAKFAST

The bed was made of the softest feathers Remy had ever lain on, large enough for four people if he'd had a mind to share. Despite the Allpriory being underground, there was no staleness to the air—he'd asked one of his cowled guides, had been informed that there were more than enough naturally circulating drafts brought in from outside.

There were windows and curtains, though there was little outside to look at but rocks. There were fresh flowers on the tables and dressers; there were *tables* and *dressers*. Remy's prejudices against caves led him to assume he would be roughing it on some stone floor for their stay, but somehow even the jewel-encrusted walls hadn't made him reconsider the wrongness of those thoughts until he'd seen the furniture. Their hooded hosts appeared to live an austere enough lifestyle, despite the opulence of the decor, and they had been content to relegate most of the Night Court's luxuries for their guests.

But despite all the glittery trappings of wealth, the castle had none of the modern contrivances that Malekh had added to the Fata Morgana. Several buckets of hot water on a small trolley were brought in for his use. Much to his embarrassment, the kindred overseeing his bath was a pretty vampire named Thaïs who was several hundred years older than Remy and had lived inside the Allpriory for most of her life.

"It's not as bad as those who live aboveground might think," she told Remy cheerfully as she dumped the steaming water into his tub. "We strive to live as simple a life as we can, but that does not prevent us from returning to the surface on occasion to find small comforts to enjoy, such as the bouquets you see here. Would you like me to scrub your back for you, Armiger?"

"That won't be necessary," Remy said hastily.

"Oh, but I should. It wouldn't be hospitable of me to leave without at least knowing everything is to your satisfaction." Thaïs picked up the sponge.

"I'm much more comfortable bathing on my own," Remy said nervously, making no move to shed his clothes. "Is your clan the only kindred living here?"

"Yes, and it's been a delight to have visitors, unused as we are to them. Those who'd lived long enough to have served the Night King haven't often found their way back since his court was sundered. The ones who do only visit to challenge the Godsflame, to brave the fires."

"Have you ever tried it yourself?" Remy asked, desperately trying to think of a way to send the girl away without giving offense. The latter had not relinquished her hold on her sponge, still looking determined to see him through his bath.

"I've had little reason. And even if I was of a mind to, it would take centuries more to believe myself even strong enough. It is one of many reasons why we chose to remain here. To turn the Allpriory into a place of contemplation and meditation, to temper and advise those eager to test themselves, and to honor

Lilith's memory, she who was the first within the courts to emerge from the Godsflame alive and whole." The wide grin she shot his way was far from innocent. "Are you quite sure that you will not be needing my help, Armiger? I'm told that I am quite thorough."

"Thank you, but I'm sure," Remy said, much more assertively this time, though unable to hide his flush. "I will bathe alone, if you please."

With a little pout, Thaïs bowed and took her leave.

As he washed the lake's excesses off him, Remy pondered his new surroundings. Thaïs's clan would have resided here for hundreds of years. The idea of spending the majority of one's life inside a cave was terrifying to him.

Another of the temple kindred returned after his bath was done, introducing himself as Altace and bringing with him a simple meal of fruits and slices of meat that he assured Remy was beef. "We are not without our own resources," he said with a laugh.

After he'd finished his meal, Remy was left with a burning need to step out of his room and poke his nose into every nook and cranny of the palace, though he reluctantly discarded the idea. There were hostile vampires similarly housed within, leaders of their own courts and likely capable of handing Remy his own arse if they were of a mind to.

He wanted to know where the others were. The Antecedents were undoubtedly keeping rival clans housed in separate wings of the palace, because Xiaodan had very deliberately brought Remy aside shortly after they'd left the throne room and warned him not to venture out until either she or Malekh came to him first. But he was growing impatient.

Remy sat on his bed and grimaced. He didn't like sleeping without Xiaodan or Malekh in a place where there were far too many vampires who would not take kindly to having both a Reaper *and* a Pendergast in their midst. As a safeguard, he'd barricaded his door with the dresser. Odds were that his paltry blockade would not even slow them, but he'd been working up the urge to do *something*, even an exercise in futility.

There was a faint sound by the closed window, a tapping noise that put him immediately on alert. Slowly he crept toward it, Breaker held aloft just in case, whipping the curtains to one side in a swift movement.

Xiaodan grinned cheerfully from outside, wriggling her fingers at him with glee.

"What are you doing?" Remy spluttered after he'd let her in.

"Our hosts said we were free to look around the temple as we liked. They must have spent far too long in isolation, to give such ill advice. I've already spotted some of the other court leaders loitering about, and I would much rather avoid them until we officially convene."

"And that led you to climbing the castle walls? Xiaodan, this room is a thousand feet up."

"I'd climb a thousand more if I had to. I needed a way to get to you without their knowledge—I'd rather they not know where you're staying until Zidan has petitioned for better arrangements."

"Where is he?"

"Talking to the high priestess, last I checked. The clan defers to him as if he has already assumed the throne, and it's pissing him off. Elke's all right—I checked on her before heading here. So are Lord Lorien, Lady Rotteburg, and the rest of the Third Court." She straightened her robes. "Zidan said that I ought to stay with you until morning."

"You think I might be attacked?"

"Just making certain you're safe." She brushed past him and climbed into his bed. "Besides, with him away, I don't like being alone in my room, either." She glanced over her shoulder and grinned at him. "Coming?"

"We do need to talk about what might happen tomorrow," she said quietly after Remy had gotten in with her, wrapping her arms around his waist and leaning her head against his chest. "It's the Seventh and the Eighth Courts that you'll need to watch out for. Raghnall leads the former—you'll know who he is, he's like a stonework fortification cursed into life—and Hylasenth leads the Eighth. Don't let his gentle disposition fool you. He can be twice as merciless as the others."

"And they're not going to take very kindly to human companions?"

"Not as badly as you think. Some keep their own share of human familiars."

"How hypocritical of them."

"Kindred exist to be contradictions. But Fanglei implied that they're willing to make compromises, should an alliance with Aluria hold—*if* Zidan takes power, that is. For now, it's promised that they'll curb some of their bloodier urges." She snuggled closer. "I'm worried," she said quietly. "Zidan acts like nothing bothers him, but I can tell this place affects him more than he lets on. I don't know what's going to happen at the gathering. Regardless of what the Sixth Court leader says, I don't see them giving up the throne without a fight."

"Neither do I," Remy said, pulling her closer. "But I'll support whatever your fiancé decides, even if he persists in keeping his own secrets. I didn't come all this way to a damn cave not to."

XIAODAN WAS already gone by the time he'd woken, which he was hoping was a good sign. He squinted out at the window before spotting cave ceiling instead of sky and wincing. Habit often had him up by dawn, but it was harder to tell in this place.

There was a knock on the door. It was Thaïs again, with a

breakfast tray bearing hot rolls, tea, papayas, and different kinds of jam.

"You didn't need to," Remy said awkwardly. "I would have come down to eat anyway."

"We thought this would be much more prudent, Armiger, given there are so few of you in our sanctuary. The other court leaders aren't prone to sit down for their meals."

"So few of us?" Ah. Humans. "Thank you. For this, and for taking the time to prepare special meals for us."

"We've learned to cook human food well enough to move aboveground if we need to. Most of us started out as human, and old habits die hard, even after eons." She paused and blushed. "I would also like apologize for being too forward last night, Armiger Pendergast. I didn't realize that you were committed to both Lady Song and Lord Malekh, and I took liberties that no host should to their visitors."

"No offense taken," Remy said, and then added warily, with a sudden burst of insight, "Did Lady Song speak to you about that?"

"Yes, and she was most kind about it, despite my impertinence."

Xiaodan at her kindest was when she was at her most dangerous, and from the nervous smile on Thaïs's face, Remy suspected the woman already knew. She withdrew from the room, and he scarfed down the meal with gusto. He would've liked to linger over it longer, but he wanted to know where the rest of his companions were and whether he should brace himself for any fresh trouble.

He found trouble all the same as soon as he stepped out of his room and made his way downstairs. He'd seen no one since Thaïs, and the Antecedents were likely few in number—he'd counted about twenty in total who had greeted them when they'd first entered the fortress. He was wondering just how many clan kindred the other court leaders had brought with them when he realized he'd stumbled into the dining hall by accident.

There was a silent war currently being waged during breakfast. Three vampires were seated at the center of a long table, with no food before them but several cups of crimson-colored liquid that Remy had no reason to believe was wine. None of them moved, save to take a sip. All watched one another.

Among them was Cao Fanglei, the Sixth Court leader. She was drinking from one of the little teacups she'd brought along instead of the glass brought out for her to use. Oddly enough, Daoming was nowhere in sight; from his brief encounter with them, Remy had somehow assumed that the two were near inseparable. She looked placid and relaxed, smiling benignly like she had not a care in the world, though the geniality didn't quite reach her eyes.

Across from her sat a massive hulk of a man in heavy chain mail, wearing a steel helm with stylized wings on either side of his face that resembled an eagle's. He looked like the type of soldier who would go to bed in his armor if he could, and carried that hard, heavy look of one who'd seen far too many battles and regretted not involving himself in more. He was drinking heavily from a large goblet, and the several empty ones before him indicated he'd been doing this for some time.

The third vampire was slender and willowy compared to the giant, and oddly ethereal. He was the palest of the three, with a fox-like face and long wheat-colored hair that hung toward his waist, and clothes that were loosely wrapped around his body like some expensive curtain. His long, slender fingers held the stem of a wineglass still full of the red liquid, suggesting that he had yet to drink from it.

It was he who spotted Remy first before the latter could retreat, a grin curling at his lips.

"Ishkibal's tits," he said. "The rumors were true after all. Malekh has finally netted a doxy of his own!"

And then the long-haired kindred was gone from the table and on Remy in an instant. The hunter felt fingers push against his chest—they were light to the touch, and it was a shock to find that they carried enough force to launch him several feet back all the same. Remy grunted when he hit the wall harder than he thought he ought to, Breaker clanging behind him. And then the willowy vampire was on him, hands thudding against the stone on either side of him and mouth opened to reveal pearly white fangs.

"He has good taste," the light-haired vampire breathed. "I'm impressed. I didn't know the old man had it in him to risk Xiaodan's ire by bringing a concubine along."

"Oh dear," Fanglei said primly, rising to her feet. "That won't do. Hylasenth. I should have told you; they don't like it when you touch him."

"Zidan isn't here, my dear Fanglei. Besides, I don't intend to corrupt him . . . too much." The vampire leaned closer, his eyes taking in Remy's Breaker with delight. "Oh, and what is this? Where have I seen this weapon before?"

Remy's fingers moved, and the scythes slid out of Breaker's steel frame, snapping out some inches away from the inquisitive kindred's face. "I don't mind telling you, right after you get the fuck off me."

"A Reaper?" The armored vampire was now standing, his face twisted in rage. "They dare bring a *Reaper* into these sacred halls?"

He reached under the table and drew out the largest battle-axe Remy had ever seen, nearly as tall as he was. It was a weapon in direct proportion to its owner's size, which, now that he was on his feet, was nearly seven feet high, and at least four inches more if you counted the ridiculous helmet.

"Raghnall," Fanglei said peaceably, unfazed that the giant looked ready to disembowel Remy. "Lord Malekh is free to bring companions of his own choosing."

But Raghnall was in no mood for a discussion. He raced toward where the other vampire had cornered Remy and swung his weapon.

Hylasenth disappeared and reappeared still holding Remy, ten feet away from where the Seventh Court leader had created a new doorway through the wall they'd just been standing at. Already the giant was turning toward them, hefting his axe a second time.

"This is no way to treat guests of the temple, Raghnall," Hylasenth said calmly, like he hadn't just attacked Remy himself. "I know that there's very little going on in that great big head of yours, but if you would at least listen to reason—"

Raghnall was not a very good listener. He struck at them again, and Remy felt another heady rush of air as he was spirited away from one location to the next, only to be dragged speedily away again by the Eighth Court king before he could get back his bearings, and all while the other court leader did his damnable best to kill them both.

And then Remy was torn from Hylasenth's grasp, and the room spun. When he could focus again, he found himself on the opposite end of the room with Xiaodan holding tightly to him this time, her eyes glaring daggers at the others. "What is the meaning of this?"

Raghnall hadn't stopped for Hylasenth, but he did for her, lowering his weapon. "*You* brought him here?" he sputtered.

"I have the right to bring a human companion if I so wish, do I not? You've brought Trin yourself."

"He's a Reaper! He wears that damned Pendergast weapon on his back!"

"As well he should. This council was called to discuss matters involving the Night Court, including a new alliance with the human kingdoms, Aluria chief among them. How do you think we would resolve that without a representative from Elouve here at the temple?"

"Any would have done, save for a vile Pendergast!"

"It is a Pendergast who is now in charge of Elouve and serves as Queen Ophelia's right hand," Fanglei pointed out. "What better emissary to send here with us, to serve as both a captive and a guarantee for the Alurians to be on their best behavior?"

Raghnall looked even more pissed at the idea of anyone being on their best behavior, but several Antecedents had arrived before he could muster a retort—among them the high priestess who had welcomed Remy and the others into the castle. Altace and another Antecedent stood behind her, looking stern.

"I understand that there are many things unresolved among the courts since we last gathered centuries ago," she said sternly. "But that is not a reason for you, Seventh, to choose a quarrel with the Third and Fourth Courts. We have offered sanctuary and safety to Armiger Pendergast knowing full well his alliance with the Reapers and with Aluria, and we will not allow the Seventh to make a mockery of our pledge."

That proved enough to pacify the giant. Raghnall's mouth moved, but no words came. "It is a sacrilege," he finally said, but put away his axe. "The Fourth Court has declined much over the years, but I did not know how far you truly have fallen, to go so far as to claim a Pendergast as your concubine."

And with that, he marched back to the table, seized his goblet, and inhaled the rest of its contents in one mighty gulp, then thundered out of the room, fist slamming into another wall as he did.

"Well now," Hylasenth said mildly. "This has been far too much entertainment so early in the day."

"Do you intend to lodge a complaint as well?" Xiaodan challenged him.

"Of course not, seeing that I am the reason your lovely companion still has his head on his shoulders. If anything, I would like some thanks for keeping Raghnall from turning him into mincemeat." The vampire turned back to Remy with a beaming smile. "Perhaps a kiss would be adequate enough reward?"

Xiaodan stepped forward. That was all it took for Hylasenth to laugh and retreat. "I am only jesting with you, my little lady. You know I would never put my hands on anyone unwilling, no matter how lovely. But you surprise me, Xiaodan. I was quite certain you would tear the arms off anyone Lord Malekh would dare take as a consort. He does not seem the sort to let his gaze wander elsewhere with you by his side."

"And what makes you think he is Zidan's consort alone?" Xiaodan asked boldly, without any trace of shame. Remy, meanwhile, had cast his gaze on the floor where he had deemed it safest, and sweated a little. "He's my captive as much as his."

"Oh, our little Xiaodan is growing up. I love this new look, my dear. Spontaneity becomes you. Bare more of your newfound claws and teeth, I would like nothing more than to see Raghnall discomfited. They will expect us to gather in an hour's time, and I am sure he will have come up with a thousand more protests to lodge with the temple clan." He bowed to Xiaodan, cast a wicked grin in Remy's direction, and glided out of the room.

"Our apologies, Armiger," one of the temple kindred said to Remy. "My name is Gibrid. While we were expecting some tension, you are still guests under our protection. There is no excuse."

"It's all right," Remy said hastily. "Seems to me that the Seventh is a known arse. Think nothing of it."

Gibrid smiled. "We thank you for your clemency, but we will strive to be more watchful in the future."

Fanglei sighed. "Children," she said to no one in particular, then turned to Xiaodan. "You must do well to keep your Reaper companion on a leash while we remain within these walls. Raghnall still remains hostile at the prospect of an alliance with the humans, and while Hylasenth is outwardly supportive, it would be dangerous to assume his objectives align with our own."

"Or that yours would with ours," Xiaodan said gravely.

Fanglei smiled. "You ought to be more than capable of speaking up for the Fourth as well, for I fear your mother will no longer be up to the task. I shall see where Daoming has gotten himself off to."

The high priestess bowed to Xiaodan. "Until the council convenes, please feel free to enjoy everything else that we have to offer."

"I'm sorry," Remy muttered once the Sixth Court leader and the temple leader were out of the room.

"We've at least given Raghnall no more reason to come after you—though I'm not quite sure he won't try again." Xiaodan looked worriedly at him, lowering her voice. "You didn't mind? When I called you a captive?"

"I presumed that things would tread along those lines once we arrived."

"Yes, but it will be different once put into practice. Raghnall is the leader of the Seventh, the Court of the Eagle. Hylasenth leads the Eighth, the Court of Tranquility; he allies himself with wherever he perceives would be most advantageous to him. None of them are to be trusted; not even Fanglei, for all her claims." Xiaodan looked up at him. "This was why Zidan was reluctant to bring you here."

"Well, had the Eight Court leader not been manhandling me all the while, I think I would have defended myself well against the Seventh Court ogre, though I'll take greater care not to have him come after me for a second round," Remy said, smiling. "But Queen Ophelia needed someone here to speak on her behalf, though more for a show of solidarity with Malekh and you more than anything else. And I rather like you claiming me for your own before the rest of your peers."

She smiled back. "You're incorrigible."

"I imagine that's why you chose me as your *doxy*?"

Malekh was still nowhere to be seen, but Xiaodan didn't seem perturbed by his absence. "He'll need time to get used to this place," she said sadly. "I know the memories weigh heavily on him.

I'm giving him the space he needs, but there's something else I want to see."

Elke was already up. She was examining the jewels embedded on one of the stone walls leading back out the fortress. "Finest-grade gems I've ever seen," she noted excitedly when they arrived. "Far better than any I've used at my shops in Elouve. It's such a shame that so few can come and admire these beauties."

"You're not still planning on stealing them, are you?" Remy asked warily.

"Of course not." Ruefully, Elke let her fingers trail down the surface of a perfectly cut ruby barely smaller than her hand. "Well, not anymore. Is there anything else to see in this temple beyond pretty stones?"

"There is one," Xiaodan said quietly.

She brought them and the other Third Court members deeper underground, to a set of stairs below the ground floor of the castle and past a no-nonsense temple clansman guarding an archway. "I asked the High Priestess Isabella for permission, and she granted it," she said as they walked down the dimly lit corridor. "This requires a court leader's consent."

"And what exactly is in here that they would station someone to guard it constantly despite the scarcity of visitors?" Aunoir asked.

Xiaodan didn't answer. She didn't need to, when they reached the end of the long hallway and a sudden flood of light enveloped them.

It was a fire, Remy saw, but one of a scope and proportion he'd never seen before. The flames climbed almost all the way up to the ceiling hundreds of feet above them, burning atop an altar built into the cave wall. There was a set of stairs nearby and a long walkway leading up into the conflagration, but there was nothing to indicate how such flames could be stoked to such a size without any kindling or ignitable substance. Remy could have sworn that the flames had a purplish tinge to them, adding to its unnatural allure.

"Preserve us," Shiragiku said softly.

"Light," Speck said, and made the sign of the Mother. "Surely this is—"

"The Godsflame," Xiaodan said, as they all stared into the fires that had burned for centuries before they were born and would do so long after they were gone.

14

FAMILIARS

The leaders had arrived at the great hall, seating themselves at the round table, chairs spaced at a reasonable distance from one another to ward off any more hostilities. The throne remained on the raised platform before them, looking even emptier than before.

Malekh had yet to appear. Raghnall's arms were crossed, the perpetual scowl still on his face, and Hylasenth was seated beside him, attempting unsuccessfully to engage the hulking warrior in conversation despite the latter having swung an axe at him earlier. Cao Fanglei was on the seat to Raghnall's left, eyes closed as if in meditation, and her husband stood attentively behind her chair, scratching absently at skin underneath his collar and looking bored out of his mind.

Song Yingyue was seated beside the Sixth Court leader. She was calm, almost serene. Remy heard Elke inhale sharply, realizing the reason when he spotted Alegra standing behind Yingyue, serving as the Fourth Court leader's guard. The dark-skinned woman started slightly, taken aback at seeing Elke there as well, but otherwise maintained her poise.

There were four more empty chairs: one for Malekh, the remaining two to represent the Second and Fifth Courts. The last remaining chair was soon occupied by the high priestess, hands folded primly in her lap. Neither Lady Rotteburg nor Lord Lorien were present. Remy wondered but chose not to dwell on it. Malekh surely had his reasons.

The court leaders were not the only kindred in the room. About three dozen or so vampires gathered in clusters within the hall, far enough from the table not to interrupt the proceedings, but close enough to intervene, should anything happen. They knew who Remy was, judging by the hostile stares. Each ruler had come with their own entourage, though no more than six or seven subordinates for each clan save for the Fourth, who had brought only Alegra and Liufei, another vampire Remy had met during his time at Chànggē Shuĭ. "There's always been a veil of secrecy surrounding the temple," Shiragiku muttered. "Likely that each liege has brought along only the most loyal of their followers."

And their own human familiars, as well. Remy was quick to spot them among the crowd, sitting on the floor and wearing little to the imagination, with sheer robes and short togas. Some wore collars around their necks as if they were pets, and on more than a few he spotted sigils tattooed onto their skin.

The humans didn't look at all angry or upset at their situation. They looked healthy enough and seemed to care little for their surroundings. At least three were more interested in rubbing themselves against some of their kindred's legs like cats.

"My darling Xiaodan," Yingyue said warmly. "There you are. Your father's been searching everywhere for you."

"Mother," Xiaodan greeted, after a pause. "I—I'm sorry. I must have missed him."

Yingyue gestured airily at one of the doors. "He headed off to inspect some of the rooms. You know his fascination for woodwork. But you mustn't worry him so, my dear. Soon it will be you who shall be leading the clan, and it won't do for you to be running off wherever your whimsies take you. After all, I won't be around forever. And who might be your companions be?"

Remy waited for her to remember him. When she did not, he faltered. "I'm, ah—"

"A representative of Aluria, Mother," Xiaodan said smoothly. "Isn't an alliance with their kingdom one of the things we are here to discuss?"

Raghnall smirked at her from across the table, and Remy idly considered taking Breaker and bashing his face in with it. "We can't very well begin when the man of the hour has yet to show himself, now, can we, Yingyue?" he asked, voice dripping with disdain. "Where has Malekh gone? It was he who requested we convene."

"Lord Malekh sought me out earlier today to brief me on the agenda he had in mind for today," the high priestess said calmly. "Rest assured that the Third Court king takes this matter just as seriously as you."

"Then where the hell is he? He's arrogant enough to bring a Reaper as his harlot," Raghnall scowled at Remy. "For all we know, he could be working with Aluria against us."

"I am exactly where I am supposed to be, Armaros," Malekh said from directly behind the man, "regardless of your opinions."

The Seventh Court king leaped to his feet, but Malekh had already blurred toward one of the empty seats, finding his place beside Yingyue, who, immersed in a world of her own, smiled vaguely at him.

"I hope my dear Xiaodan hasn't been bothering you and distracting you from your work again, Zidan," she said. "She's a spirited young woman, though not always the most considerate."

"We are wasting time, Lord Malekh," Fanglei said. "You called for this session. I understand that the location may not be to your liking, but I'm sure you know the reasons for that as well. We must discuss the growing threat of the Night Empress, as well as the unfolding situation within the kingdom of Hallifax."

"Threat?" Raghnall demanded. "Do you not remember that it is these accursed *human* kingdoms who are seeking to destroy us, Fanglei? I have tangled enough times with Hallifax in the past that he would not have lifted a finger to aid us, had the shoe been on the other foot. Even now he refuses to defend his own kingdom, retreating into his capital and leaving his citizens to their fate. As far as I can see, the Night Empress is doing the work for us."

"But is it a wise thing, to permit such murderous killing sprees?" Hylasenth pondered. "Whatever the humans intend, I do not want a repeat of the days where this land was awash in their blood and our ashes. They still outnumber us, and they are not so easy to kill as you imply. Lord Malekh's alliance with the Alurian kingdom has given us some measure of peace, has it not?"

"The Alurians were just as quick to withdraw their pact."

"Treaties can be reforged and strengthened," Malekh said shortly. "I have talked to Queen Ophelia, and she is more than amenable to resuming our negotiations."

"And once the danger is done, they will break your treaty a second time and resume their war against us, as they have done countless years past." The Seventh pointed an accusing finger at Remy. "What surety can you make that those like this disgusting Pendergast will not come upon us like thieves in the night when our guard is down?"

"He is here willingly. The Alurians intend to uphold their end of the bargain for as long as our council does not move against them. Would you be willing to do the same and send one of your people to Elouve in exchange?" Malekh's voice grew lower, but there was nothing to hide his anger for. "You tried to kill him this morning. He's a Pendergast, as you said. A trained Reaper, descended from generations of hunters. He's more than a match for a court kindred. Has he sought revenge against you for making a liar out of the temple clan's offer of hospitality? He has every right to demand recompense, by our own laws. How do you think Aluria would react had you slain one of their most prominent fighters *and* the heir of their lord high steward? He knows the importance of an alliance between us and will do nothing to destroy it. I, on the other hand, have no such qualms. Lay a hand on him again, and you will answer to me."

Raghnall looked stunned. "You challenge me to a fight? Over an Alurian Reaper?"

Malekh said nothing else, though his gaze held his answer. He'd shifted his stance to reveal the saber by his waist. "Try me, Seventh. I have had little patience these last few weeks, and it would do me no harm to exercise some of that energy to your detriment."

Raghnall's hand lingered over the handle of his axe but hesitated. After another moment, he relented and put it back down.

"Have you truly taken him as your consort, Zidan?" Hylasenth asked mildly.

Malekh's gaze swung to the Eight Court leader's face.

The other man smiled cheerfully. "You need not look so stricken, milord. Most everyone here has indulged themselves in the same manner. Despite their grievances with us, and ours with them, we have had no short supply of humans eager to share our beds. Come here, Melody."

One of the collared men inched forward eagerly, crawling under the table and laying himself at Hylasenth's feet without a trace of shame. With a wicked smile, the Eighth Court king tugged his familiar forward, until the latter was nuzzling happily at his groin.

"Hylasenth!" Raghnall said sharply. "That's enough."

"Why so shy, Seventh? You have your own human. You seem to treat her well enough, despite your ire toward mortals." Hylasenth grinned at Malekh. "And we have the Third Court king to thank for that, have we not? It was he who insisted that any familiars we keep be treated well, lest more humans retaliate. The follies of the Second Court are proof that they would fight us for such trivialities. And I found my dear, sweet Melody as a result."

He stroked at the man's hair, even as the latter began eagerly opening up his robes, and cast a sly glance in Xiaodan's direction. "Even without the marks on the Reaper's neck for everyone to see, I could smell you on him when I was keeping him free from the Seventh's rage, Third. Have you truly taken him in as your familiar? A high-ranking Reaper of Aluria for your very own? I would suppose that the Alurian queen is aware of this development, but I daresay that would not have been made public within her kingdom. Or is this all some mere ploy? Raghnall has every right to be suspicious."

The expression on Malekh's face was once more an enigma. Most of the kindred's gazes were on Remy now, as if expecting him to respond on the Summer Lord's behalf, but for the life of him, Remy was clueless. One wrong word, and he could make things worse.

Malekh turned his head slightly to Xiaodan and made the barest of nods.

"Remington," Xiaodan said calmly. After Raghnall had begun making his demands, she'd remained in the background, saying little. Now she glided forward, graceful as always, deliberate in her movements as she walked across the room and sat herself down on one of the empty chairs beside Malekh. "It is true that he is a Pendergast and Reaper both," she continued, spreading her legs just enough for all to intuit her motivation. "But here in the Allpriory, he is nothing more than our puppy."

"Well now," Remy heard Fanglei whisper animatedly. Her head was still tilted up, and she had not once opened her eyes since Remy had entered the room, but there on her face was a smile, amused and anticipatory.

"Remington," Xiaodan said again, fastening her large brown eyes on him. Her gaze was placid, but there was something odd about the way she looked at him. There was a hunger there, like she wanted him to . . .

Remy was slow on the uptake when it came to many things, but not this. A jolt of fear and embarrassment raced up his spine, overlaid with arousal.

"Remy," Elke whispered, worried.

He shook his head at her and allowed his feet to move, following the path Xiaodan had taken across the room, to kneel down at her feet in the same way the familiar had done with Hylasenth. Xiaodan's face was carefully blank as she looked down on him, an odd thing to see when she had always been so expressive. Her eyes held a question.

Remy responded by reaching out and gently spreading her legs, lifting part of her robes up only enough to give her what little privacy they had left—thank the Light for the heavy skirts that Qing-ye fashion favored—but high enough that his intentions were clear to all watching them. He could hear the muffled moans the other familiar was making, the deep sighs of pleasure from Hylasenth.

The court leaders thought little of alliances and treaties. They'd lived long enough to see them easily broken over the centuries. But as Malekh had said, what they prized most of all was submission. The power and control over another, the trust involved.

Xiaodan made a soft sound, a faint whimper only the two of them could hear, as Remy bent forward. He'd done this a thousand times before with her, wanted it a million times more. That they were doing this before an audience made his head spin, his stomach clench, but not all the giddiness he felt was unwelcome.

Underneath the table, he saw Malekh's hand graze against Xiaodan's briefly in silent comfort before moving to settle lightly on his head.

He didn't tighten his grip on Remy, didn't force him forward into Xiaodan. All the lord did was stroke his hair, his fingers warm and soothing against his scalp, and that was all it took for Remy to lose his inhibitions completely.

He didn't know how long he was there on his knees. Xiaodan was often loud with them, and while she restricted her sounds to staggered gasps and a faint wriggling of her hips as she tried to urge more of his mouth on her, Remy knew she was close. Almost as a counterpoint, he could hear the familiar and Hylasenth's grunts growing louder, and he redoubled his efforts, his tongue swirling, desperate to see to her completion.

He felt Xiaodan's whole body tense and shudder for several long moments before she finally relaxed, growing limp before him. He kissed her one last time, just as Malekh took his hand from his head, and he leaned back to look up at her, taking care not to look at anyone else—not even, oh, Light, Elke.

"Well," Hylasenth said after his own breathing had slowed. "I for one am very much convinced of the Reaper's stalwart determination to broker peace between us. What say you, Raghnall?"

A grunt was the Seventh's only answer, but the tension in the room had broken. Remy remained by Xiaodan's feet instead of moving away, the decision confirmed when it was Xiaodan's turn to reach down, her fingers brushing against the side of his face as she rearranged her robes.

"The Pendergast Reaper is *ours*," she said, the last word heavily emphasized. "Lay a hand on him, and you will answer to me."

THE REMAINDER of the session had been anticlimactic. The court leaders had finally agreed to make a concerted overture to Aluria as a council. Remy sat by Xiaodan's feet through it all, in a slight daze.

The high priestess came forward to say something quietly to Malekh. Remy hadn't been paying enough attention, but a frown crossed his features. He'd announced the meeting concluded for the day shortly after, the specifics of the negotiations to be discussed on the morrow, along with any other matters the clans intended to bring before the council. Raghnall did not deign to give him a second look as he strode out of the room.

He'd been dreading that Yingyue would attack him for daring to violate her daughter. But Xiaodan's mother was too far entrenched in her own head to take heed. She only nodded amiably along as if there was still a discussion in progress, while her eyes continued to gaze blankly at the wall before her, until Alegra murmured something gently into her ear and lifted the smaller woman up in her arms. The warrior shot Remy an apologetic look, averted her eyes away from Elke, and walked away.

Xiaodan helped him stand, then kissed him. For some reason, that felt even more intimate than what had just taken place.

"I'll explain everything later," she whispered into his ear. "For now, stay by Elke's side. She'll know what to do."

Which was why Remy now found himself in the temple gardens. He would have thought that no plants were capable of growing this far underground, but he was once more mistaken. There were green shoots taking root in between some of the cracks on the stone they stood on, and many were flowering before their eyes, ripening into thick red flowers that curved at the bottom like tulips but burst out at the tip like trapped sunflowers, with far more petals than it looked like it could hold.

"Luminesas," Elke said. "They're good for healing humans and kindred alike—wounds close faster after you drink from a distillation of their roots."

"And they need no light to grow?"

"My guess is that they take their sustenance from the nearby lake, but a few daily drops of kindred blood are all the nourishment they need. They'll feast on small insects, too, given the chance."

It made sense for the flowers here to be vampiric. Remy coughed, looking down. "I— About what happened—"

Elke snorted. "Remy, do you remember what court I belonged to?"

"The Fifth?"

"And do you remember what my position at that court was?"

"Ah," Remy said uncomfortably. "Still. We gave you no warning."

"Remy, I'm not oblivious to court custom." Elke gazed down at the flowers. "Etrienne used to beat me as foreplay," she said. "He would tie me up and show me off to his other subordinates, and I could do nothing to stop him. He thrived on torturing others. Trust me, what you and Xiaodan did was romantic by court standards."

"Elke, you don't have to tell me anything about Etrienne."

"But I do. I don't want you not to tell me anything that distresses you. I never told you of my past because I knew you would only worry, and that was my fault." She reached over and squeezed his hand. "If anything, I think you'd make a pretty capable kindred if you ever changed your mind. You've adapted far more quickly than I expected." Her nose wrinkled. "I *would* rather prefer not to see you like that again, however. You're too much like a brother to me, and . . . *ugh.*"

"Elke!" Remy sputtered, and she laughed.

"I trust that Xiaodan and Malekh know what they're doing. If anything, you've likely risen in the others' esteem. How did you know what it was that Xiaodan wanted you to do?"

Remy coughed. "The Allpriory's location was a secret, but the kindred brought their human familiars all the same. So they must be in some position of trust. And for them to realize that I was genuinely Xiaodan and Malekh's familiar, I had to do the same as they did."

Elke nodded. "I spoke with Lady Rotteburg this morning. The woman is a force of nature when it comes to ferreting out gossip. I do not know how she was able to do so here, but she shared her findings with me. Many believe you to be an Alurian spy, but none of them thought a Reaper, much less a Pendergast, would go so far as to yield so publicly. The courts do not believe your father would ever allow you to submit in such a way. The Pendergasts have acquired a reputation of being far too proud for their own good—astonishing really, coming from kindred."

"They put far too much trust in what they think constitutes pride for my father," Remy mumbled.

"I've met Hylasenth before, and he's far more subtle than Raghnall could ever be. He was using his own familiar to challenge Lord Malekh's authority. Had Malekh refused, it would have cast your position into even further question. Had he accepted, he would have lost face at having to appease a subordinate, even an Eighth Court king. So he delegated the matter to Xiaodan instead, as she holds no official position at court but acts on his behalf. Most important, they know he would never use her for something like this, even to his advantage. You have a flair for the dramatic yourself, you know."

"What?"

"Going down on your knees for Xiaodan with Breaker still on your back?"

Remy was red from neck to hairline. "I didn't even remember it was still there."

Elke's eyes twinkled. "I won't tell your father, if that's what makes you anxious."

Remy swallowed, remembering the question in Xiaodan's eyes, her willingness to put a stop to everything if Remy had shown the least sign of unwillingness. "And what if Xiaodan and I hadn't done that? Would Malekh have found another a way?"

"He could have demanded that Hylasenth's familiar attend to him instead as a reprimand, but that would continue to cast a cloud of suspicion on you. And I suspect neither you nor Xiaodan would have liked that alternative."

"How are kindred politics even more fucking complicated than Alurian?"

"We live longer, hold grudges, and use sex for ultimatums. But while Lord Malekh may not act it or want to be, and no matter how much Raghnall whines about it, the other court leaders are already deferring to him." She grinned at him. "I understand why he doesn't want the responsibility. But Fanglei's only concerned for her clan, no one really listens to Raghnall, and Hylasenth isn't to be trusted. Yingyue would have been a good choice, but she's in no condition to lead. Lord Malekh defeated the First Court once, and they're gambling that he can do it again." Elke frowned at him. "*Do you want to be involved like this? So many things can go wrong, and the council may demand more from you in the days to follow.*"

"I didn't mind it," Remy said slowly. "It would have been different if it wasn't with Xiaodan or Malekh. Being with them wasn't a humiliation like it was with Giselle and her friends. If that's what it takes to convince the rest of the courts, then I'll be their court familiar."

"I think you like it a lot more than you're willing to admit." She winked.

"Shut your mouth, Elke."

"Armiger?"

They both turned to face the newcomer, a startlingly pretty girl with gentle blue eyes and long brown hair. The collar she wore on her neck announced her to be one of the human familiars—of the Seventh Court, judging from the small tattoo she wore on her shoulder.

"My name is Trin," she said. "My apologies if I had interrupted you both. I was hoping to thank you, and perhaps be friends? It isn't easy to be human in a court of vampires, as you likely know."

"Thank me?" Remy asked blankly.

"For what you did earlier, with Lady Song. We've never seen anyone with the rank and position you have becoming a court familiar. Many in the Seventh are reconsidering how they treat humans in general, knowing Lord Malekh would no longer take so kindly to any mistreatment."

"Has your leader been abusing you?" Remy asked quickly, angrily. "If he is—"

The girl laughed. "No, though I understand why you would think that. For all his talk, my lord is not as dismissive of mortals as he'd like you to believe."

"And why tell us this?" Elke asked suspiciously.

The girl hesitated. "I think your presence here is a boon to the rest of us. It gives me hope, and I at least want to tell you that we are grateful."

"No thanks are necessary," Remy said hesitantly. "I'm doing this for—for—"

"I know. We're not so different, you and I." She bowed and turned to go, then paused. "Lord Malekh never had a familiar," she said. "That's what Raghnall tells me. And Lady Song is young by kindred measures but doesn't strike me as the type to take one in haste. When I heard they were engaged, I thought they never would. But there is no mistaking the way they look at you."

"Well," Elke said thoughtfully, after Trin had left. "That was either an offer to be an ally or a spy sent by the Seventh to keep an eye on you, I'm not quite sure which." She paused. "Remy?"

It took a moment for Remy to get his mouth working again. "Neither of them has had a familiar before?" he asked.

"YOU'RE NEARLY one thousand years old," Remy said crabbily, settling in between Xiaodan and Malekh. As he'd anticipated, both his vampire lovers had been insatiable *and* extremely possessive that night, coming to his bed instead of the other way around. The lord hadn't withdrawn from him nor he from Xiaodan, all three content to lie there and savor their closeness until Remy had started talking again.

He could hear the irritated grunt from behind him. "And why is that surprising to you?" Malekh, Remy noted, never did like it whenever he brought up his age.

"Surely there might have been *one* human to have caught your eye in all those centuries?"

"None that would make me consider a bond. Most of my relationships were temporary. I had little inclination then to find anything lasting."

Remy cleared his throat. "Technically, any bond with a human would be temporary. Like my bond with both of you."

"Do you want me to turn you, Remington?" Malekh's breath ghosted along the back of his neck. "Will you finally let one night pass in comfortable silence if I do? I may not have taken a familiar, but I've turned enough kindred in that time. Not all of them were happy about it."

"Y-you mean like Vasilik?"

He could feel Malekh's scowl burning through his skin. For the most part, Xiaodan was quiet, hands stroking Remy's face and content to let her fiancé talk.

"Not like him. Others I've turned realized they didn't want to be and surrendered themselves willingly to the sunrise."

Remy gasped. "Why?"

"The life of kindred can be one of loneliness. Not everyone finds a mate. Others could not stomach the killing for sustenance. Still more lost the passion that could only be kindled with life's brevity. But for all your talk in the past of not wanting to

be turned, you've been bringing it up unprompted rather frequently."

"I don't know!" Remy said a little too loudly. "Learning that
neither you nor Xiaodan had ever . . . You all let me ramble
on about what would happen to me as I grow older, but no
one's talking about what's going to happen to you two when I'm
gone! I don't want to leave any of you miserable just because
I'm gone."

"Remy," Xiaodan said calmly. "High Priestess Isabella has
agreed to a personal audience with us. The Antecedents claimed
at first to know nothing of mandurugo, but Zidan saw through
their excuses. We're to meet with them tomorrow, and we would
like you to come with us."

Remy stared at her in silence for a long time, then inclined his
head so he could stare at Malekh, too. "Just like that?"

"Just like that," Malekh confirmed. "And we would appreciate
if you kept yourself from falling apart until we've at least heard
what they have to say."

"You've been thinking about this just as much as I have," Remy
mumbled.

"Of course. Why wouldn't we?" Xiaodan couldn't stop touching his face, the curve of his shoulders. "You . . . did very well
today, love. I'm sorry you had to do that. Hylasenth would not
have backed down otherwise."

"I liked it," Remy said without thinking, and then immediately
began to sputter at the looks of surprise on their faces. "I mean, I
didn't think about everyone watching so much."

"Remy," Xiaodan's brown eyes sparkled as she wrapped a leg
lazily around him. "You're getting harder."

"You have even more scandalous proclivities than you let on,
Pendergast," Malekh murmured in his ear, which only worsened
Remy's current problem.

"We already know that you like to be tied down," Xiaodan

purred, running her hands down his chest. "But do you also like being commanded? Pampered and praised? Shafted?"

"Sh-shafted?"

"I am at a disadvantage when it comes to certain appendages that most men are born with, having none of my own. So I had one commissioned at my leisure."

The words were easy enough to hear, but understanding them took longer for Remy's already addled brain. "But why would you need . . ." Realization broke through. *"Oh."*

"Oh," Xiaodan agreed, shifting her hips.

"He likes the idea," Malekh murmured.

"Fuck you," Remy said, and then immediately regretted it when both vampires did.

15

THE COUNCIL

It was easier back in Elouve. He would wait for dawn to arrive before silently stealing out of Giselle's bed, then take a hansom back to his residence. Few nobles were up at that hour, and there was no one else to see his ride of shame back to Kinaiya Lodge, hating himself all the while and knowing he would repeat it again.

But few at the Allpriory slept. And since most were vampires with the ability to hear through stone walls, everyone's eyes were on him when he'd slunk forth from his bedchamber and down to the great hall to break his fast.

Xiaodan and Malekh were gone by the time he'd woken, and there was only Thaïs knocking politely outside his door, telling him that his meal was ready downstairs. It was somehow worse than when she'd been trying to flirt with him, because this time she sounded both awed and gleeful because she *knew*.

He didn't know why he was so embarrassed by his conduct, because the corridors were writhing with bodies. Privacy was apparently not a trait among all the courts, and Malekh and Xiaodan's clans seemed to be the exception rather than the rule. There were couples in stages of undress against walls and on any conceivable surface that could hold their weight. A room they passed contained sprawled shapes, participants therein in various compromising positions, but Remy kept his gaze straight ahead despite the red standing out from his cheeks and soldiered on.

"Most are from the Eighth Court," Thaïs said amiably, thoroughly unbothered. "I am told that they are notorious for such things."

"Apparently," Remy muttered, unsurprised. And then, "This isn't the way to the dining hall."

"I was asked to bring you to the Eighth Court leader. Please don't be alarmed," the woman said hurriedly when Remy reached behind him for Breaker almost on instinct. "He would never do anything to incite Lord Malekh's anger. He will not attempt any harm to you, that much I can promise."

Remy wasn't quite as sure, but it didn't feel like he had much choice. They followed the orgies down a hallway he'd never been to and into a room that was larger than the one he shared with Xiaodan and Malekh. Hylasenth himself was reclining on an overly large bed that could easily fit half a dozen, with vampires and familiars in various stages of undress lounging on either side of him. The lord himself was proudly nude, and Remy hastily fixed his gaze at a spot on the wall right above the Eighth Court leader's head.

"I had quite the interesting night," Hylasenth said, by way of greeting. "I thought at first that Lord Malekh was being deliberately deceptive. That your relationship with him and Xiaodan was a ruse, to have us think that he could be quite the deviant. How glad am I to be wrong. The sounds I have heard through these walls are downright delicious."

"If you say so," Remy mumbled, still staring straight ahead and trying desperately not to bolt. Breaker's familiar weight on his back was his sole comfort.

Hylasenth languidly rose from the bed to circle him like a lion sizing up its prey, and Remy shifted his gaze to stare determinedly at the ground. "While I am pleased to learn that some depravity does lie beneath that stern exterior, you remain quite the enigma. I find it suspicious that of all the familiars to take to their bed, it would be the Reaper son of *the* Alurian Butcher he would favor."

The Eighth Court leader reached up and tapped a finger against Breaker's handle, lightly enough not to be misconstrued as an attempt to grab it, but Remy tensed all the same. "I can think of two possibilities. Either he is in league with the Alurian queen and seeks to betray our courts, with you as his surety. Or he is a fool, and you are taking advantage of his affections to help your father take us down." Hylasenth's voice was light and pleasant, but Remy heard the threat for what it was.

"Or maybe he's just good in bed," Remy said, forcing himself to sound neutral. "If you had the chance at him, I reckon you'd do the same, and without a second thought."

"Perhaps." There was a hand on his back this time, fingers trailing down suggestively. "And perhaps I'd take you too, if you were so inclined. Surely Lord Malekh and Lady Xiaodan aren't too possessive of where you take your pleasure?"

"They don't decide what I choose to do on my own time," Remy said. "And neither do you. All I want at the moment is breakfast, so if you're done with the questioning."

A long silence from the vampire, and Remy was beginning to think he'd miscalculated when the court leader let out a long, throaty chuckle. "I can see why you have their attention. I'm almost envious." The hand withdrew. "You are Thaïs, correct? Kindly escort our famished guest to the dining hall."

"You did well," Thaïs murmured, the instant the door to Hylasenth's room closed behind them and Remy sagged in relief. "While the Seventh likes to stomp around and intimidate, the Eighth takes a far subtler approach. Lord Malekh has always been something of a mystery to the rest of us, and I suppose this is Lord Hylasenth's method of reconnaissance."

"He thought I was one of Malekh's lackeys, brought here to pretend to be his and Xiaodan's consort, didn't he?" Remy muttered. "Do you all think that?"

Thaïs winked. "Not after last night."

Thankfully, the dining hall was ruled exempt from all the debaucheries, but even here *everyone* knew, because the only meals set out were for human consumption. Kindred loitered there anyway, grinning at him like they'd been friendly from the start. A few even raised their tankards at him. Remy was ready to turn around and leave, but a small hand grasped at his arm before he could flee from their attentions.

It was the young human familiar from the Seventh Court, Trin. "I have already eaten," she whispered, "but I was wondering if you wouldn't mind my company while you do?"

"I'm not very hungry." The growl emanating from within his stomach contradicted him, and Remy flushed again.

"Don't worry. We're protected here." Trin pointed to Gibrid, Altace, and another Antecedent named Elspeth who had surreptitiously planted themselves around the dining hall. Catching his eye, Altace smiled at him and shook his head a little, as if telling him not to worry.

Trin led Remy to one of the tables by the corner, where a plate filled with sausage links, warm bread, and poached eggs awaited him. "You know there's nothing to be ashamed of," she asked softly, seating herself across from him.

"I'm not ashamed," Remy mumbled, nearly inhaling the bread in his haste to find something to occupy himself.

"I can tell that you're still very new at this. But this is more about Lord Malekh than anything else." Trin looked down at the table. "They're not mocking you, if that is your worry. Lord Malekh has held himself distant from council affairs for so long that he normally treats having a familiar as something beneath him. They're all very pleased to see that they were wrong. And . . ." It was Trin's turn to flush. "Begging no offense, but they don't believe that any Pendergast would ever go so far as to become a familiar and all that entails, just to disrupt our council. Certainly not to *two* kindred, much less to Lord Malekh."

Remy looked around as he ate. Much of the tension from yesterday's session was gone. The atmosphere was almost relaxed, even if there were still far more vampires in one space than he was comfortable with. "Were we that loud?" he burst out.

Trin actually giggled. "I heard little, to be honest. But Raghnall sulked all night, said he couldn't rest because of all the commotion."

"Fuck," Remy muttered, and shoved more cheese into his mouth.

"You'll get better at it," Trin told him sympathetically. "It's easier once you understand kindred customs better. Why, they used to have full-blown orgies at the Allpriory in the days of the First Court. Many of the kindred here have themselves been thralls to the Night King. Isn't it fascinating?"

"Not really." Remy didn't particularly want to think about orgies. "How did you become a familiar? If you would like to tell me," he added hastily.

"My parents wanted to marry me off to a man I didn't love. He was a boor and had mistreated his previous wife, and I didn't want to share the same fate she suffered, so I ran away. Stumbled into a vampire's nest a few days later. They would have killed me, had not Raghnall intervened," Trin said, a little starry-eyed. How she could react that way to such an overgrown piece of armor was a mystery to Remy. "I've been with him ever since."

"So his attempts to kill me were because he didn't like me personally, and not because I was human?"

"I believe he and some of your ancestors have had bad blood. A great-great-grandfather of yours killed several kindred he'd sired, and he himself has been scarred by that weapon of yours. He was in quite a state when he returned to our room after Lord Hylasenth and Lady Song managed to talk him out of doing damage to you *and* the temple. Kept me awake all night."

Remy choked at that.

Trin laughed again and patted him on the back of his hand. "Do you know why familiars are so important to kindred courts? Kindred protect their familiars. In exchange, we spot and head off tension between the clans, even among their kinsmen. You did a wonderful job of that yesterday at the council. It isn't something to be embarrassed over." Trin's eyes sparkled. "We're supposed to keep our masters and mistresses happy."

"Oh, Light," Remy groaned.

"Remy!" Elke burst into the room in a whirlwind of anxiety. For once, she didn't look as neat and put together as she usually did. Her hair was sticking up in all directions, and her face held more pallor to it than usual.

She nodded briefly at Trin, then slid into a seat beside Remy. "Didn't your fight with the Seventh teach you anything?" she hissed. "You're not to wander about the corridors without one of us at your side!"

"I don't need looking after, Elke. Besides, no one told me."

"I was supposed to tell you," Elke admitted, slumping down against her chair. "I told Lady Song I would be at your chambers before you'd woken, but I've had much to deal with this morning."

A hush fell over the place, and Remy looked up from his plate. The kindred had fallen silent as well, turning to see Raghnall framed against the doorway. His gaze flitted toward Trin and he frowned slightly, but made no move against Remy this time. He merely tilted his head at her, then turned to leave the same way he entered.

"I must be going, then," Trin said cheerfully, rising gracefully to her feet.

"Will you be in trouble for talking to me?" Remy asked worriedly.

"Of course not. I've already lectured him about the importance of keeping ties to the Third and Fourth Court. He won't attack you again." Trin bowed low to him, then to Elke, before following her master. Some of the kindred stepped aside to let her pass with a respectful incline of their heads.

"Sounds like she has him well under her thumb despite all appearances," Elke said, and then sighed deeply, leaning forward to rest her head against the wooden table with a faint clunk.

"Are you all right? You don't look like you've had much sleep."

"I'm kindred, Remy. I don't need sleep. This place is a little overwhelming, that's all. And I wasn't expecting you to be up so early after last night."

Remy resisted the urge to pound the table in frustration. "Did *every*one fucking hear us?"

"What were you expecting, given kindred and their senses?" Elke lifted her head. "Lady Song intends to formally ask the council today to acknowledge her as the official leader of the Fourth Court instead of Song Yingyue."

Remy gaped at her. "Does her mother know?"

"You've seen Yingyue. I don't think she even knows where she is. They may not have as many clansmen as in the past, but the Fourth Court still holds just as much sway. Lady Song is worried that the other leaders might view Yingyue as a weakness, and she wants to make sure that her court's interests are well defended."

"Won't she officially join the Third Court once she becomes Malekh's wife?"

"Yes, and that's where the potential conflict of interest comes in. They may not allow her to remain acting leader of the Fourth for long, once she shares leadership of the Third Court with Malekh. But she's determined to hold the position until they find another way. It's why they've been putting off their marriage." Elke crooked an eyebrow up. "Although I imagine that they need to discuss you as well before taking that step."

"That was part of what we were discussing last night," Remy muttered.

"I should remind you that what you have is a natural thing between three loving, consensual adults, and that it isn't wrong for you to pursue that."

"Elke."

"Seems like something's still on your mind. You do know that you can talk about it with me if you feel like you can't talk about it with Lord Malekh or Lady Song, though I don't see what could possibly—"

"Have you ever shafted someone?"

"I'm not sure what that's supposed to mean."

Remy prayed desperately to the Light that his voice was low enough for no one else to hear. It helped that most of the kindred had left the hall. "Xiaodan has a . . . shaft. Of an artificial variety. And she uses it on Malekh to . . . and I was wondering if you, uh, had done that with any of your—"

"Of course," Elke said immediately. "Countless times before. Not all men want to, of course, but there *are* some interesting ideas to use it for when you've also got a female partner." She broke off, staring at his face. "Remy," she said, grinning. "You are such an innocent, it's adorable."

A shout rose up from somewhere in the other room. Elke and Remy traded glances at each other, then were both off in an instant.

A crowd had gathered before one of the rooms. Thaïs was standing there in wet clothes, red-faced with a sponge in one hand and an empty bucket in the other. Even more scarlet was the Lady Rotteburg, her eyes bulging out of her head and a brush raised as if to chuck it at the girl. A bar of soap on the floor beside the Antecedent was proof that this was not her first attempt.

"Stay away from my son, do you hear me?" Lady Rotteburg roared.

"I only offered to scrub his back, milady," Thaïs squeaked.

"Mother!" Lord Lorian came bursting through the door, all the more comical because he was soaking wet and clad only in his braies. The crimson had spread from his face and down his chest and shoulders. "You are misreading the situation!"

"You are not to go near him!" Lady Rotteburg thundered. She cast a furious glance at the others who'd gathered to watch, and under her gaze many of the kindred wilted, murmured apologies, and tactfully withdrew.

"Is there anything I can do, milady?" Remy asked tentatively, watching Thaïs scuttle away with the others.

"No, Armiger. I have everything well under control." Lady Rotteburg rubbed at her temple. "Forgive me. I am not used to causing such outbursts. I fear this will lower Lorien's standing among the rest of the clans, but it had to be done." She cast a glare upon her son.

"She didn't do anything!" Lord Lorien protested again.

"You are not to seek her out, nor is she to stay in the same room as you in our time here. Do you understand me?"

The Second Court leader sighed. "Yes, Mother."

With a loud harrumph, Lady Rotteburg retreated back into the room.

"As bad as that?" Remy asked sympathetically.

"Was she really just scrubbing your back, milord?" Elke asked casually.

Lorien met their gazes before his eyes drifted to the floor. "She's very pretty," he muttered, and Elke and Remy couldn't help but laugh.

MALEKH DIDN'T look like he wanted to be there. He had once more eschewed sitting at the head of the table in favor of seating himself at the chair designated for the Third Court leader, deliberately facing away from the throne that was still taking up most of the unspoken questions in the room.

Remy sat on the floor in between him and Xiaodan, noting how the other familiars had positioned themselves in the same manner beside their own respective masters. The Antecedents, at least, had been solicitous enough to provide cushions in lieu of the hard stone ground, and they proved surprisingly comfortable. Xiaodan had looked ready to fight for the right to spare him a chair beside her at first, but Remy had taken Trin's earlier words to heart, refusing more privileges than the other familiars had. It paid off in the approving look that Fanglei, of all people, shot his way.

"Zidan offered to lead in exchange for the high priestess providing us with more information regarding the mandurugo," Xiaodan said softly for Remy's benefit, all without moving her lips. "He knew she wanted him to handle the council in a more official capacity, and it was the easiest way to get her to agree."

Malekh was doing something he hated for *him*. Remy gritted his teeth but otherwise kept his calm.

Xiaodan occupied the Fourth Court's seat. Everyone knew the extent of Yingyue's condition, but Raghnall had once more kicked up a fuss, arguing that Xiaodan was not capable of juggling the interests of two courts at once, and it had taken time to convince him to withdraw his protests.

Remy didn't know where Alegra was and assumed that she was at the Fourth Court leader's quarters. He spotted Elke searching the room for the tall warrior herself before her shoulders slumped in realization.

"Now we come to the matter of the Second and Fifth Courts," Malekh said.

Hylasenth nodded. "It would do well to inject some fresh blood into the clans. The demise of the Second and Fifth have been through no fault but their own selfishness, but it would be good for morale to find better leaders for them."

"And reform them we shall," Raghnall boomed, sounding far more pleased than Remy suspected any of them would have liked. "The Seventh is the largest among the clans, and we have no shortage of kindred eager to join our ranks." He raised his hand, and two of his subordinates waiting at one side of the room stepped forward. "Abel and Forshall are two of my most trusted clansmen, and they have offered to leave my court to make efforts to rebuild the Second and Fifth. You will not find their determination lacking, nor their experience."

The looks on Hylasenth's and Xiaodan's faces plainly stated that it was not anyone's determination or experience they were opposed to.

"And this is not a ploy to influence those courts to intercede in your favor on future sessions of the council?" Fanglei asked candidly and coolly.

"Did you not argue that Lady Song here is more than capable of overseeing the Third and Fourth without an overlap of interests?" The man shot her a smug smile, thinking he'd scored a point. "It's not like I will be handling the affairs of three clans at the same time, as she handles two."

"The council previously agreed to first make our selections from the former clansmen of both courts before we take other steps," Malekh said.

"Survivors?" The other vampire scoffed. "You cannot think that anyone would be willing to return after all that transpired, for the Fifth in particular. There was no love lost between Etrienne Sauveterre and many of his own kinsmen, and you would be hardpressed to find any who survived the purging *you* yourself wrought on them, much less one eager to take up the reins in his place."

"That's not quite true," Elke said, stepping forward.

Raghnall narrowed his eyes at her, displeased by the interruption. "And who might you be?"

"I am Elke Whittaker. I once served as Etrienne Sauveterre's head forger, and I am ready to take up the mantle of leadership for the Fifth."

Startled murmurs sprang up from the rest of the crowd.

"And how are we to know that you are who you say you are? I knew Etrienne for close to four hundred years, and I have never seen you at his court."

"If you knew Etrienne for that long, then you would have known about his propensity for possessiveness, milord," Elke said, smiling grimly. "He was most appreciative of my companionship and my talent at metal smithing and strove to keep me a secret to all but his inner courts, for fear that someone else may spirit me away."

"You forged Etrienne's sword," Hylasenth said suddenly. "Dawnbreaker. I have admired it many times in the past. He told me that he had commissioned it from one of King Unhurst's most brilliant smiths at the turn of the sixth century."

"He was not wrong, milord. In fact, he fancied my work so much that he murdered my king and took me as his prize."

Raghnall was still glaring at Elke, clearly pissed that his scheming was already heading south. Abel and Forshall were silent, looking to their master for further instruction. "You have yet to prove your identity," the Seventh Court leader finally said. "Words are not evidence. If there is no one else to vouch for you—"

"I do," Xiaodan spoke up quietly. "We encountered her during the Third and Fourth's final battle with the Fifth, and a few more times before that."

"And how are we to know that she isn't just some kindred you found along the way here? You've always been biased against the

Fifth, Xiaodan, and you would jump at the chance to control their court now that the Fourth is bereft of members."

"Lady Whittaker has no clan ties with me, Raghnall. Any decision she makes will be of her own choosing, and not because she was ever my subordinate." Xiaodan gave Abel and Forshall a pointed glance. "Unlike some other candidates who have been put forward."

"I vouch for the Lady Whittaker as well," Malekh said calmly, before the Seventh Court king could splutter another protest, "and confirm that she was a standing member of the Fifth Court long before our battle with them."

"I, too, can vouch for the young Whittaker," Cao Fanglei spoke up unexpectedly. "I saw the young lady quite a few times and always wondered of her position within Sauveterre's court. The Fifth refused to reveal her origins when I put forth inquiries in the past, and I long suspected that there was more to her than he let on. More than just a consort, anyway."

"It is settled, then," Hylasenth said. "Begging your pardon, Lady Whittaker, but to have survived both Etrienne, his cruel proclivities, *and* the bloody war the Third and Fourth waged against them tells me all I need to know about your character, and I would be most pleased to see you restore the Fifth to even greater glory." He looked around. "Let us make it official, then. Is anyone opposed to granting Lady Whittaker her right to the Fifth?"

No one else spoke; Raghnall was too outraged to speak, unable to come up with another counter to her claim. "If that is the case," he finally said, "there is still the matter of the Second Court. As I said, I would be happy to offer both Abel and Forshall for your consideration."

"That will no longer be necessary," Malekh said. "May I present to the court the Lady Violet Rotteburg of Elouve and her son, Lorien Cedric Tattersall." Aunoir and Deithnir were already gently guiding both forward.

"What?" Raghnall sputtered.

Hylasenth was taking this revelation less jovially than he had Elke's announcement. He was out of his chair and before the young man in an instant, inspecting his face carefully. "Be at ease, madam," the Eighth Court leader said when Lady Rotteburg started forward in alarm. "I mean no harm to him. The opposite, in fact. Tattersall, you said. Do you mean to say that this young man's father was Redwald Tattersall?"

"Yes," Lady Rotteburg whispered. It was the first time Remy had heard her sound so broken. "We were lovers. Eloped when I was still young. My father had written me off—he never knew I'd married a vampire—and we lived at the Second Court for many years, until . . ."

"Until the Alurians attacked Meridian Keep," Fanglei finished for her.

Lady Rotteburg nodded. "Redwald helped me escape. I was already pregnant then, and he sent me away to his kin, who were disguised as humans in a nearby town. He died in the siege, and I raised Lorien on my own until my father died. We had no close remaining kin, and the law Queen Ophelia passed then allowed me to inherit his estate in lieu of other heirs. I kept Lorien in the countryside, but I needed to comport my life in a way to put myself above suspicion."

And so you became a duenna and a terror in the hearts and minds of every rake, gold digger, and reprobate foolish enough to cross your path, Remy thought. *Me included.*

"If I am to lead anything," Lorien said quietly, speaking up for the first time, "I shall pull my own weight, fight as hard as I would expect any followers of mine to. I believe I can bring that much to the courts."

"And you would have me believe that you happened to find an heir to the Second Court from chance alone, Third?" Raghnall roared at Malekh.

"Redwald was a good friend of mine," Hylasenth said. "I understand why he would seek to keep this part of his life a secret, even from me and his own court. He always did his best to temper Kurdashev's flightiness. He would have made a better leader, given the chance. Save for the yellow hair, this young lad is his spitting image. However she found him, I have no doubts this is his son."

"There is still the question of whether or not he is fit to lead the Second Court."

"You are free to offer Abel and Forshall as his guides until he is able to take full command," Malekh said. He watched Raghnall's eyes light up for a few moments before he added, "All the other courts shall pledge advisors of their own. I'm sure Fanglei already has names in mind, but perhaps the Fourth and the Eighth would like to offer their own people to serve as mentors."

"The Fourth would be well glad to," Xiaodan said calmly.

"As will the Eighth," Hylasenth said.

Things were not going Raghnall's way. He looked about ready to spring from his chair and fight them all, but Trin, who was seated at his feet, laid a hand on his right knee. That was enough to soothe the man, who slumped back down with a glower.

"I believe that Lord Tattersall should be given the chance to speak first," Malekh said.

The lad bravely squared his shoulders and turned to Malekh. "I am prepared to do so, milord."

Knowing what to do, Elke slid into the chair kept empty for the Fifth, and after some hesitation, Lorien did the same for the Second Court seat. Remy saw Daoming taking Lady Rotteburg gently by the elbow and leading her back to where the other kindred were waiting.

"I see no reason not to place both Lady Whittaker and Lord Tattersall as temporary leaders of the Fifth and Second Courts respectively, and take into consideration any others who may wish to present candidates in the future," Malekh said. "Which brings us to matters involving the First Court."

Remy could feel the tension in the air again. Raghnall was still sulking. Hylasenth was frowning, and while Fanglei's features remained placid, there was a faint wrinkle in her forehead.

"The Alurians see the benefits of an alliance with the rest of the courts. There are far too many newly turned covens about, pledging loyalty to the Night Empress. There are mutations attacking human villages."

"But weren't these mutations created by the Alurians themselves?" Hylasenth said. "I see no reason to help them clean up their messes when it is clear that they made these foul abominations to use against us."

"It became our problem when the Night Empress found a way to manipulate them to attack both kindred and humans alike," Malekh said, and judging from the mutters and gasps from the other kindred, many hadn't known of this. "An evolved incarnation of these mutations tried to invade the Fata Morgana—webbed feet and scales, all exuding poison."

"Now that you've mentioned it," Hylasenth said. "My court recently defended ourselves from a similar offensive."

"We have found similar assailants back in Situ," Fanglei confirmed. "Green scales? Rows of jagged fangs?"

Hylasenth nodded. "We were able to use the inoculations you sent us to prevent them from rising up, Third, though I fear that will not be enough if this goes on for much longer. Perhaps you are right. It is one thing to sit back and wait for the Night Empress and the Alurians to see their way to a mutual destruction, but it is another to let the rest of us slide into the hellfire along with them."

"And what if the Night Empress is found to have better claims to the Night Court than Lord Malekh has?" Elke asked unexpectedly.

Remy gaped at her, unsure why she was suddenly choosing to

square off against Malekh, but Raghnall was quick to take advantage. "If the right to lead the Second and Fifth Courts are based on the seniority of its surviving members, then none of you should be able to oppose the Night Empress if she can prove closer blood ties to Ishkibal than Zidan."

"She is free to assume the Night Court's throne if she wishes it," Malekh said, in a too-tranquil voice Remy learned to expect when he was about to make everyone else angry with his next announcement. "That changes little of the danger she poses to us all. I will have no qualms about laying her and her clan to waste a second time, regardless of title."

The proclamation did not sit well with the rest of the council. Hylasenth sat with his arms folded across his chest, lips pursed. Raghnall looked about ready to have an aneurysm. Elke was careful not to display any expression on her face, and Lorien looked nervous. Remy shot him a sympathetic smile, and Lorien's lips twitched up before he caught himself and looked down at the table.

Fanglei tsked loudly. "Who are you to say that the Night Empress, too, does not wish to unite us? It seems to me that her enmity has always been directed at the Alurians, and that she chose to attack the Third and Fourth Courts because they have aided the humans. What benefit do we have from siding with the mortal kingdoms?"

"The mutations who attacked my mother's home thought that we were from Situ," Lorien said. Heads swiveled in his direction, and he looked ready to crawl under the table from their scrutiny.

"You never mentioned that," Fanglei said quietly.

Lorien cleared his throat. "I didn't know anything about the Night Empress at that time and thought it possible that the Sixth Court, being the closest, had instigated it as a ploy, to eventually ingratiate yourselves toward me. Even more so as I am likely to take on the leadership of the Second Court."

There was a tense silence before Fanglei broke it herself with a soft chuckle, her manner now relaxed. "If I still entertained any doubts that you were Redwald's boy, I have none now," she said. "It was exactly the kind of reasoning he would have come up with. I commend your mother for raising you in a way that his line breeds true. But I am most curious to know why you think you were attacked because they thought you were under my protection."

"It was something one of the attackers said."

"What?" Malekh asked. "Are you saying that one of these creatures *spoke* to you?"

"It was not so much speaking to me as announcing what they intended to do to me and my mother, milord." Lorien took a deep breath. "They called me impure. Cambion. Said none of the other courts had retained the purity of Ishkibal's bloodline. That the First Court would be borne anew of his blood alone, just as it had once been—with no other courts alive to dilute their lineage."

16

THE GODSFLAME

To Remy, the court kindred were accustomed to treating humans with condescension, having deemed them inferior stock regardless of the close relationships they themselves maintained with their familiars. To hear Lorien declare so blatantly that they, too, were considered ill-bred blood by others was met with both anger and incredulity.

"Who does this bitch think she is?" Raghnall sputtered, as if he had not toyed with the idea of joining up with the empress only minutes before. "We are of the Night Court! There is none else that could boast the purity of our lineage!"

"If she has reason to claim closer ties to the Night King than even Lord Malekh, then it would be no idle boast. The question is whether we treat it as bravado or truth." Hylasenth leaned back, a frown crossing his lips.

"Milord," Xiaodan said. "Did you by any chance catch a glimpse of the kindred's face? Most of the coven we have encountered tend to be under a strong compulsion, and rarely do they speak with their own mind."

"If I may speak, milady?" Lady Rotteburg spoke up formally

from the audience. At Xiaodan's nod, she continued. "Our attackers wore hoods, preventing us from recognizing them. Lord Tattersall saw no other identifying marks on them, though we knew little of the courts to understand what to look for. You are right when you said that the coven vampires acted like they were under some thrall, but there were one or two that appeared of their own mind, and it struck me then that it was they who commanded those kindred."

"So the Night Empress is not without her own allies, serving her of their own volition." Xiaodan frowned. "Zidan has the right of it as Ishkibal's successor, but if her predecessor was sired earlier by the Night King . . ."

"Then she has better claim over the Allpriory," Fanglei finished. "And we are therefore duty-bound to accept her as such."

"No," Xiaodan said. "This is madness." She rose to her feet, glaring at them all. "That you all feel beholden to the Allpriory is exactly what is wrong with all this, and the reason the Third did not wish to use this place as our meeting ground. Zidan has been vocal about sundering our ties completely to the temple, to grant us the freedom to rule our own clans without interference from lingering influences of the Night Court. Ishkibal has been dead for centuries. It is the rest of you keeping his unreasonable customs alive."

Hylasenth sighed. "You are far too young to understand, Xiaodan. That the clans are cordial now does not mean we shall remain so in the future. Before Ishkibal's court came into existence, kindred killed kindred indiscriminately. His guidance is what gave us any measure of peace in those early years."

"And that means naught if this new empress is prone to Ishkibal's weaknesses." Fanglei turned to regard the temple priestess, who had said nothing throughout the proceedings. "If the Night Empress comes to take the throne and proves that she has a greater claim over it than Lord Malekh, what will you do?"

The cowled woman bowed her head. "We have little choice but to accept her as Lord Ishkibal's successor, milady."

"And should Lord Malekh choose to contest such claims?"

The priestess's expression grew pained, as if she disliked the very thought of it. "We cannot go against our own laws."

"So the only way, then, would be if the Night Empress goes the same way as Ishkibal."

"You would plot to murder her?" Hylasenth asked.

"Unless you wish to see her installed on the throne instead of Malekh. As much as the idea of killing our own ruler pains the rest of you, having accepted Ishkibal's death as the only way for us to survive sets a precedent we can use now." Fanglei looked around. "Unless you are not quite as eager to see Malekh rule the Allpriory as you say you are."

"No more than I," Malekh said. "With or without the threat of the Night Empress, I intend to break with kindred tradition and dissolve the responsibilities of the throne. No one should have so much power over all the clans. It broke Ishkibal, and it will break everyone who thinks themselves capable of taking his place. For now, I will ask all your oaths to pledge against the Night Empress when the time comes. The stability of both Aluria and Kerenai are essential to our own security. Will you lend me your strength in keeping their borders secure?"

Silence met his answer. It was Xiaodan who rose silently to her feet. For a moment Remy feared no one else would rise to the occasion, but it was Elke who stood next, looking resolute. "I have no clansmen yet to speak of, having only been newly raised to the lead the Fifth," she said. "But I have spent many years in Aluria and understand all too well how necessary they are to our own survival. Kindred I might lack, but I know my weapons. I can pledge you that much for assistance."

"As will I," Lorien Tattersall said bravely, scrambling to his feet as well. "The Night Empress poses a great risk to mortal and kindred alike, and it would be foolish to allow her influence to grow."

"As I am still defending the borders between Situ and Aluria, I believe that it goes without saying where I stand," Fanglei said. "However, I would like better assurance that Lord Malekh will not immediately vacate the Allpriory throne as soon as the threat has been subdued." She smiled at the Third Court leader. "You are very clever at wrangling our oaths without giving us your own. I would extract from you a promise to oversee Allpriory matters for oh, half a decade more before you make any decisions to sunder the throne."

"I have already promised the priestess twice that long," Malekh said, with no visible change in his expression. Remy tensed at the revelation.

Fanglei smiled broadly. "Good," she said, and rose stately to her feet as well.

"The majority speaks," Hylasenth said placidly. "My own scouts have been monitoring the situation in Kerenai for the past several days. There have been no other attacks there from the covens she controls, but should anything else transpire, I will apprise you all of it immediately."

Raghnall merely grunted, the closest to an assent that could be extracted from him. "Time enough for another matter I wish to put forth to the council, then. Three from the Seventh wish to walk the fires, and I have given them my blessing to do so."

"Let us see to one of your Seventh first," the high priestess said, though with great reluctance. "And see if you are still favorable to the notion after his trial has passed."

Another of Raghnall's men stepped forward, a great bulk of a vampire not dissimilar in size and manner to his leader. "I am Edgarth of Brenwyche," he said. "Sired by the Seventh. I wish to be worthy."

"Edgarth has been my brother-in-arms for the last five centuries and more," Raghnall said, "and I would be honored to fight with him for another five and see him walk the fires as I did." He waved a hand dismissively at the other clans. "Let them watch, if they wish."

The priestess nodded. "I will tell the others to make the preparations."

"I extend the invitation to you as well, *Hierarch*," Raghnall said, with a triumphant glance back at Malekh. "And perhaps one day you too shall gather the courage to walk where I have triumphed."

"I DON'T know what just happened," Remy muttered as Xiaodan helped him back to his feet. The other kindred were quick to depart with their respective leaders, the day's session ended.

"Zidan wanted the clans' promise to help defend Aluria," Xiaodan sounded tense despite the words.

"But what about the rest of it? The one where he promised the priestess he'd lead the Allpriory for the next ten years?"

"He told me nothing of that, either."

Elke was waiting for them, smoothing back her hair nervously. "Did I do it right?" she asked worriedly after the last of the other kindred had left.

"I didn't even know you'd accepted the leadership," Remy growled. "Bloody hell, Elke."

"Before you think to lecture me, don't be getting it into your head that anyone's forced me into the position. Lord Malekh was just as surprised when I told him so." Elke paused, looking down at the floor. "Remember when you convinced Lady Song that something good can come out of something bad? Well, I intend to do the same. I don't even know if there are any kindred who might be interested in joining so new a court, but I'd like to do it right this time."

"You know that you would have been welcomed in either my court or the Fourth's if you wanted," Malekh offered as he came up behind Remy.

"I do know. But I want to rebuild the Fifth into one I can finally be proud of."

Xiaodan spun on Malekh. "And what possessed you to agree to take command of the Allpriory for a decade? The other kindred would keep your feet nailed down here in a place you loathe—"

"I decided that the risks were worth the endeavor," Malekh said. "And it was I who proposed it. The other courts would not be so willing to fight the Night Empress without extracting an oath from me to keep to the throne, as Fanglei has already pointed out. A decade is a tolerable compromise."

"I don't trust the high priestess not to find a way to tie you down here forever, for all her hospitality and kindness," Xiaodan said. "The Allpriory is what gives them purpose, and they would not appreciate the loss of it. I don't like you acceding to their demands, even if on your own terms."

"Our priority is securing Aluria's safety. Should the kingdom fall, as Kerenai is on the verge of doing, that will spell even more strife for the kindred, though they do their best to pretend our fates are separate from the mortals." Malekh took Xiaodan's face tenderly in one hand. "Forgive me for making this decision without your knowledge."

"I suspect that the Antecedents were about to paint you into a corner, and you acted preemptively," Xiaodan grumbled. "I cannot be angry, knowing I would likely do the same in your place. But what of the new Second and Fifth Courts?"

"Accepting a decade of service at the Allpriory has also ensured that I can cast a closer eye on the two courts and keep them protected. But I believe Elke is more than able to handle things."

"It *would* help to have the support of the Allpriory hierarch behind me." Elke sighed. "Bloody hell, where would I even begin to find clansmen? I have the reputation of the former Fifth leader to contend with, and that alone is likely to chase most suitable candidates away."

"I think Eugenie would be more than happy to help on that note. She knows of kindred who want the steadfastness of a court but are wary of the entrenchment of the other existing clans. They are younger, for the most part, and perhaps not as set in traditional ways."

"I will be very deeply in your favor if you can arrange things with her, milord."

"If anything, I am in *your* debt. I would have a bigger headache to deal with, should Raghnall have let either of his subordinates take charge of the Fifth."

"But what about the Second Court?" Remy asked. "Lord Tattersall strikes me as a decent lad, but I do not trust the others not to take advantage of him."

"I have already sent Shiragiku to offer her assistance." Malekh sighed, weariness creeping into his face. "Loathe as I was to capitulate to the priestess, I was at least able to glean something from the gathering."

"Aid for Aluria?"

"Yes, and knowing where the others stand with me versus the Night Empress."

Remy stared. "How? They said little about their opinions."

"It was enough. Fanglei is inclined toward our side, but always holds back until she is certain victory is imminent before making bolder overtures. Raghnall clearly detests the idea of having me at the helm, but he is not eager to tangle with the empress himself and is willing to let me deal with her until he can assess whether she is a greater threat than a boon. It is Hylasenth that bears the most watching."

"I would have thought him the most amenable among them. He didn't seem to mind turning over the throne to you."

"That is what he would like us to believe." Malekh winced. "And I suppose I am to be present for a Seventh clansman's attempt to walk into the Godsflame?"

"It sounded from the priestess that it is one of the responsibilities of those who rule the Allpriory," Xiaodan said cautiously.

Malekh turned to look fondly down at her. "I sense this is something you are most keen to witness."

"I have no intentions of walking into it myself, if that helps ease your mind."

"It does. It's best that we both be present, should the worst happen." He glanced at Remy and Elke. "And I know it would be useless to try to convince either of you to stay behind."

"Wouldn't miss it for anything," Elke said immediately.

"Like hell you're going to tell us to stay," Remy said, and then added curiously, "Is it so bad as that?"

"Worse than any frenzy I've ever had to witness." Malekh took Xiaodan's hand. The other he extended toward Remy. "Perhaps Raghnall's subordinate will walk out of the fires with nary a singe to his name, and the Seventh Court will have one more powerful kindred that we shall have to contend with in the future. And it says much if that is our best-case scenario."

THE GODSFLAME was still as intimidating as ever. It seemed to Remy that there was a more purplish hue to its color now, as if awaiting a fresh sacrifice. The Antecedents were silent and accommodating for the most part, though every now and then Remy detected a few frowns from some, as if they tacitly disapproved.

He spotted Thaïs close by. The girl had her arms folded, eyeing Edgarth warily. The kindred who was ready to consign himself to the flames showed no outward fear of the upcoming task, laughing and joking boisterously with his clansmen as if he was not about to step into an inferno that could take his life or worse. "You and your clan seem even more nervous than the one about to take the risk," he murmured to Thaïs.

The frown on Thaïs's face disappeared when she looked at him, a warm smile taking its place. "Armiger Pendegast! I had not expected you here!" The grin dimmed somewhat. "We have borne witness to far too many kindred who have failed, and it is always to us to ensure that they be put out of their misery as compassionately as possible. It sours us more than the elation that the successes could ever bring."

"I'd never thought about it that way."

"The priestess herself has tried to talk Lord Edgarth out of his attempt, but as you can see, the man is steadfast. I pray that this works better for him than others." She snuck a glance behind them, noting Malekh and Xiaodan standing not too far from Remy. Elke, he noticed, had left their circle entirely. She was standing beside Alegra—that came as a shock, for Remy had not even seen the other woman arrive, alone and without Yingyue—and the two were talking quietly, both their expressions grave. Remy sensed a trace of irritation on Alegra's part, a surprise, since the woman was typically as hard to read as Malekh.

"I would be happy to explain more of the process to you," Thaïs said. "If Lord Malekh and Lady Song don't mind."

Remy tried to work out his status as court familiar and decided it would be all right. In many ways, it was similar to the often-confusing social etiquette of the Alurian court, where he'd been treated as the heir of one of the noble families in Elouve and yet not *quite*. "I'm sure they wouldn't, and I'd like to know more."

She was quick to supply him with the information he wanted. There were certain rituals necessary before the supplicant could be granted passage into the Godsflame, and it took a good half an hour. The priestess and her fellow Ascendents burned herbs of a sweet-smelling nature before the fires, and the caves were soon filled with their scent—a relaxant to ease one's mind, Thaïs explained.

The priestess of the Allpriory murmured a benediction over Lord Edgarth. "May your journey be riddled with fire and flame to cleanse you of light," she intoned. "May you ever walk in the night of the Mother, and may her blessing grace you in all the twilights of life therein."

"Not quite the prayers we had in Elouve," Remy muttered, mildly scandalized. He was not a religious sort by any means, but the Mother walked in the Light and dispelled the darkness; to have the reverse recited with such reverence felt almost like blasphemy.

"Kindred believe that we are the closest to the Mother's image as any being can be," Thaïs said, amused by his reaction. "We believe, in fact, that the Mother was the First of the Vampires, who walked the earth as an immortal and sired us all."

The formalities finally completed, the priestess stepped to one side, officially granting Edgarth access to the flames. The kindred didn't hesitate. With one last grin back at his comrades, fist raised in the air, he walked steadily into the fiery conflagration, and disappeared promptly into its depths.

"How long does this take?" Remy whispered.

"It varies among kindred. A few return within minutes. Others may take hours."

"Are the consequences affected by the length of time?"

"No. Many emerge, hale and hearty, in the span of ten minutes, and those staggering out bereft of sanity within the same duration."

"And do you know what it is that they see within the Gods-flame?"

"Very few remember their time within. Those who do recount a vast, empty blackness, cold with none of the heat of the fire they walked into. They describe a strange emptiness within that somehow shook them to the core, as if their minds were incapable of understanding such infinity. They could feel themselves change under the gaze of that void, of how they were powerless to stop it."

"Has there ever been an incident of a human entering the Godsflame?" Remy asked before he could stop himself.

The corners of Thaïs's mouth turned up again. "I hope that this is not an attempt to announce your intentions of walking into the fires yourself, Armiger."

"Of course not. Merely wondering."

"No human has ever entered the Godsflame and walked back out again, alive or otherwise." Thaïs paused. "Save for one."

"Who?"

"The First, of course—the Mother. The first human to ever become a vampire threw herself into these flames. How or why she made the attempt has been lost to time. King Ishkibal could trace his lineage from her. The Allpriory is the birthplace of all kindred, which is why we hold it in such reverence. From the Godsflame that burns for eternity to the great Tree that stands below, we have dedicated our existence to—"

"The great Tree?" Remy echoed, latching onto the words. "The Fount? Wasn't it destroyed by the fires?"

Thaïs glanced around them. "I should not be divulging so much without the priestess's permission," she said evasively, sounding sorry she'd spoken.

Somebody screamed. It echoed through the cavern without warning.

The fires of the Godsflame flickered low, close as Remy had ever seen it to going out, and for several awful moments, darkness filtered into the room.

When the light returned, Lord Edgarth stood on the platform. He had entered the fires laughing and impeccably dressed, with every intention of returning unscathed, but the man who had finally emerged was his complete opposite. In the short time that he had been gone, his hair and clothes had become unkempt and stained with dirt, his eyes wild with madness. His fangs were bared, snarls leaving his mouth.

Remy had fought enough vampires to know a frenzy when he saw it.

The man lunged. The Seventh Court kindred closest to the flames dodged to avoid him, but one was not so lucky. More screams rent the air as Edgarth pinned one of his former clansmen to the ground, slashing indiscriminately with sharp fingers.

Remy started forward, but Xiaodan's hand pulled him back. "No," she whispered, sounding grim. "We must allow the Seventh leave to handle this on their own before we intervene."

Already Raghnall was moving, ripping Edgarth free of his victim and flinging him toward the wall. "Control yourself, brother!" he shouted. "You can fight this!"

The force of the throw and the heavy crack the frenzied vampire made when he hit stone should have been enough to kill, or at least incapacitate him. Edgarth shrugged it off, leaping back to his feet. "And if I do not wish to fight it?" he spat, and Remy was shocked to find the man still capable of speech. "Finally, *finally*, I am free of the petty dreams you impose on me. Now I live on my own terms!"

He was changing. His fangs continued to grow until they were far too large for his mouth, which compensated by expanding and lengthening in response. His nose flattened and grew, a much more bestial countenance taking over. His shape followed suit, muscles growing more prominent as his shoulders dislocated with a horrific snap, lengthening as his arms and legs extended and took on a hideous shape. The fabric of his clothes tore, unable to accommodate his new form.

"He is lost," the temple priestess said sharply. "You must take him down now."

And still Raghnall hesitated, unwilling to slay his subordinate. Edgarth took the opportunity to lunge for the Seventh Court leader with a howl, and the latter had enough presence of mind to sidestep the attack. The frenzied vampire struck the ground instead, the stone breaking apart from the force of the blow.

And still none from the other clans helped him. All were tense, though the choice to engage never seemed to materialize. Remy shot a frantic look at Xiaodan, then at Malekh, but the vampire lord slowly shook his head, though he looked frustrated at his own inertia.

Nobody had thought to inform Lorien Tattersall of kindred protocol. The newly minted Second Court leader moved to assist the Seventh; a sword flashed in the darkness, but Edgarth was faster. The weapon was torn from the younger vampire's grip as the frenzied man changed targets abruptly, and soon it was Lorien who was on the ground, the madman on him.

Only then did Malekh act. Before Edgarth's fangs could wreak damage on Lorien's unprotected throat, the transformed vampire was ripped away from the youngblood and thrown to one side. Attuned to her fiancé's actions, Xiaodan was already dragging Lorien away before the Seventh Court kindred could clamber back on his feet, and Remy was immediately by her side to assist.

"Raghnall," Malekh said tersely. "We have no choice."

"He can still beat this," said the Seventh Court king, sounding desperate. "He would never succumb to such—"

"He will be near uncontrollable if you allow him to transform entirely," Fanglei said sharply. "If you will not strike, Seventh, then one of us shall."

Edgarth was nearly unrecognizable at this point from the boisterous, confident vampire he'd been before he entered the Godsflame. A beast had taken his place, eyes mad with triumph and hate.

The vampire roared and moved to attack Raghnall again.

There was an awful ripping sound of metal cleaving through flesh.

Edgarth remained suspended in motion for a moment or so, massive paw stretched out before him as if still intent to maim his liege, who had flickered out of his reach and had reappeared behind him, his massive axe already extended and dripping fresh blood. And then the frenzied vampire crashed to the ground and the great beast's head slid off his shoulders, landing on stone only half a second behind the rest of the hulking body.

Raghnall remained where he was, not bothering to look behind him and see the consequences his axe had wrought. He only looked down at the great blade, watching the red crimson drip down.

"It is done," the priestess said quietly.

The other kindred were not yet inclined to move. Malekh didn't, and neither did Xiaodan, so Remy felt it best to follow their lead. All watched the Seventh Court leader.

Almost absently, Raghnall took out a dirty rag and began to wipe at the surface of his battle-axe until not a drop of blood remained. "He was not worthy," he said calmly, like he had not just decapitated a man he had claimed was like a brother to him. "My apologies for the mess, Priestess. If you will permit the Seventh time to dispose of our burden today, we can resume as discussed on the morrow."

17

THE FOUNT

The Eighth Court leader appeared without warning in the garden that Remy had been loitering at an hour later, had only laughed when the latter had spun around in shock, hand scrabbling behind his back for Reaper. "Be at ease, Armiger. Are we not friends now?"

"What do you want?"

"There is a series of hot springs only a stone's throw from the castle, and I wondered if you would care to explore it with me and my entourage?"

Remy would never accept such an offer, and Hylasenth knew it. "I have no interest in telling you anything about what Lord Malekh or Lady Xiaodan intend," Remy blurted out, choosing frankness over decorum.

"Did you think yourself interesting to me simply because you are with them? Can I not enjoy beautiful company?"

"Appreciate the compliment, but my answer remains no."

"Should you change your mind, just call for my second-in-command." Hylasenth's eyes ran appreciatively over Remy's form. "You are a familiar, Armiger," he said easily. "And this is what familiars do. Once you learn your place in the hierarchy, perhaps you will even come to enjoy it."

He was gone before Remy could give a snippy rebuttal, so instead he glared at the empty space the lord had occupied. "You'd have a better chance of pissing into that damn temple fire undetected than making me doubt them," he muttered.

He was still shaken by what had happened at the Godsflame. Both Malekh and Xiaodan had stayed behind to assess the damage, and it finally hit home to him the extent of the risks each kindred took. Malekh had been right to be cautious. Any hope Remy had entertained of Xiaodan finding a cure within those flames had been successfully squashed by Edgarth's demise.

Staying by the greenery helped, because it almost made Remy feel like he wasn't underground at all. Now that he'd had time to adjust, the cave walls did not trigger his same fears of narrow spaces, as long as he did not deign to look up at the ceiling and ponder the tonnage above him. But his run-in with Hylasenth had rubbed him the wrong way. He was beginning to understand what Xiaodan had meant when she had warned him about the Eighth Court lord.

"Armiger."

Remy flinched before Lady Rotteburg could say more. It was a reflex; even experienced Reapers knew not to mess with the matron, especially when one of her girls' reputations was on the line. He turned around. "Milady," he greeted.

"I only wish to thank you," she said. "For saving my son from the frenzied vampire. He is far too young to know court etiquette, and unfortunately, I know very little of it myself to instruct him."

"Lord Malekh did most of the saving, and Lady Song the rest."

"There is more," Lady Rotteburg said. The linen of her gown twisted under nervous fingers. "I have certain questions regarding some of the customs of the kindred court, and I did not wish to trouble either Lady Song or Lord Malekh after everything. Do all kindred possess marks to identify themselves as part of a certain court? Are such things mandatory?"

"Some kindred do willingly bear the crests of their court on their skin, but only those fully committed to their clan do so, as it is not a requirement. I believe that human familiars also bear the court marks of their kindred, but mainly for protection."

Lady Rotteburg frowned. "That is unfortunate," she murmured. "I am familiar with some of the crests that the court uses for their clans. The Second's was of a white rose, for instance. Many of Redwald's fellow kindred often inked such sigils on their person as their mark of privilege. It was a surprise for me when Lady Cao said that most other courts do not follow such trends."

"Is there a reason why you are so concerned about their crests?"

"One of those who attacked Lorien and I had such a crest on their person. It was tattooed on their thigh, and it was not of the First Court."

"You believe that one of the Night Empress's vassals is from one of the Eight Courts?"

"More than that. It was a sigil of the Fourth. A peony, I believe."

Remy stared at her.

"Now you understand why I hesitated to tell you sooner," Lady Rotteburg said gently. "I do not believe that this is Lady Song's doing. I thought that perhaps the coven had wanted me to see the crest as a red herring, to lay the blame on the Fourth and sow discord."

"Have you told anyone else yet?"

She hesitated. "Only one. But I do not want to tell you their name just yet. Only know that I trust them as I trust you, but no one else within this temple." And then Lady Rotteburg blushed. "I have been working in confidence with a trader of information for some time. It was on her advice that I do this." She smiled briefly.

"I suppose there are perks to being a busybody in the Elouvian court."

Not for the first time, Remy marveled at the extent of Eugenie's reach, and made a note to ask Lord Malekh to push her for details instead.

"I know that I have already asked for too much, but please take care of my Lorien. Lord Malekh and Lady Song were kind to vouch for him."

"They will make sure he is protected," Remy assured her. "As will I."

"I will always be in your debt, Armiger." Lady Rotteburg turned, and Remy saw that Trin was waiting for the older woman, smiling brightly at them. "You need to take your medication, milady!" she called out.

Lady Rotteburg chuckled, sensing his surprise. "She is a good child, whatever my thoughts on her liege. A pleasant companion to spend time with while the rest of you concern yourselves with saving the kingdoms."

"You were quite easy on her," Elke said, materializing at his elbow soon after the two women had taken their leave.

Remy rubbed at his face. "Being rude to her now wouldn't accomplish much. And I believe she's genuinely regretful."

Elke took his arm. "Follow my lead," she said softly, then kept up a deluge of mindless chatter until they had arrived within the confines of his quarters. "Doesn't that strike you as odd? That the Lady Rotteburg would choose to say all that to you out here in public where everyone can overhear?"

"I—I didn't think about that."

Elke sighed. "If I could overhear her, it stands to reason that anyone else would. It strikes me that was her intention. The Lady Rotteburg is playing a dangerous game and risking her life for something she is refusing to divulge to us. Alegra thinks she knows more than she says."

"What has happened with Alegra?"

"Nothing. She saw the Lady Rotteburg poking her nose around and was worried for her. She tried to dissuade her, but that Elouvian woman is like a hound once it's taken hold of a scent."

"No, I mean what's happened between *you* and Alegra?"

Elke coughed. "I've no clue what you mean."

"You're far cozier with each other now than when I last saw her. Something changed between you two in the interim, when I wasn't around."

The woman looked slightly uncomfortable. "She apologized."

"For what?"

"She already knew who I was when I showed up at Chàngge Shuǐ all those weeks ago, looking for you. After you'd had your lovers' spat with Malekh."

"It was *not* a—that's beside the point. How did she know who you were?"

"At Dracheholm. The war between the courts. She was the one to tell Lady Song that I would be better off dead than left alive after they destroyed the Fifth. I didn't remember, but she did. Her guilt had colored her interactions with me since."

"And I take it you've forgiven her because you're so attracted to her?"

"It's a bit more than that." Elke looked to one side, coloring herself. "She often served as the representative of the Fourth Court even before then, sent to serve as either an emissary or messenger. Long before the hostilities between her clan and mine, she had unfortunately witnessed me in varying stages of . . . shall we call it humiliation? . . . by Etrienne during her visits to the Fifth."

"Oh." Remy would much rather not know, but waited quietly anyway.

"Her rejection of my advances was in part her guilt at not having done something to stop his perversions when I was most vulnerable."

"Does it upset you? Will you still pursue her?"

"I remembered nothing of her." Elke smiled gently. "She couldn't have prevented what Etrienne did to me. I wondered why she wasn't responding to any of my overtures, and it was driving me mad."

Remy laughed. "You've just accepted a position to lead the Fifth. Surely you're giving that priority?"

Elke brightened. "Do you mean that I should ask her for her expertise? With Lady Yingyue so often indisposed, she would likely have been managing the Fourth Court in her stead. What a beautiful idea, Remy."

Remy groaned. "Elke."

A knock sounded at the door, and behind it was Thaïs, who bowed. "Armiger, milady. I was asked by Lord Malekh to bring you to the high priestess," she said, smiling rosily at them. "The Hierarch was most insistent that we make haste."

Remy and Elke traded glances. Elke's suspicions regarding the Lady Rotteburg would have to wait.

"Is it common for so many kindred to attempt the Gods-flame?" he asked as Thaïs led them back inside. They were walking through a different part of the castle now, in a wing that he guessed was reserved for the Antecedents' quarters. There was even less ornate decor here, the jewels that were the Allpriory's hallmark less prominent.

"We receive visitors wishing to take their chances every few years. Less than a quarter survive to tell the tale." Thaïs made a small, displeased noise. "Their clansmen often travel with them, usually a court leader to give their blessing. It frequently falls to us to bind the kindred and deliver the killing blow when their companions are loathe to do so." She let out a bitter laugh. "The Seventh Court king, at least, was kind enough to do the deed himself. It wears on one's nerves, Armiger Remington, watching kindred after kindred throw themselves into the flames, knowing few make it out."

"I can only imagine how you can carry that burden with you for centuries," Remy said sympathetically. "But surely it would be easier to live on the surface than remain underground?"

The look Thaïs gave him was warm. "Thank you for your concern, Armiger. As much as we enjoy our brief travels to the surface, we remain steadfast to our commitment to guard the All-priory. We are proud of what we do here, and we take the bad with the good."

They headed up three more flights of stairs. The farther they climbed, the more spartan and austere everything looked. The room they finally entered was completely absent of furniture, save for a small cot at the other end of the room and a small table with nothing but a vase of flowers beside it. Remy had seen penitents' rooms with more furnishings.

The high priestess seemed comfortable with her choice of accommodation. She was kneeling on the floor, and on either side of her were Xiaodan and Malekh, sitting on pillows. Oddly enough, Speck was present as well, looking nervous. Two more cushions lay across from them, and Remy and Elke occupied them both.

"I can understand why you asked for the Lady Whittaker to be present, as she now represents the Fifth," the priestess said. "But I am surprised to find how closely you allow your humans to be involved in affairs of the clan."

"Armiger Pendergast is more than just a familiar to us," Malekh said simply. "And human or not, Spencer is a trusted member of my court."

"Your faith in them may be absolute, but the other clans would not think it wise to make them privy to Allpriory secrets that not even they are aware of."

"The other clans aren't here, Isabella. You cannot push to offer me the Hierarch's seat and then question my orders in the same breath."

"A mere curiosity, that is all. Hylasenth has already made known his views to me, questioning the closeness of your relationship with Aluria given your reluctance to rule the Allpriory. They have every right to harbor such uncertainties."

"It was Armiger Pendergast who was informed that remnants of the Fount still exist within the temple when we all thought it destroyed. It is only fair that he hear more of what you have to say."

The priestess fixed Thaïs with a sharp look, and the younger vampire flushed guiltily. The woman raised her hand, and another aide glided forward bearing a tray that held several teacups and a pot of tea. "Chai," she said as the assistant poured the steaming beverage for them. "I believe it is not a drink you would find often in Elouve, but we have coffee if you are so inclined."

"Chai is good," Remy assured her, taking a sip. It had a thick, strong taste—milky, with surprising heat.

"As for the bloodwood," the priestess continued. "I would like to apologize for choosing to hide it from you, Hierarch. Very few among the clans remember it exists, and I thought it better to excise it from memory."

"If you are as eager to see to its destruction as we are," Xioadan remarked, "then why have you not taken such steps?"

"It is complicated. King Ishkibal despised it as well, though that did not stop him from turning it into his instrument of torture when he so wished. He took particular delight in entrapping his enemies within, relished in their cries of pain as the tree slowly drained them of blood, transforming them into lifeless husks."

Remy thought of the creature that could have been Etrienne

Sauveterre, dying inside the Dracheholm tree, and could not stop himself from shuddering.

"Few but Ishkibal knew of the bloodwood's history, or how closely it intertwined with that of the Godsflame." Isabella's gaze grew distant. "Forgive me," she whispered, though the entreaty was not to anyone in the room. "We chose to obscure the origins of the Godsflame out of fear that kindred would use the temple for ill, to harness its potential."

"You said that you knew little of the Godsflame's origins," Xiaodan said.

"A necessary deception. Long before it was our temple, the Fount was a sacred place for the mortals who dwelled within its territory. They worshiped the tree as a sacred deity, and those who broke their laws were thrown into the flames as punishment."

"Yet one survived and emerged from the fire," Malekh said. "I am aware of the tale."

"The First, yes. She wrought her vengeance on the tormentors of her clan and used their bodies as nourishment. In time, she created her own kindred and kept the bloodwood for her lairs—the Fount here at the Allpriory, and another planted farther south, where the denser soil allowed for it to thrive better than the original."

"The First was responsible for those trees?" Elke asked, looking upset.

"If she imparted the knowledge to the clan in the Whispering Isles, then it stands to reason that the Night Empress may know of it," Malekh said.

"That's why Etrienne devoted himself to the task," Elke said in sudden understanding. "It wasn't simply healing or immortality he was after, but re-creating the Fount itself."

"It would explain his notes, and why he would set fire to parts of the bloodwood at Dracheholm and study its effects," Speck agreed. He turned to the high priestess, visibly excited. "Milady, has anyone been able to divine how the First was able to survive the flames to begin with? Was it some quirk of physiology, some biological novelty on her person that the rest of her people did not have?"

The priestess lowered her head, deep in thought. Eons seemed to pass before she finally raised her head. "Perhaps it will become more apparent after we visit the Godsflame again so that you can see it with your own eyes," she said.

IT WAS Thaïs who seemed to know where the leaders of the other courts were, and she was happy to supply Remy with the information. Yingyue had remained in her room for most of the day with Liufei and Alegra tending to her. The Seventh remained in his rooms after having seen to the full cremation of his fallen subordinate. Inclined as Remy was to dislike the man, he could not help but feel sympathy. Thinking of Edgarth's transformation still made his blood run cold. It had felt far too similar to the mutations his own father had wrought on the kingdom. There was a link in there somewhere, and it all tied back to that damn bloody tree.

There wasn't a tree within the chambers that housed the Godsflame, however. Remy was certain he would have noticed it. But the priestess bypassed that chamber completely and gestured at them to follow her into another passageway beside it, one with a set of stone stairs that led even deeper underground and made Remy sweat. This was more like the caves he hated: narrow passageways and a ceiling barely taller than Malekh, making Remy feel trapped and small. Xiaodan sensed his anxiety and nestled close; her presence helped him breathe easier.

The absence of torches on the walls meant this was not a place for visitors, but Thaïs came prepared with a torch to light the path, though Remy suspected it was more to his and Speck's benefits, since the vampires could see well enough in the darkness. But a sudden flicker of light from a distance caught his eye and took him by surprise.

It was the Godsflame again. Or rather, a lower part of the Godsflame hidden by the landing of the chamber above, which meant they were directly below the platform where the known fires burned. The air felt stale and hot, sooty from the burning pit before them.

"I suggest that none of you stray too far from the torch's light," the priestess warned.

The Fount may have long been gone, but there were certainly roots here. Remy recognized the huge, gnarled vines and branches visible from the ground. Brambles grew all along the walls here, as if the very cave was made up of the tree, but all of them curled back toward where the fires burned.

"No," Xiaodan whispered, sounding stunned. "She's part of the Fount?"

It was not a tree, but a mummy. There were similarities here to the gnarled creature they had found within Dracheholm, their bare bodies more bark than flesh, but this one was nearly horrific in its beauty. It was in the shape of a woman standing in repose, arms that were more spindly twigs than skin folded across her chest. Her eyes had been gouged out, hollowed darkness staring back at them while desiccated vines wrapped around her head like wayward locks, spreading outward like tiny branches, like tapestry woven into the very walls. The vines that encircled her were much like the ones the Night Empress had worn in the Meridian Keep, and even here they bulged ripe to bursting with blood, crimson running close to the surface of the near-transparent wood.

"So," Malekh said. "Rumors of the Fount's demise appear to have been grossly exaggerated."

"Here lies the First," Isabella said. "Her immortal coil fused with the remains of the Fount, for even Ishkibal knew better than to disturb her sleep. And with her as kindling, the Godsflame burns forever more."

"But why?" Elke breathed out.

"Immortality is a lonely thing. When she believed that her life had fully run its course, she died in a place and time of her own choosing. She had hoped to inspire more generations of kindred, to ensure that her line continued in this manner, to fan the fires of the Godsflame above." The priestess sighed, looking up at the twisted face, its hollowed eyes. "This was the choice she made out of love for the new breed she had sired."

"It is not just the First that sleeps beneath the fires," Xiaodan said. She clutched at her chest, a look of pain on her face. "I can see blood running through the branches around her. Whose blood is that, and who does it nourish?"

"It is not to maintain the body itself, if we can still describe it as such," Speck said, more excited than he was afraid, and looking like he would have run closer to inspect the Fount's remains if he didn't fear repercussions. "If we suppose that the vines have the same function as those found in Dracheholm and the Meridian, then they are serving as storage of some sort. Milady, what manner of blood would you choose to keep with such—" He broke off abruptly, finally turning pale.

So did Xiaodan, whose hand was digging into her chest like she would dig out her own heart. Remy's hand closed upon her fingers before she could injure herself.

"It is the First's blood," Xiaodan whispered. "You have her blood running through the veins of the Fount."

"Yes," the high priestess said. "And it is worth more than any treasure in this world, Lady Song, for the healing properties in her blood are found nowhere else. Now do you see why we took great pains to keep this a secret, yet cannot bring ourselves to destroy it?"

18

UPON A THRONE

Elke's next words were a question. "Most of the other kindred do not know of what lies underneath the Godsflame, but Etrienne Sauveterre did, didn't he?"

"Yes," the priestess admitted, laying her hand on the bark. "He theorized how the Godsflame could have continued to thrive for so long and was correct in his assessment. He had expressed his interest in replicating the rejuvenating abilities of the tree, and we had hoped to benefit from his expertise. The results of the studies he'd sent to us were very promising. It was why I was adamant about appointing a Hierarch such as you, Lord Malekh, to have the authority to turn down such inquiries from other clans where we could not. We had not realized he had intended to use his experiments beyond simply healing."

"It didn't matter," Elke muttered. "He would have found the means to spirit some specimens away, whether he received permission or not. How far down do these roots go?"

"Farther than you or I could imagine," Altace said. "We have tried, but we could dig for hundreds and thousands of feet more and never know their true source. Not even we knew how the

Fount and the Godsflame came to be. I do not believe the First herself knew."

"You may not have been aware of Sauveterre's intentions when he took samples of this tree," Malekh said. "But surely you learned of the experiments he had later carried out?"

The priestess shook her head, idly tracing circles on the wood. "While we make short visits to the surface as necessary, we have had little inclination to explore at our own leisure. We heard of the destruction of the Second and the Fifth Courts, of course, but we thought Sauveterre's involvement with the trees ended at his death. We had no idea that the Fifth Court leader had learned to extract life from these roots and transform them into the very creatures plaguing the lands."

"Have you used any of the blood stored within these vines?"

"Absolutely not!" the priestess sounded offended. "The First's blood is sacred to us. Our role is to preserve her remains and keep the flames going."

"But none of you seem happy to let the other kindred into the Godsflame," Remy said. "If you chose to destroy what remains of the First, then surely it would burn out the fires for good and prevent anyone else from making the attempt?"

Lord Malekh smiled grimly. "And then they and their temple would lose their importance as the sacred sanctuary of the courts," he said. "And that would be a worse sin. Is that not right, Your Holiness?"

Isabella raised her chin stubbornly. "We do what must be done to protect what has been relinquished to us. Is not our willingness to divulge these secrets to you proof of our trust, when every other clan leader would kill their own for the chance to reap its mysteries? Gibard, come."

The man stepped forward, a sword in his hands. Before anyone could stop him, he slashed at his own arm, wincing as blood ran down his wrist.

"What are you doing?" Xiaodan cried out.

"Be not worried, milady," the priestess said gently. "Gibard volunteered for the task, to show you that the tree is all that we say it is."

The wounded man approached the woman-shaped tree and allowed his blood to drip onto the bark. Something shifted within the gnarled roots, and the womb-like trunk split open lengthwise, revealing an interior chamber similar to the one at Meridian Keep.

The kindred stepped eagerly enough into its confines, and the hollow closed after him.

"The Fount does not produce abominations like those Etrienne Sauveterre created," the priestess said. "Was that not what you had hoped for? While I have no evidence that Lady Song's sickness could be completely cured here, I believe it would help keep the worst of her symptoms at bay without risk."

"But how?" Speck asked. "Do those who enter become infused with the First's blood?"

"Her blood is a finite resource and not one we would use for treatment, for not even we know what the repercussions are of taking so ancient a blood. No, we draw upon our own supply. We Antecedents willingly volunteer our own at intervals, to hold enough in reserve to tend to any of us who return from aboveground with severe wounds."

It did not take long for the injured vampire to return. The roots parted again, and Gibard emerged, smiling, his arm free of wound and scar.

"I trust that you are candid with us regarding the matter, and that you are concerned for my fiancée's well-being," Malekh said evenly. "All the same, it is not a lack of trust on my part when I ask that some of my kindred inspect the Fount for themselves."

"But of course, Hierarch. Your kinsmen are free to examine the tree to your heart's content." The priestess smiled. "I would not have expected anything less. Anything to ensure that the Lady

Song will be well cared for, should she choose to indulge in the Fount's capabilities. We can even use your blood in lieu of our own, if it comes down to it. Humans can also be healed within its hollow." She looked to Xiaodan. "Have you considered taking to the Godsflame yourself?" she asked.

Xiaodan looked taken aback. "You do your best to talk other kindred out of hurtling themselves into those fires, so why suggest the opposite for me?"

The priestess chuckled, surprising Remy. "My apologies. I only ask out of curiosity, remembering how insistent you were that first day, wishing to see the Godsflame as soon as you were able. Your great-ancestress, Lilith, was one of the few to walk the flames and survive. She had a heart ailment much like yours and was weaker than most kindred before she chose to brave the conflagration. The Fount helped manage her condition before she chose the fires."

"Is that so?" Malekh sounded startled. "I was not aware of that."

"I do not think you would. You knew her as an ally and an able fighter, but not who she was before she came into her abilities as the Sunbringer. She hid many things even from us and her own clan, for times were uncertain under Ishkibal's rule, and trust a rare commodity. In fact, many assumed she already wielded the sun long before she walked into the Godsflame. Unwilling then to give other clans reason to find weakness in her, we tried to maintain such illusions. She was a cambion herself."

"She chose to walk into the Godsflame in the hope of growing stronger?"

"You knew Lilith yourself, my lord Hierarch. Did she ever strike you as one who would put her life in danger simply to gain strength?"

"She had enough determination of character that I did not think she would need more."

"She would not have told you her worries. You were still the

First Court's high executioner, and she was wary that you were but a spy planted by King Ishkibal to monitor dissent among the Fourth. It took time for her to learn trust from you, and you with her. But she knew full well that Ishkibal would kill more kindred if permitted to run untethered, and she was desperate. She thought it a manageable risk, given that her heart shortened her lifespan even without." The priestess sighed. "Even then did she defy the odds. And with her emergence came the birth of the abilities that you yourself have been able to harness, Lady Song."

"Not so much anymore, I fear," Xiaodan said.

"Yes, which is why I wondered if you were willing to travel the same path as your forebear did. But that is not for me to decide." The priestess watched the flames a few seconds more. "Does my explanation satisfy you, Hierarch?"

"It does." Malekh bowed to her. "Another favor that I owe you for, Priestess."

"That you have agreed to serve as Hierarch, no matter how temporary you hope the position to be, is thanks enough."

Remy didn't like the implication behind the words, and neither did Xiaodan, her eyes narrowing.

"I have more unfortunate news to share," the priestess said. "We have not been idle in our search for the Night Empress, as you asked. There have been sightings of her along Vierre; Elspeth and Altace found suspicious covens in the area, though they have yet to attack any of the nearby villages. What is it that you wish us to do?"

"Has anyone seen the Night Empress among those kindred?"

"No. It is possible that she is still recuperating from the wounds she sustained in your previous battles with her, and that these covens are awaiting instruction."

Malekh considered this. "Continue to monitor for any signs they might strike, and if there is movement, bring the news to me regardless of the hour."

"It shall be done, Hierarch."

Xiaodan lingered behind as the others departed, staring at the temple priestess. "Lady Isabella," she said. "If the Night Empress did present a greater claim over the Allpriory than my fiancé and decided that he is to be killed, would you follow her orders?"

The temple priestess regarded her, eyes sympathetic though her words were not. "We have striven for eons to ensure that the clans will not be so divided as it was in the time of King Ishkibal's court," she said firmly. "We will not allow anyone else, no matter how valid their claims to his throne, to destroy what we have striven to preserve all these centuries. We wish for peace more than anything else, Lady Song. We have learned such lessons the hard way."

Xiaodan nodded but didn't look as convinced. "I think she is doing this for more than just to preserve tradition," she said quietly to Remy as they left. "And she never did answer my question. We'll need to keep an eye on her as much as we are everyone else."

Lord Lorien, Lady Rotteburg, and Shiragiku stood waiting when they emerged from the chamber, the former relaxing upon catching sight of them. Lady Rotteburg was curious as ever, trying to sneak peeks inside. Remy was not sure she would have liked what lay within, for all her nosiness, but the horrifying shape of the Fount would not be visible from her vantage point, at least. The priestess remained inside, conversing with her fellow clansmen.

"I wish to thank you for asking Shiragiku to aid my mother and I, milord," he said formally. "Already I've gained much insight from her tutelage—and am in awe of her accounts of human and kindred existing harmoniously within the Third Court. It is something that I want the Second to emulate."

"Shiragiku is one of my trusted lieutenants and an able administrator," Malekh said, and the woman flushed with pride. "She has much more guidance to offer, if you are agreeable to it."

"Milord?" Trin emerged from the shadows, looking bashful. "I understand that the Second has already been introduced to some of the advisors of the other clans, but Raghnall sent me on his behalf. He wanted to send Abel and Forshall, but I convinced him that the Second needs friends more than they need advisers."

"And the Seventh agreed to this?" Xiaodan asked suspiciously.

Trin smiled. "When I asked him to, yes. I hoped that this might be a way to apologize for my court's actions. Raghnall means well, but he often lets his temper get the better of him."

"It sounds like you handle him well."

"He trusts me. However he behaves, he is sincere about seeking peace, even with the mortals."

"I believe her, milord," Lady Rotteburg said warmly. "The more I learn of the hierarchy of the Seventh Court, the more inclined am I to believe that Trin is a notable influence there and means what she says."

"If Lady Rotteburg trusts you, then so will I," Malekh decided, and the young girl beamed happily.

"Milord," Shiragiku said. "Lord Tattersall has asked for advice regarding the recruitment of possible kindred to his court, and I thought you could advise him on where to start."

While the others talked, Trin sidled closer to Remy. "I want to apologize personally to you again," she said. "I was honest when I told you I wished to be friends."

"Do you ever think of it?" Remy asked. "Allowing your lord to turn you?"

Trin looked down at her hands. "He has made the offer, but it is I who hesitate. I am afraid that I will be different as kindred than I am as a human. That what first drew him to me could push him away in the end."

Remy inhaled. "You've just put my own fears into words so simply, when I did not know how to express them."

Trin grinned and patted his hand. "That your kindred are willing to wait is testament to how well you are loved. But I owe it to my own lord to be unwavering and sure when I give my answer. I hope the same for you."

"It is settled, then." Malekh said. "My associates will seek out those interested on your behalf. With all the current chaos, I believe there will be many wanting for the consistency and security a court can bring them."

"As always, you are most kind, milord," Lorien said gratefully.

Lady Rotteburg said nothing. She was staring at something behind her son and frowning thoughtfully to herself. "A coincidence," she muttered. "Such habits are common enough."

"Milady?" Xiaodan prompted. "Is anything wrong?"

After a moment, Lady Rotteburg's face cleared, though the wan smile she shot Xiaodan's way was unconvincing. "It is of no matter," she said. "I am sure it was unimportant."

"THE HIGH priestess never answered my question," Xiaodan muttered, cuddled against Remy. "She said she wanted to keep the peace, but never denied she would stop the Night Empress from taking the throne if she had closer connections to it. Her main priority seems to be maintaining the temple's significance to the courts, as Zidan suggested. Her own clan's importance would be greatly diminished otherwise."

"She does seem particularly single-minded when it comes to her clan," Remy admitted.

"If her kin is more important to her than the Allpriory, then it is the continuing stability of the latter that protects the former." Xiaodan's head was buried against his chest, but Remy could feel her scowl all the same. "Sometimes I wish we'd convinced Malekh better that he needn't be here. That we could have found another way without him being beholden to the Allpriory."

"He was doing what he could for you." *And me*, Remy thought. "Bastard has a bloody noble streak larger than the Morgana."

"That's what makes it worse." She shifted in his arms. "He's late. He promised to come to bed hours ago."

"Kindred business? But surely your courts have evolved beyond paperwork?"

"Kindred like seeing oaths written down on paper. They can be just as bureaucratic as an Elouvian." Xiaodan paused. "We *could* go look for him."

"What are the chances that he would just tell us to bugger on back to our room?"

"Extremely high."

"He won't be happy to know we'd be skulking about the castle," Remy warned, eyeing his clothes folded across one armchair.

Xiaodan was already climbing out of bed. "He'd be furious," she said thoughtfully, finding a heavy robe to wrap around herself. "He'd tell us it isn't safe to be wandering around kindred territory not our own."

"Probably going to punish us," Remy agreed huskily, already warming to the idea.

Xiaodan's eyes danced. "More likely he'd punish you and make me watch," she said, and laughed softly when Remy couldn't stop a short, terse groan.

The threat didn't stop them from leaving their chambers. They encountered no one else in their side of the castle wing, and Remy once again speculated that the temple wings had been separated by clan to prevent bloodshed. Xiaodan and Malekh's quarters, he realized, were closest to the throne room; the priestess had no use for subtlety.

There was a glow of candlelight emanating from within. Remy saw broad shoulders and a muscular back as Malekh bent over several sheafs of paper, facing away from them. The man let out a low, long-suffering sigh and straightened.

"I expect you are both here because of urgent matters," he said, "and not out of whimsy."

"You said you would be joining us soon," Xiaodan accused, and then glanced down at the parchments on the table. "What are these?"

"Reports I requested of the Antecedents to monitor the movements of the coven we suspect are led by the empress. Altace is serving as our scout aboveground, and I expect news from him soon. And then there are the current conditions of the Allpriory, so I may familiarize myself with its maintenance and the supplies they require to maintain its upkeep. Observations of the other courts, as summarized here. It would be safer to take stock of any unusual behaviors or activities, in case the Night Empress has planted her own spies among the courts."

"They're not going to like that," Remy said.

"It was standard practice in Ishkibal's day. If they're so keen on falling back on old customs, then they should give me no protest on this." Malekh ran a hand through his hair. "I'll be along shortly."

"No, you won't. I know you well enough, love." Xiaodan picked up one of the parchments. "Is there any way we can help you speed up the process?"

"I'm almost finished. It would do no good for you to forsake your own rest."

"On the contrary, I think you need it the most out of us three." Setting the piece of paper back down, Xiaodan drew closer to the throne, staring up at it. And then, to Remy's shock, she stepped onto the dais and plunked herself down on the royal seat.

"Xiaodan," Malekh began, wary but not angry.

"It's a throne, my love. Nothing more than that. You have no wish to sit on it, and I understand. But there's no need for you to look at it as if Ishkibal's spirit might rise up from it still. Don't give him any more power."

The earnestness in her voice, coupled with the worry, was enough to bring a faint smile to the lord's face. "It is not Ishkibal that plagues me when I look at the throne." He turned away from the table and closed the distance between them. Slowly, he knelt before Xiaodan, taking her hand, and the familiarity of the movement, the ease in which he crouched by her feet and found space there, made Remy wonder if this was something he had done often at the height of the First Court's rule. It was reminiscent of how he himself had sat by Xiaodan's feet during the council's sessions.

"I do not know if I can lead the kindred," Malekh said softly. "You know that I have no love for rule. My founding of the Third stemmed from necessity rather than ambition. If anything, I would think you a better fit to rule in my stead. I would much rather while away my days in my laboratory than play at being king."

Xiaodan only nodded, sure enough of herself not to play at humility. "And I would take that burden from you if I could. Even so, you cannot tell me that you are unmoved by the centuries within these walls. There was a reason you were so reluctant to come here."

Something sparked in Malekh's gaze. "Then perhaps you will help me to make better memories of this place."

"I have yet to sup," Xiaodan said slyly.

"In here?" Remy blurted out. He cast a slightly panicked look about him, though he could find no evidence of either eavesdroppers or voyeurs.

But hadn't he seen his share of kindred and familiars alike along corridors and inside open rooms for anyone to see because of that blasted perverted vampiric need for public displays of subjugation, even if they were pleasurable ones?

Xiaodan leaned back against the throne, parting her legs slightly for them both.

Bloody Light, but these vampires were corrupting him.

And Malekh, despite his paperwork, appeared willing to indulge. He let Xiaodan lean forward and sink her fangs into the curve of his neck, offering her sustenance. Remy's mouth watered at the sight of the vampire lord so vulnerable, head thrown back and eyes closed as he allowed his fiancée to have her fill. And when she finally pulled away, Remy watched, entranced, as small droplets of blood clung to her mouth, a small trickle running down one side of her chin.

He hadn't realized he'd climbed the dais with them as well, his feet moving of their own accord. At the crook of Xiaodan's finger he bent, copying Malekh's position so that he was on the other side of the throne in a similar posture. She kissed him sweet and slow, allowing him the faint taste of Malekh's blood. It burned through his veins like the sweetest aphrodisiac, stronger than any bloodwaker he'd ever consumed.

"Please, puppy," Xiaodan said, but within that pleading lay a command.

It wasn't long before his stays were unfastened and his breeches gathered at his feet. He loomed over Xiaodan as she guided him into her, their groans in unison as he thrust impossibly deep, the angle by which she was splayed and the position he was now in an advantage. Her teeth were on his neck now, that pleasure-pain spiking through his senses until the only thing he wanted was to keep her satisfied even if it killed him.

He couldn't stop the moan that tore through him, unspeakably loud, at the sensation of the suddenly oil-slicked fingers of Malekh behind him, the sound bouncing across the room. "You're too noisy, pet," he heard the lord whisper, but the fingers drove mercilessly into him all the same, as if daring him to repeat the action. Remy did, louder than before.

"They're going to hear him," Xiaodan said breathlessly, caught between a gasp and a giggle.

"Let them hear us ruining him," Malekh murmured, leaving Remy drawn taut and tight against his touch.

She reached up to her neck and drew a thin line across the nape. Spellbound, Remy watched as blood trickled out of the small cut she had made before she was drawing him even closer, encouraging him to take from her the same way she'd taken from Malekh.

And Remy feasted, the sweetness of her keeping him silent even as Malekh's fingers withdrew, were quickly replaced, until soon he was a writhing, senseless heap between them, both his lovers beginning a rhythm they had perfected with each other over the years and now sought to instruct him with.

He knew that they would be a sight to anyone passing by, defiling King Ishkibal's throne in this manner. He no longer cared about the consequences, only the brightness and love in Xiaodan's eyes as she beheld him, and Malekh's harsh breathing behind his ear, the possessive way the man's hand anchored at his hip. And when the lord paused long enough to turn his face to his, Remy felt the burst of flavor on his tongue as Malekh granted him another taste. Caught between the two people he loved most in the world, he no longer cared about prying eyes, his vision whiting out until he thought he would go blind.

He sagged between them after what must have been hours, the amount of blood he'd consumed from them no substitute for natural vampire stamina. He heard Xiaodan hum, felt her press his head against her chest as he slumped against her. "Did this help your dislike of thrones, love?" he heard her breathe to Malekh, who responded with a rare laugh.

"Aye," the lord murmured, his fingers burning a line of heat down Remy's back wherever he touched. "Perhaps we should try once more to make sure I am done with such repugnancies."

HE SHOULD have slept soundlessly that night, body ridden to exhaustion and satiation as only Malekh and Xiaodan could wring from him.

Instead, he stood in a burning field, the smell of acrid smoke and flesh heavy on his tongue. There was a village burning before him, houses collapsing from their own weight, succumbing to the quickly spreading flames.

The Night Empress took little stock in their surroundings. She was staring at him, mouth partly opened in surprise.

Malekh and Xiaodan were beside Remy, each looking startled to be there as well.

You love them, the Night Empress said in wonder.

19

THE HUNT

Morning came with Altace's return to the temple, bearing grim tidings. "There is fresh movement among the covens," he reported to Malekh. "They're headed back west, in our direction. They are becoming more brazen, making no attempt to hide themselves."

"If they've been mobilizing since last night, then they would have arrived at the lake by now," Xiaodan argued. "Unless they've become very adept at hiding themselves. Not likely, since there aren't as many places in which to conceal themselves in the terrain just aboveground."

"My father would have already been alerted to their actions if so," Remy said. He, Elke, and Xiaodan sat within the adjoining room of the chambers he now shared with Xiaodan and Malekh. He was the only one of the three making use of the table as intended, wolfing down the breakfast fare. Malekh was absent, having left to consult with the high priestess on the defenses the Allpriory possessed.

"Certainly they're up to no good, but I'm not going to entertain any speculations just yet without other information on hand." Xiaodan cast a worried look at Remy. "Malekh thinks that you were able to pull us into your dreams due to the bloodsharing. But it wasn't quick enough for me to take stock of where we were. You saw the empress standing before a burning village? Do you remember anything more beyond what you've already told us?"

"I didn't have time to understand much of it." Remy took a fortifying gulp of wine. The Antecedents had not questioned him when he'd asked for a bottle, though it was Elke, of all the hypocrites, who chided him for indulging so early in the day. "But it *felt* recent, like she was reacting to me as it happened. She didn't initiate it."

"What did the Night Empress see that startled her so? Did she say anything to you?" Elke asked.

Remy flushed. "It's of no consequence—beside the point." He glanced at Elke, who was looking at him a touch too serenely. "You know," he said, resigned.

Elke convulsed into gentle laughter. "Even if I'd heard nothing, it's quite obvious from your scent."

Remy wanted to crawl under the table and die, because it was even worse than he imagined. "You *heard* us? You can *smell* it? I bloody bathed!"

"I'm sure your lovers were well enough aware of their surroundings to have defended themselves, should anything have happened, but Alegra and I nonetheless did a fairly good job, pointedly turning any vampires away from the great hall under the excuse of not interrupting the Hierarch and the Fourth Court leader at work." Elke's eyes gleamed. "Though I neglected to mention that *you* were what they were working on."

"*Alegra* was there?"

"We tried to give you as much privacy as we could, given the circumstances. As Xiaodan is now the Fourth Court leader, even if only during our time here, Alegra insisted that she be afforded constant protection just like her mother. In fact, she's standing outside the door right this instant, to discourage eaves-droppers."

"You and Alegra have been spending more time with each other," Xiaodan said with a smile. "I take it that you are reconciling whatever it is that troubled you two before?"

"Of a sort, yes," Elke said, the slight pinkish cast on her cheeks saying everything.

"I'm glad to hear it. As to the matter regarding the Night Em-press." Xiaodan folded her arms and scowled. "I would like to be-lieve for your sake that she intends no harm, Remy. But we must be prudent and assume that she is once again trying to infiltrate your dreams in a bid to win you to her side."

"I'm not sure she is in as much command of this as you think," Remy mumbled into his bread. "I had a vision of her digging her way out of her own grave, panicked and disoriented, and I do not think it was an attempt to deceive me. I felt her fear and bewilder-ment as if they were my own."

"If she was revived shortly after her death, then she would have had twenty years to learn," Xiaodan said. "Even if Wikaan do not remember their own vampires."

"We should take advantage of my link to her. Getting into her mind could tell us where she is at the moment, even divine where she might strike next. It worked before." Remy closed his eyes. "There was a statue," he said, after several moments' thought. "Of a flock of birds in midflight. It was partly razed by fire, but enough of it remained intact to recall it in my mind's eye, even though I've never seen it before."

Xiaodan was staring at him. "Verlouze," she said promptly. "A village in Kerenai territory. That statue is the highlight of the town's plaza, carved by an artisan who was born there. Ten birds with their feet tied to a carriage behind them, soaring through the air? Inspired by an old Kerenai fairy tale, as I recall."

"Yes, although most of the carriage had not survived the flames."

"That is proof enough." Xiaodan stood. "I'll need to talk to Altace."

"How did you know, milady?" The man was astounded when Xiaodan asked. "I had only just returned from making a report to both the priestess and to the Hierarch, and I had spoken to no one else of it. Yes, Verlouze was the place the coven was last sighted at."

"All the more reason for Pendergast to take his medication rather than letting it lapse another night," Malekh said grimly when they found him next. "The temple clan may not have the same reach as Eugenie's informants, but we should be informed early enough of her movements through their own sources without the need to endanger you."

"Except you can learn of the Night Empress's activity within minutes, as opposed to the hours it takes Altace to return," Remy argued. "Light, Malekh, didn't you say you could find a way to yank you and Xiaodan into my dreams so you could see for yourself?"

"What would be irresponsible is forcing you within reach of the Night Empress for her to compel you a second time," Malekh said sternly.

"I don't think she wants to compel me anymore. Not after that first time." He had felt her horror and her guilt when he'd told her he had killed Naji because of her machinations.

You love them. It had not been an accusation, nor from anger. She had merely spoken the words as if she had not entertained the idea before.

"I cannot stake the well-being of everyone else here in the Allpriory on a maybe," Malekh said after a pause. "We can attempt contact in a controlled environment of my choosing, with both my kindred and Xiaodan's in attendance."

Remy brightened. "Truly?"

"If it shall take that woebegone look off your face, then yes. I know you well enough. We can try it your way later, once preparations for the Allpriory's defense have been completed. Isabella believes that the Night Empress will be attacking the village of Cardan soon enough, and that is only a hundred miles away—no large feat for a coven to traverse. While the other kindred have pledged to our cause, I would like to see them putting their words into action for true."

"How did I look at him?" Remy asked after Malekh had gone.

Xiaodan grinned mischievously. "Like an adorable little puppy wanting his master's attention. You don't seem to be aware of it when you do that, but Zidan most certainly is."

Puppy. The word she'd breathed into his ear last night.

Malekh's had been not quite as innocent-sounding, filthier somehow. *Pet.*

Remy swallowed.

"Are you sure about this?" Xiaodan asked, mind already on a different track. "I trust you, Remy. But I can't trust her."

"This is the best option we have, and you know it."

Xiaodan wrinkled her nose at him. "Incidentally, they found the vampire that your father uses as his messenger. He waited at the lake's edge for close to an hour, taking no pains at all to hide himself."

"Of course he would learn the Allpriory's location," Remy muttered.

"He did bring us news confirming the covens' occupation at Cardan. We know now why they've taken some time to get here— your father's army has been engaging them, slowing down their progress."

Remy tensed. "Is he all right?"

"The messenger swears Lord Pendergast was hale and hearty when he left. Malekh intends to lead a small contingent to render assistance to the Alurians. He would prefer that you stay here at the temple, but he also knows you have every right to accompany us if you wish to."

"You already know my answer." His leg jiggled underneath the table. He didn't want to worry for his father, but . . .

"I know." Xiaodan's smile was bright and unwavering. "I've already laid out your Reaper clothes on our bed. It's about time the other kindred saw just how well you use Breaker."

REMY'S ASCENT to the lake's surface was just as nerve-wracking as when he'd been dragged down with Malekh. He broke through the waters sputtering and gasping, grateful when the lord towed him firmly back to shore rather than let him flounder alone. It wasn't quite the best impression to make in front of the other clans, especially when decked out in Reaper black, but Remy let himself be pulled toward to firmer ground with as much dignity as he could muster.

The helhests were waiting for them, fortunately; having to cling to Malekh's back while they charged into battle would have killed what little remaining respect for him they had.

Peanut kept pace with the other vampires as they tore through the plains. The Sixth, Seventh, and Eighth Court leaders had sent representatives from their respective courts to aid them, including their seconds-in-command: an easygoing kindred named Krylla who served as Hylasenth's right-hand woman; a Seventh Court giant named Grager, and Si Daoming. Elke and Alegra had chosen to remain behind to guard the Lady Rotteburg, while the kindred leaders preferred to remain behind and observe before truly committing themselves to the cause.

Reassured that his mother was in good hands, Lorien Tattersall had insisted on accompanying them, and Xiaodan promised to keep an eye on him.

"My mother talked a lot about you," the Second Court leader said after they'd stopped briefly to get their bearings.

"She did?" Remy asked, taken aback.

"She never thought that you were a true cambion, although some of the court in Elouve said so." The boy's eyes were shining. "And still you held your head high, never shirking from the responsibilities and duties laid out before you. She said you were someone that I should aspire after."

That nearly bowled Remy over, given how brusque and suspicious she'd always been of him back in the city. "Ah," was all he managed to say.

"I heard about what happened." Lorien flushed. "The mob at Elouve, what they tried to do. It was my mother's greatest fear, to be discovered that way and have me come to harm. I am sorry."

"You defended your home—and her—valiantly," Remy said. "And that you are here speaks much of your character. I'm glad to have you with us."

The youth smiled. "Lord Malekh has been most kind. He offered me use of his other Third Court territories while I decide where to build my own clan. Fighting by his side is the least I can do. But I should let you rest." He bowed awkwardly, and Remy watched him leave. "You see a bit of him in the boy, too, don't you?" he muttered, though Malekh couldn't hear.

It was no more than an hour later when they crested a small hill and beheld the Alurian army camped below. The tents and the state of their campfires indicated they'd been gathered there at least half a day, though none of the soldiers seem any worse for wear. There was a larger contingent of Reapers now than before. Garbed in their black coats, they lingered on the edges of the camp, on the lookout for any signs of attack.

He'd been hoping that his father would forgo the use of any

more mutations, but his hopes were dashed when he spotted Grimesworthy lurking just outside of the periphery of the camp, motionless, like some great tree trunk sprouted on the ground. With him were two dozen more of Quintin Yost's experiments, just as unmoving and even more repugnant, their lack of humanity obvious in their flayed limbs and tumors, shunted as far away from camp as the soldiers dared.

A few Reapers spotted them and called out an alarm, and within moments the camp was a flurry of activity: hunters snatching up their fire lances, soldiers scrambling for swords and bows. From one of the larger tents a man emerged, and even from this distance, Remy recognized his father.

"Stand down!" Lord Pendergast called out calmly. "This is not an attack, these are reinforcements!"

Many of the Reapers paused, unwilling to give up their weapons now that they were on hand, but Xiaodan was quick enough to head off any unpleasantries. She blurred back into view right before the encampment, keeping just outside the boundaries, radiating a harmlessness that Remy knew better than to believe. "Lord High Steward," she greeted. "When we received word of your encounters with the First Night coven, we wanted to rush to your aid in all due haste."

Remy's father laughed. "We fended them off well enough. Without their accursed witch they posed little danger to us, though more to bolster our ranks will always be welcomed." He gestured again, and his fighters reluctantly lowered their weapons. "I trust, then, that your council has been successful?"

"That remains to be seen, Lord Pendergast," Grager said abruptly. He, too, remained outside the circle of Alurians, eyeing them warily. "I am Grager, second to Lord Armaros of the Seventh. I've never met the Night Empress myself, but I am here to test her mettle, and yours as allies. Whether or not this becomes a more permanent agreement will depend on what you do next."

Lord Pendergast raised an eyebrow, unintimidated. "A step in the right direction, for as long as you do not get in our way. We hold no love for kindred as you well know, Lord Grager, but I am willing to set aside our differences for as long as you fight with us against the First Court. I mean to destroy the Night Empress, with you or without."

"Then we are, for the moment, in accord," Daoming said cheerfully, stepping in before Grager could utter another word, with Krylla at his heels. "Felicitations, Duke of Valenbonne. I am Si Daoming of the Court of Cultivation, and my companion here is Krylla of the Court of Pleasures. You must forgive our abrupt companion. We were surprised to find a vampire under your employ, and that he was well aware of the location of our council." He paused, as if choosing his next words carefully. "Some of the other kindred had gone so far as to venture that your young son has been supplying you with information of our activities."

Lord Pendergast snorted. "I would be a very incompetent lord high steward indeed if I had not been able to ferret out information through other means. To your credit, we would not have found your temple at all had these not been . . . more interesting times, shall we say, and I am sure you have protocols in place to dissuade us from exploring further. I have not had contact with my son since his departure from the Third Court's domain, but I do employ skilled scouts. Enough to know that the Sixth Court has been populating the villages from here to Elouve with kindred pretending to be mortal, keeping track of my army's movements as we traveled west."

Daoming showed neither agitation nor concern at that. "I am impressed. Though I must confess that there is nothing standard about those great hulks you have guarding your camp."

"Oh, those old things?" Lord Pendergast asked with a lazy wave of his hand. "Just a few odds and ends we picked up along the way. Quite a burden to bring along, if I may be frank, and a reasonable cause of concern among my own men, but more than worth the trouble. One more vampire dying at their hands is one less for my soldiers to handle." He chuckled. "You'll get used to them in time. I am as ever grateful that you would rush to our assistance, milord, but we have, unfortunately, seen neither hide nor hair of the enemy since yesterday. The covens that rushed to attack us are fewer in number than those we encountered in Kerenai, though the men I have left stationed within Hallifax's kingdom tells me that they have seen even fewer. At any rate, Yost has returned to Elouve to develop more mutations, should they be needed."

"We have reason to despise the Night Empress ourselves," Daoming said. "She has been responsible for many atrocities committed in and around Situ, and my mistress is not one to take such matters lightly. We are not without our own scouts, who suggest that a heavier contingent is set to make landfall along these parts soon enough. Until we are able to corroborate such reports, we would be more than pleased to offer you our company—within reasonable distance of your own camps."

"I think that would be best. I am most pleased to see that kindred can be just as noble as one from the Alurian court." Lord Pendergast gazed at the scowling Grager.

The Seventh's second-in-command grunted, heels clicking together as he shifted into a soldier's stance. "We, too, pledge ourselves to defend the Alurians—for now." And with that threat, he spun around to return to where the others from his clan stood waiting.

"It seems that you have found yourself in quite esteemed company, Lady Song," Lord Pendergast remarked.

"Don't I know it," Xiaodan said wearily.

"I must confess," Krylla said conversationally, "that I have never found myself allied with the Alurian army before. My sire bade me commend Your Grace for the efforts he has undertaken to ensure that the covens in Kerenai are put down as swiftly as possible. As his territory adjoins King Hallifax's to the north, he has been just as determined to slay the Night Empress's minions from the other end of the kingdom."

"It is my honor to have helped alleviate his problems in however small a capacity," the duke said wryly.

"He is also quite taken with your son, Lord Valenbonne. He was pleased to learn that the practice of familiars is being looked upon with more favor in Aluria, despite the misunderstandings that have stemmed from the past. Had Lord Malekh and Lady Song not claimed him so thoroughly, he would have been moved to make an offer himself."

Inexperienced as Remy was with intrigue, he recognized the bait for what it was. He felt Xiaodan pause beside him, though not so tense that it gave her away. For his part, he let himself relax.

"Did he now," said Valenbonne, somehow managing to convey a sword's blade despite the calm of his tone. He allowed a faint quirk of his eyebrows, as if pondering why Krylla would need ask him such a trite question.

"I have yet to see him in a fight myself, though if he comports himself in the same way, I would be more than impressed. Fierce as he is, he is quite the docile little thing at Lady Song's feet, and it's quite a beautiful thing to see. The noises he makes in the throes are quite exquisite. That weapon strapped across his back is enough to give one nightmares, however. I'm told you wielded it yourself enough times in the past. The Seventh in particular has crossed blades with it and knows the names of every kindred to have fallen before your blade."

"As well as we know the names of every Reaper and hunter who have gone down from a vampire's bite," Valenbonne said. "Which is why it is a fine day to cast those differences aside and take down another that poses a far greater danger."

"Yes," Krylla conceded. "On that, we are of one mind. I only thought to warn you, Lord Valenbonne, that there are some among the clans discontented by this turn of events—those who would rather seek to treaty with the Night Empress than look to the Alurians as allies. I speak for the Eighth when I say that we have no intentions of breaking our oath, but it would do well to stay on guard. As things stand, we cannot let our alliance falter, lest everything else descend into chaos."

"It seems you have yet to rein in some of the more dangerous members of your council, if this kindred's words are to be believed," Lord Valenbonne said once the Eighth Court vampire had walked away.

"It's not so easy as it sounds," Remy found himself snapping before Malekh could say a word. "She's trying to warn you of the Seventh and his clan."

"Not just the Seventh. I suspect that some of her own kindred are of the same mind as Lord Raghnall, though diplomacy prevents her from saying so aloud. They will honor their vows for today, but tomorrow may demand a different treaty." He smiled grimly at the look on Remy's face. "Did you not think I would be aware of their leaders' names? Raghnall of the Seventh, Hylasenth of the Eighth, Fanglei of the Sixth. And Queen Yingyue, of course. The Marquess of Riones is a competent administrator. He has put Astonbury's chaos into some semblance of order, has selected the best runners to draw more information as we can about these courts." He nodded at one of his aides, who went scurrying off. "We will need to speak of how we shall be coordinating our efforts with what little light still remains, Lord Malekh."

"I will leave you two to your discussion, then." Xiaodan placed a hand on Remy's arm. "Shall we?"

Remy nodded. He had so many things he still wanted to say to his father, but no idea how to go about it.

But Lord Pendergast only nodded briefly to him, dismissing him immediately. The bow he presented to Xiaodan was low and florid.

"It strikes me that he is embarrassed, just as much as you," Xiaodan said, once they were out of sight.

"I have never seen him ashamed of anything, and I doubt that he would start now."

Xiaodan hummed thoughtfully but said nothing else.

The kindred were wise enough not to draw nearer to the camp despite their newfound alliance, but Xiaodan had no such compunctions. She strode past the tents like it was she who was their commanding leader, and not even the Reapers dared stop her. A few even went so far as to mutter "milady" when they were within hearing. It wasn't much, but Remy, who had been expecting hostility, was relieved by the bare minimum they were providing.

The only real friendly face among the soldiers was the Marquess of Riones, who sprang to his feet with a wide smile when he caught sight of them, all but tripping over himself in his eagerness. "You're a fine sight to see, old friend," he said cheerfully enough, but Remy saw the bloody smears on his boots and the rips in his coat. Anthony Castellblanc was very particular about his clothes and would never suffer for them to be in this condition.

"Bloody Light, Riones," he said. "My father said all you'd had were light skirmishes, but that isn't the case, is it?"

Riones gave an embarrassed shrug, like he'd somehow been found wanting. "It was, at first. Pockets of coven few enough not to cause undue worry when we were in Kerenai. But Lord Valenbonne thought the scarcity in numbers meant they were merely distractions and gave the order to pack up. Hallifax finally pulled his head out of his ass enough to muster some kind of defense beyond his capital, and your father thought not even the king's soldiers could muck it up." He looked around. "Still don't know why he chose this place to bog us down at. Not quite Aluria, is it? A bit north past her borders, but not quite anyone else's territory, either. Nothing of note here, though it's a good place to see incoming attacks. No woods to speak of, flat plains save for that small hill over yonder."

"Your commander is a wise man who knows his history," Xiaodan said dryly. "This place has served as neutral grounds many times in the past between human and kindred, though I'm told those cease-fires never last long."

"Truly? They never tell us any of that in Reaper training," Riones confessed, scratching at his beard.

"Those truces were few and far between. I only know of them because it was Zidan who arranged for half of those stalemates, and it was how his court and Aluria's got to talking in the first place." Xiaodan glanced around at the other soldiers nearby, who were intent on not looking their way. "Is there anything about those covens you can tell me without receiving censure from Lord Valenbonne?"

The man guffawed out loud. "I'll tell you gladly, milady. If Valenbonne's right, then you might have to face them with us soon enough. The covens all wore scarlet robes, as expected, but many of them were young—far too young. Remy, do you remember all those reports you received about children going missing?"

"Surely you don't think—"

"Ah, but I do. Once I made the connection, I started looking through some of the files you've already perused, and even more that you hadn't had the opportunity to. Not all of the cases were abductions. A disturbing number of runaways, for instance. I sent some of my men over to interview those families, and they admitted that many of those boys and girls were not happy with their home life for a variety of reasons, many of them heartbreaking. It took a lot not to punch a few of those parents in the face, knowing what I knew."

Hadn't Vasilik done the same? He'd boasted of taking in children for his court who'd been mistreated by their families. It pissed Remy off that the man had, for once, told the truth.

"Your father won't say it out loud, Remy," Riones went on, "but he's worried about you and happy that you've all arrived to help, as much as he'll insist the Alurian army have come well prepared. We've even seen a few of those bloody faces they've been hiding under their cowls. We've even sketched out some of the ringleaders—"

"Incoming kindred!" The shout echoed across the campsite. "We're under attack!"

Riones grabbed for his fire lance and Remy drew out Breaker. Xiaodan, as always, was faster; she reappeared on the other side of the encampment, where soldiers were already leveling their weapons at the hooded vampires that came hurtling forward . . . bringing the Rot with them. They were huge, lumbering creatures, perhaps two dozen in total, and though they lagged by the enemies' rear, they were moving far more quickly than Remy would've liked.

He heard his father cursing loudly even as he began to issue orders, saw the other kindred engaging with the vanguard. Reluctant as some of the clans had been to offer aid, they attacked in full force, meeting the crimson-clad kindred without hesitation.

But unlike the reports they received and Riones's own account of their recent battles, there were far too many vampires, as if the Night Empress had finally committed to a full-scale attack. Remy saw Malekh in the lead, cutting down foes before turning to deal with the mutations. Valenbonne's own thralls were lumbering forward to meet their coven counterparts, and there was a roar of triumph as Grimesworthy ripped one mutation's head from its many necks.

"Shit," Remy said, and ran.

20

A BETTER CLAIM

The Rot-spawned creatures, as expected, were even more revolting up close, but surprisingly fully formed. Remy's past experiences had been of creatures made from decaying skin and walking sores much like the ones his father controlled, Grimesworthy being the sole exception. But these mutations, while monstrous in feature, didn't look like melting, unfinished creations. They looked like fantastical beasts sprung from some demented bestiary, and their similarity to the ones that Remy had fought outside of the Fata Morgana confirmed exactly who had sent those monsters.

These, too, had scales and sharp claws and were roughly ten feet tall, but with terrifying new additions. Heavy horns added another two feet to their height, and their mouths were ringed with massive fangs that extended a meter or so past their jaws. Several were multi-headed, in alarming pairs of twos and fours. They looked to be a combination of the dragons from old storybooks and upright, walking snakes.

Malekh ignored the covens and focused on the scaled mutations. One tumbled to the ground sans heads, the torn appendage landing with a thump a few feet away. The body continued to flail about, limbs contorting as it struggled to stand. The Summer Lord ripped through another, and only then did it become more apparent that they were like the mutations of old; lesions bubbled up from their wounds, scales shearing off to reveal the same symptoms as those afflicted with the Rot.

Xiaodan was right behind Malekh. A punch was enough to crush the monster's head completely.

The rest of his father's corpses joined the fray. Grimesworthy drove his axe toward one of the beasts, the force enough to cleave its body in two. It fell to the ground, but the wound immediately began knitting together. Lord Valenbonne drew his bow, took aim, and shot it in the chest. The creature shuddered and remained still.

Remy was still too far from the wave of mutations, so he focused on the approaching kindred instead—and froze.

Riones was right; they were far too young. Faces that could not have been older than sixteen or seventeen years, maybe even younger, transformed into baleful red eyes and long fangs. Remy remembered the caves at the Dà Lán, when Vasilik had trapped him in a cavern full of children even younger, using Remy's past against him, confident that he would not fight back.

Remy gritted his teeth and fought back this time.

He didn't want to think about who he was killing, about how Breaker's scythes were coming down on skin and neck, blood spurting up as they tried to defend themselves. Didn't want to think about how he'd done this over ten years ago, fighting for his life in a cave by Elouve, how similar it was to the fellow novices who'd been turned that day and had attacked him in their frenzy. These weren't the Reaper recruits he'd trained with. They had chosen to become kindred, even if they'd been misled.

And then Xiaodan was by his side. "Zidan may need some assistance," she said, even as she cut down another without Remy's initial hesitation. "There are far too many creatures there even for him and the clans."

She was giving him a lifeline, and he seized it, grateful. "Thank you," he breathed as the coven shifted their target, likely recognizing her. Xiaodan flashed him a brief smile before she withdrew, luring them away from Remy so he wouldn't have to relive his past yet again.

Grimesworthy was more than a match for his current opponent, but one of Lord Valenbonne's other creations wasn't as lucky, torn limb from limb by the scaled creatures surrounding it. Fortunately, the coven mutations that had already gone down hadn't come back up again; his father likely treated their weapons with an antidote similar to what Malekh had created to ensure they could not be revived. "These Rot have poison!" Remy shouted, plunging one of his scythes deep into a monster's chest, sending it stumbling back.

His father nodded; he had put away his bow in favor of his battle-axe, which he now slashed at the same beast Remy was harrying. Remy had never fought alongside his father in battle before, but the man had taught him everything he knew. Their moves flowed together, borne from the same techniques, the same practices. They made quick work of the creature, Valenbonne slashing at its head and massive shoulders while Remy focused on its lower extremities, until finally it sank down. His father let out a shout, and an arrow buried itself into the fallen corpse, ensuring that it would never rise again.

Remy knew colossi well enough; they could control other lesser mutations despite being mindless drones themselves, using some basic instinct to herd them together and take charge. The colossus controlling this particular group was easy enough to detect: larger and bulkier than the rest, its scales blacker than the bluish hues of its minions, and with six heads and long necks joined at the shoulders like some demented hydra. The other court kindred were at Malekh's side, fighting off the rest of the Rot while the Summer Lord moved to confront the colossus. The grotesque creature proved far more difficult to defeat. Malekh's saber damaged it little; the blade should have easily sliced through its skin, but the colossus simply batted it away.

Remy rushed to the lord's side, noting that Lorien had done the same. The younger vampire was proving himself handy with a longsword, and he settled himself to the right of the monster, distracting him with slashes that nonetheless did only as much as damage as Malekh's had. Remy thrusted forward with Breaker to make his own attempt; it was like hitting a steel shield.

Xiaodan had taken out her share of coven; leaving the rest for Lord Valenbonne's men to handle, she flew across the battlefield toward them, eyes narrowed at the gigantic mutation.

"Don't do it, Xiaodan!" Remy yelled, even as he redoubled his efforts. He resorted to his knifechain instead, whipping the spike through the air. It bounced off the colossus's scales like a toy.

Xiaodan wasn't listening. Her brows were drawn, and she hunched over in concentration. Remy slid back to her side, cutting down any other vampires taking advantage of her distraction. "Don't do it," he said again.

"I don't think we have a choice," Xiaodan said, already breathing hard from the exertion.

Frustrated by their lack of progress, Lorien moved closer, swinging his sword hard. The creature had turned its focus to Malekh, and the edge of his blade caught onto its horn, cutting off a hefty piece. A black, vile liquid spilled down from the wound.

With a roar, the colossus whirled back, enraged, and struck out at the Second Court leader. The boy's sword was still raised in the air, and Remy knew he would not be able to bring it back down in time.

Malekh was quicker. He caught the blow that had been meant for Lorien, and a hard shove sent the colossus stepping back.

Blood ran down the front of his coat, but Malekh paid it no attention. He swung his saber, this time targeting with deliberation what Lorien had cut off by accident. The creature was too slow to block him, and another horn broke away, more of the black substance flowing down one of its heads. Now that he had a target in mind, Malekh made swift work of the monster, rendering the rest of its heads hornless.

The colossus staggered. This time, when Malekh shifted his aim to strike across the mutation's stomach, the flesh was cut open immediately. It howled, but Malekh had scented weakness and was relentless. Remy did the same, using his knifechain to score more wounds across the creature's back, the flesh now tearing easily where it had once been like stone.

Malekh moved in for the final kill, severing the monster's necks seemingly all at once with a wide sweep of his saber. The thing gagged, choking on its own blood, and then fell.

The other beasts staggered, dropping to the ground as dead as their leader. The mutations that Remy's father controlled paused, looking around hungrily as if craving more to fight.

The rest of the enemy coven retreated rapidly, leaving only their dead and the cheers from both soldiers and Reapers in their wake. Lord Valenbonne remained where he was, ever watchful, eyes scanning the area around him.

"There's something else here," he said tersely. "I can *feel* her."

He stepped forward, away from the others, even as he forwent his axe and took out his bow again. He turned to the right and shot an arrow into nothing.

A figure plucked it out of midair.

Someone in the same scarlet robes as the attacking coven materialized before them.

Malekh was at Remy's side in moments, as was Xiaodan.

"Come no farther, witch!" he heard Grager holler.

The woman reached up and let her hood fall to her shoulders, and once more Remy found himself staring at his mother's face. "How far have the courts fallen," Ligaya Pendergast said coldly, "to see them side with humans against the Night Court."

"It is you who are the usurper, to so falsely claim rights to the Allpriory when you have nothing but foul mutations and untried bloodlings for your court!"

The woman laughed softly. "I, the usurper? It is you and your clans who seek to put an impostor on Ishkibal's throne." Her gaze met Malekh's, her tone now mocking. "You were nothing but a dog at the Night King's feet, a plaything. I am more than what you are, more even than what he was. I am descended by blood from the First Who Walks in the Night, who stepped into the fires of the Godsflame and emerged as the foremost kindred. I am the queen of the Wikaan Court, and four of the eight clans conspired with Aluria to kill us."

"Hearsay!" Krylla gasped.

The Night Empress spread her hands. Wings grew from behind her—one, two, three pairs now, all black as night. Where once Remy had thought them akin to bat's wings, feathers now adorned them, spread about her like she was some unholy angel sent to purge the kingdom. It was exactly like he'd seen in the murals on the Allpriory's walls depicting the First of the kindred.

Xiaodan had planted herself between the others and the Night Empress. "No," she said.

"It was your sunbringing that gave me life, sweet child," Ligaya said. "The pain hollowed me out for days, but in the end, I was reborn anew. Much like your ancestor who emerged from the Godsflame whole, light thrumming in her veins." She turned to the other court leaders. "Do you still think to deny me the right to the Allpriory?" When you have the very proof of the First running through me?"

Xiaodan was tired of talking. She made for the other woman's unprotected face with one fist raised. But the First Court empress's wings folded around her, immersing her in a cocoon that proved resistant to Xiaodan's attack. The younger woman gasped and leaped back, clutching at her hand, cut by the razor-sharp feathers.

"Ligaya," Lord Valenbonne said. "You utter fool."

Grimesworthy had not been idle. He and the other mutations under the duke's control lumbered forward, less concerned with the sharpness of the Night Empress's wings than Xiaodan. They clawed through the cocoon, and for a moment, Remy thought they might succeed from the huge chunks they were ripping from it.

The Night Empress unfolded her black wings just as quickly as she had curled them about her, and the other two mutations alongside Grimesworthy were immediately vivisected, clumps of flesh and bone falling to the floor. Only the former valet remained upright, though deep gashes along his sides bore testament to the attack, even if Grimesworthy neither bled nor indicated any pain.

"Ligaya," Lord Valenbonne said. Remy's heart lurched when his father stepped forward, striding toward his former wife as if she had never threatened his life. He was moving as well, catching up to the older man.

"You are being ridiculous, Ligaya," Edgar Pendergast said. "You would embroil all of Aluria into chaos simply because you despise me so?"

The Night Empress bared her teeth at him. **This goes beyond just you and I**, she rasped. **This is for Wikaan, and you know as well as I what Aluria did there.**

"Please," Remy begged his mother, all too aware of his father's eyes on him, the scrutiny of the other kindred. How many battles would have to be fought, only to end with him pleading with the Night Empress for a humanity he was no longer sure she had? "You told me that you abhorred war, that you wanted to stop. Whatever recompense you feel is owed you, surely we can find a way without any more bloodshed. Didn't you tell me you wanted to live the rest of your days in peace, like your Alurian ivy?"

Blank golden eyes stared back at him. **What useless drivel are you spouting, little bloodling?** The Night Empress's hand raised, forming claws.

"Touch him and I will kill you here and now," Xiaodan snarled. Her hands glowed, and her eyes flashed silver.

The Night Empress hesitated at the sight. Her arm lowered. She stepped back and shook her head, as if fighting off something unseen. "No," she croaked, and something desperate flashed across her expression. "I cannot—I will not—"

"Mother," Remy said, and reached out.

He was in her mind, and she was in his. Images blurred confusingly together: images of the Fount and the Godsflame, of a man who sat on the Night King's throne, the rage when he turned his gaze to Remy . . .

The connection broke.

With a shrill scream, she tore toward the skies, leaving Remy staring after her.

"AN UNEXPECTED development," Lord Valenbonne conceded, "and a remarkable one. What does this mean for Lord Malekh's claims over the temple? Are they bound by their own laws to turn the Allpriory over to the Night Empress instead?"

There had been several casualties and many wounded; the two Alurian mutations who'd been disemboweled took nearly an hour to knit themselves back together, much to Remy's disgust.

"Most of the clans have no reason to trust the Night Empress," Malekh said. "And they would be loath to accede to one they consider an outsider, whatever her claims to the First are." He pinched the bridge of his nose with one hand. "That said, I cannot trust the other clans. There have been enough incidents in the past where court leaders have reneged on their oaths for personal interest."

"But what possible benefit could they receive from supporting the Night Empress?" Lorien exclaimed. "She is determined to destroy all court kindred, or at least relive the days of the First Court and force us to submit to her rule. Surely they would never again subject themselves to such treatment?"

"You talk quite splendidly for someone newly raised to the court," Lord Pendergast said dryly, and the youth flushed.

"King Ishkibal had the strongest claims of any of us then, and still we forced him from his throne," Malekh said. "We can do so again."

Lord Pendergast nodded grimly. "If that's what it takes, then by the Light, let it be. That was not my wife. It speaks in her voice and wears her flesh, but it is not her."

"Pendergast," Malekh said to Remy in a quieter tone. "Tell me what you think we need to do."

Remy swallowed. "We have to stop her by whatever means necessary."

The Third Court lord nodded and took half a step toward him before seeming to remember where they were. He gave Lord Pendergast a curt nod. "I will need to talk to the council," he said shortly. "Should you receive any more reports of further attacks, then it would be best to send your kindred messenger to us at due speed. Tell him to remain by the lake, and someone will attend to him quickly."

Lord Valenbonne's mouth quirked into a smile. "I see that very little gets past you. And if we are choosing to be honest with each other now, tell me, what are your intentions toward my son?"

Remy stiffened. "Father."

"It is no secret that you and your fiancée are more than just fond of him," Lord Valenbonne continued, ignoring Remy completely. "Do you intend to turn him into your official court familiar before the day is out? Some whore that you can pamper and spoil, or discard eventually when you have no further use of him? I allowed him his time to indulge the infatuation he has for you both. But there is only so much a father can tolerate if you wish to parade him before the other courts like some strumpet."

"While I have no intentions to remain as the Hierarch of the Allpriory," Malekh broke in coldly, "my position as the ruler of the Third Court is well assured. It has always been my intent for Remy to hold the same privileges and responsibilities that I wield within my own clan in the same manner accrued to Lady Song. Whether or not he is willing to accept a more official title is something we have yet to discuss, but we are willing to leave the decision up to him when that time comes."

Lord Valenbonne cocked his head, a faint grin on his features. "A Pendergast ruling the Third Court, Lord Malekh? Surely there will be some protests among your own kinsmen."

"Elouve would be less tolerant, I suspect. I have long since taken in both human and kindred within my territories, Lord Pendergast. However the other leaders choose to complain, they have no jurisdiction over what I do within my own borders, and they understand that our respective court sovereignties are what I am defending."

Lord Pendergast was staring at him. "By the Light, you truly are serious," he said. "You *do* wish to install a triumvirate to lead your own court, with Remington as your third."

"I understand that it is human custom in a courtship to ask for blessing from one's parents," Malekh continued, unperturbed. "I am informing you now out of respect for him, not requesting permission."

"Well now," Valenbonne said, faintly bemused. "What say you, Remington?"

Both were looking at him with similar expressions on their faces, Malekh genuinely inquisitive, Lord Valenbonne with just a touch of amusement. This was worse than fighting the Rot.

"Father," Remy finally managed to choke out, "might I have a word with you in private?"

Malekh took a step back and nodded at Valenbonne. "I will have a word with the rest of my kindred," he said, "and we can discuss Remington and other matters afterward."

21

LIKE FATHER

Malekh left, and with him Remy's urge to kick the man in the shins for the public display. He followed his father into the large commander's tent.

"Quite an unusual man, that vampire lord of yours," Lord Pendergast said conversationally. "For all his unflappable air, I detected a hint of nervousness from him. You, on the other hand, have never been able to hide your emotions from me."

"You're not angry?"

"I had hoped that you would know to place some distance between you and they, the same as you did with the Duchess of Astonbury and her friends. There is some merit to being involved with a powerful kindred court—far more advantageous than being married to any other noble house in Elouve that comes to mind, in fact." He raised his hand, chuckling at the look on Remy's face. "There is no need to act like it's an insult, Remington. I am merely stating facts. Do you know that the priests have started spreading rumors again?"

Remy froze. "About me?"

"No, about me." Edgar Pendergast folded his hands behind his back, gazing down at the papers neatly piled on the small table. "Many refuse to see my miraculous recovery as anything short of witchcraft. They are saying that I, like my only heir, had succumbed and become kindred myself. I was quick to shut down such talk, of course, but I do not doubt that such chatter will rise again before long."

"I am sorry."

"There is no reason to be. I have never paid much mind to what they think of us. It is the queen and Aluria I serve, and fools always come with the territory." He paused. "While my opinions of most kindred have not changed, I am willing to make an exception for Lord Malekh and Lady Song. But surely that is not the reason why you asked to speak to me away from their ears?"

"I don't know what you intend to do with the alliance Aluria has forged with the kindred," Remy said grimly, "but I want you to honor your end of the bargain. I don't want you to betray the clans as soon as this matter with Mother is over and done with, and I won't have you going back on your word after you'd pledged to work with them."

"You think I would turn traitor?" Lord Pendergast shook his head. "Of all the people to fall for, Remington. Two vampires, each a ruler of their own court, in the middle of a war. Are you sure that this is the path you're willing to take? You will never be able to return to Elouve."

"Oh, but I'm coming back to Elouve," Remy said heatedly, "and I'm bringing both of them with me. I'd take Xiaodan out to a ball and dance with her. Bring Malekh back to the Ministry again and give him the run of the facilities there, to his heart's content. I'm perfectly content to show them off, not hide them like the partnership embarrasses me. I give even less of a fuck than you about what they think of me, and I'm not going to hide who I love just because the ton are the fools you say they are."

Lord Pendergast watched him carefully, though for what,

Remy didn't know. "Very well," he said. "I do not intend to betray the kindred unless they do so first, and it seems to me that likelihood is greater. While I believe both Lord Malekh and Lady Song honorable, at least as much as kindred can be, I have no such compunctions with their other companions. Should they prove us false, I will have no qualms about cutting them down. And I expect you to honor Aluria first and foremost. Protect your lovers, if you wish. They will be valuable allies with or without the other courts' backing. But Ligaya—" He frowned. "There is more to this than what it appears."

"What do you mean?"

"That wasn't your mother, Remington."

"You've been telling me that ever since she—"

"No, I mean she *isn't* your mother. The kindred we faced at Elouve and even at Meridian Keep had some of Ligaya's spirit, but this was someone else entirely. Something else."

"What did Aluria do to Wikaan, Father? Any mention of it sets her off."

Edgar Pendergast rubbed at his nose, sighed. "I always told you not to believe those bloody historians, Remington. Liars, all of them. Aluria professed to have saved Wikaan from the vampires that made a resurgence there decades ago, but it's a rather careful wording of what truly happened. There were fresh sightings of a vampire clan within the Whispering Isles, true, but they were peaceful for the most part. They claimed no rulership of Wikaan, however, made no steps to seize power or pose a threat within and outside its borders. I should know. I was there."

Remy stared wordlessly at him.

"It was where we met," Lord Pendergast said. "She was not born in the main archipelago, but along one of the smaller islands dotting the peninsula. An islet really, one of those small fishing villages that you would think little of visiting, the ones you could walk from end to end in the space of an hour. I had traveled there based on reports of this so-called coven, to determine whether they might pose a threat to us. I was forced to take shelter at the nearest hut when a storm broke without warning: a hut I thought abandoned, until I saw her by the fire she was only beginning to kindle."

Lord Valenbonne paused. He looked different now, Remy thought. The hard look his father often wore softened visibly, a trace of a smile faint on his lips. "She was not very happy to find a Reaper in her home, despite my apologies. This small woman threatened a hunter with her little kettle, saying she would brain me unless I told her what I was doing in her home.

"She kept the pot trained on me until the rains lightened enough for me to leave, even after I told her who I was and how I meant her no harm. Even when we started talking about other matters, of the food she was cooking and her begrudgingly sharing some with me. Long before the storm had passed, I knew I would make her my wife. She was still none too pleased when I returned a few hours later armed with flowers instead of Breaker, though she relented a little more each day after, with every new visit I made."

Remy was silent. This was not the tale he'd been expecting from his father, who looked almost like a different person as he recounted his story.

"I courted her for months. She was the leader of her tiny village, but admitted she looked forward to my visits. Wound up spending more time in that small hut than in Elouve in those months. It was the happiest I've ever been."

"What happened?" Remy asked quietly when his father stopped.

"King Beluske and Aluria happened." Lord Edgar Pendergast said with a grim smile. He stopped before one of the two wooden chairs within the tent, but made no move to sit, content to remain behind it, a hand resting at the backrest. "In the course of my reconnaissance, I sent letters telling him that the Wikaans were peaceful. That the one historian who knew anything told me those kindred had warred with the Night King and long since sundered their court willingly, choosing to live simply among the mortals. Not even I could detect any kindred, so integrated they would have been within these communities with none the wiser, not even their family or friends. Ligaya didn't even know that Wikaan vampires still existed, that they had a court of their own. Unlike the Eight Courts, Wikaan kindred chose who to turn." He let out a humorless bark. "Ironic, don't you think?"

"Despite my reports and pleas, King Beluske chose to invade. He gave the Reapers permission to slay anyone who resisted, under suspicion of being kindred. He decreed that I had spent far too much time there, that my objectivity was colored by my feelings for the locals. So he sent Astonbury to take command instead, and the attack took place without my knowledge.

"The small island Ligaya lived on, along with many others, was utterly destroyed, family and friends scattered to the winds if not outright killed."

His father shook his head. "I did not know Beluske's plans until the bloodbath had already begun. I could not go against the king's orders, but I protected Ligaya, spirited her away. I told her it would be easier for her to live with me in Elouve, that she would enjoy being a duchess. I didn't know until much later how much anger and resentment she harbored against me and Aluria, nor that she would be despised by the Alurians for hailing from what they now call the Witching Isles. Astonbury was particularly vicious, delighting in the scandal. She drew away from me, little by little, over the years, no matter my entreaties."

It explained Astonbury and Valenbonne's longstanding hatred of each other.

"I thought time would help her heal, but it was not to be. I started hearing rumors. How she had been spotted with another man, some stranger in Elouve no one else knew. Speculations that it was a foreign count, or a merchant, or even a bloody stable hand. That she'd taken in a lover, multiple bedmates. It drove me mad with jealousy, and still I could not let her go, even knowing she hated me to go to such extremes." Valenbonne's voice was steady and even, and yet he gripped the back of the chair with such force that the wood creaked under his grip. "I was willing to look the other way, to believe the gossip was false and that she would be honest with me in the end. Until the day I learned she'd eloped. My life ended that day. When we found her body months later, I was still numb. All that remained was my own hate."

He looked at Remy, regal and proud. "You look too much like her, and all the love I had for her had burned up so that I had none more to spare."

Remy swallowed. "Why didn't you give me up, then?" It was not uncommon for noblemen to reject bastards, even their own, and have them brought up in some other establishment, fostered by others well paid for the task. No one else in Elouve would have batted an eye, would have thought it cruel or out of the ordinary.

He wondered why his father had never taken another wife. Never thought to make another heir.

Something crossed his father's expression. "There is something you ought to know about Pendergast men, Remington," he said instead of answering Remy's question. He moved toward the tent's exit, lifted the flap open. Outside, the kindred were preparing to leave, and the other soldiers were already breaking camp, intending the same. The skies had darkened, the clouds gray and heavy with hints of stars filtering through their haze. Lord Valenbonne looked up at the scarce pinpoints of light. "Your great-grandfather fought countless kindred, only to die in a duel protecting his lady's honor," he said. "His grandfather before that was killed protecting his wife and child from a coven that swept through northern Aluria, though their marriage had been dissolved years before. My own father lost to vice and drink; a slow death, as he was unable to comprehend a longer life without my mother, who passed long before him. If there is one thing you should know about us Pendergasts, Remington, it is that while we take betrayal poorly, we feel too strongly for it to matter. Be careful with the Lord Malekh and Lady Song. Never love anyone so much that it makes them the death of you."

THE RIDE back to the Allpriory was slower than when they'd set out. The kindred were not so eager to return when they came bearing bad news. Malekh himself seemed willing to linger, letting the others enter the lake while he remained on the shore with Xiaodan and Remy, to give the latter time to steel himself for the dive.

"I did it without meaning to," Xiaodan said. "I think that the closer I am to her physically, the more I am able to draw from the sun inside her that she took from me."

"And if you tap into it and wind up hurting yourself more you hurt her?" Malekh asked.

Xiaodan looked chastened. "Well, what else can I do? It's the only way I can think to get back my powers, even with how she was."

"How she was?"

"Something about her was wrong," Xiaodan said slowly. "Even though I can feel the sun burning inside her, she was so cold. Nothing like our previous encounters."

"My father thinks along those same lines," Remy muttered. "And so do I, for that matter. She was different this time. She didn't even remember the Alurian ivy she'd kept."

"We *were* in battle, Remy. She might not have remembered in the heat of the moment."

"She loved that plant. She lectured me about it in one of the first dreams I shared with her. But she acted like she didn't know what I was talking about."

"The rest have departed," Malekh said. "Are you ready, Pendergast?"

"And what the fuck was all that shit you said to my father?" Remy blurted out. "About my role in your court."

"Did you intend to turn it down?" Malekh asked.

Remy colored. "I should. Just because I'm with you, doesn't mean I want to be some blasted ruler! I don't know the first thing about leading anyone."

"You do," Xiaodan said. "You were wonderful with Renzo and the others at the Fata Morgana."

"It sounds like a position for someone more . . . permanent," Remy said, the words sticking to his throat.

"Are we going to start this again?" Malekh asked gravely. "We want you however you want to be with us. I apologize for saying such to your father before we had the chance to talk to you."

"You have no obligation to do anything for his court or mine," Xiaodan added. "You're perfectly free to represent Aluria in any future affairs—"

"I'd rather leave the politics to you two," Remy blurted out. "But. I could . . . train some of the others again? Help with supplies? I'd be happy to serve as a go-between for Aluria, but I have no wish to go back to Elouve. I want to stay in either Fata Morgana or Chàngge Shuǐ, or travel between them. Wherever you both are."

They stared at him. Finally, Xiaodan cleared her throat. "We weren't expecting you to make a decision so soon," she said, her voice light.

"Shouldn't I have?"

"No," Malekh said quietly. "This pleases us."

Never love anyone so much, his father had said, but it was far too late.

~

MALEKH WASTED no time summoning a quick council to gather all the court leaders together, and Remy knew how much of a headache that was going to be. With the Night Empress's claim, there was a chance Raghnall and Hylasenth would renege on their oaths, whether out of spite or a desire to uphold custom. Even Fanglei was something of a dark horse, for all her assurances.

Malekh had waved off Remy's attempts to help. None of the other familiars would be in attendance, he was told, and it would be far better for him to return to their chambers and wait.

There, Remy dozed off without intending to and found himself in paradise.

He was sitting on a beach with the clearest blue waters he'd ever seen, slender trees with large, fanlike leaves swaying in the breeze above him. He watched the waves lap at the shore a few feet behind him, the sun warm on his face.

He turned. Small huts were lined up neatly in a row along the sand. Smoke rose from a small campfire beside one. A large cooking pot simmered cheerfully over the fire, and the smell made his stomach growl.

"Was this where you lived?" he asked.

Yes, said the Night Empress from behind him. **It was a simple life, but a peaceful one.**

She moved to the pot, taking a bowl from midair, and ladled soup into it. **Come. It may not warm your belly for true, but perhaps it can soothe your soul.**

Remy perched himself on a nearby rock and accepted the bowl. It tasted sour and tangy at the same time, with bits of chopped meat and vegetables floating to the surface. It tasted real. "It's good," he said.

He basked in her companionable silence awhile, neither of

them wanting to speak. A dog came to bark importantly at them, then trotted away. From a distance, he could see fishing boats hauling in the catch of the day with their nets.

"To answer your question," Remy said. "Yes. I love them. Does that anger you?"

No. It is clear that they are devoted to you.

A heartbeat. Two. Three. "Father loved you. When rumors circulated that you had eloped with someone else, it broke his heart."

He braced himself for her rage, did not expect her melancholy. **He sent reports to his king, swearing he would protect my home. He spirited me away and left my family and friends to their fate, to live among those responsible for their deaths. Fond as he was of me, he despised vampires more.** Her voice turned pensive. **I had not expected people to think I would take a lover, when all I wanted was reassurance that I was not turning into what my husband hated most.**

"Etrienne Sauveterre found you," Remy said with a sudden, awful realization. "Was it he who put that First Court sigil on you?"

No. Not he. The Night Empress hunched over, face wracked with pain. **There is something you must know, but I . . . I do not remember. Why can't I remember?**

"You were not yourself when you fought the other kindred today," Remy pressed on.

I recall little of the battle. But why? Why? I am most myself in these dreams, but I cannot reconcile this version of myself to the reality of me. When I took in the vampiress's sun—oh, it burned me, yet its pain made me aware that I am not myself. But the thought does not always flare so brightly, and then I do not remember. What was it? What has—

She rose to her feet without warning and crossed over to where Remy sat in an instant. Before he could defend himself, she had taken his shoulders and began shaking him hard.

Wake, the Night Empress cried. **You must wake, my Remy. Danger is close, and death draws near, wanting. Wake! Wake.**

Remy startled awake on the armchair he'd fallen asleep on and had little time to clear the cobwebs of his mind before he beheld the shadow before him, poised to strike.

He bolted out of his seat to hit the floor as a dagger flashed in the near darkness, the hilt embedding itself into the backrest. Remy scrambled to his feet, his first instinct to grab for Breaker, only to realize that he'd kept it leaning on the side of the bed several feet away, and his would-be killer was far closer than that.

He dodged again when the assassin struck at him, the blade narrowly missing his side as he made another mad dash for his weapon. The knife slammed into the floor in front of him as the killer moved in between him and his scythes, and Remy flung himself backward to avoid the next swipe. The fires had burned down low, and he couldn't see much of the intruder, only a robe and hood. He ducked down, the blade sailing past his head, and then made a desperate grab at his attacker's wrist. A deft flick and the knife skittered to the floor.

The assassin had likely more arsenal, so Remy risked turning his back on his attacker to make the final leap for Breaker, grabbing on to it like a lifeline and spinning back around with it firmly in his grip, finally ready to fight back.

But the room was empty. Whoever the attempted killer was had fled in the interim, leaving him with nothing but the faded embers of the fireplace and the encroaching darkness.

22

IN THE SHADOWS

Xiaodan was horrified. She'd alerted the other court leaders and a hunt had begun, but not a glimpse of the mysterious assassin had been found. Raghnall had been dismissive enough to suggest that Remy had had nothing more than a bad dream, had Remy not remembered the dagger he'd kicked under the bed. It had no design carved into its hilt, no crest or heraldry to indicate who it belonged to, but the blade was sharp and well maintained, crafted to cause damage. Now each court was mounting their own defenses to ensure that they would not be attacked in the same manner.

"Whether he be Reaper or Pendergast, he's only a familiar," Hylasenth said laughingly to Xiaodan, intent on annoying the Fourth Court leader. "It strikes me as odd that only he would be targeted by this would-be killer. Surely it would be easy to find a replacement?"

"If any harm comes to Remington, Malekh will murder the whole world," Xiaodan said. "Including you and your clan, and I will help him." And Hylasenth knew better to tease again after that.

Oddly enough, Raghnall was furious to learn of the Night Empress's closer claims to the throne than Malekh and had confronted the priestess once the council's session had ended. "And you think to simply let her have it?" he bellowed. "Do you think she would leave even the Antecedents well alone once she rises to power?"

"We have little say in the matter," the temple priestess murmured. "Such is our laws. You have chosen a Hierarch, and for now, that is who we obey."

"You're rather het up, considering you weren't so happy to see the Third take charge," Hylasenth drawled.

Raghnall eyed him suspiciously. "You are far too calm," he accused. "What is it that you know that the rest of us do not?"

"Oh, do be quiet," Fanglei said irritably from where she sat. "While the woman may have claim to take the Allpriory, there are other means to prevent her from doing so. Her death will halt all claims, as King Ishkibal's did."

"So you ask us again to commit regicide?"

"Do you want to spend another few hundred years chained to the feet of a tyrant?"

The Seventh Court leader glared at her but refused to answer.

"We are getting ahead of ourselves," Xiaodan said quietly. "It is still the majority of the council that dictates who to install as Hierarch, does it not? Not even the Antecedents will protest."

"Unless she chooses to attack the Allpriory and take it from us by force." Malekh turned to the priestess. "Can I count on you to coordinate with us to see to the defenses of the temple?"

The woman bowed. "You can, Hierarch."

"And can I count on the council's cooperation?"

"The Sixth pledges to fight with the Third," Fanglei said immediately.

"You shall have the Eighth's assistance and all that is necessary to stave off her forces," Hylasenth promised.

Raghnall glowered at them all. "The Seventh shall not be found wanting," he said shortly.

Malekh and Xiaodan shared a quick look, before the latter reached for Remy's arm. "It would be best if we leave them be for the moment," she said quietly. "There is some trouble with my mother."

"Did something happen?" Remy asked with alarm.

"She is unharmed, but acting stranger than she usually does. Alegra's concerned."

Remy hadn't seen Song Yingyue since the first council meeting, before Xiaodan had taken over her duties. According to Alegra, she rarely strayed from her quarters, often staying listless on a chair by the window, gazing down at the rocks outside. Now he was stunned by the change that had come over her in the last few days alone. She lay on the bed with her face pale, eyes closed and breathing shallow, all color leached from her features.

"I shouldn't have brought her outside of Chàngge Shuǐ, council or no council," Alegra fretted. "She sleeps most of the time now, and when she wakes, she thinks we're back at the Fourth and asks frequently for her husband. The tea the Antecedents offer seem to calm her down, but . . ."

"She doesn't recognize this place?" Xiaodan asked anxiously. Remy squeezed her hand.

"She doesn't recognize anyone, milady. Not even me," Alegra sighed. "The unfamiliar surroundings are likely making her worse. I am sorry. She was lucid when we started out, insisting that it was her duty to attend the council."

"It's not your fault," Xiaodan said. "She would have refused to stay behind. I'll handle everything; your priority now is seeing to her needs and ensuring she's protected. I'll go—"

Yingyue jolted out from the bed, eyes wide and staring at the wall across from her. Xiaodan stepped back, alarmed, but her mother didn't see her, only continued to stare ahead.

"Milady!" Alegra said, reaching for her mistress. "What are—"

"Xiaodan," Yingyue hissed. "Don't do it, Xiaodan!"

She was far too quick. She shot out of bed and was on her daughter in an instant. Xiaodan was fast enough to block the hand that had been reaching out for her, but Yingyue's touch gentled, brushing against her skin instead of clawing at her neck as Remy had expected.

"Don't do it," Yingyue gasped, her eyes fixated on her daughter's. "Your life is not worth it! Do not step into the flames. Do not bring the sun to bear on her. Do not . . ."

She sagged against Xiaodan, unconscious before she could even finish her sentence.

"ONE MORE worry on our minds," Xiaodan sighed after she left her mother's chambers. "I would like nothing better than to have Alegra bring her home, but with the Night Empress so close, I worry about the trip back."

"Was she talking of the Godsflame?" Remy asked.

"No, she was not yet born when the Night Court was sundered. As far as I know, she's never been to the temple herself." Xiaodan looked down, hand tracing through her clothes at the heavy scar on her chest. "When her condition grew worse and she started dreaming more frequently, we dismissed them as nightmares, but now . . ." She bowed her head. "Her dreams are clearer than she is nowadays. But I won't be stepping into the Godsflame. She needn't worry about that."

Elke was waiting for them outside the door, her face ashen. "I need to talk to you both," she said briskly. "Lord Malekh, too, if he's available."

"What's happened?" Remy asked curiously, already on alert.

"Not here," Elke hissed, casting a furtive eye about. "The walls have ears. As odd as it will sound, I think the Fount would be the best place to discuss matters."

The group that assembled before the Fount consisted only of the Third Court, with Aunoir and Diethnir stationed outside the chamber to ensure there would be no eavesdroppers. Speck was already inside the chamber when they arrived. Remy wasn't even sure he'd stepped away from the place, save to steal a quick bite to eat or catch some sleep. "I can say with absolute certainty that the priestess is being truthful about the First's blood, Lady Song," he said. "The veins housing the First's blood do not intersect with those that power the healing cocoon and they serve only as some means of storage, albeit an even far larger one than I expected."

"Have you even slept, Speck?" Xiaodan asked.

"Oh, 'twas no trouble at all. I placed myself within the cocoon to experience it firsthand."

"Spencer," Malekh said with deceptive calm.

"Only after I was certain it would be safe!" the human doctor squawked. "The notes the Antecedents have provided us are impressively efficient and match everything we have observed so far. In truth, they have been storing a far more ample supply of blood than I thought. Centuries of it, from my reckoning. A fount of healing, it truly is."

"As much as I commend your zeal," Xiaodan said. "I would like to delay my own foray into this hollow until a later date."

"But milady, the priestess thinks you have come to be healed."

"Even better. Let's pretend I have, so we can talk here without anyone interrupting or spying on us."

"I think Lord Raghnall is thinking of murdering Remy," Elke said abruptly.

"Wh-what?" Remy spluttered, caught by surprise. "I understand that he has no love for me and he's made that clear enough times, but what makes you think that?"

"You never did believe me when I told you that I could ferret out secrets in Elouve just as well as any Alurian spy. The Seventh Court has been far too quiet as of late, which aroused my suspicions. They are not the type to stay hidden for long, yet they have been holed up on their side of the palace, ostensibly to mourn their lost comrade. I thought to see for myself what they could be scheming and overheard the Seventh's desire to be rid of you."

"Are you certain, Lady Whittaker?" There was barely contained anger in Malekh's voice. "Have you ascertained why?"

"It has nothing to do with you or with Remy, milord. Odd as it sounds." Elke frowned. "I think it has more to do with the Night Empress."

"They were not pleased to hear that the Night Empress has a greater claim to the throne than I."

"I think it's more than that." Elke bit her lip. "I have reason to suspect that they might have had a hand in the scandal over Lord Valenbonne's wife twenty years ago."

"Do you think the courts all worked in tandem to mislead my mother? That they had a hand in spiriting her away to become the Night Empress?" Remy demanded. "Then why would they be so opposed to her now?"

"I'm still working out the why of it, but I'm convinced they played a part. Perhaps they only wanted a pawn to put on the throne, to have her under their thumb, but then she proved unwilling and they killed her, which triggered her resurrection."

"Why do you suspect the Seventh in particular?" Malekh asked.

"I heard Raghnall and Grager talking inside the former's room. Grager sounded distressed. He said that he'd never met the Night Empress before, but it was clear that he recognized her. Said that she was the same bitch that Raghnall had asked him to hunt, the one Sauveterre had taken in."

Remy froze. "So he knew who she was. That's why Raghnall was so furious to find me here at the Allpriory."

"Apparently, they've already spent months plotting to kill her."

"What?" Remy all but shouted, only to be hushed by the red-head.

"Grager was pissed that his lord hadn't told him everything. *I didn't understand then why you thought her important enough to kill,* he said. *I certainly didn't expect her to be the Night Empress— she barely even put up a fight—so pardon my shock when I saw her standing before us with those bloody wings. It's a wonder she didn't recognize me.* Raghnall told him to shut his trap about it, because if Lord Malekh heard, he would break the Seventh Court as he'd broken the Second and Fifth—*especially since his little plaything's her son.*"

"Why did he want to kill Ligaya Pendergast?" Malekh murmured. "She wasn't the Night Empress then. None of us knew what she would become."

"There were rumors about my mother," Remy said slowly. "That she was often sighted in Elouve with strangers, and it gave rise to whispers that she was taking lovers. My father certainly believed them."

"So we must find out who these strangers were."

"That was over twenty years ago."

"Not long enough for people to forget. It seems that I'll be requiring Eugenie's assistance again."

"You mentioned something about the Night Empress, Remy," Xiaodan murmured. "About how she was briefly able to come to her senses once she absorbed some of my sun. It suggests that perhaps she is not the main instigator of these events."

"Are you suggesting she might be compelled herself?"

"It would explain quite a bit. How she was able to gather hundreds, even thousands into her coven—a daunting task for even experienced kindred, much less one who was unfamiliar with her own heritage. Her dream state seems to be where she's briefly able to break free of the rage consuming her." A familiar telltale glow sprang from her palms, the light holding steady for several more seconds before wavering. With a wince, Xiaodan let it flicker out. "I still can't hold it for long," she said and then grinned. "But a far improvement from before, when I couldn't manage so much as a spark."

"You are not to push yourself," Malekh said sternly.

"Spoilsport," Xiaodan said fondly, wrinkling her nose at him.

"Lord Hierarch?" Thaïs had arrived, this time without her usual cheerfulness. The Antecedent's face was pale, and her eyes red-rimmed like she'd been crying. It must have been bad for both Aunoir and Diethnir to have allowed her inside, the latter two already looking grim.

Malekh looked at her, immediately on alert. "Did something happen?" he asked sharply.

Thaïs took a deep breath. "I am sorry," she whispered. "But they were found dead in your room, milord."

LADY ROTTEBURG had not gone quietly. Her fingernails were bloody, evidence that she'd tried to fight off her attacker until the very end. Despite her crimson-soaked clothes, she looked peaceful in death, as if the final blow had caused her little pain.

Trin was still alive, though bleeding profusely. Her wide eyes were trained on the ceiling, looking at nothing even as her chest heaved and shuddered painfully.

Raghnall was by her side, his fangs buried against the side of her neck.

Lorien was near inconsolable. He'd spent the last hour cradling his mother in his arms, looking down at her face. He said nothing.

The Seventh Court leader raised his face from his human familiar. Blood trickled down his chin, but he made no move to wipe it away. Expression still blank, he stood, Trin nestled in his arms. Without so much as a word to the others, he strode with her out of the room.

"It was Lord Raghnall who found them," Altace said quietly.

"No one could have gotten into the palace without our knowing," the high priestess said, for once sounding rattled and ill-composed. "None of the Night Empress's kindred could have snuck into the Allpriory and done this without being caught."

"Someone put them here, in the chambers Malekh and I occupy," Xiaodan said softly, brow creased. "A warning and a taunt. But if no one from outside can really get in, then . . ."

"Someone from another of the courts would be a logical conclusion," Malekh said quietly.

The temple priestess made a small sound of distress. "That can't be, Lord Hierarch. The only one to oppose your leadership was the Seventh Court, and surely they would not kill one of their own familiars to prove a point."

"He didn't," Elke pointed out. "He found Lady Trin in time, albeit to turn her before she could succumb to her injuries."

"Relinquishing authority to me doesn't mean that they want to see me on the throne," Malekh said. "If I could turn the reins over to anyone else, I would. But to kill another to spite me, or try to implicate me in a murder, as well as the assassination they attempted on Pendergast—"

"Don't you lock me in our chambers," Remy said, alarmed. "Do not stick me into our bloody room while there's some bastard roaming the palace attacking everyone else. I can take care of myself, and I'll be more useful on patrol."

"I am not going to restrict your movements," Malekh said irritably. "I know well you would never agree, no matter how valid the reasons. The temple has been compromised. We could leave the Allpriory and conduct court somewhere else."

"And be ambushed out in the open?" Xiaodan said sharply.

"We'll be much more vulnerable on the road, whereas whoever this is can only infiltrate the Allpriory with a limited number of assassins. We need to coordinate with the Antecedents and sweep every inch of the palace to root the killers out from hiding." She scowled. "And I'm not going to stop until we find them. Trin and Lady Rotteburg didn't deserve this. There's a chance that the familiars of the other courts may also be targeted. We must tread carefully."

"I'll help you," Lorien said, looking up from his mother. There were tears trickling down his face, anger intertwined with grief. "All Mother wanted was to keep me safe. She thought coming here would do that." He choked, then continued. "Let me join in your hunt. I want to personally ensure that whoever did this never harms anyone else again."

Malekh gazed down at him and sighed. "I have stationed both Antecedents and guards from the other clans together to monitor every exit of the Allpriory. With a representative from each court present, there will be little opportunity to do more damage, should one of the clans be the guilty party. The entrance leading into the lake has been kept under watch since yesterday."

"But if that is true," Xiaodan said, "then the killer is still here with us, and likely has been from the very start."

Remy stared. "Then we know them?"

"We will find the guilty party," Malekh said sharply. "We will question every clansman and learn who was responsible, and I will start my inquiries with the Seventh Court."

Lord Raghnall, as it turned out, had some questions of his own once he had returned. "Who hates you so much that they would dare raise a hand to the other courts in order to get to you?" he asked, and the axe in his hands told Remy that he would not allow Malekh to step past him until he'd gotten his answer.

"I am sorry about your familiar," Malekh said quietly. "I take full responsibility for the lapse. I cannot—"

"Responsibility?" the Seventh Court leader roared. "And by that do you mean to keep shielding the killer from all repercussion?"

"The killer? Lord Raghnall, what are you talking about?"

The man jerked his axe in Remy's direction. "But who else? Did you seriously think you would continue to hide it from us? This fucker is the Night Empress's very own *child*. Who else but he would kill in her name, to diminish the other courts so that she could finally seize power from within? Are you so besotted by him that you are willing to let them destroy everything the kindred stand for? Or are you yourself a traitor, sent to aid and abet the First Court all while pretending to oppose her?"

Malekh stared at him. "You are mad. We are not in league with the Night Empress, and neither is—"

Raghnall was no longer willing to let him finish, rushing him with a full-throated bellow. Remy grabbed at Xiaodan without thinking, some intuition attuning him to her intentions, and she yanked him out of harm's way, both reappearing at the end of the hallway while the larger court leader attempted to cleave Malekh in two.

"You almost had me fooled, Malekh," the Seventh Court leader snarled in between swings. "You protested far too much against taking control of the Allpriory. Pretended you were only doing so for the betterment of the council. You are just as power mad as the rest of us. Does the thought of becoming Ishkibal's heir excite you so much that you would willingly resurrect the Night Empress? You want to sunder the courts, just as you have always said—only to re-create it in your own image."

Malekh didn't even bother with a reply, nor did he deign to fight back. The hallways were still not conducive to axe swinging, and Raghnall promptly demolished another section of wall to complement the gash he'd already made downstairs.

Malekh flickered out of view, reappeared behind Raghnall, and the heavier man froze when the sharp tip of the Summer Lord's saber came to rest upon the back of his neck. "I will give you no excuses for the deaths on my watch," the lord said quietly. "You have every right to place the blame on my shoulders, and if you wish to seek me out again after all this is done, then I will not deny you the opportunity. But there is a traitor within this temple, and I intend to take apart every stone until we root out their identities. I want to see them pay as much as you, whether this was done by the Night Empress's hand or someone else's. I swear to you by Lilith's grave that I had no role to play in this, nor did Pendergast. I need your wits about you, Raghnall, to see your court through this tragedy."

Raghnall said nothing, fist gripping tightly at his axe as if he still meant to deliver a blow at Malekh once an opening presented itself.

"Think, man," Fanglei snapped. Her short figure had filled the doorway, having witnessed the last moments of their fight. "What reason would Lord Malekh have to target your court? And why would he do it so blatantly, using his own chambers for the discovery? More likely it is someone else eager to split the ties between you, keep us unbalanced and unsure so they can attack when we are at our most vulnerable. Help us find her killer."

Raghnall's grip on his axe loosened. "I promised her," he said. "I promised that until she made her final decision, I would not turn her. And now I had no choice but to go against my vows, and she will hate me for it. For the sake of the oath I made to the council, I shall stay my hand. But if you turn out to be the villain in all this, then I will strike you down with neither mercy nor hesitation." He strode away without another look back.

"Well," Fanglei sighed, once he was gone, lowering her voice. "Another crisis averted. Lady Rotteburg was quite the busybody at times, never one to stick to her chambers when she should—her weapon always was gossip rather than a sword. And she was not the only one attacked."

Malekh's head jerked up. "More deaths?"

"No, thank the Dark Mother. But Yingyue's young guard has admitted an attempt made on her life last night."

"What?" Elke's head snapped back up. "Someone tried to hurt Alegra?"

"She is safe for the moment. While taken unawares, the assailant did not count on Yingyue herself barreling out of her chambers, roaring for blood. Landed a cut on the attacker before they escaped, she claims." Fanglei frowned. "I have instructed Daoming and the rest of my kindred not to stray alone along these corridors for as long as the killers are still loose. I agree with the temple priestess that one of her minions is hiding within the temple undetected."

"Far more likely," Malekh said, "that one of the other courts are keeping secrets from the rest of us."

Fanglei eyed him, nodding. "So you are of the same opinion. I would have singled out the Seventh immediately, but he doted on that young human. For all that he is capable of, he is not one to lay a hand on his own kindred simply to allay suspicion, especially at so great a cost."

"There have been no reports from the Eighth Court of any similar attacks."

"None from the Sixth, either," Fanglei said. "Though we have not brought any familiars. If there is anything within my capacity to do, Lord Malekh, I shall oblige."

Some of the Antecedents had arrived, a few eyeing the new hole in the wall with dismay. "I would first ask the Second what he would wish for his mother," Malekh told them.

"There is very little anyone can do for her now, milord." Lorien still wore his anguish heavily, but a grim determination had taken precedence. "Allow me to accompany you in your investigations instead."

Malekh nodded. "We are on our way to question the Fourth Court, and then the Sixth and Eighth in turn. I would be glad of your assistance."

"Good." Lorien gently stroked his mother's face, and a sob tore from him without his meaning to. "Rest well, Mother," he whispered. "Find your peace with him now."

ALEGRA WAS expressionless as always; not even a near assassination could shake her composure. The same could not be said of Elke, who was gripping the other woman's hand so tightly Remy feared she would break it.

"It happened far too quickly for me to realize what was happening," Alegra said. "I had stationed myself in front of Lady Song's chambers while she slumbered. I had a full view of the corridor on either side, and it would have been impossible for me not to have sensed anyone nearby, no matter how quickly they moved." She frowned, far more perplexed by this than the attempt on her life.

"Were you drowsy?" Lorien suggested.

He received a flat stare for his offense. "I do not drowse," Alegra said stonily.

"Fortunate that I was there," Song Yingyue said, sitting on an armchair and sipping languidly from a teacup.

"Mother," Xiaodan said gently, reaching out to take her mother's hands in her own, looking happy when the woman made no move to pull away. "Can you tell me everything you remember from the night before?"

Yingyue frowned. "Why? Did something happen? I was lying in bed, wasn't I, Alegra? A nice heavy wine for supper. And then tea. But I didn't want to bother you, my dear. You're always rushing off with a hundred other important things to do, and I'm no invalid. I can perfectly make my own cup. But I couldn't find that little teapot I liked, with the wisteria painted on it. And so I opened my door to where you stood guard to ask. You turned to look at me, and I saw . . ." She paused, puzzling it out. "A shadow. It lunged for you, I remember. We were at the Allpriory. Nasty kindred lurking there, hoping to throw themselves into the Gods-flame for the Dark Mother knows what reason. That temple's not to be trusted. Didn't think to chase the shadow down, more's the pity. Would have made a sight, wouldn't it, tearing down the hall in nothing but my pantalettes." She chuckled.

"Can you show us where the shadow emerged from?" Xiaodan urged.

"Of course, my dear. But let me finish my tea first. I was worried that we had run out of my special Darjeeling blends, but as it turned out, I had misplaced that, too." She took a small sip of her cup. "I visited the Allpriory once before. Oh, you didn't know, my dear? It was back when Jairette was still alive. She was the Fourth Court's leader before I was, and the most prominent healer in the days of the Night Court after Lilith. It often fell to her to tend to the injuries the other kindred sustained under King Ishkibal's reign, often dealt by his own hand. The deaths took a toll on her and Lilith in those years, she told me. For every life they could save, there were three or four they could not. She admired Lilith very much. Lilith's weak heart was no barrier to her own talents as a physician, and Ishkibal had turned her for that alone. She had many consorts, I'm told—her love split among many, but no smaller for it. They adored her, and she them in equal measure."

She gazed at the wall, her expression unfocused. "I never thought Lilith would ever ally herself with you, my dear Zidan," she continued in a soft, dreamy voice. "After all, you were responsible for many of the deaths she had hoped to avoid."

"It didn't take her long to convince me of her cause," Malekh said. "There were many who wished for freedom, same as I."

"Not as many as she would have liked, but it says much about her character that those who swore fealty to her stayed on to serve the temple, to ensure no one else who thought themselves the next Ishkibal could seize the throne. You must be more careful wandering around the castle by yourself, Alegra. The walls listen to Ishkibal. Their tongues whisper secrets to him still." She dropped her hand, and then seemed to come to herself again. "What?" she asked, looking around with alarm. "Where am I?"

"Mother," Xiaodan said, "we're at the Allpriory, and you—"

Yingyue flew to her with a scream, grabbing Xiaodan by her neck and pinning her to the floor. "Vile woman!" Yingyue screamed. "They will hunt us down! They will break our clan and destroy us! We must cleanse you!"

Alegra and Malekh were on the older woman in an instant, forcing her to release her grip. Alegra clapped a hand to her lips, halting her rant. Remy saw Yingyue swallow, as if the warrior had forced something into her mouth. Malekh kept her immobile, not relinquishing until her struggles grew weaker and she slumped down in his arms, unconscious once more.

"Well," Xiaodan said, making no move to rise from the floor. "Somewhat back to normal, I suppose."

23

AFTERSHOCKS

Elke brought Remy to the temple forge while the rest of the kindred prepared to sweep the Allpriory for the culprit. It was not as large as her old one at Dracheholm had been but was enough to keep her busy. Several swords and daggers already hung from the wall, gleaming in their novelty. The fires were still burning, meticulously tended to by Alegra.

"Lady Yingyue is still fast asleep," she said with a sigh. "Giufei will send me word once she awakens."

"All well and good," Remy said, "but what are you doing here?"

"As it turns out, Alegra has a penchant for seeing me work the forge," Elke said slyly, and the expression on Alegra's face turned even more wooden. Elke picked up her hammer and tongs and set to work on a blade, the sharp ringing echoing through the cavern. Her voice lowered. "This will ensure that no one can overhear us. Alegra thought it important enough, and I trust her instincts."

"With the Antecedents and other kindred constantly surrounding Lady Song and Lord Malekh, I thought it would be prudent to reach out to you first," Alegra confirmed.

"Lady Rotteburg was worried about something," Remy said.

"Sometimes it felt like she was on the cusp of telling me, only to change her mind at the last moment."

Alegra and Elke glanced at each other. "I saw her skulking about in the few hours leading up to her death," Alegra said slowly. "She was conversing with several familiars from the other courts, along with a few of their kindred."

"And you think that has something to do with her murder?"

"Remy," Elke said patiently. "What was your impression of the Lady Rotteburg back at Elouve?

"She was always something of a gossip, I suppose, but that's not uncommon with many of the other matrons of the ton."

"She was a busybody. She always needed to know everyone's business—to better protect her charges from the libertines and despoilers of lady's virtues, she always claimed. I don't see her changing just because she's found herself at kindred courts instead of Elouvian ones."

"She approached me two days before," Alegra said. "Asked me about Lord Hylasenth and his kindred."

"What? Why?" The promiscuous, hedonistic Eighth Court leader seemed to represent everything the matron would despise.

"I assumed at first that she was helping her son navigate kindred politics by making the acquaintance of the other lords and ladies," Alegra said. "But she was more interested in Krylla than anything else. Wanted to know if I'd known her long, and if she'd been involved in any of the wars against Aluria. She said that as I was loyal to Lord Malekh as well as Lady Song, that she thought to trust my opinion on the matter."

"Krylla? Hylasenth's second-in-command?"

"The very same. When I asked her why she was so interested in the woman, she became evasive. Said that she was invested in seeing her son succeed as leader of the Second Court and would like to know more about those who would claim to guide him along that path. Krylla, I believe, made such an overture. And then I made the mistake of asking her if she was all right."

"Was she injured?"

"No. This was following her outburst at Thaïs, accusing her of seducing her son. The Antecedent has always been overtly friendly, but I don't think she meant Lord Tattersall any harm. Lady Rotteburg nonetheless held a grudge against the poor girl after that."

"Ah," Remy said with a flinch, remembering his secondhand embarrassment for poor Lorien.

"Then she muttered something about tattoos and asked me if the Fourth Court required its clan kindred to be marked, as those in the Night Court had been. She knew that it was not a prerequisite of the Second but had seen a tattoo on Krylla's shoulder and wondered if all the other courts did the same. I told her that most of the Eighth have themselves marked not out of obligation, but as a show of pride, and that the other courts do not make it a requirement." Alegra frowned. "But it seemed my answer only confused her further. I suspected that she wanted to ask me more, but Lord Lorien came along at that moment, and she left with him. I never saw her again until we learned of her and Trin's deaths."

"And here's my theory," Elke said. "I think someone killed Lady Rotteburg because she realized something no one else did. And Trin was unfortunate enough to have been with her when she was murdered, and so they tried to silence her as well. Lady Rotteburg was not otherwise so important that someone would go out of their way to target her."

"It could have been done to affect Lord Lorien," Remy said.

"Lord Lorien barely has a court to rule over. His authority as of this moment is still inconsequential. If this truly is the Night Empress's assassin, they would not risk their life to infiltrate the palace simply to murder the parent of a Second Court lord who's barely even consolidated his position. Lord Malekh has had a guard stationed over Trin despite the Seventh's protests. If anyone saw the killer, it would have been her, though we need wait till her frenzy passes, if it does."

"Will she make it?" Remy asked worriedly. He liked Trin, for all his suspicions that she might be a spy for Raghnall.

"I hope so, though one can never tell until it is over."

"What if they meant to murder her instead, and the Lady Rotteburg was the one unfortunate enough to be there?"

"It is true that Trin has some considerable influence in the Seventh, but no. No, I think the Lady Rotteburg was their true target for two things: her nosiness, and the fact that they also chose to attack Alegra."

"Me?" Alegra sounded surprised.

"It strikes me as desperation—like the killer wasn't certain if the Lady Rotteburg, too, divulged her secrets to you, and wanted to take you down before you could pass that information along to anyone else."

"And what about me?" Remy demanded. "I was attacked, too, and I don't know anything."

"You were frequently seen in Lady Rotteburg's company," Elke said seriously. "The killer targeted everyone she looked to have confided in. I don't think it's a coincidence."

Remy groaned. "I don't like complications, Elke."

"It's why I'd like for us to stay together until Lord Malekh sweeps the temple clean. In the meantime, we must piece together what it is that Lady Rotteburg knew that would give our killer a reason to target you both. Let us start with Lorien, then Krylla. I suppose neither of you have anything else that needs doing today?"

"Lady Yingyue is in Giufei's capable hands," Alegra said. "I can perhaps spare an hour or two, if only because I wish to see this resolved as well."

"Even if I had anything planned," Remy added grumpily, "you nipped it in the bud when you told Malekh I'd be accompanying you."

Elke grinned. She finished her hammering and skipped to the wall of weapons, selecting a few daggers and extending them out hilt-wise to Remy. "I thought I'd make more for you to use, given your habit of losing knives as quickly as you do chains."

"That wasn't my intention," Remy grumbled again, but accepted the gifts. They felt lighter in his hands than her usual, albeit still with the excellent precision work she was known for.

Elke coughed, suddenly red-faced. "Alegra, I know you asked me to work on your battle-axe, so I scoured and melded it as best I could. I'm sorry I haven't had time to do more—"

"There is no reason for you to apologize. If anything, I am in your debt." The woman took the axe and gave it a few practice swings. Her face softened, then lit up in a smile. "This is beautiful work, Lady Whittaker. I am honored."

"The debt can be repaid," Elke said, still coloring, "perhaps with dinner once we have left the Allpriory behind? If you intend to return immediately to Chàngsē Shuǐ, Caranelia is only a day's run from your castle. We have quite excellent chefs. "

"But why? We are kindred—we have little need for human sustenance. If it is your wish that I go and warm your bed to express my gratitude, then you only need ask."

Elke stared at her, open-mouthed. Remy had never seen her so blindsided before. "Uh," she began. "I . . . that is, I wasn't—"

"Say yes," Remy said wearily. "For the love of the Light, Elke, just bloody say yes."

Elke tried again. "I . . . yes?"

Alegra nodded. "It's settled, then. But first, we question Lorien."

"What's happening?" Elke asked, sounding dazed as the other woman moved toward the door. "Did she just . . . ? Did I?"

"She's straightforward, if nothing else," Remy said, grinning.

"I didn't expect such an offer. Or even the suggestion that she was interested."

"If my own relationships with kindred have taught me anything," Remy said, "it's that I never think long enough to overthink myself. Now, we'd best get going before someone tries to stab one of us again."

LADY ROTTEBURG'S body had been cleaned and readied for a funeral, but Lord Tattersall didn't want her buried at the Allpriory. There was a spot in their country estate that she'd always loved to have picnics on, Lorien decreed, and he intended to inter her there as soon as possible.

"She was always protective of me," he sighed. "After she learned of her illness, that only doubled. I wanted to make her last days as painless as possible." His fists clenched, tears threatening to spill out of his eyes again. "Couldn't even do that, could I? How am I to lead a clan if I can't even protect those closest to me?"

Remy sat beside him feeling awkward. Malekh and Xiaodan had also arrived; all corners of the Allpriory had been upturned, with no assailant found lying in wait. For once, none of the other kindred were in attendance, and so Remy had relayed to them all he could of his conversation with Elke and Alegra. Xiaodan had immediately departed with the two women to question Krylla, leaving Remy with Malekh and the Second Court leader. "Is there anything she told you in the hours leading before, even if you think it's of little importance?" the lord asked Lord Tattersall.

Lorien frowned. "Nothing I can recall. I tuned out too much of what she said: little matters like who was courting who in Elouve, what outfits some debutante wore to upstage another. Here in the Allpriory, she was mostly worried that we wouldn't be comfortable, questioning the cooking and bathing customs." He reddened a little. "I thought it best to let her have her way for the most part. I should have—"

Malekh laid a hand on his shoulder. The younger man leaned against it, as if it could carry his whole weight. "What lord can I be, if I can't even protect my own mother?" he whispered.

"I had a brother," Malekh said after a pause. "He was headstrong and determined, always wanted to prove himself. He was still young when he came to my court and always felt the lack of gravity he thought should come with age. And I . . . I couldn't protect him, either."

Lorien looked up at him, blinking.

"Why, then, should I be the leader of the Third Court, much less the Hierarch of the Allpriory, if I could not save him? What claims do I have to such positions when I consider myself too weak to do them justice?" Malekh met his gaze. "But this is not the first time that I was powerless to save someone I cared deeply for. And I fight every day to ensure that will be the final time, though that is likely impossible. Sometimes there are circumstances beyond our control. Sometimes we make the wrong choice, and all we can do is learn to live with the consequences. If you intend to be a good lord to your people, then this is something you must learn, again and again."

Lorien took a deep, shuddering breath and nodded. "Thank you, milord. I . . . there is something else I must tell you. I thought little of it previously, but my mother was furious about the bath incident. I thought it was with the poor girl who'd offered to wash my back, but she told me afterward that it was actually about the vases."

"Pardon?" Malekh asked, taken aback. "Vases?"

"Aye. All eight of the courts' crests have been added to the design of the vases in the temple. She knew that the Second Court's crest was that of a white rose but had little knowledge of what the other clans' symbols entailed."

"And so she wanted to know more?"

"Yes," Lorien sighed. "Admittedly, I had little knowledge of it myself, and thus offered to find out if she was so adamant, only for her to insist that she would conduct her own inquiries into the matter. She said it would not do for the next leader of the Second Court to be asking things he was already supposed to know." His head dropped into his hands. "I should have done it myself."

"Was your mother often inquisitive about such trivial things?"

"Oh yes—she always said that nothing is inconsequential— that might as well have been the family motto. I wondered why she seemed so fixated on it—there are matters much more pressing here than crests."

"She saw something amiss," Malekh said. "I don't know what it is yet, but I will find out." He paused, as if planning his next words carefully. "I am sorry for your loss, Lord Tattersall. If there is anything you need, we are at your disposal."

"No, you have done far too much for us already," Lorien sighed. "The only measure of peace I have from this is that . . . well, we both knew she didn't have long to live, and we were both steeling for when it would come. Perhaps a reprieve from the longer, painful illness she expected." He looked straight ahead, eyes blazing. "But even that gives me little comfort. Find her murderer, milord, and I will be in your debt."

XIAODAN'S INTERROGATION of Krylla had not gone as well as Malekh's. While sympathetic over the death of the Second Court leader's mother, she claimed to have never engaged in conversation with her at either the Allpriory or at any point before that. Xiaodan thought she was genuine enough in her surprise to take her words at value. "Unless she was a consummate liar," she admitted, "I'm inclined to believe that someone had killed the lady before she ever had the opportunity to reach out."

"Aren't we focusing too much on what Lady Rotteburg said?" Remy asked. "I don't think anyone would seek to harm her just for learning court crests."

"I don't know. It seems innocuous enough, but it must have played a role. I trust Lord Tattersall's instincts with regard to his mother. She must have thought it important. Therefore we must do the same."

Remy took a deep breath. "You're not going to like what I'm about to say. But it's time we consider letting me reach out to my own mother to ask some questions."

Xiaodan paused. "Remy, there are far too many unknowns to such a step."

"You've all swept the palace and turned up nothing. There may be more deaths coming, and it will lead to the peace that Malekh's been trying so hard to fight for, to disintegrate, and both kindred and Aluria will fall. If my mother is the one responsible, I can try to reason with her. But she was the one who saved me. She forced me awake, just in time to dodge the assassin."

"He may have a point," Malekh said.

Xiaodan spun on him. "You actually *agree* with him?"

"We have limited other options at this point. We've been able to send him into these dreams before with minimal risk. Speck can monitor Remington's physical condition and determine whether or not to wake him." Malekh looked to Elke. "There is a favor I must ask of you."

"Say no more," Elke said promptly. "Alegra and I will stand guard."

"Rest assured that nothing will get past us," Alegra said calmly.

"Then let's get started," Remy said to Malekh. "Like hell if I let them put the blame on you for this."

"Very well," Malekh said, and his face softened just a smidgen.

MALEKH HAD left them momentarily to consult with Altace, looking grim when he returned. "It seems that the rest of the Night Empress's coven is set to make landfall at our shores at dusk."

"What?" Remy leaped to his feet from the armchair he'd been hunched at. "Why didn't the Antecedents say anything about this?"

"Because they don't know what's coming, either. My sources are elsewhere."

Xiaodan stared at him, perplexed. "What sources?" she asked. "On the surface? Did Eugenie send word?"

"She did, but with information we already had."

"There's no one else we've remained in contact with, unless Agatha has managed to send someone very discreetly, or—" Xiaodan stopped and glared at him. "Lord Valenbonne's vampire messenger?"

"He's a resourceful lad. Observed that I would emerge from the lake during certain times in the morning and endeavored to wait for me when I did."

"And so you began swimming back aboveground to meet with him."

"Lord Valenbonne is a sound tactician. He decided that I would be receptive to any information he was willing to provide."

Xiaodan frowned. "Now what?"

"I have instructed the Antecedents to prepare the usual defenses. It matters little if the First Court somehow already has access to the Allpriory, so we must use what time we have left to reach out to the Night Empress first."

They chose to barricade themselves at the quarters Remy shared with Malekh and Xiaodan. Elke and Alegra stationed themselves between their bed and the door, while the other Third

Court kindred took up positions near the window, the only other point of entry—or attack.

Remy felt self-conscious, even more so when the time for bloodsharing came. None of the other kindred thought it unusual for their lieges to be sucking at his neck and he at theirs in turn, but Elke had taken pity on him, demanded that everyone else retreat from their chambers temporarily to give them privacy for the deed. It took effect as intended; not even Remy's nervousness could stem the surges of lust boiling inside him, and while his vampire lovers composed themselves far better, there was no mistaking the way their gazes strayed to him and to each other, as if they were ready to jump him the moment the opportunity arose, audience be damned.

"That won't be necessary," Speck said cheerfully, gesturing at the syringe he held in one hand. "One shot of this, and you'll be out like a light. I'll be reviving you with another shot in an hour's time—or should anything go awry. As agreed, I will wait until you display extreme signs of agitation before I rouse you again."

Remy lay down on the bed with a grunt. "I'm as ready as I'll ever be, I suppose. Whenever you wish to begin."

The needle was longer than he anticipated and hurt like bloody bollocks going in, but the effects were almost immediate. Remy felt his limbs slacken, drowsiness overcoming him before he could even ask if it worked. All too quickly their private chambers, wavered out of view as he sunk into darkness.

Only to find himself at the center of a burning village, surrounded by acrid smoke and the sound of people screaming.

His instincts kicked into gear, and he began to run toward the sound, straining to see someone, anyone he could help, while fighting down a wave of panic.

He spotted a figure in the distance and scrambled toward it.

The woman was sitting on the ground, staring in dismay at the flames before her. She was dressed in a simple white robe, one he'd never seen on her before. Even more surprisingly, she was weeping.

Must it come to this? he heard her whisper. **So many deaths. So many more will die.**

"It must," another voice said. Remy saw another kindred dressed in scarlet beside her. "You saw what they did to your people, to your home. How could you still forgive them?"

He is my husband. I have a child with him.

"No," the cowled figure spat. "You were his brood mare. He thought you a far more docile bride than the Elouvian women he courted in the past. He left you for dead, didn't he? Cut your babe out of your womb like you were some dying sow. And still you make excuses for him."

I lied to him.

"You were only trying to save your people," the hooded one stressed. "He would have stopped you, had he known. The Fifth helped you, didn't they? They suspected who you were long before. Only they protected you."

I am no one, the Night Empress said bitterly.

"You are the last hope of your people. You were powerless then, when they invaded your land." The other figure gestured around them. "Will you sit back and do nothing again?"

Slowly, the Night Empress stood. Gone were her white robes, and in their place was her familiar scarlet. Her eyes had turned resolute, furious. **No**, she said, and the scenery before them flickered, to be replaced by the city of Elouve at a greater distance. **I will kill every last one of them.**

She whirled around, facing Remy. Some of the tension left the woman's shoulders. **Remington**, she said in a softer voice.

"No," the hooded figure hissed. "He is an illusion. An attempt to take your resolve, to probe for a moment of weakness. He is not your child. He fights for your enslavers, just as your former husband does. To save him, you must kill the Alurians and the kindred who wish to ally with them."

"No!" Remy shouted. "They're lying. Mother, it's always been me. I want to stop this bloodshed. I'm sure there's another way."

There is none, came the anguished reply. **Can you resurrect those I have lost to the Alurians' greed? And the kindred courts tried to murder me long before my blood ever awoke. They hunted me, wishing to eradicate every drop of blood that Ishkibal still had in this world, no matter that I was innocent. Only the Fifth offered me sanctuary, and even that was to experiment on me, to test the extent of my abilities. They sent me into the fires, and I lived. I will not allow them to go on while my own are dead and buried. I will not.**

Black wings emerged from her back. The landscape shifted again, into something more familiar: the plains only several miles away from where the lake leading into the Allpriory glittered.

"Mother," Remy cried out.

The Night Empress turned toward the waters.

. . . And something small and quick darted out from nowhere, targeting not the Night Empress, but the hooded figured beside her. There was a cry of pain as the latter took a step back, raising their hands to ward off the sudden flurry of attacks, and failing as Xiaodan punched them harder, sending them stumbling away.

The Night Empress bared her teeth and hissed, turning to Malekh, who stood several feet away. **You turned my own child against me**, she hissed. **You** *murdered* **me in those caves.**

"I did not know who you were," Malekh said quietly. "I never compelled Remington, but I am sorry for the rest."

You ripped my life from me.

The Night Empress struck, and Malekh ducked her blow. Again and again she lashed out, but all too nimbly the Summer

Lord dodged, intent on evading her without a counteroffensive.

Xiaodan was equally preoccupied, her opponent less adept at protecting themselves. They cried out again when a blow from Xiaodan landed across their ribs with a shattering sound, and they stumbled back, clinging to their side.

"*You've* been compelling her," Xiaodan said. "All this time, we thought that she was in charge, acting on her own—but that was a falsehood. Who are you?"

Despite their pain, a soft laugh escaped from beneath the figure's hood.

An anguished groan from Malekh. The Night Empress had not struck another blow, but the vampire lord had fallen to his knees, dazed, shaking his head if to clear it. The Night Empress had raised a hand toward him, brow furrowed.

"No!" Remy cried out, darting forward. The compulsion broke; the woman turned to face him, ignoring the gasp of relief coming from Malekh.

"No!" he cried again, feeling that telltale heaviness steal over him, locking his muscles and rendering him unable to move. "Please, no!"

He couldn't do it again. He remembered Naji's blank eyes, the look of hurt surprise on the youth's face, Remy the last thing he saw.

A startled cry. The Night Empress reared back, staring at him, and the beginnings of his compulsion dissolved as well, giving him back control of his own body. "I didn't mean to—" she said, shaken, and Remy realized she had seen into his mind, tapped into his anguish at the memory. "Oh, Remington—"

Another scream. The hooded figure leaped back. They clutched at their stomach, moaning weakly. Red brighter than the crimson fabrics of their robes dripped onto the floor.

"Get out of her head," Xiaodan said. She was glowing. Her hands were raised in fists before her, and a dazzling light was sparking from them, far brighter than what she had been capable of when she was awake. For a moment, he thought that she could channel the sun again, turn it on the figure and turn them into so much dust.

But within moments, the Night Empress was between Xiaodan and her target, the same glowing light emanating from her hand as Xiaodan's.

"You took part of it from me," Xiaodan said. "We only both survived because I didn't give you all of it."

You took from me in equal measure, the other woman returned.

"Have you planted spies inside the Allpriory, Lady Pendergast?"

I need no help to get rid of vermin like you.

Remy dashed to the fallen hooded figure, but Malekh was already ahead of him. He took one look at the robed stranger and made a sound of surprise. "You are—" he began.

With an angry cry, the Night Empress turned and leaped for Malekh, faster than Xiaodan could react. Remy saw the nails reaching out, beginning to close around the Summer Lord's throat . . .

And Remy shot awake, screams escaping his mouth. He realized he was face-first into something warm and soft—Elke had thrown her arms around him, holding him to her shoulder until clarity returned.

"You're all right," she breathed. "It was only a dream, Remy. You're back now."

Remy drew a shaky breath, enough to mumble out his thanks as his senses acclimated to his surroundings. Then he turned his head to see Xiaodan slowly sitting up, blinking. "That was a close call," she said with a nervous laugh. She looked over to Remy's right, where Malekh lay. "Zidan, what was . . ." She trailed off, face turning pale. "Zidan?"

Malekh hadn't awoken. Remy grabbed his hand; his skin was clammy to the touch. He shook him, softly at first, then with growing intensity when he realized his attempts did nothing. Malekh's eyes remained closed; by all appearances, he looked truly dead.

24

TRAITORS

Remy had demanded that Speck put him back to sleep so he could find Malekh, but every attempt was unsuccessful. He would jerk back awake from a dreamless sleep with no Night Empress to confront, and he couldn't ignore the growing horror churning in his gut. The lord slept on, despite all their attempts to rouse him.

The news outside the temple remained grim. The high priestess had informed Xiaodan that several vampire covens were approaching the lake. Xiaodan had been adamant that no one tell the Antecedents or the other kindred of Malekh's condition, and her instructions to inform the other courts about the developing situation aboveground and prime them to defend the temple, should the attack come, was accepted without question.

Though she put on a brave face before the priestess, Xiaodan was a different story in private. She didn't stop cradling Malekh in her arms, staring down at his face like willpower alone was enough to wake him. "I know you're in there," she said hoarsely, tracing a path down one side of his cheek. "I know you can hear me. You have to wake up. We can't do this without you." Her voice broke. "I can't."

Remy had chosen a different route, throwing all his anxiety and worry onto poor Speck, who was horrified that nothing he did could bring back his lord. "He isn't dead," the young physician said, pacing the floor in a nervous fit. "He would have been reduced to ashes otherwise. But if his mind is afflicted, then we're treading in unknown territory. The only theory I can surmise is that whatever the Night Empress has done to him, he's fighting it off."

"Fighting it off?" Remy was incredulous. "*This* is what you describe as fighting it off?"

"Had the Night Empress succeeded, he would likely be awake and under her thrall, trying to murder the rest of us." Speck paused, thinking hard. "I can perhaps take the inoculation I made for you and modify it to suit Lord Malekh. It's not a guarantee, but anything more complex requires ingredients from the Fata Morgana laboratory. That he is unconscious is a good sign, though it may not appear so."

"It's not a good sign at all, especially when everyone is waiting on him to lead the charge against the revived First," Elke said worriedly. "Did not the priestess say that they were already amassing by the lake's shores?"

"However large this coven is, most would find it difficult all the same to infiltrate the temple," Alegra said. "The waters will slow them down, and they can be picked off in the caves. Lord Malekh deigned to activate the outer defenses—he said it was integral to defending the Allpriory against would-be intruders in Ishkibal's time, and he places faith that it is just as effective now."

"Except Ishkibal didn't fall to any outsider kindred, did he?" Elke muttered. "He lost because both Lilith and Lord Malekh attacked from within. History repeating itself, but this time against us. What do we do now?"

"What he would have done," Xiaodan said, looking up with a determined set to her mouth. "He would have told us not to waste any more time on him. I know his plans, and I know what he intends to do. The trick is to keep the other courts in the dark, to say that he is preoccupied with strategy and I am issuing the orders in his stead. I've spoken up for him enough times that we can probably pull it off, but it's best not to let them foster any suspicions."

"Elke and I will watch over him," Alegra said. "And Speck will continue to monitor any changes to his condition."

"We can't leave him with only you two guarding him," Remy protested.

"You underestimate both our capabilities," Elke said gently. "Your place right now is with Xiaodan, fighting whatever bloody abominations that woman has chosen to unleash on us this time. The more you kill out there, the fewer will reach us. What would Malekh have asked of you?"

"To protect Xiaodan. He'll be particularly unpleasant, should I let anything happen to her." Remy scowled at Malekh's still figure. "Don't let anyone near him until Speck figures this out."

"And I will," the doctor said determinedly.

Remy found Zidan's valise easily enough, and Xiaodan took out a sheaf of papers within, spreading them out on the bed beside her sleeping lover while taking care not to dislodge his head from her lap. "He had no desire to return to the Allpriory, but his memory is eidetic; he knows every arsenal King Ishkibal once employed to defend the place, likely because he had to circumvent most of them in the past."

She gestured at a piece of paper: a broad sketch of the cavern outside the temple and another that laid out the palace structure. "All the crossbow clusters and spiked traps are here. We'll need the Antecedents to coat them with Zidan's formula to keep mutations from reviving. And these are key spots within the cave and near the temple best for ambush."

She turned her attention back to Malekh, stroking his face. "What are you doing in there, love?" she sighed. "I'm not so sure I'm capable of this."

"Yes, you are," Remy said, laying his hand on hers. "And the bastard's going to be proud of you when he wakes. But right now, we need to leave him to Elke and Alegra and see to the rest."

Xiaodan nodded, lips tight.

"We'll die before we let anyone harm him, milady," Alegra swore.

"I don't want it to come down to that, either." She bent and kissed Malekh on the forehead, then gently laid his head back onto the bed.

"You better be up when we get back," Remy muttered to Malekh's unconscious form, allowing his knuckles to brush against the man's cold cheek before reluctantly standing. "Because if you make Xiaodan cry again, I'm going to kill you."

"ABOUT TIME," Fanglei grumbled when Xiaodan and Remy appeared. "Where's Lord Malekh?"

"Making sure we leave nothing else to chance," Xiaodan said calmly. "Are the others ready?"

"Hylasenth's got the archers stationed on the rocks above us, as Malekh instructed. Grager and his men will serve as our frontline. Raghnall is still keeping watch over his familiar, which I suppose is for the better. The traps secreted within the outer caves should slow any invaders down. Even Lorien, bless his heart, is ready."

"The Third Court lies closest to the Allpriory. Help from them should arrive sooner than most."

"I hope so." Fanglei smiled briefly. "I've always found it ironic that the Fata Morgana is but half a day's away from the temple, and yet its lord is the most invested among us in seeing it fade into obscurity. I always wondered if he chose to build his own domains so close in order to keep a careful watch—to warn whoever takes up the throne whom they need to contend with."

"It may not seem like it to the others, but he has always put the best interests of the kindred first."

"We've all tried to in our own ways, child. But sometimes what we think is best differs from his."

Remy stood beside Xiaodan, only half listening to the conversation. He hefted Breaker from one hand to the next, not quite sure what else to do with his hands as he waited.

"I'd rather you stay inside the temple," Xiaodan said quietly.

"Not while you're all out here fighting, I won't," Remy said, struggling not to glance up.

"It is good to see you looking healthier, at least," Fanglei told Xiaodan. "Priestess Isabella admitted to worrying over your health when we shared a cup of tea. Full wore out the table wood with her fingers fretting."

Xiaodan frowned. "Did you—"

"Incoming!" The call rang clear across the cave. At the same time, loud splashing noises erupted from the underground lake as several creatures came loping out of the waters to meet them.

These were new kinds of mutations, like an attempt had been made to improve upon the ones they had last faced. These hulks had the same scaly appearance, but the horns carved at the sides of their heads were longer, sharper. Their teeth extended cruelly from their mouths, and their faces had broadened, eyes flattened against the side of their heads like a lamprey's. A strange antenna hung from atop each of their heads, and every move they made triggered a spark off it like bottled lightning.

"Fall back!" Xiaodan shouted. "Move away from the lake!"

The dozen or so creatures yowled. Their antennas blazed,

more light rippling out as they struck the damp ground before them, sending shock waves their way.

Many of the kindred fell, stunned by the unexpected blast. Remy would have as well, but Xiaodan had snatched him up and darted away from the radius, sticking to drier ground. The mutations themselves appeared immune, using the pause to lumber forward.

"Altace reported that they brought no mutations," Xiaodan all but snarled. "A lie; the Night Empress could not have hidden so many of these blasted monsters."

Fanglei had received a mild jolt, having stationed herself by the lakeshore, but she recovered swiftly, staggering back to her feet while her husband helped her up. "Take out their antennae first!" Xiaodan roared to her and the others. "Relay that to the Eighth! And tell bloody Grager not to move forward! Not with his damn soldiers in all that chain mail!"

Hylasenth's clan quickly received word; arrows sang through the air, striking many of the mutations and severing their antennae-like appendages clean off them. The Seventh's second-in-command was reluctantly retreating, he and his kindred positioning themselves before Fanglei and her soldiers. "None of the traps have been set!" he roared at them. "They're in a position to swarm us if we don't hold them back."

"I want you to keep them busy," Xiaodan said grimly, "and I will see to securing the temple."

"We will hold the line," Fanglei promised. "There may be worse waiting for you back at the palace. Take some of my kindred; you ought to have company."

"No; you will need all you can to keep them from advancing." More mutations had surfaced, and Hylasenth's archers were targeting them next, aiming for their antennae. "Grager, have your clan bring the wounded behind our defenses. I would like to know what the conditions are aboveground, if you have anyone skilled enough to get past these fiends."

"I do not mean to brag, milady, but I am more than stealthy enough for the task."

"I can accompany him," Krylla offered. "I can be quiet when I need to be."

Xiaodan nodded. "Don't engage any of the mutations in battle. Your priority is to make for the surface and see what else we have to deal with. Lord Valenbonne's army moves decidedly slower, but send word to him. I will make arrangements within the temple."

"I'm coming with you," Remy said.

"And I with you," Shiragiku said. "Queen Yingyue is still inside her chambers. I understand that she is well protected, but we must confirm her safety all the same."

Remy and Xiaodan sprinted back into the Allpriory, Shiragiku close behind. There was no one waiting for them within the great hall, but Remy's senses were on full alert. Each of the courts had left a few of their own stationed within the temple walls; the absence of anyone about was worrying.

Xiaodan made for her mother's quarters first and saw the Fourth Court matron in fine fighting form. Much to Remy's horror, one of the mutations had managed to get inside without anyone the wiser. Yingyue was holding her own, using her spiked chakram to cut deep gouges into its skin. There was no water here for the Rot to take advantage of, but the antenna continued to blaze with lightning, making any closer contact with it fatal.

Remy fell back to the new daggers Elke had given him, as Xiaodan took her mother's side. The room was far too cramped, giving them little space to fight. The creature took advantage by spraying a radius of sizzling levin around itself.

Xiaodan moved, forcing the creature to turn its back on Remy. He flung his knives, watching with satisfaction as the first blade cut its antenna cleanly, leaving a short stump, while the other embedded itself deep at the back of its head.

The beast yowled and lifted its arms up. It was just enough time for Lady Yingyue to shove her circular saws into the monster's face. Toxic black blood spurted up, Giufei yanking her mistress back before it could get onto her clothes and skin. Xiaodan had snatched off one of the curtain rods and shoved it hard into the mutation's stomach, punching a hole right through it. It stumbled away from them.

"Let's see if you're still as smug about the lightning if it comes from someone else," Shiragiku said, charging her fire lance. The tip of it gleamed with a familiar white-hot glow, and the resulting blast that came spiraling out of it turned the mutation into an inferno. It careened wildly, clung to the side of the wall before losing its balance, and sank down to the floor, where it soon stopped moving.

Giufei darted forward, a syringe in hand. "Lord Malekh gave us ample supply," she said, plunging the needle into the Rot-spawned creature and watching the thin layers of gelatin-like substance spread across its form. "I'm so glad to see you, milady. A few more minutes and we could have been—"

"Nonsense," Yingyue said, using some discarded cloth to wipe her chakrams free of the monster's blood. She frowned as she examined her weapons, watching a faint steam rise from the metal as the poison stained the surface. "I am perfectly capable of handling such vermin." She turned to Xiaodan. "Still, it would have been far more challenging had you not shown up in time, my dear."

"I . . ." Xiaodan began, taken aback.

"The Allpriory has been compromised, has it not? Curse these fools. I would not have thought they would want your head so badly that they would destroy this temple to see you mounted on their wall." Yingyue squared her shoulders. "I cannot sit back and watch while they bring the Allpriory down around us."

Xiaodan stared at her, opened her mouth, and closed it again. "Thank you, Mother," she finally said with only a slight tremble of her lips. "We must speak to Isabella and determine the extent to which the Allpriory has been breached."

"Isabella?" Lady Yingyue scoffed. "What would she know about the attacks?"

Xiaodan looked at Remy and Elke. "This is no coincidence. Someone sent a mutation specifically to my mother in the hopes it would kill her. Whoever it was knew enough of the temple's wings to bring it to her very door. We must hurry; we may have been compromised for far longer than we thought."

They returned to the quarters where Malekh lay sleeping, but neither he, Speck, Alegra, or Elke were there. "Why would they have left?" Remy asked, stamping down his panic. "Malekh was in no shape to be moved."

"There are no signs that the room has been disturbed," Elke said. "It could be that Alegra decided that they move somewhere safer."

"If he dies," Remy said, "I'm going to fucking murder him."

They scouted briefly where the priestess and the other Antecedents kept quarters, but the rooms were empty.

"They'll be at the Godsflame," Xiaodan said. "And the Fount. Protecting those above all else."

They encountered no one else on their way to the temple's underground, Remy training his eyes on the semidarkness before him. When they finally emerged from the narrow caverns, he did so with some relief.

That relief quickly turned to horror as he beheld the Night Empress before the roaring flames, gazing into its center.

Malekh, Elke, and Speck's unconscious forms lay sprawled nearby. Alegra was still alert, but on her knees between the Night Empress and the others, holding her side.

"No!" Yingyue shouted, already moving, weapons raised. She

leaped onto the platform and swung her blades at the Night Empress.

She was easily flung back, hitting the opposite wall hard and sinking down with her back against it. Giufei let out a terrible cry and rushed to her side.

"Ligaya Pendergast," Xiaodan said, sounding far too calm.

Finally, the Night Empress turned, her eyes finding Remy as if it were a reflex. "It is over," she said. "I have your temple. The throne is mine by rights." But even as she spoke, she swayed on her feet, as if about to buckle under her own weight.

"You're compelled," Xiaodan said. "Aren't you?"

"Silence," the Night Empress gasped, reaching a hand to her head and lowering it again.

"Is Malekh inside your head, too?" Xiaodan asked. "He's fighting you there, just as we're fighting you here, isn't he? I want him back."

She was on the other woman in an instant, faster even than Yingyue had been. This time it was the Night Empress knocked off the platform, though she sprang back to her feet without pause, countering with a punch that could have taken out a full wall. Xiaodan ducked and made another strike, but the Night Empress blocked it with even swifter ease.

"Mother!" Remy shouted. Shiragiku was loading up another round on her fire lance, though she hesitated, the muzzle far too slow to track the movements both combatants were making. "Slow down enough for me to hit her," she muttered. "Come on, Lady Xiaodan."

Xiaodan snapped into the Night Empress with a strong uppercut, and that was enough for Shiragiku. The fire lance roared into life, light gathering at its tip for a few brief moments before she released it into one huge blast.

Someone screamed, and it was neither Xiaodan nor the Night Empress.

Thaïs was on fire. She had flung herself in front of the First Court leader before anyone else could react, scrambling from her fallen position on the floor to dive into harm's way. She hit the ground hard, parts of her body blackened from the lightning, the rest of her broken and bleeding.

Xiaodan froze, stunned by the sight. But Remy, still staring at Xiaodan, saw the temple priestess approaching her with a knife in one hand. This time, it was his turn to jump.

He must have gotten faster since leaving Elouve, because he blocked the dagger before the temple priestess could plunge it into Xiaodan's back, though not fast enough to avoid it cutting into his own arm. He swung Breaker on instinct, scythes jutting out, and one of them caught the high priestess up from her collarbone and right across the face. Blood spurted on his clothes as she let out a wail and fell back, clutching at her cheek and her ruined neck.

Altace, Gibrid, and Elspeth, the others Remy thought he could trust, now surrounded them. Gibrid punched Alegra, who went down, as Altace pressed a knife to Remy's throat.

"What's happening?" Remy panted. "Why are they not up there, fighting alongside the others?"

"Because they never intended to," Xiaodan said. "They were our traitors all along."

"But they wanted Malekh for Hierarch!" Remy choked. "They all but pressed the responsibilities onto him!"

"Well, we couldn't have gone and said we didn't want him, now, could we?" Altace said wearily. "But the Third was smart enough to see through us."

"We have no intentions of killing him, milady," Gibrid said. "Only wanted him out of the way. Armiger Pendergast being the Night Empress's son, we thought you would all come round eventually. We were not lying when we said we hoped to avoid bloodshed."

"Avoid bloodshed?" Remy shouted. "You killed Lady Rotteburg! And you attempted the same with me and Alegra and Trin!"

"Far easier for everyone to believe that one of the kindred had a vendetta against the humans. If Lord Malekh could barely protect his own familiar, then what hope could they have for him to lead the council?"

"Oh, you nearly did a good job of convincing everyone," Xiaodan said, still far too calm for Remy's comfort. "The council would have chucked him over, had there been another candidate they hated less. But you killed her for another reason entirely. I suppose it was you who orchestrated the attacks on Kerenai?"

"Her hatred for Hallifax ran too strong. We pulled her out of her rampage, but the damage was done. It was your sun, Lady Song, that weakened our hold on her. We did not realize she could find her way to her child in her dreams until much later."

"I don't understand," Remy said weakly. The silent figure of Thaïs was crumpled at his feet. Deliberately ignoring the knife pressed against him, Remy slowly inched his way down, Altace following once he realized his intent.

Thaïs was still alive, though gravely injured. Most of her hair was gone, and the smell of burnt flesh turned his stomach. One eye slowly opened to look at him. "Remy," she said weakly. "I am sorry."

"Why did you do this?" Remy asked, pained. "You were my friend."

"And you are mine."

"Why did you kill Trin and Lady Rotteburg?"

"Because she recognized the crest tattoo on Thaïs's leg, bearing the temple clan's sigil," Xiaodan said. "That was the real reason she attacked Thaïs at the bath before she could stop herself. I wondered why Lady Rotteburg was so evasive. She would have had to tread carefully, knowing she was in their territory. The attack on her estate . . . Remy told me that she mentioned a certain mannerism the leader had, a habit of tracing circles on surfaces with their finger—just as Isabella does. And if Trin survives the frenzy, it will only be a matter of time before your secrets are revealed. Raghnall guards her too well for you to get past him." She turned to the priestess. "You claimed that Etrienne Sauveterre approached you, hoping to experiment with the Fount," she said. "But it was *you* who approached *him*. It was easy enough to replicate the infusions necessary to control the mutations using his experiments. It was not the Rot-infested creatures that you wanted to control, but the Night Empress. You sought to make her an unstoppable colossus."

"What?" Remy choked.

"It was easier when you were physically at her side, where you could guide her actions—much like Lord Pendergast and his own creations. But you cannot be there all the time, and in those periods where you are gone, she breaks out into an uncontrolled frenzy. What we thought was a deliberate attack on Kerenai was actually the Night Empress untethered from your possession. And then there were the periods of lucidity in her dreams, the only place where she could be most like her true self."

"You ruined her," Isabella said accusingly.

"You approached my mother when she lived in Elouve," Remy said, finally piecing things together.

"She was the closest descendant of the royal Wikaan bloodline. The babaylan passed down their blood through their village rituals, but most are so unfamiliar with their own history that they do not understand the significance of the act."

"You killed her, and then revived her using the Fifth's bloodwood," Remy hissed, angry.

"Not Sauveterre's bloodwood," Xiaodan said. "The Fount. A mix of the First's and what they preserved of Ishkibal's blood was infused into her. It explained Spencer's observation that there seemed to be a larger blood supply there than you implied. You needed a leader to unite the clans, but Raghnall is too hotheaded, Hylasenth too hedonistic. You don't trust Fanglei, and my mother is too far gone to be of any use to you. Zidan you despise most of all for willfully destroying other courts, just as you feared."

The high priestess simply nodded. "The Fifth's experiments proved that it was possible to resurrect a facsimile we could control, and we found it even more efficient to infuse a Wikaan kindred with the Night King's blood. We are not without our own scientists; one of us worked closely with Etrienne. Do you not see that we are doing this for the betterment of all?"

Xiaodan's eyes flicked toward the Night Empress. "You took her from her own grave, then subjected her to the Godsflame without her consent, did you not?"

"We could not allow her to perish when she was the best choice to bring the Allpriory back to its former glory. She'd been killed in the chaos following the fight at the Fifth's lair." The priestess turned accusingly to the unconscious Malekh. "Likely by him! But by the Dark Mother's grace, she survived these fires."

Xiaodan's eyes narrowed. "It was you who sent Zidan those corpses over the years, pretending they were killed by First Court vassals."

"All for a greater purpose."

"Do you still think you can win this fight, Isabella?" Alegra breathed. "You and your fellow Antecedents would be lucky if the other courts don't tear you limb from limb, once they realize what you've done."

"No matter. The Rot shall take care of them."

"You have no idea how to exorcise Zidan from her mind," Xiaodan said. "That's why you haven't killed him yet. Eliminating his physical body may lodge him permanently in her head. You've invested too much in the Night Empress for her to die on that chance."

"Let me talk to my mother," Remy said to her.

"No," Xiaodan replied, at the same time the temple priestess said, "What do you intend?"

"We're connected, mind to mind. I won't harm her; I just want to get Malekh out. The same thing you want."

"Remy," Xiaodan said.

Remy flashed her a reassuring smile. "Trust me."

Elspeth laid Malekh out on the floor. "I'll kill him if you try anything else," she threatened.

"Wouldn't dream of it." Altace took Breaker away from him, and Remy stepped closer to his mother. When no one protested, he took another, and then another.

His eyes flicked briefly toward Malekh's form, wondering if he was close enough to make a running leap and grab him so that Xiaodan was free to attack the other Antecedents.

"Remington," his mother whispered. And then all of his schemes fell away as he felt her in his mind, driving down deep, and the rest of the world swam away.

25

UNFETTERED

He was at Kinaiya Lodge. Everything was exactly how he remembered it: the watercolors on the wall, his collection of plants, the tables and furniture where he'd always placed them. There were no signs of the scorch marks the mob had inflicted. No other evidence that the city had hated him.

He stood before the painting of the Night Empress on his wall. No, not the Night Empress, his mother. Ligaya Pendergast smiled benignly down at him, and in an earlier, more innocent time, he would have imagined that was how she might look like surrounded by the Three of the Light's grace, happy and peaceful and free.

But that wasn't the reality of his mother. He'd loved the idea of her because he'd had no other memories of her to make, but his mistake had been believing her flawless.

The silence in the room was unnatural. He turned and noted one way in which Kinaiya Lodge was different—there were no doors leading out. Someone was intent on keeping him here.

Remy reached out from behind his back and found the familiar cold steel of Breaker, hefting it into both his hands. "No," he said, then lifted it up to slash at the portrait of his mother.

It fell away easily; behind it, a fierce fight took place. The rest of Kinaiya Lodge faded away, and Remy saw Malekh in combat with the Night Empress. Both looked exhausted, neither giving in, and he wondered if they had been at this ever since Malekh had fallen unconscious.

"What are you doing here?" Even in his subconscious state, Malekh was ungrateful. His clothes were torn, his face bloodied. The Night Empress was similarly battle worn. Remy's arrival was enough for both to take pause.

I was made a vessel to exact my own revenge, the Night Empress hissed. **Their enemies are mine.**

"They consider me their enemy. Am I your enemy, then, Mother?"

Bright red eyes gazed back at him. **Remington.**

"I cannot let you harm Malekh or Xiaodan, Mother. The Antecedents threw you into the Godsflame without your consent. They will use you to rule the courts, and you'll be nothing more than their puppet. Is that really what you want?"

The scarlet-clad figure hesitated. Rather than press his advantage, Malekh waited, sword at the ready but no longer braced to attack.

I— the Night Empress began, then cut herself off with a cry. She hunched forward, fingers pressed against her temple, face twisted in agony.

"She's been having these spells since we started fighting," Malekh said. "Not long enough for me to subdue her, but enough to know that she suffers from a prolonged frenzy from the Godsflame."

"You were aware?"

"Only after being trapped with her here for this long. How much time has passed?"

"Nearly a day. Everyone else is fighting mutations outside the castle, but Xiaodan, Elke, Lady Yingyue, and I are outnumbered by the Antecedents inside. They orchestrated all of this—they've compelled her."

Malekh rubbed at his eyes. "I should have known. The possibility crossed my mind, but I had dismissed it too quickly—they all seemed so loyal to the throne rather than to Ishkibal."

"Ligaya," came the priestess's voice, startling Remy. He saw the hooded figure materialize out of nowhere, the same one he'd seen in their last shared dream. "I will grant you that which you so dearly wish for," the woman said.

Remy didn't see anyone move, but instinct made him dodge all the same, and a sudden, crippling pain in his side sent him to one knee. He clasped at the injury, feeling blood drip in rivulets down his leg.

"Remington!" Malekh leaped in front of him, slashing at the seemingly empty air before them and hitting something. The priestess jumped back, a long dagger in her grip covered in Remy's blood.

"How are you still standing?" she snarled.

No! cried the Night Empress.

"Your child will be here with you forever," the temple priestess offered. "And as such, you *both* shall rule."

Isabella moved forward again . . . and the knife slid from her hands. She gasped and staggered back, looking down at the hand that had driven itself through her chest. "O Holiest One," she whispered, mouth filling with blood.

No, the Night Empress said. **Not this way.**

And then the dream was gone.

Remy lurched awake with a gasp, hands scrabbling toward his hip, trying to staunch his injury there only to find his clothes clean. Alegra and Elke were awake, the latter guarding him closely.

"They came straight for you," she panted, "and Xiaodan fought off anyone who dared draw close, until the priestess awoke screaming."

The high priestess lay on the floor, eyes wide and clutching at a chest that was also bereft of wounds. But his relief came when he saw Malekh stirring.

The Night Empress had gone still before the Godsflame, staring up at its fire.

"Ligaya," the priestess wheezed, climbing painfully back to her feet. She shuffled toward the other woman, hand raised pleadingly out. Xiaodan was already by Malekh's side, face pale. She turned to Remy. "It's over," she whispered. "She's lost."

"How can you know that?" Remy wheezed, still trying to catch his breath.

"They thought to kill your physical form," Malekh said weakly. "But there's something else inside Ligaya's mind."

"Ligaya," Isabella said again. "Please."

The Night Empress turned to look at her. She smiled gently. "Isabella," she said, her voice no longer traveling in echoes. "Thank you."

She grabbed the temple priestess by the throat. The woman's eyes bulged as the Night Empress slowly lifted her. Though Isabella was taller, her legs kicked several inches off the ground as Ligaya Pendergast's grip tightened.

And then the Night Empress turned and flung her into the wall. Again and again she drove the other woman into the unmercifully hard stone, the horrifying sounds of breaking bones and tearing flesh agonizingly loud. Eventually, Remy's mother was holding something that barely resembled a human or vampire. Only then did she drop her burden in bloody remains to the ground.

Gibrid let out a furious shout, charging the Night Empress. The woman turned, red eyes blazing, and grabbed the man's head with both her hands, crushing it easily in her grip. The other Antecedents made their own desperate attacks, but the latter showed no signs of tiring.

"They weren't just using compulsion to control her," Elke said, stricken. "It was to curtail her strength as well, Bloody Light."

The Night Empress tore through her enemies easily, leaving broken bodies and torn limbs in her wake. When she turned to Remy, he saw that even the whites of her eyes had turned crimson.

Light surrounded Xiaodan as she channeled the sun; her face was strained and her fingers trembled, but the blaze around her only grew stronger.

Snarling, the Night Empress lunged at her.

She was blocked by a furious Yingyue, who slashed with her chakram, forcing the vampiress back. "Do not touch my daughter," the Fourth Court matron roared.

The Night Empress surged forward and was blocked again in turn. Both women stood slicing away at each other, neither giving ground. Shiragiku and the other Third Court rushed to help Yingyue, to no avail; Shiragiku staggered back, a jagged cut across her stomach from the Night Empress's nails.

Remy was already at Shiragiku's side, hands pressed firmly over her wound in an attempt to staunch it. Alegra and Elke doggedly kept up their assault, doing marginally better than the others, though still no match for Ligaya.

Yingyue staggered back and the Night Empress rushed forward, hand raised to slice the clan leader's head clean off her shoulders.

"No!" Xiaodan shouted.

Light and fire swept through the cavern, crashing into the Night Empress, who howled in pain. Xiaodan sank to the floor, panting heavily with a hand clenched against her chest.

The Night Empress pawed at the flames that burned her clothes, dousing them with a swipe of her hand. Weakened but still upright, she turned to Xiaodan, who was struggling to summon another blast of light.

Yingyue's chakram cut right through the Night Empress's midsection.

Roaring in pain, Ligaya Pendergast spun and drove her hand into Lady Yingyue's stomach, right through her back.

Yingyue gagged, blood pouring from her mouth. Alegra let out a horrified cry as she rushed to her mistress's side.

The scream that burst forth from Xiaodan was heartwrenching, and the halo of light around her became nearly blinding. When the Night Empress leaped for her, she raised her hands, her own face a mirror to the other woman's rage.

There was an explosion the instant they made contact. The Night Empress was thrown into one of the cave walls, which shuddered as the stone crumbled, sending her sprawling into the cavern beyond.

And Xiaodan was thrown straight into the Godsflame.

"No!" Malekh roared, finding just enough strength to get to his feet . . . and to throw himself into the fires as well.

Remy cried out and started after them, but Elke's grip tightened on his arm. "No, Remy," she said.

He tried to break free. "But they could be—"

"There's a possibility that they can survive the Godsflame, but no human save the First ever has. You can't risk it, Remy! Not even for them."

Still bleeding, Shiragiku limped to the destroyed wall, but there was no one waiting for her within. The Night Empress was gone.

Remy stared at the Godsflame, heart pounding. They were the strongest vampires he'd known. Surely, surely . . .

Elke's arms circled his waist. "*Please*, Remy," she wept. "Don't."

The flames leaped up, an otherworldly sapphire for several moments before returning to its orange intensity. Xiaodan and

Malekh appeared in a heap on the platform before them. Swallowing his cry of relief, Remy stepped forward.

The snarl was his only warning.

He was on the ground with Elke crouched in front of him, a hand clasped to her bleeding shoulder.

Xiaodan's teeth were bared, hair in wild disarray. There was a look of fury in her eyes Remy had never seen before, bordering on madness. Her hands were gnarled like talons, and she was glowing brighter than the sun had ever shone down on Elouve.

Frenzy.

The word shot through his brain, panicked and terrified. She'd succumbed to the frenzy.

Xiaodan leaped for Elke, who barely dodged the blow as she drew the vampiress away from Remy. "No!" he shouted, snatching up Breaker from where it had fallen out of Altace's grip. He shook out his knifechain and ran . . . only to be blocked by Malekh. The man's eyes were red and his fangs at their fullest, his features nearly unrecognizable.

"Malekh." Remy said his name slowly. "I know you're in there. That you don't want to hurt me."

A hiss from the Summer Lord, but he did not attack. Remy risked taking his eyes off the man's face, watched as Malekh's fingers dug down hard into the stone ground, leaving grooves in their wake. As if he was forcing himself to remain still.

A flash of hope bolted through Remy. "I know you can do this, you bastard. You like me too bloody much to—"

It must have been the wrong thing to say because Malekh was on him in an instant. Remy only had enough time to bring up his knifechain, shoving the links at Malekh's mouth to keep him from reaching his throat. Malekh's face was only inches away; there was a telltale snap as one of Remy's chains broke, the strongest steel Elke could find, unable to endure the vampire lord's strength.

"Fuck, Malekh!" Remy lifted a boot and kicked desperately at the man's chest, feeling like he'd broken a toe instead. His hand scrambled for the knife still attached to the link, finding it just as Malekh bent lower. "I'm not going to die knowing you'll feel guilty for killing me on top of everything else!"

It wasn't a fatal wound by any means. Malekh's shoulder was the closest target he could reach, and even then, Remy winced when the blade dug deep into the vampire's flesh, as if he'd just been stabbed himself. And he couldn't stop his cry of pain when the vampire responded in kind, teeth biting down hard on his arm.

And then he was no longer on the ground but in some empty white space where the fog closed in around him, thick and unyielding.

This was different. Malekh was several feet away, on his knees and bent over in agony. A little beyond him lay Xiaodan, thrashing noiselessly on the ground, still aglow.

Remy forced himself to move, crawled the last few feet to reach them.

"Kill me," Malekh rasped, a pained sound. "It's the only way."

"If it's all the same to you, I'd rather not." Remy grabbed at Malekh's head and pulled him closer, with no idea what the fuck he was doing or if he was doing it right, but determined to do it all the same. "You are coming back to me, both of you," he said fiercely, bracing his forehead against Malekh's. "And you're going to do it because you are stronger than this, and I fucking love you. You haven't spent more than nine hundred years dicking around only to let some goddamn fire be your downfall. Come back to me, you arse. Come back to—"

He didn't expect Malekh to seize him by the neck and bite down, but this time there was no pain, only the breathtakingly, sickeningly sweet pleasure he remembered when they couldn't keep their hands off each other. He let himself go limp, allowed the vampire to have his fill, and when Malekh finally raised his head, his eyes were a bright gold.

"Xiaodan," Malekh rasped.

"I'm scared," Xiaodan sobbed, curled up into a ball and glowing so brightly they could barely see her within the light. "I can't do this. I can't."

"You can." Ignoring the spasm of pain on the side of his neck, Remy took her gently in his arms, ignoring how the light hurt his eyes. "You promised me you would fight to stay by our side, and I'm holding you to that."

Xiaodan's hands found his shoulders, squeezed them, almost digging into Remy's flesh. "I'm not myself. I could hurt you."

"Nothing you can do can ever hurt me more than leaving me." Following Malekh's lead, Remy tugged her closer. And then again that pinprick sweetness, that spike of ecstasy as Xiaodan's fangs sank deeply into him.

And then the pressure was gone, and Remy was on his back, the cave ceiling looming above. Malekh was on his feet, no longer primed to attack. He was licking his lips, where traces of Remy's blood still lingered. "Are you all right?" he asked, and for once his usually devastatingly calm voice sounded like it was packed full of cotton.

Remy was still bleeding slightly. Malekh tore a strip of cloth from his shirt, tying it like a tourniquet on his upper arm just below the wound.

"Are you finally sane?" Remy asked weakly, touching a finger to his neck.

Xiaodan was no longer fighting Elke. Instead, she sat with her back against the cave wall, crying quietly as she cradled her mother in her arms.

"Oh, sweet child," Yingyue whispered. "Are you yourself again?" And then she chuckled weakly. "A fine thing to say, when I have not been myself for so many years."

"Mother," Xiaodan begged. "Don't leave me."

"I've been leaving you on your own for so long. I can do this one last thing for you, at least." Gently, Yingyue lifted a bloodied hand and placed it against Xiaodan's cheek. "Do not cry for me, my beautiful daughter," she breathed. "Only rejoice that I will no longer have to live caged inside this body. I go now to where your father is, but know that I—we—are so . . ."

Her hand dropped, and an errant breeze swept her from Xiaodan's arms, ashes dancing into the wind.

"Xiaodan," Malekh said.

"No," Xiaodan said, though her tears still flowed freely. "I—I'm glad she doesn't have to suffer now."

"I don't know what you three did just now, but I am glad for it," Elke said, sounding weary. The wound on her shoulder was a mess, but she managed a shrug at Remy's stricken expression. "It looks worse than it is."

"I'm sorry," Xiaodan said wearily.

Remy winced when Malekh tugged the strip of cloth tighter. "Someone needs to see to you and Elke, Malekh."

"It barely stings." Malekh took the dagger still buried in his arm and pulled it out with barely a wince. "You should have driven it into my heart."

"And lose the chance to rub it in your face how right I was not to? I think not."

Malekh leaned in close and kissed him thoroughly, robbing him of his next boast. Those who emerged from the Godsflame came out more vicious, Remy had been told, but Malekh's hands on Remy remained gentle, and there was a newfound softness in his eyes. He helped Remy to his feet so they could check on Xiaodan, who had not moved from her spot, still looking down at her hands.

"I could have killed you and Elke," she said, horrified.

"But you didn't," Remy said, sinking down beside her.

"I don't remember much. Only an anger I've never felt before."

"Was it Remy's blood that helped you and Lady Xiaodan survive the flames?" Elke asked.

"Our regular bloodsharing may have established a connection where no other vampire who had entered the Godsflame could . . ." Malekh paused. "Was that your secret after all, Lilith?" he asked quietly. "Was that how you survived? You shared your heart with many who loved you dearly, after all."

"More than that. Otherwise, most kindred with such blood bonds would have made it through the frenzy with ease."

Xiaodan lifted her head. "Because we love him?" she asked softly. "Because our blood is different from that of other kindred, and it flows through him, too? Because Remy has his own ties to kindred? How simple, and how terribly complicated." There was still a hazy ring of light about her when she turned to Remy and gave him a kiss, and he could feel the exhaustion spilling out of her in waves. "I feel a bit more like myself again. Zidan?"

"I don't feel any different, but now may not be the time for introspection."

"What has happened here?" Fanglei had finally arrived, looking about at the strewn bodies with mounting horror as she pieced together what had happened. "The Antecedents?" she choked out, displaying more emotion than Remy had ever seen from her. "They betrayed us?"

"Unfortunately so, though most of the carnage you see here was by the Night Empress's hand. How fare the battles outside?"

"The mutations and the coven have retreated. The Alurian army has arrived by the lakeshore and are engaging the rest. By a stroke of luck, they were within a few hours' ride from the lake when Grager and Krylla found them."

"More than just a stroke of luck, knowing my father," Remy muttered.

Malekh grimaced. "We were in far greater danger here than outside the temple. Xiaodan—"

"I know what you're going to say, but I refuse to sit and recuperate in my rooms while the rest of the courts return. They will not be happy when we tell them about the high priestess and her Antecedents." Xiaodan swayed slightly as she stood, waving off Remy's attempts to help, then folded her arms. "See? I will rest later, but for now, I am just as capable of meeting them as you are."

Malekh pinched the bridge of his nose. "The Antecedents may no longer have control of the Night Empress, but that does not mean she is powerless. If anything, now that the shackles are off, she may be even more dangerous."

Speck groaned, stirring as Malekh gently lifted the man up.

"Milord?" the young physician asked, eyes fluttering. "Are you . . . finally awake?"

"More than ever," the Summer Lord told him. "And you did a fine job protecting me, Speck. I am grateful."

"Good," the man sighed, eyes closing again.

"What are you doing?" Elke asked, aghast, when Remy scooped the still-breathing Thaïs up. "Remy, she tried to kill you."

"She's in no shape to do so now." He looked down at the frail vampiress in his arms. He wanted to be furious, to hate her for what she'd done to his mother, for what she and her clan had nearly cost them. But he could muster nothing for her beyond pity.

"Why?" Thaïs whispered. "I do not deserve your kindness."

Remy didn't know either. All he knew was that he was tired of so much killing. "Just because you say you don't deserve it, that does not mean I cannot give it," he finally said. It was a poor answer, but he had never been much good at those anyway.

26

A NEW DAY

The other court leaders listened with grim faces as Malekh relayed what had happened that day. "I knew Isabella could be overzealous," Hylasenth said. "But to think that she would conspire against us with the Night Empress herself?"

"She tried to kill Trin simply because she was in the wrong place at the wrong time?" Raghnall demanded, his expression hard.

"At ease, Seventh," Hylasenth said. "We want no further bloodshed today."

"And it was she who killed my mother?" Lorien was moving deliberately toward Remy, who still carried Thaïs in his arms.

"Lorien—"

"Be at ease, friend." He looked down at the injured woman. "Why?" he asked, voice pained. "Why would you all follow in such madness?"

"Because it is the only way," Thaïs whispered. "We were optimistic at the beginning, when the sundering of the First Court promised to pave a better life for us all. But though the Night King was gone, kindred turned upon one another, their greed and lust for power further diminishing our numbers. We are all now are but a tenth of our number during the Night King's reign, and it emboldened the humans to take up arms, to learn how to exterminate us. Isabella thought that if she could put someone of considerable power on the throne, but not so strong that she could not keep them under her eye, then everything that had led to Ishkibal's fall could be averted. She truly believed it. I am sorry, milord. Please take my life."

"You may not have been the hand that slew my mother, but I hold you responsible all the same," Lorien Tattersall said. "That said, killing you will not bring my mother back, nor anyone else the Antecedents have murdered. I will find a more fitting punishment, but live you will."

Thaïs seemed to wilt further against Remy. "Then I will accept whatever measures you choose," she whispered.

Tears fell from the Second Court leader's face. With a grimace, he dashed at his eyes with a sleeve. "As a first condition, you must tell us everything you know of the Night Empress and her other lairs. Where does she keep most of her coven? Will she continue her siege against the Allpriory or look elsewhere for targets?"

"Rulership of the Allpriory has always been Isabella's objective, not Ligaya Pendergast's. With her compulsion gone, I am sure she will not return here again. Not even my priestess knew of all the empress's comings and goings."

"How much of these attacks was of my mother's volition, and how much your priestess's doing?" Remy asked quietly. "The siege at Elouve? The attacks in Kerenai?"

But the girl could only shake her head, even that slight movement looking painful. She closed her eyes with a sigh.

"Ironic, that she who could compel armies was compelled herself," Hylasenth noted.

"You are just as culpable," Xiaodan said.

"Pardon?"

"You and Raghnall hunted her for years. Isabella admitted as much. You knew that she was of the First's bloodline, that she belonged to the clan of the Whispering Isles. The Night Empress claimed it was both Alurian and vampire together that attacked the Wikaan kindred, and she was telling the truth."

"My dear," Fanglei said. "Had you or Malekh known, you would have surely opposed it, and there would have been far more kindred like her."

"So it was your idea," Malekh said.

"They did nothing to provoke you!" Xiaodan seethed. "The Wikaan vampires spent their lives in hiding. They only wished to defend themselves against Ishkibal, not to rule any throne! They would have spent the rest of their lives on their island in peace."

"You are far more naïve than I thought," Fanglei said coldly. "Hylasenth, Raghnall, Etrienne, and I agreed that no opposing seed of the First should be permitted to live—though Sauveterre, it seems, played us false. And yes, we did so without informing either the Third or Fourth Courts. Or the Second, as we knew Redwald had the ear of its leader."

"So this is why you wanted me as Hierarch," Malekh said. "As boldly as you claim that your choices were for the good of the council, you are less inclined to face the consequences of them and would rather have let me deal with the aftermath."

"You always had first right to claim the position of Hierarch," Fanglei said smoothly. "We merely chose not to contest it."

"The irony is that we thought to eradicate the Wikaan bloodline by purging the isles," the Seventh said, "and only through our folly did the Night Empress rise against us."

"Surely you cannot agree with the Third and Fourth now, Raghnall?" Hylasenth asked.

"Our decision may yet cost me Trin." Raghnall leaned forward and closed his eyes. "And even if she survives, I shall regret what happened to her for the rest of my life."

"How long have you known that the Night Empress was my mother?" Remy asked, dreading the answer.

Fanglei sighed. "We knew a descendant of the Wikaan clan was under Etrienne's protection, though we could not determine her location after he and his court perished. We did not know she was Alurian and also Lord Pendergast's wife until rumors of their elopement occupied the gossip of the Elouvian courts. It stank of the Fifth's machinations."

"Would you have killed me?"

"Beluske was willing, but he died before we could talk of the matter further, and his successor, Queen Ophelia, argued against it. She and Xiaodan were friends, and your fiancée proved a much more frustrating influence than even her father. You, we knew better than to touch. Your father guarded you closely, and we knew any attack on you would start a war with Aluria that we could ill afford. Well and good that Lord Malekh took to you, and in the short span of our acquaintance, I've found myself growing rather fond of you as well."

"If you worry that we still have reason to take your life, know that the time for such attempts have long since passed." Raghnall sounded weary. "Should the Night Empress be unwilling to parlay, then we will have no choice but to resume our fight against her, considering the threat she poses to the council. As for the rest of her progeny, we hold no grudges. We have lost far too much already in this endeavor, and I have no wish to risk more."

Hylasenth watched the other man walk away and sighed. "The Seventh is right, as jarring a change as that is," he said. "There is little that can be done now. We thought to stamp out a threat for the betterment of our clans and failed to do so, but we shall see all this through to the end. You have the Eighth's support still, Malekh, and I pray that you know the best means to end this once and for all."

"And you?" Malekh asked Fanglei. "What do you intend now?"

The old woman sniffed, plucked some invisible lint from her sleeve. "Our goals remain the same. Take out the Night Empress, unite the courts. Who was in the wrong can be argued afterward. No harm shall befall your precious human—for as long as you keep the throne, of course."

"Is that a threat, Fanglei?" Xiaodan asked stiffly.

The Sixth Court leader flashed her a smile. "Merely a promise. Now then, what are we to do next?"

THE MUTATIONS had been dealt with, their corpses inoculated and collected, to be burned once Valenbonne issued the command. Remy's father surveyed the bloody field with some satisfaction. The soldiers not made to work on collecting the grisly bodies were setting up camp some ways from the lake.

"There's a chance she might return," Valenbonne said amicably. "I believe one of their leaders—Lady Fanglei Cao, was it?—has offered use of the underground temple for our lodgings, but as friendly as they are now, I doubt that I nor any of my men will want to sleep in kindred territory. And a little bird told me that the Night Empress made her way inside easily enough."

The *little bird* was currently lounging by the lakeside, looking bored out of his mind. Though the other vampires eyed him wearily, the young messenger gave no indication of giving a damn.

"The kindred aided Aluria in conquering the Whispering Isles," Remy said. "And they were hunting for Mother long before she allegedly eloped with one of the court. How much of a hand in it did Beluske have—did His Highness grant them permission to kill her? And how much of it did you know?"

Edgar Pendergast said nothing for a while, watching as his soldiers continued to stack corpses in piles before them. At least a quarter of the dead were First Court kindred; the rest had fled with their mistress, possibly the instant she'd left the Godsflame. "It was at Beluske's insistence, after the kindred came to make the offer—the Eighth Court leader, on behalf of the Sixth and Seventh—*despite* my misgivings and Ophelia's strenuous objections. I had lost my faith in His Highness long before, and when I learned that he'd tried to conspire with the kindred to kill my own wife, it was the last straw. He died suddenly, did he not?"

"Father," Remy said, stunned. "You—you didn't—"

"Beluske was not one to care for his own health. He enjoyed the soirées and banquets, favored his wines and his roasts far too often. So when they declared him dead of an unexpected heart ailment, no one saw reason to question it."

"But—"

"Queen Ophelia was a far better ruler than he could ever dream to be, and his death was nothing but a boon to the kingdom. Beluske never informed me of his cooperation with the vampire courts." Edgar Pendergast's voice grew quiet. "I only wanted to bring her away, to protect her. Not once did I realize that she herself was kindred."

"She was trying to protect you," Remy said.

Valenbonne let out a bark of laughter. "You think far too highly of her, considering the devastation she's already wrecked in two kingdoms and the vampire courts besides."

"She watched you because even then, she wanted to find a way to be with you. She was frenzied for most of the two decades she had left, and the temple priestess's hold on her made it even worse, but she had her lucid moments, and she spent them watching you."

"No," Valenbonne said, though the faint unexpected lilt in his voice gave him away. "She hated me, Remington, long before she died. I would have given her everything within my power if only she had stayed with me, trusted me. If she wanted another lover, I would have looked away, if only she had come home to me at day's end. But she left. There was nothing she could find in me to stay."

"Father—"

"Prepare the bonfires," Valenbonne told Riones, who'd come running up. "The coagulants we shot into the mutations should be more than enough to prevent their resurrection, but I'd like them burning as hot as you can manage."

"There is another option now, milord," Xiaodan said as she stepped toward them. She held out her hands, and they glowed briefly.

"Well," Lord Pendergast said. "By all means, and my congratulations, Lady Song. I had wondered why you were looking rather rosy today. I take it that the temple did wonders for you during your stay?"

"Unfortunately so." Ignoring his quizzical look, Xiaodan raised her hands toward the piles of corpses before her. Light sizzled out from them, and in the space of two seconds, the dead the Alurians had piled up disintegrated so thoroughly that nothing visible remained.

There were startled gasps from the soldiers who hadn't expected it, but Riones slumped with relief. "If only you were with us at Kerenai, milady," he said. "We discarded the ashes as best we could with Lord Malekh's antidote, but I was still left worrying what to do should the bits of bone stitch themselves together and rise again."

"I am greatly indebted to you, Eugenie," Malekh said gravely to the information gatherer, who approached them.

"Think nothing of it, Lord Malekh," the woman said cheerfully. "I worried that the lord high steward would refuse to work with a simple vampire, but he was most accommodating. After all, if we intend to become members of the Fifth Court, then it is only natural that we strive to work with the humans."

"You intend to join the Fifth?"

"The Lady Whittaker would be glad for our services, I think." Eugenie smiled wistfully. "Paolo and I had never been members of any court before. But I rather think I would I like being a part of something that I have cause to believe in. That is, of course, if the Lady Whittaker doesn't mind me bringing a familiar along."

"I'm sure she won't."

"Did you hear that, Paolo?" Eugenie called out joyfully. "We're the Fifth kindred now!"

"Ha," her beloved said, glaring at the spot where the corpses had been, as if somehow this was their fault.

THE KINDRED had retreated to the temple underground, and Malekh and Xiaodan with them. Remy chose to linger with the soldiers' camp instead; so many things had happened within the Allpriory that he could not be sure that he would ever be comfortable spending the night there after this. Several tents had since been set up for their use, his father having intuited his discomfort, which was a new aspect to their relationship that he also found disconcerting.

Elke had made use of that hospitality. Remy had seen her quietly sneaking into the tent Alegra had chosen for the night and thought it best to leave his best friend well alone. Alegra had been quiet and withdrawn since Yingyue's death, and as much as he worried for her, he knew Elke would better know how to ease the woman's pain.

He felt no pressing need to retire himself. He'd offered to take a shift to stand guard over the encampment, an offer Riones had received with horror and a flat-out refusal. Resigned in the face of the man's stubbornness, Remy had instead retreated toward the edge of the camp, looking out over the lake. There were lesser clouds in this part of the region, and the stars were a sight to behold, having little opportunity to see them in Elouvian skies.

"Copper for your thoughts?"

Riones was back, holding two steaming mugs in his hands.

"None so valuable as that," Remy said, accepting one. "Thank you."

"Hot chocolate," Riones said. "My mother used to whip up a huge batch of it, especially when the winters grew something fierce back at Castamanas. Always keep a few packets with me on the road. It's a source of comfort to me during trying times, and I hope it bodes the same for you."

It was thick, sweet, and creamy, just the way Remy liked it. "Elouve feels all the safer with you in charge of affairs, Riones."

"The highest of compliments, given your contributions to its betterment, Aphelion." At Remy's raised eyebrow, Riones chuckled and took a sip of his drink. "You call me Riones all the time. It should not be so surprising that I would call you by your title."

"*Marquess of Riones* suits you. *Marquess of Aphelion* feels like clothes that would never fit me."

"Aye, you always seem more at home with *Reaper* or *hunter*. Or *familiar*." Riones grinned. "So. Really? Lady Song *and* Lord Malekh?"

Remy winced. "Be honest with me, Riones. How have people reacted to that in Elouve?"

"Quietly, given the way the last mob was dispersed. The priests are still on their high horses, but barely anyone pays them attention now." Riones raised his head, surveyed the night sky. "There are many who do appreciate you and what you've done for them," he said. "Some you've never met, and so you know little of their high regard for you. Others have had time to reassess since the attack on the capital, though they are hard-pressed to admit it when they've made it their personality to turn their nose down on you for so long."

"I suppose," Remy said, thinking of the Lady Rotteburg.

"There are those who care not a whit that you're consorting with the Third and Fourth Court leaders. Bloody hell, Lord Malekh and Lady Song helped us repel all those vampires in Elouve, and they all know it. I'm happy for you, my friend. You seem content with them, and that's all that matters, eh?"

Remy smiled. "I appreciate you, Riones."

"Have you any notions of returning in the future, if we are lucky enough for a longer respite? You could take back your official duties as Reaper, perhaps accept a greater role in the administration of the kingdom? Her Majesty has been very pleased with your work."

Remy took a sip of the cocoa. "Lord Malekh and Lady Song have both asked me to join their courts," he said quietly. "In a similar capacity."

Riones's eyes widened. "I suspected that it was serious, but—are you sure, Remington? Not that I would begrudge you any of this if it is what you want, but you told me you were never one for politics, and you'd be jumping headfirst into a pool of chaos."

"I think they might be worth all that," Remy said, looking back up at the stars. "I've never felt at peace in Elouve, or anywhere else in Aluria. With them . . . I think this is what home is supposed to feel like."

Riones laughed softly. "You've got it bad, Remington. Lucky bastard. Tell those two to stop by Elouve every now and then, once the dust settles. I still owe you that drink."

"I will," Remy said, "though my choice of beverage by then might not be one you will find so easily in taverns, should I finally give in to temptation."

He waited, expecting Riones to recoil from him in horror. The man's eyes looked stunned for a brief moment as the words sunk in, but soon enough he was smiling again. "I can always ask Lady

Whittaker where she finds her stores," he said, "and I'll open a bottle of my best wine so we can celebrate all the same."

REMY WAS nearly asleep inside his tent by the time they returned. He only remembered the sudden burst of warmth about him as someone tucked him into the crook of their arm and felt another settle against his chest. "Took you two long enough," he mumbled.

"We never had the chance to thank you yet, did we?" Xiaodan whispered. "For keeping us safe."

"S'all right."

A low hum behind him, and then the sensation of a mouth pressed against the back of his neck. Remy groaned. "Get your own cot," he groused. "We all can't fit in this one."

"No," Malekh said, voice just as rich and thick as the hot chocolate Remy had imbibed with Riones. "Try as you might, you are bound to us now."

27

AN ENGAGEMENT

It was morning, and Lord Valenbonne was relaying final instructions to his men. The kindred had returned aboveground, with the courts assigning trusted vassals to keep guard over the Allpriory.

Remy wasn't sure what they intended to do with Thaïs. Lorien had asked her to be placed under his care. The youth had shown no signs of wanting revenge, but Remy couldn't help his concern.

"Mother wouldn't want me to harm her," the Second Court leader told him. He was to return to the Lady Rotteburg's estate to put the woman's affairs in order before rejoining Malekh. "I suppose she was as much a victim, brainwashed by the priestess for centuries. She's been deeply remorseful, and I'm inclined to believe her."

"You're far too kind for this," Remy said, and then gave a little start, remembering the times Elke or Xiaodan had said the very same thing to him.

"I suppose. But kindness has to start somewhere, doesn't it?"

The other court leaders, too, planned on returning to their respective domains to prepare. There was no reason to believe that the Night Empress would act differently than when she'd been under the priestess's thrall, though the prospect of having to face his mother again hurt.

He hadn't been able to see Trin again before the Seventh Court had departed. Likely she was still suffering from the frenzy, but he felt sad not to have known. Raghnall had been even more abrupt and curt than usual, stonewalling Remy's questions.

Malekh intended to return to the Fata Morgana to make his own preparations, while Alegra was to make for Chàngge Shuǐ to inform the others of Yingyue's death. "They will be shocked and saddened, but not surprised, I think," she said quietly. "And as selfish as it is of me to say, I cannot help but think of it as a final reprieve, after all the years she's mourned and suffered."

Xiaodan had said even less about her mother's passing. Unsure of how to approach her, Remy had chosen to hover by her side to the point of painful obviousness. He did not want her to grieve alone again like she had back at the Third Court.

"I know what you're doing, Remy," Xiaodan finally said after an hour of him tailing her like a shadow. "I am perfectly all right."

"I am certain you are," Remy said.

"Eugenie has very kindly offered to use one of her many residences as a temporary stronghold while I figure out my court," Elke told them. "As I want build my own clan, I want to rid it of the stain of Etrienne's legacy once and for all."

"And I expect you to be frighteningly competent at it, given your successes in Elouve."

"I appreciate the vote of confidence. The other courts are to depart in a few hours' time. Immune as they are to the daylight, they are loathe to travel in the morning. Fanglei has been most insistent about meticulously packing all that her clan had brought to the Allpriory. By the Light, what does one do with sixteen pairs of slippers and two dozen silk robes? I have only seen her wear linen since we've arrived at the temple."

Remy took the opportunity to explore the Allpriory for the last time, knowing he would never set foot back inside the temple given the choice. He should not have been surprised to see his father already inside, looking at the empty throne with a faint jeer on his face. Grimesworthy stood beside him, quiet and as intimidating as always.

"Is that it?" Edgar Pendergast asked. "All the blood they've shed over eons, this is what it boils down to?" He laughed. "Well. Not so different than we do in Elouve, eh, Remington? Though we call ourselves lord high steward when they would call themselves kings. And where is this Godsflame that I've been hearing so much about? You need not look so sour about it. Lord Malekh has given me permission to view this monstrosity they've been keeping a secret, and after all we've done to help defend this place, none of the other courts protested. I'd like to see the accursed fires that resurrected my wife at least once in my lifetime."

Remy was too tired to argue. He led him to the Fount and toward the platform where the flames continued to burn with its odd blue hues, indifferent to the violence that had taken place in its sight hours before.

The bodies of the Antecedents had been brought away, and he didn't inquire about how they were disposed of. He thought of the temple priestess's zeal, the devout desperation that had festered inside her all these centuries.

"What do you intend to do next?" he asked his father.

"Keep some regiments in the area to ensure that no one claims the Allpriory as their own. Some mutations still linger, and I would destroy whatever nests survive. But I suppose the better question is, what do *you* intend to do?"

The answer came readily enough. "I'm returning to the Third Court with Malekh and Xiaodan."

"Oh? So you intend to renounce all the positions Queen

Ophelia has been itching to give you, to be nothing more than their consort?"

"They treat me as far more than a consort. More than what anyone thought me to be at Elouve."

He was expecting Valenbonne to be angry. But the man only continued to stare into the ghastly fires. "They tell me that this is where the first vampire was born," Valenbonne mused. "That they walked into the flames and emerged unscathed, with powers no human reckoning could have imagined. A brave feat, they said. But I wonder, who would choose to throw themselves into such a terrifying conflagration if despair did not motivate their actions? They said she was a criminal condemned by her own clan, didn't they? Ironic to find herself walking out whole and unharmed, cursed with her new immortal life?"

"I would not put it above you to try the same thing," Remy said guardedly, watching his father as the light cast shadows over his face.

Valenbonne chuckled and took a step back. "Not on a whim, no. You may think me foolhardy, Remington, for allowing Quintin Yost to experiment with my body, but I had little to lose then. Now, I have much more to gain by not surrendering myself to fancy."

He took pause. "No. That was not how I should have described it. I was infirmed and close to dying, of no use to anyone. Had I met my death quickly in battle, I think I would have faced it with as much grace and dignity as I could muster. It is a weary thing, to be a burden."

"A burden?" Remy echoed, surprised.

"That is of no matter," his father said, smiling contentedly to himself. "We have thwarted the Night Empress for today, and her mutations litter the ground above and below. It is a good day."

~

FANGLEI'S SUBORDINATES rushed back and forth from the temple, carting the rest of their leaders' trunks and other miscellany—Elke had not exaggerated when she said that the Sixth Court queen had brought far more possessions than she'd bothered to use. After parting ways with his father, Remy had avoided their mad rush, heading immediately to the chambers he shared with his lovers on the western side.

Malekh and Xiaodan had yet to finish packing their belongings for the journey back home. Neither were the disorganized sort; Remy saw with a guilty flush that his own meager items were strewn more haphazardly about than either of theirs. It was quick work to clear away the rest of his belongings; after a moment's deliberation, he began attending to theirs as well.

The effects of their bloodsharing hadn't completely gone away. The lust had dimmed somewhat after everything else, but now that he was holding their clothes, their possessions, parts of it flickered back to life, brought back by the scent of them that still lingered in their chambers. Long before he'd met Malekh, he would have scoffed at the idea of vampires bearing scents, for not even his bloodwaker-imbued sense of smell could detect them. But now they were as familiar to him as breathing. He had not touched any bloodwakers since their journey began.

Malekh had brought relatively little, as always. A few changes of clothing, all in neutral tones of gray, brown, or black, and a few cleaning implements for his sword, most tucked away inside a second valise. And then there was the oversized kit where he stored all the medical equipment he liked to bring along in cases of emergencies, but that was the extent of the lord's vanity.

Xiaodan was a different story. While she hadn't had the trunks upon trunks of clothing and items that Fanglei had, she'd brought along a pretty qipao for formal occasions and sensible shirts and breeches suited for traveling. A few hair ornaments, a few bottles Remy recognized for her skin, though the thought of Xiaodan worrying she might break out in spots made him smile. Several jewelry boxes, one smaller than the others. He opened it, wondering briefly if it was fragile, so he could wrap it heavily in some cloth before—

It was a simple gold ring, bright and polished. Remy stared at it wordlessly.

He had seen one on the dresser of their chambers at Fata Morgana. Had Malekh fashioned a replacement in case one of them lost theirs? But they never wore them.

He knew enough about courting rituals, had seen many a newly engaged woman flaunt her ostentatious jewelry in a bid to incite envy. But the rings were simple enough that it would cost very little to—

There was the sound of a throat being cleared behind him. Remy turned to see Xiaodan and Malekh by the doorway: the latter leaning against the frame, the former looking aghast. "Y-you shouldn't have seen that," Xiaodan spluttered.

"I'm sorry. I thought it would be faster if I were to pack the rest of your things."

A chuckle from Malekh. "No sense in delaying it now, Xiaodan."

"Delaying what?" Remy asked.

"Remy," Xiaodan said seriously. "Do you know what that is?"

Remy looked down at it again. "A ring?"

"Yes. And what do you think it's for?"

"I suppose it's something supplementary, should you accidentally lose the ones you have or need the originals cleaned."

"Remy," Xiaodan said, with all the patience of the Mother. "It is a simple enough design that a warm soak is enough for polish. And we never mislay our possessions."

"Oh," Remy said, perplexed at why she was taking the time to explain to him the intricacies of their jewelry. He'd never worn many himself, except for some function or other.

A strange sound erupted from Malekh. On any other person, Remy would have thought it was laughter.

"The ring isn't for Zidan or myself," Xiaodan said gently. "We'd been hoping to ask you when things weren't as chaotic as they've been the last several hours."

Remy stared blankly at her. "Ask me what?"

Malekh remained amused. Xiaodan sighed, crouching down beside him. "Remy, I swear to everything you consider holy that sometimes you are the densest person I have ever met. It's *yours*."

Remy looked down at the ring. It did look about his size. Xiaodan must have been very good at estimating, or had she measured his finger when he was asleep?

And then, finally, he understood.

"Me?" He didn't mean to sound like he was choking on thick wool, right on the verge of regurgitating it back out. Neither seemed offended. Xiaodan looked worried, while Malekh was having the time of his life.

"Actually, we were planning on asking Raghnall for the honor," the lord said. "Of course it's you, you oblivious arse."

"You don't have to answer now," Xiaodan said hurriedly. "Malekh was overhasty in talking to your father about involving you in the Third and Fourth Courts, and I don't want to—"

Remy leaped for them.

Xiaodan was pinned to the floor beneath him, Remy taking her unawares for the first time while he peppered kisses onto her mouth and neck. With his other hand, Remy grabbed at Malekh's collar and yanked him to them, lifting himself up from the woman to fuse his mouth with the Summer Lord's.

"A yes, then?" Malekh murmured.

"I don't need a wedding in Aluria," Remy breathed. "I don't *want* a fucking wedding in Aluria. I don't need a wedding at all. Just the two of you in bed for a week, and if I'm still walking by the end of it, I'll sue for annulment."

"Oh," Xiaodan said. She lifted a hand to cup at his face, peering into his eyes. "We should have been more careful, Zidan. He's still under the influence of the bloodsharing."

"You were caught up in a particularly nasty frenzy," Malekh said. "As was I. Surely Pendergast can forgive us the momentary lapse."

But their hands were already moving, divesting him of his clothing. A particularly hard tug from Malekh sent one unlucky boot flying into the corner of the room with a muted thunk.

"We'll ask you again once you're of sounder mind," Xiaodan said against his throat, teeth nipping playfully along the base. "For now, we intend to take very good care of you, puppy."

"I want Malekh's arse for my wedding present," Remy continued, and the lord finally, truly laughed.

"MILORD? MILADY? Oh, hell, I didn't mean to—"

Remy cracked an eye open. Both Xiaodan and Malekh were already up, talking in low tones as they moved about their chambers, sorting the rest of the belongings that Remy had tried to pack before he was interrupted. Lazy bastard that he was, he'd been content to lounge about in bed and polish off the rest of the plate of fruit that had been sitting in their quarters before all hell broke loose, not wanting them to go to waste. He glanced over and saw Elke doing her best not to look in their general direction, as they all three had felt little need to put on clothing.

"Lady Whittaker?" Xiaodan asked, startled. "I thought you'd already left for Eugenie's."

"Left and brought my arse back here running again. We hadn't time to do much there before one of Eugenie's pigeons came soaring in with a fresh report. The First Court is moving east toward Agathyrsi, milady. There's no time."

"Agathyrsi?" Malekh whirled, eyes flashing. "Does she intend to attack the Fata Morgana?"

"I would very much hope not, but all indications point to that."

"They cannot have recovered so quickly." Malekh was already pulling on his shirt and reaching for his breeches.

"Didn't Riones say that there were close to ten thousand children who'd gone missing in the course of ten years from Aluria, Kerenai, and the surrounding areas? The Night Empress has all the numbers she needs—especially if those who succumb to the frenzy can be turned via the Rot." Elke was pale. "I've already called on the other courts, but I do not know how long it will take them. Eugenie's is the closest to your court, and they've already been alerted. I apologize for overstepping my bounds, Lady Song, but I told Alegra to bring everyone from the Fourth that she could spare."

"You did the right thing, Lady Whittaker." Xiaodan was already pulling on her own clothes while Remy was scrambling to find his. "We didn't get through to her, then," she said, voice pained. "I thought that perhaps—"

"If Ishkibal's blood still runs through her veins," Malekh said, "it is not an unforeseeable outcome."

But they'd hoped not, for his sake. "She's still frenzied. I'll get word to my father; he cannot have traveled very far." Remy finally spotted his shirt half-hidden underneath the bed. "He still had plans to survey the area, in the event of any stragglers, and was heading toward the Fata Morgana himself. No doubt he's left his vampire messenger near the Allpriory, waiting to see me leave. I'll send word to him, and they should be at the fortress only an hour or so behind us."

"Remy," Xiaodan said, sounding troubled. Malekh watched him with the guarded look that Remy knew all too well.

"We'll finish this one way or another," he said, curbing his despair. "No more regrets. If she still wants to fight in the end, then we'll give her the battle she wants."

THE VAMPIRE messenger appeared after Remy had shouted for
him a third time, looking bemused. "Must you call me *an under-
sized piece of shit* every time you try to summon me?" he inquired
politely, not at all affronted by Remy's lack of etiquette.

"Maybe if I knew what your fucking name was," Remy said,
then barreled on when the latter gave no sign of giving it, "Tell my
father to make haste to the Fata Morgana. The Night Empress is
on the move and intends to make her next siege there."

"Even without the temple clan's influence?"

"It's complicated."

"I shall send word immediately." The messenger hesitated. "I
have no love for the courts, as you very well know. I have always
thought your Summer Lord's penchant for seeing humans and
kindred coexist far more optimistic than what the reality requires.
But after seeing the odd arrangement he has with the humans
within his domain—perhaps it's possible after all." And he was off
before Remy could formulate a reply.

28

SURROUNDED

Remy was glad to see the last of the Allpriory behind him, but the thought of the upcoming battle cramped his gut. Neither he, Xiaodan, or Malekh were in the mood for much talking, and Peanut, sent back by Agatha once she received the news, sensed their unease. It would take half an hour to reach the Third Court, Malekh had said. Remy had turned down his offer of resting up at intervals, determined only to get to the Fata Morgana despite the dizziness that came with riding distances few humans could handle on undead horseback, though experience had tempered some of the nausea.

It was with relief that he finally spotted the imposing fortress ahead, a first glance telling him that it was not on fire or overrun. That was the extent of the good news, because Fata Morgana was completely surrounded by what looked to be thousands upon thousands of coven and mutations alike.

The residents within had already activated many of the weapons Remy had previously seen. Hedgehog-like spikes jutted out all over the walls, and many of the mutations who'd attempted to scale them wound up brutally impaled. But for every fallen Rot, there were several more eager to climb the fortress in search of victims, not caring or stopping even when the spikes caught more of them in the chests and gullets.

"We won't be able to get inside," Xiaodan said tersely.

"We can't, lest we compromise the safety of all within."

"Zidan, we can't handle them on our own. There's far too many."

"We only need to hold for another hour more. Elke has pledged to return by then, as will Lord Valenbonne and his army. And if the Night Empress realizes that I am here, she can be persuaded to leave and give me chase instead."

"Absolutely not!" Xiaodan snapped. "No more noble sacrifices, Zidan."

"The fortress was constructed to withstand a siege, but not against mutations who would never be persuaded to stop attacking once they'd begun. We must lure them away long enough to give the castle a reprieve and allow reinforcements to arrive."

"Then two targets will prove much more tempting than one. Some of those mutations and quite a few covens move very quickly, and you will be hard-pressed to fight them all off on your own. You taught them to defend themselves well whenever you're away, and that's what they're doing now. My place is with you, as it always has been."

"If you lose the sun again—"

"Then I'll take it just as well as I did the last time. That I can channel it again is something we must take advantage of. I am stronger now than I've ever been, and I am staying."

"And me?" Remy objected.

Xiaodan paused. "You won't be able to move as fast as—"

"But that's what it's here for, eh?" Remy reached down and patted Peanut, who let out a pleased nicker. "I'd say three targets are better than two. Easier to split them up, keep them running in circles. I'm a better rider now than I was before. And protest all you want, but you know my place is with the both of you, too. Or do you intend to withdraw your proposal?"

"They are not for you to engage with," the Summer Lord said roughly. "Avoid fighting and concentrate on keeping out of their reach. I've taken Peanut into more than a few battles myself, and it will know what to do. Keep them far enough away from the Fata Morgana. Ride all the way back to the damn Allpriory if you have to."

"I've a mind to run all the way to Situ and dump the rest of them in Fanglei's lap," Xiaodan muttered.

"Only until help arrives," Malekh told Xiaodan, but it was onto Remy he yanked into his arms. Startled, Remy allowed himself to be pulled off Peanut's back and into his embrace. The Summer Lord was chilly against the bracing air, but his chest remained warm.

"Trust Peanut and keep safe," Malekh said roughly. "Do not fight the mutations, Pendergast, or I'll be stripping your arse raw later."

"You act like that's a punishment," Remy said, grinning. "Let's go and have at it while it's still light enough."

Malekh muttered something inaudible, then drew Xiaodan closer as well, far more gently than he'd done Remy. "We're not going anywhere," she told him, and Remy finally saw what she already had—a faint tremble to Malekh's solid form.

"I know," Malekh finally said, the too-low husk of his voice giving him away.

It was Xiaodan who charged first, giving the nearby coven enough time to recognize her before she was atop one of the other mutations, her blows so violent that she all but punched through the back of its head. The monster dropped, and the other behemoths turned toward her, smiling bloodily with their overlarge mouths and tusks.

Xiaodan took off, and thankfully they followed, just as Malekh cut cleanly though a group of coven unaware of his approach. Dozens of bodies fell before the hulks turned to him as well.

Malekh took off in the opposite direction from where Xiaodan had disappeared, slowing down long enough to gut a few more every now and then, encouraging others to follow.

Unsure as Remy was of how these Rot were being controlled, it was clear that they had been primed to attack either Malekh or Xiaodan on sight. A good third of the mutations had taken up chase, though many of the coven remained.

Remy targeted them instead. It was a novel experience, using Breaker while on horseback. He adjusted accordingly to the now-familiar vertigo, taking care to keep Peanut out of range while he proceeded to brain the nearest vampire with his knifechain, then drew close enough to behead another with a flick of his scythes. Soon enough, he had his own set of admirers at his heels, drawing another good chunk of the horde away from the fortress. Peanut only ran faster, quick enough to outpace the others if it had a mind to.

Until it reared up without warning, a shrill cry leaving its mouth. Remy turned and spotted the spear sticking out from its rump just as the helhest stumbled and fell, taking its rider with it. Remy was on his feet in an instant, stepping in front of the wounded steed to face the mutations racing for him, the snarls from the coven as they scented victory.

His mind riffled through his options and found only two. He could flee. Use Peanut as a distraction while he got away. The mutations would be attracted to the fresh scent of blood, even if it was from an undead mount, and they were likely to give in to their instincts instead of chasing him farther.

"No!" Remy said aloud, and his grip on Breaker tightened.

One of the Rot was already making for the injured helhest, but it paused at his shout, as if struggling not to obey. Just like when the previous horde had attacked the Fata Morgana.

"Listen," Remy said, putting every ounce of will he could muster into his voice. "It's them you want." He gestured at the rest of the approaching mob, its fellow mutations and Night Court coven. "Kill them," he breathed, and maybe it was going to work after all, because that familiar throbbing pain in his head returned every time he was fool enough to attempt this, that rush of blood making him lightheaded as wordless voices crowded in again.

The giant brayed and lifted its meaty fist. It came down and brained one of the coven who'd drawn close enough, the blow likely turning his insides into liquid mush as the youth crumpled, eyes wide and sightless long before he hit ground.

The behemoth was not the only one to answer his plea. A good half of the Rot who had chased him were already turning on the other vampires and even some of the mutations who hadn't yet been swayed. Remy stared, dazed, as a free-for-all broke out, and then turned to Peanut to assess the damage. He knew little about the care and feeding of helhests, but the spear that crippled Peanut did not look fatal.

He blocked an incoming attack by another coven youth who'd snuck past the mayhem. The boy had had some training, but not enough to face his opponent. Remy angled Breaker and plunged one of the blades into his enemy's chest, forcing back the instinct to be merciful. The coven youths reminded him of the Elouvian Siege, the fellow novitiates he'd had to kill, but he was wiser and older and sadder now for the experience, had learned the hard way from the turned children in the caves at the Dà Lán, and this time he refused to hesitate.

"Some fresh mess you've gotten yourself into." The zweihänder came spinning out of nowhere, cutting into both a mutation and a coven vampire's necks at the same time, and nearly nicking Remy before he dodged out of the way. The momentum sent the heavy blade sinking into the tree behind them, but the vampire messenger simply planted a foot against the bark and pulled it back out with relative ease.

"I told you not to swing too hard!" Remy shouted at him, sending his knifechain spinning into another vampire's face.

"I'm still not quite accustomed to its weight, truth be told. And I see you're attempting thralldom again."

"Shut up." A mutation lunged for Remy, and a mental shove from him sent another hulk at it, the latter viciously tearing into its fellow. Most of the coven were no longer bothering to attack the mutations, all focusing on him instead. The vampire messenger was doing surprisingly well, cutting down those drawing close enough to him.

Remy took advantage of the confusion to spike a few through the skull with Breaker's knifechain, ignoring the rising pain in his own head. "Where's my father?"

"Close. Human speed can't catch up to kindred, even with bloodwakers."

"Is that why you're here? I don't believe my father pays you to fight for him."

"This is more than just a paycheck." The messenger cleaved through another vampire. "I owe you and your Third Court lover for saving my life, and I don't like owing anyone for anything."

"Never call him my *Third Court lover* again and we'll call it even." Even with the messenger at his side and the score or so mutations he'd managed to grab at, they hadn't a prayer's chance of making it out in one piece, and with Peanut hindered, they had little else to fall back on.

He was almost sure that he could do it again. He hadn't seen the Night Empress on the battlefield, but he could feel her, knew she was somewhere nearby, just lurking along the periphery and watching the fighting unfold. And she could sense *him* as well; a cloud of miasma dulled their connection, the frenzy upon her not quite absolute, but enough to dictate her actions, suppress her will until it felt nothing more like a fragile length of string he could barely reach for.

She was getting closer; he could feel her in the spaces around him, sadness and longing and anger intertwined, and behind that a coiled, lurking fury, the overwhelming hatred that had kept her alive for so long.

And then she was standing before him, clad in her usual scarlets, face obscured by her hood.

"Mother," Remy cried. "Fight it!"

Slowly, the woman shook her head. **What is there to fight, my sweet child?** she asked, the words coming harsh and cruel, as though another spoke through her. **I no longer know where I end and he begins. He gives me what I need. I will see Aluria lost to ruins.**

"I'm sorry," Remy said, wrapping his fingers loosely around the tip of one of his scythes—enough to feel its sharpness, but not enough to bleed from it.

And this time, when that familiar lullaby once more stole into him, he relaxed, letting the song wash over his mind, letting himself steep into the growing darkness. He felt warm and safe, his mother's presence gentling his fears and anxiety, sinking him further into her control. It was safe here. He did not have to think or worry or wonder, when all he needed to do was nod and obey and follow.

The Night Empress drifted closer to Remy. The vampire messenger, to his credit, tried to defend him, but the woman had merely flicked him away like a mosquito, sending the youth crashing hard into a nearby tree. The mutations had been of no consequence to her as well; one by one, she felled them easily, casually tearing them apart with her bare hands, ripping a head off one, slicing the arms and torso of another, eviscerating one more, simply because they were standing between them and she had others to spare.

Smiling, she reached out with her bloody hands, tenderly tracing the sides of his face, looking into his fog-glazed eyes. **We can be a family again, my Remy,** she breathed. **Just you and me.**

Something wet was sliding down his fingers—his own blood. He'd gripped the scythe hard just as he felt his mind going under, and the jolt of pain was enough to make Remy come back to himself, enough to partially snap out of her influence. He could almost sense the surprise from his mother's end as he slipped from her grasp, but already he was forcing his mind elsewhere, forcing himself to think about Xiaodan crying in the Third Court spire, ashamed and worried about how she'd failed protect them; about Malekh, who never slept because it made him vulnerable, holding him in bed with his eyes closed. Both of them separately and then together; sparring, fucking, traveling, in love. He was in love.

Another flash of surprise, though this time it did not come from his mother. A stray thought that felt like Xiaodan's, startled but penetrating through the fog, toward him.

Remy?

"The fuck if I'm going to let bloody Ishkibal be a part of our *family,* Mother," he snarled, and then hurled Breaker at her with all his might.

There was a horrific sound as the scythes went through the Night Empress. She let go of him and stumbled back, eyes wide as she clutched at the weapon protruding from her chest. With a tearing, wrenching sound, she ripped it free and flung it to one side. Remy was certain he'd pierced her heart, but she was alive despite the gaping wound. When she turned back to him, it was Ishkibal he saw looking back; the hewn teeth and patrician nose, the heavy brows and the hooded eyes of the fresco at the Allpriory, superimposed over his mother's features.

Vermin, the vampire king howled, a voice carrying nearly to the heavens. **You dare think to best me?**

Remy very much dared, because he'd snatched Breaker off the

floor and come barreling at the First Court king again, this time catching him in the side. Ishkibal roared.

Remy ducked the blow, but it didn't matter. The sheer force of it sent him sprawling backward like he'd been punched anyway, wind knocked out of his lungs. He staggered back to his feet, but the king was on him again, and this time his fist connected with Remy's ribs, and he was sure they'd all been broken in one swing. He fell back down again, painfully gasping for air and certain that the next strike would kill him.

But Ishkibal—no, Ligaya—was backing away, hands against her face and teeth clenched. Remy could hear her screaming inside her head loud enough that it entered *his* head, though the agonizing pain running up and down his body occupied more of his attention.

"The bloody Mother's tits," the messenger said, dropping to kneel beside him. "I was sure you were done."

"Never been better," Remy gritted out as the man's hands probed carefully at his torso, the messenger flinching at what he'd felt.

"You're in no shape to fight. I'll carry you out."

"We're not leaving Peanut behind."

"Who the hell is Peanut?"

A sudden sizzle of lightning hit the ground before the Night Empress and then Xiaodan appeared, her face falling when she spotted Remy.

"Nothing I can't survive," Remy rasped, hoping he wasn't lying.

"Lord Valenbonne's arrived. Leave Peanut to me. You, bring him north of here, by the westward plains."

"I'm not going to leave you, either," Remy protested weakly.

"I'll be all right. Go and—" And then Xiaodan cut herself off to lunge forward. A swipe of her arm knocked the zweihänder out of the vampire messenger's hands, and another punch propelled him several feet backward.

"Xiaodan?" Remy asked, stunned. "What—?"

He stopped when the messenger slowly got to his feet; his eyes were dull, mouth slack, and he shuffled toward them with a snarl. Xiaodan lashed out again and the youth went down for good, rendered unconscious. "She's compelled them," she panted. "Where is Malekh?"

And then she froze, eyes wide. With a low cry, she clutched at her head, shaking violently.

"No!" Remy shouted. "No, you goddamn bastard! You stay the fuck away from her!" His hands scrabbled for his Reaper, but he had no strength to hold it up. All he could manage was the knifechain, which he threw toward the First Court vampire like a javelin.

The woman caught the blade easily between her fingertips. Her cruel smile was fully Ishkibal's. **Worthless little mortal,** he mocked, then threw it back.

The knife went right through Xiaodan's palm. With a small hiss of pain, she pulled it out.

You will die by my hand this time, Lilith, Ishkibal purred. **And he will die by yours.**

Remy saw Xiaodan's eyes glaze over again, saw her turn to him. Her hands found their way around his throat and Remy gagged weakly, unable to push her away.

"Xiaodan, please."

Her grip tightened, strangling hm, and Remy could no longer breathe.

And then Xiaodan let go of him, turning to throw herself at the other vampire with a cry of pure rage. There was an answering roar of agony as the Night Empress doubled over, arm hanging uselessly off one side.

Xiaodan was glowing. She was a bright ball of light that was blinding to look at. "No," Remy gasped out, though nothing emerged from his throat more than a feeble croak. The last time she'd taken in this much she'd nearly died, her abilities gone, and he didn't think she would be so lucky again.

A pair of arms folded around Xiaodan's waist. "Xiaodan," came Malekh's low tones, calm and assuring. "Calm yourself. Slow breaths. Your heart is beating too hard, you'll come apart from that alone."

The light dimmed as the woman relaxed in his arms. "She made me hurt him," came the vicious, anguished sob against Malekh's chest. "She made me—"

Zidan, Ishkibal rasped.

Malekh took everything in in an instant. "I should have known you would find a way to survive," he said bleakly.

Long enough to kill you, my prized warrior, my most favored. You who turned your back on my court. Your hand I will use to slay your own and swear fealty to me again.

Remy felt the compulsion drifting toward Malekh, felt it hit. The Summer Lord jerked back as if it was a physical touch, and then held himself still for several seconds.

Remy didn't know how he'd reached out, but he closed his eyes and found himself standing at Chànggē Shuǐ, in one of the towers overlooking the sparkling lake of the Dà Lán some miles away. He could feel the warmth of Xiaodan's hand in his. On his right, Malekh's coat swirled close, brushing against him.

And then the vision was gone, and when he opened his eyes again, there was only the pain, somehow worryingly more muted than it was before.

"No, Ishkibal," Malekh said wearily.

The punch he threw could have rocked the whole world. It knocked Ishkibal off his feet, and this time he did not get back up. His and the Night Empress's blood stained the ground, but Remy was too tired to wonder if they were both dead, if his scythes had finally done the trick or if either Xiaodan or Malekh had landed the final blow. All he wanted was to close his eyes and sleep.

"No," Xiaodan said, shaking him back awake, and Remy's ribs throbbed again. "Stay awake for me, Remington. There are physicians in Lord Valenbonne's army. I'm bringing you to them."

"Is Peanut all right? Father's messenger? I think I can stand. I've had bones broken before and this is no—"

"Even deprived of air, you are still incapable of shutting up, Remington." But the lord's touch was tender when he lifted Remy into his arms.

"Where is he?" He could hear his father's voice, tense and angry. "Lord Malekh, I had thought you would do better than to see my child to harm."

"I'm fine, Father," Remy said, twisting out of Malekh's hold. "I can stand on my . . ."

Pain bloomed up his neck and it wasn't from his rib cage. He was on the ground again, had only a second to realize that the others had been thrown back as well, like a hurricane had swept through the area without warning. And then the Night Empress was on him, eyes red and lips pulled back and then there were her fangs, long and cruel as she bit down on him, feeding ravenously.

29

SANCTUARY

Remy was sure he was dead, but he'd been wrong about that before.

He had a hazy vision of his mother standing in the dirt behind a small hut, staring at the ground. He was under the impression that she had buried something there, but the vision faded quickly when he attempted to focus.

And then there was a thick wall of wood before him, close enough that he could observe the rough grainwork in excruciating detail, a multitude of imperfections and striations marring the surface. Not furniture then, or at least not one of any quality. Ideally, it would be easy enough to splinter, to break himself out.

Because he was enclosed by it on all sides, giving him only a few inches on either side and above his head. Almost, he thought, like he was inside a coffin.

Remy. It was a thought, but it was not his own. It sounded like Xiaodan calling from somewhere far away, with the unmistakable presence of Malekh by her side. He reached out to that voice and found the wooden barrier again. He pushed. It creaked under his fingers.

We will find you, Xiaodan said. *We will.*

He pushed harder.

He felt weak, like he'd been running for days and fighting for even longer. But although he wasn't at peak strength, the wood gave way easily, almost disintegrating once he applied firmer pressure.

With loud crackling noises, the rest of his prison broke apart.

Remy staggered out, lifting his hand to shield his eyes from the bright sunlight. He braced himself for another attack, expecting to stumble headfirst once more into danger.

But any threat appeared to have long since passed. He was on a sandy beach close to the water's edge, waves lapping placidly at the shore. Palm tree leaves rustled overhead, waving in the breeze. Detritus littered the ground, enough to make walking difficult. Not all of them were made from driftwood or other natural means; there were thatches of straw and stone, but also walls of slate and what looked to be some kind of quartz.

Wearily, Remy turned to look behind him.

He'd seen this place before: the trees, the beach, the water. But the houses that should have been there were gone, leaving only flotsam and jetsam. There was no one else in sight.

A large bloodwood tree stood there instead, the trunk split open to reveal the hollow he had walked out from. But the opening was slowly knitting itself back together, the wood re-forming as he watched.

Remy picked up a stone from the ground just a little larger than his hand, and of a considerable weight. His fingers closed around it, crushing the rock with little effort.

"Fuck," Remy said, and pawed frantically at his throat. He could feel no injuries at his neck, nor anywhere else. His ribs twinged, but of a mild soreness rather than of broken bones.

He cupped a hand to his mouth, trying to feel the sharpness of his teeth, then tracing their shape with his tongue, before realizing his folly. The sun was warm overhead, with no clouds to bar its light; exposed to its rays, he would have been killed immediately.

That did little to ease his mind.

He spied some wisps of smoke drifting up from behind a copse of trees. With no other options, he traced their source.

A large pot hung over a campfire, a savory smell drifting out. The Night Empress was seated on the sand, heedless of the way bits of it crept up her robe. Her cowl was down, and in that moment she looked just like Ligaya Pendergast had in life, human and sane. The hut he'd seen in his vision loomed behind her, threatening despite its smallness.

Much to his shock, his father was leaning against a tree and watching the flames. His axe and his fire lance lay beside him; he was not swinging it at the Night Empress like Remy expected him to, though it remained within reach.

His own Breaker was on a rock by the small fire, waiting for him braced against the stone.

Neither of his parents spoke. Ligaya hummed to herself happily. Lord Pendergast kept a careful watch on her. Remy was convinced this was all still a dream.

"Are you awake now, Remington?" Ligaya Pendergast asked, looking up at him with a smile. "Gave me quite the fright. You shouldn't be wandering about these sands in the dark. There's no telling what you might stumble over, especially after these last few storms."

Something was wrong. Remy's eyes flicked toward his father, who shook his head slightly though his gaze remained trained on his former wife.

"I'm sorry," Remy said slowly. He settled himself on the rock Breaker was propped against.

"You shouldn't fret too much, my dear," his father said, compounding Remy's shock. "I taught him, didn't I? I'll keep an eye on him, don't you worry."

"I still think you're too hard on him in training. But I suppose you know what's best." Ligaya stirred the pot with a wooden ladle and tried a spoonful. "Needs a bit more peppercorn," she sighed, standing up. "Don't wander off, Remy. You still need some food in you," she said, and then promptly disappeared.

"What's going on?" Remy asked quietly.

"We appear to have caught her during a lucid period," Edgar Pendergast said tersely. "She's been this way for over a day now, but there's no telling how long it will last. Saying something she might not want to hear can cause her to regress, so I suggest you play along."

"How long have *you* been here?"

"About thirty-four hours or so."

"Nearly two days. Light above, what the hell did you two even talk about for two days?"

"Nothing. Everything. She doesn't remember the invasion, nor her time in Elouve. It's for the better. She's . . . happier here."

"Am I . . . ?" It was hard to say the words. "Did she turn me into . . ."

"No," Lord Pendergast said quickly. "I thought the same when I arrived, but she . . ." He paused. "She is in no condition to lie. Lord Malekh's accounts of the Fount suggest that this bloodwood functions in the same manner. You were in bad shape. She swore there would be no lasting effects on you. It seems her village used it often in the past. Are you in pain?"

"I feel perfectly fine," Remy said. "Where are Lord Malekh and Lady Song?"

"On their way here, if their blasted three-legged horse can find its way back to them. Took some time to clear out the Rot infesting his court."

"You *rode* Peanut?"

"It was the fastest way, though the Summer Lord neglected to mention the vertigo that comes from the experience. The kindred spread themselves thin to search for you, but I had a hunch, theo-rized that the Night Empress still had something of Ligaya inside her to bring you to where she was always the happiest. While the rest of my army will be slower to catch up, I have no doubt that Lord Malekh and Lady Song will be here soon enough. Ishkibal's blood does not run through the tree here, and so you remain un-compromised."

"She tried to kill me."

"The blood of Ishkibal that runs through her veins tried to kill you. Her horror that he had nearly succeeded was enough to bring her out of her frenzy. Whatever I think of her, I know she would never harm you in her right mind." Lord Valenbonne's voice dipped. "She's returning. *Play along.*"

"Fresh tamarinds," his mother said happily, adding the ingredi-ents into the pot. "This was your father's favorite stew, you know. Asked me to make one nearly every day during his first week here, until *I* was well sick and tired of it."

"I was never any good at cooking it myself," Edgar Pendergast said, tone deliberately calm. "Chopping up the meat was my main contribution."

Still wary, Remy took the last few steps to take the soup from his mother's hands and return to his spot beside the fire. It was hot and filling, and he'd drunk nearly half of it before realizing how hungry he was. "It's wonderful. Thank you."

"Fortunate that we still have the tree," the Night Empress said, latching back onto the previous subject despite her husband's admonishments. "It would have taken far longer for you to heal otherwise."

"How long have you been using it, Mother?" Remy asked care-fully. The bloodwood was not so far away that he could not see its outline against the horizon.

"My people know it as a sacred tree to be cared for, though I am aware of little beyond that. It was our island's special secret."

Ligaya smiled at him. "I was gravely injured once as a child and re-membered waking up inside it. How warm I felt, like I was strong enough to take on the world. Though a friend of mine suffered a broken arm, and the tree did very little for her. I've always won-dered why. It is such a relief to learn that it worked on you. The Alurians were none the wiser when they attacked . . ." She paused, frowning. "Why am I talking about Aluria?" she asked, and Remy froze. "Who attacked?"

"Ligaya," Edgar said sternly. "You are thinking too much again of the Elouvian affairs I've long left behind. When I . . ." He hesi-tated. "When I abandoned all that and agreed to remain here with you and our son, it was you who exacted a pledge from me to talk little about my old life."

"That's true," Remy's mother conceded. "I was sure you would not last a month without returning to Elouve with some excuse, insist that we would be better off there than here, even after all these years." She smiled at him, love in her gaze. "Thank you for taking a chance with me, beloved."

An odd expression took over his father's face: regret, pain, and nostalgia all coalesced into one. "I wouldn't have had it any other way, Ligaya."

"Would you like some more stew, Remington? And it would do you good to have another yourself, Edgar."

"Is that what this is?" Remy asked, after Ligaya had gathered their empty bowls and walked off again. "Her delusion that neither of you left the Whispering Isles, that you both raised me here?"

"An old promise I made to her that, seeing as the invasion pro-ceeded as Beluske planned, was untenable to keep."

"You would never have given up Elouve," Remy said disbeliev-ingly.

"It was a foolish notion." Lord Edgar Pendergast cast his gaze toward the horizon. "It would be easy enough to disappear, I sup-pose, but suspicion would fall upon the kindred here as the cause for it, and Beluske would have sent his army earlier than he already had. Better to head off such concerns by first dismissing the initial reports of any vampires lurking within the islands outright, then immediately casting similar suspicions elsewhere. There were enough covens to the southwest back then, far enough away yet close enough that it would have been natural to continue the search for me there. Astonbury would have delighted in staging such an investigation to find me, only to call it off quickly in a matter of days, deeming me lost."

"You thought this through," Remy said. It should not have been so surprising a notion. His father was a meticulous planner who left nothing to chance. But that he had planned on shirking his duties and leaving Elouve for his wife was what astonished Remy.

"It was a foolish notion," Lord Valenbonne said again. He looked heavensward this time and allowed his eyes to fall shut— just an old man, quietly basking in the sunlight. "No point in mourning the road not taken."

"LORD MALEKH told me everything," his father said later. He had drawn Remy toward the sand for what he claimed was a sparring session, and Ligaya watched happily from afar as she attended the washing.

He was faster than Remy expected. Though Remy now had the advantage of the added strength he'd acquired from his stay inside the bloodwood, his father was smart enough to take that into account, goading Remy into overreaching more than he ought to and taking advantage. Remy had refused to use Breaker, so both had fashioned makeshift weapons from the surrounding driftwood.

Lord Valenbonne blocked his attack and followed up with a counterblow to Remy's shins that made him flinch, though he remained standing. "He told me of Etrienne Sauveterre's experiments," the old man said, "and how the high priestess encouraged it, luring Ligaya away in the first place and fostering suspicion in our minds, all because of the foolish notion that my wife would better serve as the Night King's puppet. More reason for me to despise the courts, to sunder any alliances in place and exterminate them all."

"But you won't," Remy panted. He sent his woodpiece flying toward his sire's head. The latter sidestepped and tried to hit him in his side, a strike Remy dodged.

"I was a part of a terrible campaign led by my own king to annihilate kindred who had done nothing to deserve their fates. Whatever you may think of me, it would be hypocritical to claim that it was only our lives ruined when I was part of something that destroyed others. If Beluske had not sought to invade the Whispering Isles, perhaps the high priestess would have not discovered Ligaya's bloodline and left her well alone."

"I would have expected you to attack Mother first and ask questions later, regardless of whether I was inside the bloodwood."

"I finally understand her part in all this. It was not what we thought."

Lord Valenbonne stepped back so suddenly that Remy, who was already in midswing, nearly tripped forward when his weapon met air.

"She never betrayed me," his father finally said. "All this time, I was so convinced. As much as I wanted to hold on to that hate, to remind myself of what I had worked tirelessly for, for decades—all of it fell away upon that revelation."

Nothing about Lord Valenbonne's expression had changed. His father was not one to show emotion, much like Malekh, and Remy wondered briefly if that was why he was constantly watching the latter for any minute signs of affection, why he liked how easy Xiaodan was to read.

"Why haven't you killed her yet?" Remy asked quietly.

"Are you so eager to see your own mother dead?"

"You've told me so many times she was no longer my mother. The logical thing to do is to kill her before she reverts to becoming the Night Empress again. You should have done it before I even emerged from the bloodwood."

"Will *you* do it, Remington?" His father's weapon met his, the crack loud as they made contact. Both pieces of driftwood splintered abruptly, breaking off near where their hands gripped their surface. "Are you willing to stake her in my place?"

Both leaped away from each other, his father breathing hard. Remy couldn't answer.

"Not yet," said Lord Valenbonne. He turned back to pick up his axe where he had left it. "Not while she's still Ligaya."

He rushed toward Remy again without warning. Remy ducked the blow and lunged forward.

His father's stance shifted, aiming for something above him.

The coven vampire staggered backward, though his head was already rolling on the ground from Valenbonne's swipe. Almost at the same time, Remy yanked Breaker off his back, scythes shooting upward, and thrust both blades into the maw of a mutation that had emerged from the trees behind Valenbonne. Its body sagged diagonally, following the sharp cut he had made, and sank to the ground with a revolting squelch.

"I have none of Malekh's antidote with me," Remy said.

"I do, but in limited supply." There were only three other coven vampires, scouts searching for their mistress rather than the main force. Valenbonne made brutal work of them. The last turned to flee, but Remy's father lifted his axe and split the back of the kindred's head like a ripe melon, the rest of him splattering onto the sand.

"What's going on?" Ligaya stood frozen some feet away, eyes wide and visibly trembling. For a moment, Remy feared that she would remember and come tearing after them, but she clutched the pan in her hand tightly and looked around like she was ready to brain vampires of her own.

"It's all right, Ligaya," Valenbonne said wearily. "That appears to be all of them."

"You said there were kindred still around, but I did not know they were so violent," Ligaya said, still trembling. "Edgar, do they know you're here? Are they after you?"

"They are not from the island, but you know that I can handle myself well, and so can Remy." Abandoning his axe, Lord Pendergast closed the distance between them, and Ligaya stepped into his arms with relief. "I won't let anything happen to you," Valenbonne said. "You know that, Ligaya."

Remy watched them together: the small smile on Ligaya's face as she rested her head on his father's shoulder, and Lord Pendergast's still-expressionless face, even with his arms gently holding her close.

THEY ENCOUNTERED two more groups over the next day. Not many to worry over, but to Remy it was a sign that their days were numbered. He and his father had taken to setting traps in the area to alert them of any intruders and took turns watching his mother for any signs of the Night Empress returning. The length of Ligaya's lucidity both troubled Remy and made him foolishly hope that it would remain for good.

Another mutation had been among the last group, dead only thanks to more of Malekh's antidote. "If only Grimesworthy were here," he muttered. "But he would frighten your mother far worse."

"They're all still acting like they're compelled," Remy said. They'd moved the corpses to the other side of the island before setting them on fire. "If the Night Empress herself isn't aware she's doing that, shouldn't her hold on them disappear?"

"Do I look like an expert, Remington?" Lord Pendergast grunted, striking his flint. "Mayhap you'd be better off asking Lord Malekh."

They watched the carcasses burn. This was the longest he'd ever spent with his father since his youth, Remy realized.

"He is embarrassed," Ligaya told him, once all the riffraff had been either buried or burned. "I know his tells well enough. I know that you and he have not always seen eye to eye, but it seems he is trying to be better. More lumpia?"

Remy and his father handled as much of the work as they could, but his mother loved to cook and had claimed their meager pots and pans as her sole dominion. There were wild pigs about that Remy had been able to hunt, and they ate with their hands in Wikaan fashion, but he had no idea where she'd found all the spices in their decidedly limited larder to make everything taste so good.

He took the plate and took his sweet time cramming the fried rolls and the rice into his mouth, trying to come up with a response.

"Has he mentioned anything?" he finally asked.

"You know your father—he's not one to voice his concerns out loud. Though he has expressed some misgivings about two lovers who've been courting you."

Remy choked.

Ligaya cheerfully thumped him on the back. "I've been hoping you would tell me yourself," she admonished gently.

"I—I'm sorry, Mother. I've been meaning to tell you, but it's a rather awkward thing to bring up."

"As long as you're happy and they treat you well, then I have no complaints. Given my unconventional relationship with your father, I am not one to talk." Ligaya's eyes sparkled. "I at least hope to meet them soon?"

"I . . . of course."

"Edgar isn't unhappy you're seeing them, if that's your worry. But he is concerned that you haven't had as much time together to repair the rift between you two. He's admitted that he hasn't been the best father but is at a loss as to how to go about mending it."

Remy stared down at his food, blinking rapidly in shock.

"I told him that he couldn't change the past, but he should at least strive to find ways to give you happiness in both the present and in the future." Ligaya grinned impishly. "And should that happiness lie toward the two nobles courting you, know he will not stand in their way. It strikes me that your admirers have already sought out his blessing, but perhaps I am already saying too much, my dear Armiger."

"He told you?"

"He said that you were adamant about the title, and while he did not understand it at first, that you should be referred to as such. Was he wrong? He has been ever the optimist."

"No. Light, he's actually right this time." Remy leaned over and hugged her tightly, relishing in the smell of the sun and pine on her skin. "But optimism is not a word I would use to describe Father."

"He was not always so dour. He had high hopes for Aluria, convinced that he could change the world and make it better for all of us. I know he still believes that, underneath all his grouching." Ligaya Pendergast took a dainty bite of her lumpia. "It's easy enough to give up hope, especially when he has had so many kindred to deal with. Vampires he's had to fight, friends he's had to see killed because of what he does." She tilted her head toward Remy. "I trust that you know what a drawn-out frenzy means. In your years as a hunter, I suppose you would have seen a good many yourself."

Remy clenched his bowl tighter. "There was a girl who was turned that I had to kill, but she had periods of lucidity where she would visit her mother without ever endangering her."

"Edgar never got used to that. When he would return from such missions, he would shut himself up in his room and drink himself into insensibility, till I made him swear that he would never touch spirits after those hunts. He was already a heavy imbiber, and I feared it would ruin him."

"And he never did touch alcohol," Remy said, startled. He had never once seen Edgar Pendergast drink, even before he'd become infirmed.

"I've been having strange dreams as of late," his mother said. "I suppose that is what has made my thoughts somber the last couple of days. But I want to tell you how proud I am of you, Remy. It is not an easy profession that you and your father have undertaken, but you do so much good for so little praise. If only there was more I could do to help."

"Sharing meals and days with you is enough," Remy said, only barely keeping his tears at bay. "Though I won't stop you from ripping a new one into my father if he's off being a bloody bastard again."

"Are you fond of the Third Court king? And the young lady from the Fourth Court?"

"I—yes. I am very fond of them."

"Then that is all I need to know." Her smile faded. "The safest course of action would be to kill me while I still have my wits about, of course. Before I am compelled to attack either of you again."

Remy's head whipped up to meet her gaze, but all he found in her eyes was calm acceptance. "You remember," he whispered.

"And refusing to act on what that entails, yes, though I do not know for how long. I fear that it would break your poor father's heart again, and I have no wish to see that."

She looked back at the bloodwood. "I used it often, when I was the babaylan of my village. I thought nothing of it then, never knew of its ties to the Wikaan kindred. We worshipped it, believed it was a gift from the Mother. It was not until I was awakened as kindred myself that I realized it for what it was. You could tell him that I reverted while we were talking, and you had no choice."

"No!" Remy was on his knees before her, clutching her hand in his. "Please don't ask that of me. Not—not while you're you. Not while he's still hoping, too. It is not in either Father nor I to give up. Malekh has done miracles before, and he can do one again."

"If I could but promise you that," Ligaya said. "But I cannot. If Ishkibal reaches out to claim what is left of me, then swear to me that you will find the one who will strike me down without hesitation. I was not meant to live for this long, and in this way."

She knew enough to know that he could not kill her by his own hand. "Only after every avenue has been pursued and found wanting," he said.

The Night Empress let out a long, shaky breath.

Oddly enough, he was not surprised to find the tears falling down her face, the relief they clearly brought her. "Oh, Remington," she said, and wept, and for the first time, Remy could hold her like he had always wanted.

"I ASKED her not to tell you," Lord Valenbonne said stonily.

"But why now?" His father knew nothing of Ligaya's awakening, of her memories of the Night Empress. It had not seemed Remy's place to tell him.

"It is easier to reflect when you are of sound mind and body, rather than the wreck I was for years, pushing everyone away." Lord Valenbonne still wouldn't look at him, staring at a small unopened bottle of lambanog before him like it was the most fascinating thing in the world. Remy's mother, it would seem, was an expert at distilling the spirit and had a higher tolerance for alcohol than either of them. "I ask for no forgiveness, nor do I expect it from you," he said roughly. "You are far too like Ligaya, willing to let bygones be. I did not want the world to break you the way I watched it break her. So I made you tougher. Strong enough to withstand all they could throw at you. So you could see the world as it truly is, even if you lost something in the beholding of it."

Remy finally found his voice. "Mother doesn't forgive so easily, if these years have been any indication."

Lord Valenbonne looked at him then. And laughed loud and long as opposed to his usual bitter and cynical, and Remy, to his surprise, found that he was laughing as well.

The scream that rang out stopped them.

Neither wasted time running back to camp to find Ligaya on the log she was sitting at where Remy had left her, huddled in a ball with her hands over her ears.

Grimesworthy loomed over her. Behind it stood Quintin Yost and dozens of coven kindred.

"I was wondering where you'd been, milord," the doctor said conversationally. "I *can* tell you where Lord Malekh and the other kindred are. A simple matter to spread rumors of sighting you back at Kerenai, far enough so that we can talk without interruption."

30

THE SUN

"Stay away from her, Grimesworthy!" Valenbonne demanded, and the giant obliged, backing a few steps away. "What are you doing here, Quintin? Tilda and Riones couldn't reach you in Elouve—"

"And surely the great lord high steward would have deduced the answer by now." Gone was Yost's jovial demeanor, a cruel mockery replacing it. "Or must it be spelled out for you?"

Lord Pendergast froze. "They said that the temple priestess spoke of other clan members outside of the Allpriory. You worked with Etrienne Sauveterre."

"The Fifth kept a good many secrets from his own court, I one of them. I thought to return to the Allpriory after Dracheholm was destroyed, but chose to remain behind and see what other chaos I could sow. It was I who realized your wife's lineage and convinced Sauveterre to use her as his final experiment, for he was just as keen to raise whatever semblance of Ishkibal that he could control. And of course, when word reached me that the Duke of Valenbonne's heir had survived, I thought it would be quite fun to see if the child would manifest the same potential as the mother."

"You bastard," Valenbonne seethed.

"I healed you, didn't I? My desire to see you in good health had always been genuine. The more success I had with you, the higher the chances of doing the same with Remington." Quintin smiled and his fangs protruded, eyes flashing red.

"Grimesworthy!" Edgar Pendergast shouted. "Kill him!"

Grimesworthy did not move.

"You can command your mutations, no doubt," Yost said. "But you forget that you have given Remington the same privileges— and in his veins run Ligaya Pendergast's as well. Did you sincerely think that I would allow you free reign of my precious toys without a way to control them myself? Isabella wielded the Night Empress like a hammer because *I* allowed her to. There are far more drugs in my armament than the tonics I used to keep you alive, Valenbonne."

Ligaya's eyes were crimson. With sickening cracking noises, wings burst once more from her back, slowly unfurling.

With a roar, Lord Valenbonne raised his axe and struck at Quintin Yost, who managed to narrowly avoid the blow. Undeterred, the old man swung a second time . . .

And Grimesworthy caught it easily in its massive grip.

"Grimesworthy!" Lord Valenbonne shouted. "Let go!"

Grimesworthy did not let go. With an almost careless flick of its arm, it sent the axe flying away.

With a loud curse, Lord Valenbonne fell back to his fire lance, the weapon charging to life. Grimesworthy moved toward its former master, only to be stopped when the spike at the end of Remy's chain hit it squarely in the face.

More vampires emerged at Yost's unspoken signal, closed in. Valenbonne discharged his fire lance at them, keeping them at a distance for the moment.

"I've wanted to kill you ever since I learned what you really are," Remy snarled.

Grimesworthy shifted its focus to him. It was not as fast as those he had encountered in the past, but what it lacked in speed it made up for in sheer endurance, pace unrelenting even as Remy's knifechain continued to savage its face and chest, leaving deep gouges in its wake.

Lord Valenbonne cut down any more kindred to draw close, and once the fire lance finished recharging once more, he snatched it up, aimed at Grimesworthy, and fired without pause.

The blast quite literally tore through the giant. A fountain of blood erupted around Grimesworthy's middle, leaving a hole right in the center of its chest. That did not slow it down.

"In your and Yost's quest to perfect your manservant," Remy said, stabbing another coven vampire through the head. "Did you by any chance leave *any* kind of disadvantages for us to exploit?"

"Grimesworthy will still fall to the Lady Song and her sunbringing abilities," his father responded. "And fire may cause him more damage than conventional weapons. I would have told you that my hold on him was absolute, but damn Yost. He likely introduced something else to the transfusions that weakens my control of it."

"Any suggestions as to how to *un*weaken it?"

"A few. See if you can take command of it."

"What?"

"You share the same blood as Ligaya. If her grip on it has strengthened, then the same goes for you." Edgar Pendergast charged Yost without warning, but the doctor batted the lord high steward easily away, with enough force to send the other old man back to the ground with a sickening thump.

Remy swiped at Yost with his links before the physician could move in for the kill. When the vampire turned his attention to him, Remy veered to the left, away from his father, and Grimesworthy followed. "Stop," he ordered, not quite expecting the mutation to obey—and also not expecting the sudden surge of pain that went through his head, nearly making him drop Breaker. It felt like someone was trying to stab him from inside his brain.

But Grimesworthy wavered where it had not with his father.

"Stop!" Remy commanded again, trying to put all his will-power into the word, and the pain only increased. He dropped to his knees, Breaker still held out in front of him, as futile as the act was. But Grimesworthy paused again, one trunk-like leg raised in the air that had yet to plant itself back down to the ground, suddenly immobile.

"Fascinating," Yost said. "I took particular care to isolate your blood from hers. That you are still able to give it orders—perhaps the Night Empress has imbued you with more of herself than she let be known."

"You're lying," Remy said, gritting his teeth through the agony. Grimesworthy had finally succeeded in putting his foot down but could not take another step beyond that. He was trying to push the now-unwanted presence out of his mind, but it only served for the pain to bear down harder in response, threatening to overwhelm everything else.

The Night Empress was still writhing on the ground. Through the haze of pain, Remy could see something coursing through her veins underneath the skin of her arms. The other coven had paused in their attack, staggering back.

"It is true that passing down kindredship among the Wikaan clan requires consent, but certain aspects of vampirism need no permission." A foot shoved itself into Remy's back, and he grunted as he fell. "Much as I would like to bring you back alive for a more concise dissection, you have become far too dangerous, even for a prized specimen." His head was yanked up. "Know that I am grateful for your contributions to science, Remington," Yost said, readying his dagger.

And then let go of it abruptly as a surge of heat went up Remy's back. He scrambled away, turned to see Yost screaming from inside a ball of fire. Lord Pendergast had thrust a burning stick into the doctor, a now-empty bottle of lambanog in his other hand.

Yost spun and rolled onto the ground, frantically trying to douse the flames. Pendergast dragged Remy back to his feet. "Protect your mother," he instructed, then turned to face his former undead vassal.

Grimesworthy feared the fire more than it feared the blade; it lurched back as Valenbonne swung the flames into its face.

"Mother," Remy said urgently. Her trembling had subsided, but she continued to stare emptily into the space before her, eyes blank.

His father had shoved the makeshift torch into the bloody hole in Grimesworthy's chest and the mutation began to burn in earnest, flames melting its face. For the first time, Grimesworthy grew visibly aggressive, flailing wildly, attempting to strike anything within reach.

Parts of Yost's skin had melted away, showing bone and worse underneath. Half of his face was nearly gone, but what remained was livid with rage. Remy moved to face him.

But this time, the dagger Yost hefted and threw was not toward Remington, but past him, at Ligaya.

The woman stiffened, the hilt buried deep inside her chest. With a stunned cry, Remy raced toward her.

Ligaya's eyes were red with fury. Her feathers rose in thick, heavy plumes until they nearly blanketed her. And when she looked up again, it was not the Night Empress that was staring back. Superimposed upon her face were another's features: male, harsher and cruel.

"Lord Ishkibal!" Yost exulted.

The black wings spread, feathers sharp. With a howl, they darted out from his body like knives in all directions.

Remy dove behind a rock, which exploded from the force, and then behind a tree, never stopping. Valenbonne stepped behind

Grimesworthy, who bore the brunt of the attack and was soon riddled with deep cuts.

Ishkibal lunged for Remy, whose enhanced agility was all that kept him from being gored as sharp nails raked the air where he once stood. Remy plunged Breaker into the First Court king, the scythes burying into his midsection. A hard shove from the vampire knocked him several feet away.

Strong as he was, Ishkibal was still struggling to maintain control of the Night Empress's body. Refusing to think about his mother, remembering what he had promised her, Remy angled Breaker and charged.

Ishkibal's hand shot out, gripping Breaker's blades before he could deliver the kill. As hard as Remy tried to push, the Night King held fast despite the blood running down his wrist. Inexorably he began to push back, forcing the blade closer to Remy.

A small dagger slid out of Remy's sleeve and into his palm. The cut was not as deep as he had hoped, but it was enough for Ishkibal's grip on his scythes to break. With an inhuman roar, the Night King struck out, catching Remy in the stomach and throwing him several feet.

Remy gritted his teeth, the pain coursing up and down his body. He was aware of Ishkibal moving closer, and he rolled over with a grunt, trying to get back on his feet despite the agony.

A hand grabbed his neck, and Remy found himself choking as he was lifted up, boots dangling off the sand so that he was at eye level with the Night King's gaze. Ligaya Pendergast's body had transformed, and Ishkibal now stood nearly seven feet tall, all remnants of his mother gone.

I will destroy you, the Night King snarled, and his grip on Remy's neck tightened.

There was a loud shot. Part of Ishkibal's shoulder was blown off, loose tissue and muscle all that connected it to the rest of his arm. Remy fell.

"Get away from him," Lord Valenbonne said. Ishkibal turned to reach for him, and this time it was Grimesworthy who blocked his path. He was no longer alight, though the stench rising from his blackened form was vile. Now obedient to Remy's father, he drew back a meaty hand and punched Ishkibal squarely in the face.

Both behemoths traded blows for several minutes, neither side giving in. Lord Valenbonne dragged Remy away from the fracas, firing shots back at Ishkibal whenever he could. "How?" Remy gasped out. It felt like his lungs were on fire.

"Not quite certain myself. Perhaps the Night Empress's own blood grew weak enough to break him free of her control—or of Yost's. How are you holding up?"

"Like my skin's about to melt right off me."

"Stop whining. You'll be fine." His father handed him his axe, then took Breaker.

"What are you doing?" Remy choked.

"Seeing if I still remember how to use this bloody stick."

Grimesworthy was on the losing end. It had lost its right arm somewhere along the way and had fallen back on blocking what it could of Ishkibal's attacks. Valenbonne destroyed the handicap by lopping off Ishkibal's own arm just as the latter was raising it to strike again.

The fight was now waged on two fronts, Valenbonne and Grimesworthy taking turns to spark Ishkibal's ire from in front and behind. With Breaker at hand, Valenbonne danced underneath its flying spikes at just the right time to jab the Night King at vulnerable spots, causing the vampire king to retreat.

Once the dizziness had passed, Remy righted himself up and spotted Yost. The doctor had climbed back to his feet and was limping toward his father.

His father's fire lance had fully charged. Remy grabbed it and took careful aim. The blast hit the center of Yost's back, sending the vampire falling on his face.

Remy limped to where his prone form lay, dragging his father's axe behind him.

"You cannot kill me," Yost hissed, when Remy raised the weapon. "Only I know how to bring your mother back for true."

Remy froze.

Yost gave a bloody smile. "You can consent to take her blood and become the kindred you never wanted her to be. Take all the power within yourself, and Ishkibal will lose his influence. Your mother will regain her humanity, and you will be all the better for it. I can help you. Neither Elouvians nor the eight courts will ever look down on you again. Think of how much I could do for you. With your strength and my experiments, we could—"

Remy's axe drove down, literally cutting Yost off before the physician could shove a syringe he'd been hiding underneath his coat into Remy.

Ishkibal was winning. Lord Pendergast had dodged most of his attacks, though not without injury. Remy could see that his father's coat was torn, blood seeping out from several places where sharp blades had cut into the cloth. Grimacing, he headed in their direction.

"What are you doing?" his father shouted.

Remy didn't answer, only raised his arm and threw the battle-axe with all his might. It cleaved into Ishkibal's back with a force that should have cut him in two.

And then he was on the ground, the horrific weight of the Night King on top of him, hot breath fanning against his neck. He struggled to push him off, but clawed fingers grabbed his throat and slammed him back to the ground hard enough for his vision to blur.

And then the weight was gone from him abruptly.

Ishkibal was writhing on the ground, the syringe Remy had taken from Yost still stuck to his arm, its contents now empty.

Lord Pendergast, too, lay on the ground.

"No!" Remy gasped, crawling toward his father. There was an ugly gaping wound on the man's chest from where he had shielded Remy from Ishkibal's hit.

With all his strength, Remy shoved his hands against the wound, willing the blood to stop pouring out.

"Remington," Lord Valenbonne croaked.

"Do not speak! Save your strength!"

"At ease, Armiger." There was a smile on his father's face.

"You cannot have worked so hard all these years to find a cure to your infirmity only to give up now!"

"I should have died the day I realized you were still at the Elouvian fields, fighting within those caves." Lord Valenbonne closed his eyes and shallowly gulped in air. "Survive, Remy."

Ishkibal screamed. His body was once more awash in flames, only this time Xiaodan was before him, trembling with rage. Her gaze traveled to Remy, then down to his father.

She turned and shot Ishkibal full of fire a second time.

Lilith, the Night King spat, enraged. He barreled into her without warning, sending them both into trees that tore straight from their trunks from their combined force.

With heavy moans, the coven started forward again; their eyes were red, features twisting. Remy realized with horror that they, too, were transforming.

Malekh appeared in lightning flashes around the coven, striking a good many before their mutations could fully form. Another shot rang out, levin crackling through several vampires' bodies before they tumbled down, but Elke was already recharging her lance, face tight with worry, even as Alegra stood before her, defending her from any more who dared come closer.

"They're here," Remy panted, glancing back down at Lord Valenbonne. "Father, you'll be all right. They're—"

But Lord Pendergast's eyes were closed, and his chest no longer rose and fell. Remy stared at him, the blood rushing through his ears and drowning out all the other noises on the battlefield.

The beach came alive with court kindred as they swarmed the covens. Raghnall was chopping the vampires into pieces with his battle-axe, and Hylasenth was darting around with his daggers, slicing up even more. Lady Fanglei was calmly disemboweling the would-be mutations with no more than her nails, Daoming at her side. Lord Lorien and, surprisingly, Lord Pendergast's vampire messenger fought back-to-back, the latter much more proficient now with the zweihänder.

Speck had joined Remy, though the look on the young human's face told Remy all he needed to know. "I'm sorry, Armiger," the doctor said quietly.

Remy swallowed and laid his father gently back down onto the ground.

"I—I have something for you." Speck fished out a small vial from his pocket. "A tonic of sorts. Lord Malekh had synthesized this when we stopped briefly back at the Fata Morgana. It was created with some of the Night Empress's blood—just enough that you can reach out to her even in your waking moments, should it be necessary. He was working on it near nonstop while we were at the Allpriory, but we were only able to find the rest of the ingredients at the Third—"

"And I presume that he was testing it out on himself and Xiaodan?" It explained how he could hear the two of them while he had been asleep inside the bloodwood, and Speck's sheepish expression confirmed it.

"Fuck it," Remy said, uncapped the cork, and drank. Then he gently transferred his father's body to Speck, wiped at his mouth, and stood.

He followed the trail of flames in the wake of Xiaodan and Ishkibal's battle and spotted them both still punching each other past the group of palm trees they had felled near the water's edge. Xiaodan was glowing like she'd never had her sunbringing taken away, and Ishkibal seemed to flinch at the light, though the blows that he rained down on her were no less deadly.

But even as the Night King stood, Remy could still feel *her* somewhere within the vampire's form. The familiar warmth of his mother swirling around him, drawing him closer.

Remy focused his mind and let go.

"We do not have enough time," Ligaya Pendergast said. They were standing inside Blackstone Manor, where Remy had not been in many months. This was his father's room; there was the blazing fireplace that kept the room insufferable in its warmth, the assorted books on the shelves, the myriad of medicines on the side table. Only the armchair beside the mantelpiece was empty, a blanket and a wooden cane leaning against it. The sight of them brought a fresh lump to Remy's throat.

"Remington," his mother said sharply. "Pay attention. Lilith killed Ishkibal by channeling all the sun that she had into him, and it brought about her own demise. You cannot let the same thing happen to Lady Song."

"I won't, Mother."

Her smile was sad despite her resolve. "I have my own fight with Ishkibal to bear. The drug you gave him is doing its work—it is the same one that kept me docile for so many years. I will do what I can, and you will do what you must out there. Go to them, love. They need you."

And then Blackstone Manor was gone, and Remy was racing toward Xiaodan, who was so bright that he could barely see anything else. Her light wavered when Remy grabbed hold of her arm.

"You can't sacrifice yourself the same way Lilith did," Remy said hoarsely. "Malekh will never know what to do with himself if you die, and I'll be even worse. She's helping us so you won't have to."

"She?"

Another burst of bright light raked through the area, accompanied by a sudden searing heat, but none of it came from Xiaodan.

Ishkibal was screaming, scratching at his own face with his claws, and the light blooming from within it was even brighter than what Xiaodan had been channeling.

"I understand," Xiaodan said suddenly, and her light flared even more beautifully. She was not directing it to attack the Night King, but channeling it *into* him instead.

"Ligaya," Malekh said hoarsely, reappearing beside them. Remy nearly scowled in annoyance at how quick the man was to figure such things out.

Crazed now, Ishkibal dug into his own stomach as if trying to pull out his own entrails, but he only flared brighter, brighter—

And he burst.

Bright rays of light streamed out from his eyes and open mouth, more warping his body as the sun burned away the Night King's blood. Ishkibal fell to his knees on the ground, wailing something in a language Remy did not understand.

Malekh stepped forward, cold gaze on his former liege. He stood there for several moments, watching the old vampire ruler burn.

The Night King looked up at him. **Zidan**, it rasped. **Whence hadst thou hated me?**

"I have let go of the hatred I once bore for you and myself," Malekh said, raising his saber. "I have nothing left to tell you, only the hope that you may find your own peace, as I have."

His aim was true. Ishkibal's head dropped from his shoulders; with a final shudder, the body went still.

Xiaodan had fallen to a knee, bracing herself against the

ground with one hand as she struggled for breath. "I'm all right," she gasped as Remy lifted her up. "Just been fighting longer than I should have."

"And when has that been a surprise?" Remy chided gently, refusing to let go.

"Whatever hold the Night Empress—or the Night King—had over their coven has been lifted," Fanglei said. Most of the First Court vampires sat up with a blank, dazed look from prone positions on the ground.

"Is it over, then?" Raghnall asked, sounding far too weary for one who typically enjoyed the thrill of battle.

"Aye. The mutations have ceased. Without their masters, they are nothing more than grotesque statues." Grimesworthy had stopped moving after Malekh had taken off the Night King's head. It remained rooted where it stood, mangled body as still as stone, its eyes absent of any seeming sentience. Hylasenth gave it an experimental swipe of his sword and shrugged when that produced no reaction. "I imagine that all other mutations are in the same condition."

"Then it is over. Let us go," the Seventh barked at his fellow court kindred. "There is nothing more for us here."

"Are you both all right?" Malekh asked quietly as he approached Remy.

"You look like shit," Remy said in response. Xiaodan sighed.

A crackling noise made them turn, Malekh moving in front of Remy with his sword out again. All around them, the other kindred were moving in place, their own weapons at the ready.

King Ishkibal's head had re-formed against his body, but in his place was the Night Empress, cradling Lord Pendergast's still form.

"No," the Night Empress said. "I will not fight." She looked up at Remy with Ligaya Pendergast's eyes. "This is not over," she said. "Please."

Remy took in a deep breath. "I—I can't—"

Gently, Xiaodan touched Remy's cheek. "It will not take too much from me this time," she said, "and I will not suffer you to do it."

Swallowing hard, Remy nodded.

With no trace of her previous exhaustion, Xiaodan walked to where Ligaya knelt. "I'm sorry," she whispered.

Ligaya only smiled.

"Mother," Remy whispered.

"I release you from all the vows of the Wikaan before me," Ligaya said. "My gift is for you to accept or deny, freely given for as long as you live. And live you will, my Remington, for the rest of us who could not."

The Night Empress's death was neither violent nor prolonged. When Xiaodan sadly brought the sun to bear, the fires burning against her fist, Ligaya Pendergast only closed her eyes and let out a gentle sigh. Behind them, the bloodwood was caught in the flames; its thick vines moved to wrap around its mistress one final time, as the Night Empress and Lord Pendergast burned to ashes.

31

HOME

Rebuilding a kingdom was a whole bloody fucking pain in one's nethers.

The truth behind King Hallifax's cowardly retreat into his capital had finally been brought to light. The old king had succumbed early on in the siege, long before anyone had even realized that mutations were abound. Panicked, the generals in his army had elected to keep news of his death a secret, each operating independently of one another but with little organization. It was the Seventh Court that had successfully rescued many from the towns and villages abandoned by the very kingdom who had sworn to protect them, had offered them sanctuary among the territories north of Aluria. Remy waited for reports to filter in of Raghnall finally losing his temper in the face of so many humans, but none came.

Unfortunately, all this required a good deal of paperwork, something Remy had neither the patience nor the resolve to see through. He glared at the stack on his desk and wondered if he could get away with having Elke read through most of it for him. Even more unfortunately, she was on a private excursion with Alegra, ostensibly for advice to rebuild her own court and castle, though he suspected that this was just another opportunity for her to seduce the woman before more responsibilities piled up.

"How do you get anything done?" Remy complained when the Marquess of Riones carefully toed the door open to saunter in, though his bad mood lightened noticeably when he saw that it was mugs of coffee the man had in his hands rather than more documents. Riones looked as refreshingly at home in this austere backdrop of bureaucracy as he did in the battlefield, though he had opted not to wear his hat today and already had his sleeves rolled up in anticipation of more work.

The other marquess only chuckled, setting down Remy's share of caffeine on his table, careful not to dislodge any of the other sheaves. "It takes some getting used to, but I find it relaxing to look through reports and not worry about getting bloodstains on your coat. And as glad as I am for your volunteering, you are here as an honored guest and not as another paper pusher. You are under no obligation to be overseeing and sorting out reports."

"I want to. I have to."

Riones said nothing, though his expression softened. Remy forced himself to go through the rest of the papers on his father's desk. Queen Ophelia had protested the old man's departure from Elouve, he'd learned, arguing that he could lead the army from his office just as well as from the vanguard, but his father had refused. He would not ask his own men to do what he could not because of his privilege, he'd told her.

And based on the reports written up after his death, it was clear that he had saved a goodly number of those men from death. How his strategies had paid off despite their novelty. How his decision to secure Kerenai, despite it not being Alurian territory, and rescue what people they could had prevented the coven from finding a better foothold in Aluria. How his mutations, repugnant as they were, had been instrumental in turning the tides against what should have been overwhelming forces.

Despite the more than twenty years of infamy that the Pendergast name had suffered through, Lord Edgar Pendergast had regained their reputation in only a matter of months. And Remy's, by relation. Everyone had been quite respectful since his return, though whether it was genuine or out of deference to his father's passing, he wasn't sure.

There *had* been one incident; a metal cabinet one of the administrative staff had been struggling to relocate had toppled over when an overenthusiastic clerk had pulled too hard at the pulley they had jimmied up for transport. Despite standing at the opposite end of the room, Remy had run and caught it easily in his grip. He was later told by an awed Riones that it had weighed well over four hundred pounds and that no one had even seen him move.

For all their newfound politeness, Remy knew they were always going to fear him. It had been nearly a week, but his mother's kindred blood ran strong in his veins, and he wasn't sure how long it would take for it to ebb, if it ever would. He was navigating unknown waters at this point, being his own creature that was neither vampire nor completely human.

"Aphelion," Riones finally said in an oddly formal tone. "There is something you ought to know. Nothing that needs worrying about," he clarified quickly when Remy shot a wary glance his way. "I worked with your father long enough to understand some of his eccentricities, and in the last few days before we departed Elouve, he had become obsessed with organizing his reports and ensuring that all pending concerns of the administration be resolved before we left. At the time, he insisted that he was not like his predecessor, that he was not one to leave things unfinished before undertaking a protracted journey, but something about his resolve struck me as odd. Even the most trivial matters he would not leave incomplete, though he had been more lax about those in the past. I did not realize until recently that he was . . . he was . . ."

"Putting his affairs in order," Remy said. "As if he was not expecting to return."

Riones nodded unhappily. "I doubt that he intended to die, mind, but his lord high steward was not one to leave things to chance."

Remy thought of the training his father had put him through—not enough to break him, but enough to survive the worst of what he knew Elouve could bring. "I thought you would have cleaned out his offices by now, or at least moved some of your own possessions in from the smaller room you've been working at."

"I'm comfortable where I am. And I'm still having second thoughts about accepting Her Majesty's offer. Short as his time as lord high steward was, he left an indelible mark on the position, and there will be high expectations for anyone thinking to succeed him."

"I have faith that you will do just fine, Riones." Remy located an envelope at the bottom drawer of his father's desk, brown and unmarked.

"I thought you ought to take first look at whatever's inside," Riones said hesitantly. "It was so carefully set aside from the rest of his paperwork that it felt like a personal matter."

Remy opened it and took out a few sheets of paper. "A will," he said slowly. "It would be best if you look through it for me, Riones. You know that I'm no good at these things."

"It's straightforward enough, if unusual," Riones said after scanning the documents for a few minutes. "On the event of his death, the title of the Duke of Valenbonne and all its estates are to be passed down to you as his sole heir—though a will would not have been required for that, having already been codified in law. But it also states that you are free to bequeath the position to any relative of your choice for so long as they remain citizens of Aluria—or allow it to revert back to the queen. It particularly stresses that any decision once made becomes final and absolute. I do not know if this will hold up in the court of law, but Her Majesty herself is cited as a witness, and it is her signature inked on this paper."

"As you said, he was not one to leave things to chance." Remy studied the document again after Riones had handed it back to him. *Bequeathed to Armiger Remington Adrian Pendergast*, it said, and *for no more than two hundred years, as long as he remains of sound mind and body.*

"Giving me two hundred years to make a decision," he muttered. "Like you already know what I intend to do. Of everything we've argued over, this is the one thing you're determined to dig your heels in on, Father?"

"Pardon?" Riones asked.

"Nothing," Remy said. "He really *did* think of everything."

"It's still your call to make, Aphelion. It could easily be your things we move in."

"You keep foisting the position on me like you don't deserve it better," Remy said.

Riones's shoulders slumped. "Well. Just a last half-hearted effort to get you to stay, I suppose. The lord high steward hadn't completely gotten rid of all the fools and lackeys in Her Majesty's administration, and I'd rather not like to make a go of it alone."

"It's not like I'm never going to return to Elouve, Riones. I've no intention of shirking the rest of my duties, and I am not relinquishing my position as the new Duke of Valenbonne. If you need help kicking some of the bastards out, send me a pigeon. Or let one of Eugenie's informants know. We could even do it now, while I'm feeling frisky."

Anthony Castellblanc grinned at him. "Reckon we've got time. The soldiers are where they ought to be, and there's no longer kindred to worry about—much. And tonight I'm buying you that drink I promised, to raise a glass to your father while we're at it."

It had been a while since Remy smiled, but he did so now—a pained one at first, flickering on his face like sputtering candle-light in a dark room, but growing brighter as it learned to find its way across his features. "I'd like that, Anthony."

THERE WAS no body for the funeral, but Queen Ophelia had de-clared three days of mourning all the same, and a monument set up by the Ministry of Archives to honor Edgar Pendergast's mem-ory. Probably the way his father would have wanted to go, and Remy made his peace with that.

Several offers had been made to purchase Kinaiya Lodge—no doubt by noblemen looking to boast of owning property that had once belonged to the lord high steward's heir. Remy disappointed the ton once again by withdrawing the residence from the market with plans to transform it into a small school for underprivileged children instead. He'd located the son of Miss Grissell's brother, who had become a schoolteacher himself, Elke having thoroughly vetted his credentials. The man accepted the position with ner-vous excitement and promised to bring three more staff members in for Remy's assessment.

The man was at least ten years his senior, but Remy felt so much older nowadays.

The former lord high steward's vampire messenger found him staring up at the memorial before the Archives. He was wise enough to have left his zweihänder behind and kept his hood up. "He was not a bad lord to serve," he said matter-of-factly, looking up at the stone himself. "A shame, though."

"It makes you a free man once more," Remy said, "without need to answer to anyone else."

"I could say the same of you, Armiger. I merely came to pay my respects, nothing more." The messenger allowed a few more seconds to pass before adding, "I have petitioned to join the Second Court, just so you know."

"You said you didn't believe in the necessity of the eight courts."

"I'm still inclined to think so. But I find nowadays that I am beginning to like being proven wrong." The man looked at him and grinned, then vanished before Remy could form a rebuttal.

He had not been expecting Trin. The Seventh Court leader was nowhere in sight, to Remy's great relief, but his former familiar was here. None of Remy's other colleagues thought to breach his privacy as he stood and meditated quietly before the memorial, but in their short time as acquaintances, he knew she had a habit of overstepping if she thought it necessary, a trait Raghnall no doubt appreciated.

"I felt like I owed you, given the abruptness of our last conversation." Trin didn't look any different, if a little paler. Her face was partly hidden by the parasol she held over her head despite the cloudiness of the day, but her expression was sad as she glanced up at the monument. "I am sorry for your loss."

"Thank you. And not to be impolite, but I sincerely thought you would have more pressing problems to deal with than journeying all the way here to offer condolences."

"I insisted. You'd be happy to know that, save for a raging thirst the first few days, I am of the same mind as I ever was when I was human."

"You're not mad at him?"

"He thought I would be, too. But given the circumstances, I can't fault him." Trin's voice softened. "He offered to unmake me, and I knew how greatly that pained him to say. But now that I have been through the frenzy intact, I thought that I owed him to learn what it's like to be kindred first."

"You're braver than I am."

"I'm as brave as anyone can be given the situation, same as you are." Trin smiled at him and proffered a hand in his direction. "As my circumstances are something you are also deliberating, I thought it might help to talk. Or about anything you'd like, really."

After a moment, Remy accepted her grip. It was warm and strong. "I'd like that very much."

ELKE FOUND him next. He could smell the light scent of her, jasmine mixed with something earthier, heard the silence of her footsteps. She looked up at the stone statue and sighed.

"I'm keeping Loxley House and the other manors," Remy said. "He was fairly explicit that I had to if I wanted to keep the position."

"You never cared much for the dukedom," Elke said. "I half expected you to give it all back to Her Majesty."

"He gave me a couple hundred years to make the decision, so I'm in no hurry. I had been adamant about not wanting any position of authority, but Queen Ophelia is far too wise not to dangle a few tempting ones in front of me." Experimentation on the mutations had been indefinitely placed on hold at Remy's request, all efforts to be redirected toward finding cures for maladies—a process that carried far less risk to the population. Neither he nor the queen had wanted another Quintin Yost.

Her Majesty had acquiesced, in exchange for Remy agreeing to keep his title as Aluria's official emissary to the courts, along with another more ambiguous position. It would enable him to travel the lands as he wished without the restrictions of a desk and paperwork, yet have enough authority to serve as her counsel. The compromise had suited his aims well.

There was a teasing sparkle in Elke's eye. "I would have suggested to Lord Tattersall that he rent out one of your properties for his Second Court, but it seems he is adamant about using the Allpriory for his headquarters in the meantime."

"What?"

"His intentions are far nobler than the priestess who lived there before him, that much I can assure you. He seeks to *demystify* the temple—his words, not mine. Another council will be made to decide on what to do with the jewels within and whatever else he might find, but they made no protest to have him settle there until a better location is found. I do believe that the courts have finally reconciled themselves to the fact that the Allpriory need not be the symbol of their unity. There also remains the Godsflame to watch over and protect, lest someone stumble into it and cause further trouble. Lord Lorien has barred the chambers entirely, to prevent anyone else access."

"He's a good choice to lead the Second." Remy paused. "I did not expect you back so soon."

"Alegra still has pressing duties with the Fourth, and she's keen on helping Xiaodan reorganize. The Second and Fifth Courts are not the only ones to benefit from a growing interest in joining their rosters." Elke smiled. "I am already working with many of the merchants here to continue my jewelry business. It should be more than enough to fund the necessities of my court."

"You'll come back here, even after they tried to kill you?"

"You could ask yourself the same question." Elke shrugged. "If I held a grudge against everyone who's ever wronged me, my hatred would encompass cities. Some things you just have to let pass in the course of long lives. But what about you, Remy? What do you intend to do?"

Remy looked up at the memorial. "I think I'd like to take a trip," he said.

Elke understood. She snaked an arm around his waist and leaned on his shoulder as the sun, a rare sight, rose from behind the Archives, rays falling on the memorial and bathing it in a soft glow.

HE'D STOPPED for a visit at both the Third and Fourth Courts first, a feat that he accomplished with a completely healed Peanut in only three days. The sprouts at the Fata Morgana in particular ran the gamut of emotions, from delight at seeing him again to awed astonishment when he recounted his last few days, to disappointment when they learned he would soon be leaving. And a thrill when, after their incessant badgering, he admitted that he would likely stay for much longer next time.

The Fourth Court received him with no less joy, though theirs was tempered by melancholy and mourning for the death of Song Yingyue. There were new faces there that Remy had not seen before, a dozen more than when he had last left.

"Most of them are from the coven the Night Empress—err, the Night King? Or was it both of them at once?—compelled. They have since recovered and, hesitant as they are, agreed to a probationary membership. Not bad people, really, just misled for the most part, and they seem genuinely contrite. Xiaodan has offered them sanctuary here while they decide what to do next, though several have already asked to stay and become part of the court." Gideon nodded, a fervent hope in his eyes. "I never thought I would see the day that we would have a second chance, and we owe it all to you three. I am so sorry to learn of both your parents' passing, Armiger."

"I think they're happier now," Remy said, and surprised himself by believing it.

Finally he visited Naji's grave, the headstone shinier in its newness than those nearby. He sat beside it with a flask of wine that Giufei had cheekily handed to him in the pantry minutes earlier and took a long swig.

"I'm sorry," he said, remembering their conversation here not all that long ago. "I don't know how to give myself the space to mourn, for all the blather I tried to lecture you with the last time. But I'll visit whenever I can. I'm gonna seat my arse right here and drone on about nothing, and you've no choice but to listen. You ought to know how I'm getting on, how Malekh and Xiaodan are. Because you'll never stop being important to them. To all of us."

Remy got to his feet and tipped the rest of the flask's contents on the ground before the gravestone. "And don't you bloody dare try to push me away," he told Naji, the constriction in his heart easing up just a little.

THERE WERE people on the island. Remy had not seen anyone else when he'd last been here, though the resulting fight and the emergence of great and terrible mutations were likely the cause of the locals' distance. Their history would not make them friendly to strangers.

But they approached him all the same. "Alurian," a man Remy supposed was their leader, ventured warily. Some of the men and women had spears, plain swords, bow and arrows.

"Yes," Remy said. "But I'm not here to harm anyone. That's the last thing I want."

The man looked at Remy, sitting on a log before the remains of the fire that Ligaya Pendergast had cooked at, had served him stew, and seemed to understand. "Babaylan?" he asked.

"Babaylan," Remy confirmed, and then pointed at himself. "She was my mother."

They showed him the small village they had built in the days after the Alurians had tried to destroy their little peninsula. It was a thriving community that had started with nothing more than

wood and sand, to grow into an impressive settlement tucked farther inland, away from invaders and threats. "We came from the
babaylan's tribe," explained the leader. Survivors of the invasion,
their livelihood made with fishing, bamboo, and sugarcane. They
had kept to themselves in the years after the Whispering Isles had
been overrun, not even when representatives from the kingdom
had come calling for trade. Even when their fellows had taken up
their offer once they found that the Alurians were no longer bent
on further annexation.

A change in policy was what Remy wanted to call it. Queen
Ophelia rejected her father's campaign and replaced her soldiers
with merchants, but that would mean nothing now.

"I want to help," he said instead, and that was what he did.
Mulched down the bamboo plants and added manure as fertilizer
where needed, set up fire lines because the season had turned out
drier than expected. Checked the fish pens and cleaned out the
flotsam. Rolled up his sleeves and trousers and waded into the
rice paddies farther inland; cut out the rice stalks and hung them
out to dry, and then stripped the grain from the stalks and stored
away the hull to use later for—much to Remy's amusement—
brewing alcohol. But still more popular was distilling lambanog
from the coconuts they frequently harvested, using the same rice
hulls for its fuel.

"Lambanog is part of a babaylan ritual," one of the women
told him as they sat by one of the fires and ate freshly grilled fish
and tomatoes. "The old leader would cut their hand and let their
blood dilute in the wine for the next babaylan to drink from.
Mother to daughters and sons, cousins to nephews and nieces."

And from her innocent recounting, the mystery was solved.

The woman smiled at him. It occurred to Remy that she was
very pretty. "Forgive me for being so bold," she said, "but I was
wondering if you have a sweetheart waiting for you."

Remy smiled back and thought of the odd vision of his mother kneeling on the ground behind her small house, the soil around her disturbed as if from digging. "I have two," he answered.

Later that night he dug up the ground himself and unearthed a tightly sealed bottle of lambanog. There was a small package beside it wrapped in twine, but it contained only a small book full of his mother's handwriting, papers still white in their newness.

He recognized the ingredients in one of them. *Sinigang*, his mother had written in her flowing script. *Tomatoes, guava, unripe tamarind, distilled fish sauce, onion, pig's shoulder.*

Green chili pepper had been added but was heavily crossed out. Another set of handwriting dominated farther down the page, bold and masterful strokes that Remy was used to seeing in Elouvian reports than in family recipes being passed down to him.

No green peppers, his father had written. *They make my nose run.*

The blackened remains of the bloodwood was all that was left of his parents. Remy sat before what was left of its dead stump, and finally allowed himself to cry.

THEY FOUND him three days later.

"Would have been great if you two had helped instead of gawking at me," Remy growled. He'd stripped off his shirt in lieu of the now-sweltering heat and had been shimmying up trees to great success, given the number of coconuts now on the ground around them. He still had Breaker strapped to his back, refusing to take it off even if it made him a comical sight.

"Just admiring the view," Xiaodan said airily, eyeing him with open appreciation. He would have thought her eyes would assume its notable silver color now that she had reclaimed most of the sun. But they remained her natural steady brown, and he found he liked that better. She looked good—better than good. Remy feasted his eyes hungrily on her form before turning to Malekh, who wore his usual dark clothes and cloak because he was incapable of sweating.

"The council has officially reached a concord with Aluria," the Summer Lord said. "The leaders are intrigued by the notion of actually using willing participants to slake their thirst— within reason, with guidelines drawn up by Aluria—as well as experiments to improve the palatability of animal blood. There will be more agreements in the coming days, one of which is the courts' request to discontinue the experimentation on mutations, but Her Majesty stated that you'd already effected that change."

"And if anyone chooses to ignore that law, you can bet I'll be back at Elouve to make them choke on their vials," Remy said. "That isn't the legacy Edgar Pendergast wanted to leave behind, even if he instigated this whole fucking mess."

"I'd like to think," Xiaodan said, "that the only legacy that he ever wanted to leave behind was you."

Ignoring his state of sweat and stinkiness, she stepped into his arms and kissed him. Remy felt Malekh move closer, though he stopped short of touching them. "What do you intend to do here?" he asked.

"Knock around for a bit," Remy said. "Try to piece together what my mother was like, what her family could have been like. I'll stay a couple of days more. And then afterward, home. To the Third Court. Or the Fourth, if Xiaodan still needs to finalize things there." He thought of the bottle of lambanog now carefully tucked away in his coat and felt better than he ever had.

Time. All he had now was time. And them.

"Xiaodan was insistent that we do this appropriately," Malekh said, in that slow, deliberate drawl of his whenever he wanted Remy's attention. "But she wasn't sure how to make the approach, whether it be before the rest of the Third Court or in our private chambers.

"I thought at first that you would prefer somewhere without any curious eyes watching," Xiaodan said, "and then I remembered you saying how you wished you had been able to be more open about our relationship, as opposed to the secrecy you needed at Elouve. In the end, I couldn't quite decide."

"I suggested that it would be easier if we asked you for your approval first—"

"And now it's no longer a surprise!" Xiaodan complained. "I would have liked to see the look on his face."

"Any attempts to keep him unaware were gone the instant he found the ring, love."

"Are you both saying what I think you are?" Remy asked thickly.

"We said that we wouldn't hesitate to ask the moment the threats to the kingdom were dealt with." There was a soft smile on Malekh's face, foreign yet familiar.

"Are you going to get down on one knee like a proper suitor and . . . bloody hell, I didn't mean that you had to actually do it!" Remy reached out to yank at Malekh's arm to keep him upright. "I am—" He choked on the words. "I am—"

Happy.

He was happy.

Xiaodan and Malekh waited, the expressions on their faces all he needed to know.

"Here is as good a place as any, I would think," Remy breathed, and stepped forward to join them.

Acknowledgments

I want to take a moment to express my overflowing gratitude to everyone who has played a part in bringing this vampire-filled fantasy book to life. This project was a labor of love, inspired by my deep passion for vampires, horror, and everything that goes bump in the night, and fueled by the burning need to have this duology finished before the rest of the world goes to shit, as one does.

First and foremost, massive shoutout to those bloodsucking creatures of the night who have captured my imagination for as long as I can remember. Every sentence, every scene, and every spine-tingling moment is an ode to the tales and stories that have inflamed my imagination from childhood, and if there are any of you actually out there in the world today, call me.

To my incredible literary agent, Rebecca Podos—I owe a debt of gratitude that I can never fully repay. You saw the potential in my twisted imaginings and opened doors I couldn't have opened alone. Your unwavering belief in my vision has been a guiding light on this publishing journey. Without you, this book might still be buried in the shadows. Thank you so much.

A massive thank you goes out to my editor, Amara Hoshijo, and the amazing team at Saga, who took my raw manuscript and transformed it into a work of art—Jela Lewter, Yvonne Taylor, Chloe Gray, Laura Jarrett, Cassidy Sattler, Tyanni Niles, Jackie

Seow, Carloline Pallotta, Emily Arzeno, Ashley Cullina. Your keen eyes and meticulous attention to detail have shaped this story into something far better than I could have imagined. You've challenged me, guided me, and helped me find my voice and I am very grateful for it.

And last but never least, a heartfelt thanks to all my fans who have supported me along the way. Your enthusiasm, encouragement, and unwavering support have meant the world to me. It's your passion for all things dark and your embrace of my peculiar musings that have fueled my late-night writing sessions and kept me going through the long nights writing about Remy, Malekh, and Xiaodan.

To everyone who has been a part of this twisted journey, whether through kind words or feedback, I am forever grateful. As always, your presence has transformed this solitary endeavor into something shared and cherished.